Lilli Marlene

Lilli Marlene

by

Ronald Simpson

The Pentland Press
Edinburgh – Cambridge – Durham – USA

© Ronald Simpson, 1995

First published in 1995 by
The Pentland Press Ltd
1 Hutton Close
South Church
Bishop Auckland
Durham

All rights reserved.
Unauthorised duplication
contravenes existing laws.

British Library
Cataloguing-in-Publication Data
A catalogue record for this book
is available from the British Library.

ISBN 1-85821-276-6

The excerpts from the song *Lilli Marlene* are gratefully reproduced by permission of Peter Maurice Music Co. Ltd., London WC2 0EA. © 1944 Apolloverlag, Germany.

Typeset by Carnegie Publishing, 18 Maynard St., Preston
Printed and bound by Antony Rowe Ltd., Chippenham

Underneath the lantern by the barrack gate,
Darling I remember the way you used to wait;
'Twas there that you whispered tenderly,
That you lov'd me,
You'd always be,
My Lilli of the lamplight,
My own LILLI MARLENE.

Time would come for roll call, time for us to part,
Darling I'd caress you and press you to my heart;
And there 'neath that far off lantern light,
I'd hold you tight,
We'd kiss "Goodnight",
Lilli of the lamplight,
My own LILLI MARLENE.

Orders came for sailing somewhere over there,
All confined to barracks was more than I could bear,
I knew you were waiting in the street,
I heard your feet
But could not meet;
My Lilli of the lamplight,
My own LILLI MARLENE.

Resting in a billet just behind the line,
Even tho' we're parted your lips are close to mine;
You wait where that lantern softly gleams,
Your sweet face seems,
To haunt my dreams,
My Lilli of the lamplight,
My own LILLI MARLENE.

Chapter One

A large ornate clock mounted above the Edwardian façade of a jeweller's shop opposite showed the time to be nine fifty. The morning sun, creeping up as it was from behind a distant building, cast its light and shade upon the streets of clean and unclean stonework that is London.

Mabel, the cleaning lady, paused for a moment to rearrange one of the curlers in her hair, before unclipping it completely and placing it in a pocket of the floral apron she wore. After a casual glance around the boardroom, she bustled briskly from here to there, collecting together her cleaning materials, before moving towards the half closed door. Just as she was about to reach it, it opened fully and a tall, lean, bespectacled man entered, carrying a large folder of papers under one arm.

'Ah . . . good morning, Mabel.'

'Good morning, Mr Peters.'

'Have you much more to do?' he enquired.

'No, sir, I have finished everything there was to do and I was just about to leave.'

'Well done, Mabel, your timing is spot on, and may I say how nice and clean everything looks.'

'Thank you, sir; I will be off then, if that's all right with you?'

'Certainly, Mabel, and would you tell the trolley lady, we will have our coffee in here this morning. After all, we don't want to miss our elevenses, do we?'

Mr Peters moved in front of the heavily burdened Mabel, opened the door and allowed the embarrassingly thin cockney lady to pass through.

Robert Peters, Robbie to his friends and associates, manoeuvred himself slowly around the large elongated table that dominated the boardroom and awkwardly lowered the bundle of papers he carried onto its highly polished surface. After separating and distributing several paper files around the table, he settled into a chair at the head of it and began to scan the pages of other paperwork in front of him.

There was a half-hearted knock at the door before it opened and five men meandered in.

'Good morning, Robbie.'

'Good morning, gentlemen; I hope you are fit and ready to go this morning?'

There was the inevitable mixture of comments from the five as each moved towards his customary position around the table. Another tap on the door followed and three more people entered to the exchange of further greetings and personal remarks. All, having settled into their chairs, continued with the banter of conversation until Robbie looked at his watch, lifted his head and spoke.

'Thank you, ladies and gentlemen, for your punctuality. Now, shall we commence where we left off at our last meeting? Monica, would you refresh our memories, by just reading out the concluding remarks noted at the end of that meeting, please?'

Robbie turned his head to face an attractive young woman to his left, smiling as he did so.

The woman thumbed over some papers, found what she was looking for, then read out the details as requested.

'Thank you, Monica.'

Having completed her resumé, she looked up to face Robbie in anticipation, half expecting him to request further detail.

In the absence of any immediately obvious characteristics, Robbie Peters was known more for his composure than his occasional capricious outbursts, for he was in fact a quiet, talented man who spoke little about himself, but was always happy to encourage and participate in any conversation that concerned his work. In spite of this self-contained quality, he had both a very pleasant personality and all the right qualifications to justify his position as a television programme director, in which capacity he now sat before his assembled production team.

'Now, ladies and gentlemen, you have all had some time in which to consider the points raised at our last meeting, so has anyone any ideas we can kick around and hopefully develop? Alan, have you had any further thoughts on the subject since our last meeting?'

'No, Robbie, I am sorry but you did set us a rather difficult task.'

'What about you, Ned, did you have any luck?'

'I did have one idea, Robbie, but I finally rejected it as being unsuitable.'

'Ah . . . Gregg, perhaps you have something for us?'

'Well, I am not sure, Robbie, for if you recall I was not at the last meeting but in Germany, and as I only returned yesterday, I am not quite sure what it is you are expecting from us by way of ideas.'

'I am sorry, Gregg, your absence had slipped my mind, so perhaps in view of this and the poor response so far, it might help everyone if I go over the reasons for these two meetings again. Well, as you know, the series of programmes that we have been working on for some considerable time, covering the last war, is well advanced and hopefully will be ready for the launch sometime later this year. As I have mentioned before, this has been, and continues to be, the most ambitious project we have handled to date and our finance people, feeling that there will be no shortage of sponsors for the advertising time allocated to the series, have for once been unusually tolerant, considering our current budget overspend.

'That aside, however, our position to date is that after some eighteen months of research and planning, we have almost completed the film editing and narration sequences of the series and soon hope to submit the whole project for approval from our people upstairs. Subject to getting the go-ahead, we intend breaking down the project into programmes of one hour duration, and, with a bit of luck, schedule them into the peak viewing period on Friday nights. The series will be spread over twenty-six consecutive weeks and generally speaking, much of the film material of twenty-five of these programmes is already in the can, but we now have a problem and this concerns our proposed last programme.

'The problem, well, how do we complete what promises to be an outstanding and unique series? How can we round off the series so that the final programme has all the necessary impact and excitement to at least match the other twenty-five programmes that precede it?

'As you know, it was our original intention to produce a series of programmes that were factual, uncompromising and without bias or prejudice. Thus the film excerpts we have put together from around the world of actual battles, events and incidents, have all, by their nature, demanded factual narrative only and have therefore denied us any opportunity to comment on them in any way. In other words, it has all been quite serious stuff, but I feel that the final programme needs to be different: it needs to be more humanised, it needs to show that war is about people and not just about statistics. But most of all, it has to suggest in some unspoken and subliminal way that we must never again allow the greed and the power of some to involve and destroy the freedom of others. It needs to depict not just the elation of final victory, but the tragedy and despair of final defeat. It needs to touch upon the depravity and subjugation of war, the sadness, the fear and even the regret of war. But above all, it has to focus upon the fantastic camaraderie that developed amongst ordinary people who, through circumstance, had to face the carnage that is war.

'We already have in our possession filmed material covering the victory celebrations of people in towns and cities throughout parts of Europe and America, which, of course, we initially intended to use for the final programme. But, whilst this obviously shows both the symbols and the gestures of celebration with the coming of peace, I am beginning to think that the material is unsuitable for the type of programme I now have in mind, but having said that, I am myself still uncertain as to the type of programme that would exactly fulfil what I do have in mind.

'This then, Gregg, is the reason for this second meeting, for whilst this was all discussed at our previous meeting, we failed to come up with any really worthwhile ideas. So what I have been asking is, can you or anyone else come up with a uniquely different idea for this last programme?'

'Well, Robbie, I think I am a little out of my depth here, so at the moment I don't believe I can offer any immediate suggestions.'

'I know the problem, it is not easy. To be honest with you, I think we were all hoping you might put your finger on something we could at least chew over, but you do see what I was hoping to achieve, don't you?'

'Yes, I think so, but it is going to be extremely difficult to match any idea to your expectations, Robbie, especially for a programme of only one hour duration.'

'What I have just outlined was not so much about my expectations but more perhaps my hopes, because I do not for one minute think we could deal with every facet of that review in any single programme.'

'Well, I don't know whether it will be of much use, but I have had a feeling for some time that there is a lot of good material by way of untold war-time stories going to waste out there.'

'Tell me more, Gregg; after all, I'm not looking for total solutions or even miracles, just seeds if you like, or in your case perhaps even feelings.'

'Well, as you are aware, for well over a year now I have been travelling around the UK and Europe researching material for this series. This of course has brought me into contact with quite a number of people, some of whom have intrigued me with personal stories of their own experiences during the war. So much so, that I have for some time thought that these stories should be written down in book form for posterity, but I have also thought that some of them would make very good television material. Now, in view of your request for suggestions, I am beginning to wonder whether this latter idea might be what you are looking for. So, merely as a matter of interest, Robbie, what sort of dates are proposed for the transmission of these programmes?'

'It has been tentatively suggested the series should start about October and finish the following March or April, but nothing is definite.'

'Could the start be a little later, say in December or thereabouts?'

'Possibly, Gregg, though I do know the authority doesn't like to introduce new material just prior to the Christmas period, but why the question?'

'Well, it would be ideal if what I have in mind could be planned so that this final programme would coincide as near as possible with the twenty-fifth anniversary of Victory in Europe Day, next May.'

'Let us hear what you have in mind first, Gregg; we can deal with any incidentals later, providing we decide to proceed further.'

'Well, the thought that has occurred to me in these last few minutes is, why don't we put on a show? A reunion type show that reflects upon the past but at the same time celebrates the present, a show that reunites, not just old comrades, but also old enemies.'

Whether the pause was intended or not, it happened, and Robbie, perhaps feeling that Gregg might be on to something, urged him to continue.

'Supposing we put on a live show at somewhere like the Albert Hall and invite people from different European countries to attend this show as part of the audience. People who actually took part in specific events of the war, members of the forces from all the countries involved, for instance, even perhaps some of the participants in the filmed incidents we have already prepared for the series. Taking this one step further, supposing some of these people were actually to take part in the show itself, not as artistes you understand, but as themselves, reliving, and in some cases re-enacting, those individual moments of war in which they had once found themselves intimately involved.

'We, that is, the viewers, could share the suspense of their experiences, their fears, their feelings then, and, with the passing of time, their reactions to those events today.

'Let me give you an example. Let us imagine for a moment a situation in war-time France where a German army unit had a task to carry out. Let us also assume that a group of Resistance fighters were out to sabotage this imaginary task and in fact did successfully do so. Would it not be both a moving and a fascinating experience to bring these total strangers, these one time antagonists in war, together for the first time?

'We could arrange to have their individual experiences acted out on stage as short plays, weave them in between musical acts and other items that reflect the period and perhaps even end up with a show that actually achieves all of your stated ideals, Robbie. Such a show would, I am sure, also serve to enrich the goodwill that currently prevails throughout much of Europe today and at the same time it would highlight the pleasures and enjoyment we can all share, when peace and understanding is on everyone's menu of the day.'

'Well, well, well. It was only a few minutes ago that I heard you say something about being out of your depth, Gregg, Now, whilst I can foresee certain problems with the idea, I have to admit it does have possibilities. However, be that as it may, let us hear from some of the others. What is your reaction, Alan?'

'What can I say, Robbie? I have some reservations, of course, but I have to concur with Gregg that the idea is a fascinating one.'

'And you, Ned?'

'Why am I reminded of Stratford's beloved Bard and more particularly the soliloquy from his *Henry V*, how does it go now?

> And gentlemen in England, now a-bed
> Shall think themselves accurs'd they were not here
> And hold their manhoods cheap whiles any speaks
> That fought with us upon Saint Crispin's day.

If we are to share the personal memories of others on their individual St. Crispin's days, we shall have to tread very carefully. The idea in principle, however, is a nice one, albeit I shall have to learn how to hold my own manhood a little more cheaply.'

'Thank you, Ned, your answer was itself a soliloquy. What about you, Margaret, have you anything to say?'

'Yes, I have, Robbie, for Ned's brief mental jaunt into English literature disturbs me a little, especially as he neglects to mention two other relevant lines also included in that same speech. "Then will he strip his sleeve and show his scars, and say, These wounds I had on Crispin's day." My point being, I am not sure that this idea of Gregg's will work, for can you really see anyone wanting to reflect upon such bitter memories? Let me labour the point further by saying, there are many people out there who, having experienced their own St. Crispin's day, have no arms to cover with a sleeve, let alone to expose to the view of others.

'There are others who no longer have the physical or mental ability to indulge themselves in these implied glories of battle and if they could, they would find little pride in displaying their torn bodies, their blindness, or any other disability that, by the Bard's poetic definition, are their medals of war. Perhaps I sound somewhat cynical, I am not, but as you may or may not know, Fred my husband was badly cut up on the D-day beaches and God only knows what he must have gone through that day and every day since, for like many others his wounds may have healed but his mind has not. Try as I will, I have never been able to get him to talk to me about it, so I am sure he wouldn't speak of it to others, especially in public. I am of the opinion, however, that if he could open up, it would perhaps help to release some of the turmoil that goes on inside him, for even after all these years, I can still at times see the pain there in his eyes.'

'Margaret, I am sorry, it was most foolish of me to bring you in on this conversation, I should have remembered.'

'There is no need to apologise, Robbie, for I have learned to live with it by now and I was merely using it to express an alternative point of view in response to Ned's remarks and your invitation to comment.'

'And a valid point of view it is, Margaret, but you may recall I did myself say that I could foresee certain problems just a few minutes ago and this was one of them. In fairness, though, we have not yet heard exactly what Gregg has in mind. Furthermore, I am sure that we are all quite aware of our responsibility to produce programmes that avoid unnecessary extremes or outright bad taste. So, Gregg, perhaps we should hear what you have to say concerning this point of Margaret's for it does at least pin-point one possible failing of your idea, does it not?'

'Well, yes and no, Robbie, but let me first say how much I sympathise with Margaret here, for, sharing a home with a mother who was widowed by the war and missing as I have the love and companionship of a father,

I can easily understand how she feels. In view of Margaret's remarks, however, I wonder whether my suggestion has been misinterpreted in some way. You see, my idea was not intended to create situations, which by their nature could be considered as being provocative, macabre, or even indelicate, but more specifically to highlight just a few of these untold stories that owe their origins to the fascinating irony of war.

'Robbie, a few minutes ago I described an imaginary example of what I had in mind. Can you bear with me if I take my explanation one step further and relate to you an actual event involving someone I know? It will, I am sure, clear up the points that concern both you and Margaret.'

'Why not? After all, this was the reason for the meeting in the first place.'

'Thank you, Robbie. Well, it was in the early days of my research in Germany that I found myself one evening sharing a dinner table with three German gentlemen I had come to know. As the evening went by and the conversation became a little less flippant, the subject of war somehow came up, reticently at first, I have to say, but less so as the restraints of the past gradually came tumbling down.

'It was one of these men, known to me as Kerkner, that held us all spellbound as he told us of an incident in his life whilst serving with the German forces in Italy, more specifically at Cassino. The town of Cassino, as you most probably know, lies at the near end of a fertile valley which runs through the centre of the country towards the heel of italy. But the monastery of Monte Cassino lies remote to one side of the town and, as the name suggests, was built upon a high peak well above it

'Well, apparently, Allied troops consisting mainly of Polish and British divisions, which had first been involved in the invasion of Sicily, were landed at Salerno some fifty or so kilometres south of Naples. From here, they were to push forward up the valley towards their ultimate objective, Rome, but had become bogged down on the outskirts of Cassino by a heavy concentration of German troops defending the town. Now, because of the very high ground surrounding the area, there was no easy way out of the valley and therefore, no way for them to by-pass the town, so the Allied forces were left with no other option than to consolidate their positions and continue to pound the area with heavy artillery. This barrage which, it would appear, intentionally avoided the monastery, was backed up by intermittent Allied infantry attacks on the town and these were to continue for many months before the final battle to take it was to succeed.

'Kerkner explained to us how, because of certain agreements, the monastery was supposed to be out of bounds to German troops, but apparently, whilst there were no gun emplacements on or around the mount, they did at times surreptitiously use the area in the vicinity of the monastery as a vantage point from which to view the Allied positions. Well, after giving us this detail, Robbie, Kerkner went on to tell the three of us around the table that evening, his story. He went on to say,

' "One evening, after a particularly intense day of shelling, I along with four of my section were posted up on the mount to keep watch and report back on any unusual enemy activity around the area. I had just started to get used to the feeling of comparative silence brought about by a lull in the gunfire, when the shelling started again. Now, having done this watch duty many times before and not being allowed in the monastery itself, my comrades and I had established our own safe spots, where we could take shelter from the debris that often flew around on those occasions. I myself would slip over a low peripheral wall around the courtyard of the monastery and with care, so as to avoid becoming silhouetted against the night skyline, I would slide down the slope of the mount on my backside to a very large overhanging rock which, by reason of its shape, afforded me some protection.

' "On the particular evening in question, there was a lovely clear moonlit sky, so as soon as the guns started, I quickly picked up my rifle, carefully slid down to the rock and made myself comfortable. I suppose I must have been there for some thirty minutes when, unexpectedly, there was a lull in the gunfire. In the silence that followed, I heard a rustling noise coming from somewhere in front of me. Thinking that it was most probably a hare or some other animal, I slowly eased myself forward on my stomach, until I could see around the lower edge of the rock, where to my utter surprise and disbelief, I suddenly came face to face with a British Tommy. It seemed like an eternity before I could come to terms with my situation, for my rifle was neither loaded nor easily to hand. But I could see his rifle and bayonet there beside him and I was conscious of his eyes peering out from under the rim of his helmet. A shudder of fear passed over my body as I lay there, fully expecting him to react in some violent way, but somehow, it seemed as if he was reading my mind, for we both remained absolutely still. Then, cautiously, after a minute or so, the Tommy's hand began to move slowly away from his side. Thinking that he was about to reach for his rifle, I tried to react, but I couldn't for my body felt as if it was in the grip of an unseen hand that had somehow held me rigid in its grasp. But instead of moving towards his rifle, he took something from his tunic pocket and within a second or two, he was holding it out in front of me. It was a packet of cigarettes and with a nod of his head, he was inviting me to take one from the packet.

' "There I was, without either the strength or the ability to think or act for myself, moving my hand forward in a dream-like way towards this stranger with a packet of cigarettes, conscious of the possibility that any moment I could find myself with a knife lodged between my ribs, and yet somehow convinced that this gesture was in fact the act of a genuine friend. I took one of the cigarettes from the pack and put it between my lips, then, as if out of thin air, his hand was there in front of me holding out a lighter. Still aware of my vulnerability and still disbelieving the reality of my situation, I cautiously took the lighter from him, shielded it from the night behind the lapel of my greatcoat and lit my cigarette before passing it back to him.

' "Then the Tommy, like myself, ever conscious of its glow in the night, lit up his cigarette behind the lapel of his coat and then, again to my surprise, he shifted the weight of his body to one side, extended his right hand forward and with a simple gesture, invited me to shake his hand. My mind was in a complete turmoil as I tried to come to terms with the mixed feelings of caution and relief. I couldn't stop shaking and I was still numb with fear, yet, in a strange sort of way, I knew that there was something about this man, this enemy, that I had never experienced in my life before. So much so, and in spite of my fears, I was so elated by this stranger's beneficence, that as I gripped his hand I willed him to understand my deepest gratitude and thanks. Well, gentlemen, I have never forgotten that night, for even to this day I can still see that blackened face, that dented helmet, that battle-stained uniform, all of which told me that this man was my enemy and yet which, in reality, marked him out as a friend."

'Well, Robbie, there were tears in Kerkner's eyes as he told us his story that night, but he went on to explain how both he and this Tommy fellow continued to share the silence of their unstated friendship, until the guns eventually ceased firing, some hour or so later.

'But the most fascinating part of this story to me was when Kerkner went on to explain that, as the guns became silent, the Tommy again pulled out his cigarettes and with a pencil wrote something on the packet. He then passed it to Kerkner with a gesture that suggested he keep both the packet and its contents, then, without further contact, the Tommy slid off down the slope into the obscurity of the night.

'Now, Robbie, perhaps like me and my other two companions listening to Kerkner around that table that evening, you feel the need for answers, but unfortunately there is very little more I can add to that I have already told you, other than perhaps Kerkner's final words on the subject that evening, for he went on to say,

' "I have thought about that incident many times over the passing years, for whilst one often faces the possibility of death in war, it was never so near to me as it was that night on Monte Cassino. I have also asked myself just as many times, what the Tommy was doing up there that night; why did he not attempt to kill me and did he manage to survive the war himself? You see, gentlemen, the question I have had to live with since that time is, would I have the same mercy towards him as he did towards me that night if our roles had been reversed? Faced with that question today, I am sure it would be yes, but if we had never met that night on Monte Cassino, would I have never known the quality of his mercy or have felt this empathy with others, as I do today? You see, there was a lesson to be learned there that night, gentlemen, and I am not ashamed to say, I learned it well. Now, the only hope that I still have is that this Tommy fellow, whoever he was, survived the war and that perhaps, somewhere, some day, some time, we shall meet again.'

A Cenotaph like silence hung over the boardroom as Gregg completed his story and it might have continued, had it not been for the trolley lady entering the room.

'Ah . . . Gladys, how welcome you are.' Robbie looked smilingly at the white-coated woman. 'And, contrary to what you may have thought as you came in, Gladys, we were not asleep, just contemplating. Now, I don't know about the rest of you, but I could certainly do with a coffee after that rather emotional story of Gregg's.'

Everyone else seemed to concur with Robbie's remark, as they waited for the trolley lady to pass the cups of coffee along the table.

'Gregg.' Alan, still with an amount of biscuit in his mouth, spoke. 'Did Kerkner ever tell you what was written on that cigarette packet that Tommy gave him that night?'

'Yes, in fact, on another occasion some time after that evening, Kerkner actually showed me the packet, for he had kept it all those years and it was something he obviously treasured. The writing on it had of course faded with time, but was quite discernible under a magnifying glass, for the pressure of the pencil must have slightly engraved the smooth surface of the packet. The message simply said, "The best of luck mate" and was signed F. Johnson. It was, incidently, on this occasion that Kerkner told me of his long and continuing quest to find out whether the Tommy had in fact survived the war and then repeated his ongoing hope, that they would one day meet again.'

'So is it a story without an end, then, Gregg?' Margaret enquired.

'Oh no, in fact I believe it will eventually have a happy ending and even perhaps another beginning. You see, it was Kerkner's story that first started me off recording such material. That was over a year ago and I am glad I did so now, especially if it helps to solve our problem here today. But apart from that, I realised that travelling throughout Europe and the UK as I do, I was in a better position to try and find this Tommy character than Kerkner, so I vowed to myself then and there that I would endeavour to bring about Kerkner's hoped-for reunion, if at all possible.'

'Does this mean that you have since found him and perhaps want to use the show as a form of catalyst, to bring these two together again?'

'I hadn't really thought that far ahead, Robbie, for, to be honest with you, I have not as yet actually located my man, although I do know he did survive the war and at that time did return to London where he lived. But certainly, now I think about it, it would be wonderful if we were to use both the story and their possible reunion as part of our show; that is, of course, providing I can find him and you decide to proceed with the idea.'

'But one swallow does not a summer make, Gregg.'

'I could not agree with you more, Ned, but as I have already mentioned and using your own analogy, I do have several other swallows in my nest and all, may I say, with the same intriguing plumage of Kerkner's story.'

'Touché. I yield to your thoroughness and knowledge of birds, Gregg.' Ned, half smiling, continued, 'In a more serious vein, though, it is quite obvious that we really do have something worth pursuing with this idea of yours, but that aside for a moment, I am also captivated by the way you appeared to have traced this Tommy fellow as far as you have, so how does one go about such a quest?'

'Well, without a Christian name to begin with, it was difficult, but I began by first visiting the British war graves cemetery at Cassino, then I searched through the records of those souls buried there. There were several Johnsons named in the records, all of which I listed, but for some unknown reason at the time, I had the feeling that none of these would turn out to be the man I was hoping to find.

'So I then pursued my enquiries through certain associations, including the Red Cross and War Office records, eventually ending up with a short list of some eight likely persons with the name of Johnson, all of whom had served on that front. I have now, by hook or by crook, reduced the list to one and I feel in my bones that this has to be Kerkner's Tommy, whom hopefully, I shall soon be meeting.

'You see, Robbie, taking this story as an example of what I have in mind, I think both you and Margaret here would have to agree that it does in no way glorify victory or wallow in tragedy. But it does go to show those often long term effects that war can have on people, and it is within their memories that one finds these unique untold, or unexplained, cameos of human contact that are the essence of good, and in this case relevant, entertainment.'

'Oh, I do see exactly what you are getting at, Gregg, but I am still aware of the delicate line we would have to tread if we are to pursue this concept of yours, even without all the other problems we have yet to face and overcome. For instance, whilst your idea has all the requirements I was seeking, it would involve the authority in a high capital cost project, just for a one night event, and I feel that it may be this high cost that might ultimately kill it. I know that I intimated earlier that our finance people have shown us a great deal of tolerance over the project this far, but what you have suggested could result in quite a substantial expenditure without any chance of ever recovering it, even assuming we leave out the question of profit.'

'I have been considering this as we have talked, Robbie, so let me digress a moment and ask, how many regions are to be covered by the series, when it eventually goes on air?'

'What is the position on this, Peter?' Robbie directed his attention across the table towards the head of engineering.

'Currently it is proposed to have a three region spread over, Robbie. Fortunately these are the regions that bring in the greatest revenues from advertising; even so, I can't help feeling that the possible cost of such a project could be greater than any income expected from it.'

A half questioning, half sympathetic look appeared on Robbie's face.

'Yes, I hear all that Peter said, Robbie, but the way I see it, if you decide to take up my suggestion, then such a show would be as much about Europe as it would be about the UK, so in my opinion, it should also be seen throughout Europe. After all, we now have all the technical facilities in place to handle such an event and there have already been some shared programmes to date which have proved to be successful, so why hang back? Why not try and get the complete series pumped out all over Europe, then there will be no money problem.'

'You don't let go easily, do you, Gregg, and whilst I am not hostile to such persistence, you are obviously unaware of the problems one has when dealing with international agreements and contracts. That aside, have you stopped to consider the fantastic planning that this Euro idea of yours would need?'

'No, Robbie, although I would have thought, with the available material I have already collected, we should be more than halfway there. Of course I realise that if we are to eventually put on a show along the lines I have suggested it won't be easy. But it was you, after all, who encouraged our participation, by pointing out that this is our most ambitious project to date. So all I am saying is, let us try to make it just that.'

'All right, let us hear from around the table. Alan, do you see any reason why we shouldn't go ahead along the lines Gregg suggests?'

'I did mention earlier I had some reservations, Robbie; however, I still like the idea and feel that with certain compromises we have the ingredients of a really good show.'

'So what reservations do you have?'

'Well, first, if we are to proceed with Gregg's idea, I think the venue for such an event needs to be more compact than the Albert Hall casually suggested by him. In fact, in view of the many technical problems that arise with outside broadcasts, I think it would be best if we were to use our own television theatre for the show.'

'Nice point, Alan, so, bearing in mind the amount of equipment you might have to use, what sort of audience numbers are we likely to achieve?'

'Probably about a thousand, Robbie.'

'Back to you and your diary, Gregg. You said you have further material and names of people who might be persuaded to become participants in this show of ours. What sort of numbers are we looking at?'

'I have over fifty different incidents in my little book, Robbie, but we would no doubt only need four or five of these at the most for the show. As for the people, well, I have about a hundred names so far, but I suggest that our prospective audience could be drawn from those service clubs or institutions that are directly concerned with ex forces personnel.'

'Alan, I believe you have further points to make.'

'Yes, two in fact. My first being this question of the audience and the mix of languages we would be faced with. For if these invited guests are to be selected from different countries throughout Europe, they will need to understand what is going on around them, so we have to consider how best to deal with the language problem. In principle this doesn't represent a hurdle, for we can install inductive loops to carry the necessary translation via headphones to those of the audience that require the facility. But in view of the time and planning required to get it right, I would have to know in advance the likely number of people who would need the facility, and of course, the different languages that are to be translated. So this must be taken into account in the early stages of negotiation, if we are to go forward with the project.

'My other point concerns the accommodation of these guests from around the world together with the necessary guides and translators to care and attend them whilst they are in this country. We shall need to know the proportion of the total audience that will be from the Continent and the type of accommodation they are likely to require: for instance, will we have to lay on an assortment of igloos, tents, mud huts and the like? . . . I jest, of course.'

'I hear what you are saying, Alan, along with your humour, but I think Trenchard here can best answer that one.'

'Obviously anything can be arranged, given the time, Robbie, thus the organisation and accommodation will represent no major issue. For instance, our own artiste's accommodation block can house quite a few people and I would suggest that the local hotels will be able to cater for the rest.'

'Right, let's stop and recap on what we have so far. We have the theme and certainly the material for our final programme. By using our television theatre we can avoid the need for outside broadcast staff and at the same time have all the necessary range of equipment to hand. We have the required facilities to link with the Continent, albeit one of our first priorities must be to ascertain whether our European counterparts find the proposals worthy of their consideration, and there seems to be no problem in housing and handling the number of guests that are likely to attend. What is still missing however is the consensus of opinion as to whether we should or should not proceed with Gregg's proposals. So let me return to my still unanswered question and again ask, am I to take it as read that we should accept the challenge of this potentially unique last programme?'

Robbie scanned the faces around the table and awaited a response.

Some moments passed before he continued. 'Ned, what say you?'

'No question at all, Robbie, I say let's go; it is an exciting idea.'

'Peter?'

'I am with Ned, Robbie.'

'So are you all happy with the proposals so far?'

Robbie looked at each one in turn as each gave their nod of approval.

'Right, shall we say that unless we come across some insurmountable problem that forces us to abandon the idea, we all agree to the proposals. Now, I would like to discuss the format of the show itself, for we may be able to use some of the material that we already have to hand. Ned, as Head of Production I think you should perhaps put your penny's worth in first.'

'Right, Robbie, but please bear in mind the limited time I have had so far to consider the subject, so any ideas that I put forward at this stage will be only off the cuff. First, the point that Gregg mentioned earlier concerning the proposed dates for the series I see as very relevant, for ideally the 25th anniversary of Victory in Europe Day, coming as it does in May next year, would be the perfect time for this final show of ours to go on air. This would also allow us adequate time in which to put the event together.

'Now, from the limited discussion we have had on the subject so far, I think that what we are looking for is a show which reflects the style, mood and music of wartime in such a way that it will recapture the overall feel and perception of the period. A show that has to be seen through the eyes of the many different nationalities involved in the conflict and viewed from their many different standpoints. For instance, if I were asked to pinpoint typical music of the period it would be that of Glenn Miller, whereas people in Europe would, at that time, have known very little of either the man or his music, so we do have to avoid the trap of producing a show that has simply materialised out of our own nationalistic viewpoint.

'I also think that it would be best if actors were to act out Gregg's mini-plays, rather than the individuals whose stories we aim to portray, for we cannot expect people who have probably never been on stage before to openly live out their highly emotional memories in front of millions of people. This will also give greater impact and poignancy to any intended reunion of people on stage that is likely to take place at the end of each play. We will inevitably come up against other delicate situations such as this, if we are to follow through with the unique theme of this proposed show. For if we are to bring together a considerable number of these highly sensitive people, we must never lose sight of the possibility that some of them may still have prejudiced views about the war. We have to remember that most people living throughout those years were by circumstance, either directly or indirectly, involved in what was effectively an ordinary people's war. For as Margaret mentioned just now, some of our potential visitors may still carry the mental or physical scars of those times. We also don't want to produce a show that is unbalanced by an excess of compassion, pathos and tears, so it must have its fair share of laughter and fun. It is this finite balance that I see as being the greatest challenge to our perceptive and creative artistry and, providing we get it right, I am sure that we will all be able to share in the pleasure of a job well done.'

'Nicely put, Ned. Your observations confirm that we do have an unusual show in the making. Having said that, how do you see it progressing?'

'At the risk of being predictable, Robbie, perhaps I should start with the beginning of the show. You see, I visualise the audience seated within the theatre, brought to silence by the dimming lights of the auditorium. At this point, the orchestra could play a medley of music suitable to the occasion, and perhaps we could quietly sound off a warning siren against this musical background.

'Then, after a minute or so, we should cut the siren effect, allowing only the music to continue as the curtains rise. I can then visualise off stage spots cutting the darkness of the auditorium, picking out the motionless figures on stage as each, dressed in the garments of their different occupations, remains symbolically frozen in a pose, depicting their different skills. The initially slow opening music should then perhaps be speeded up as the stationary cameos break into a dance, intentionally choreographed to show the changes in their clothing as they don the uniforms of war. This developing scene continues, until all on stage take up their face to face positions with those of other nations. Then the dance ends as each group exits stage and the curtains lower. After this opening number, Robbie, I envisage that we keep the mood of the show in a sustaining light-hearted vein for at least fifteen minutes or so, then we can venture into the first of these reunion-type mini-plays suggested by Gregg here. I think that we should also endeavour to stagger these different mini-plays between other less intense items, such as dance, mimed comedy and the like. That way we can avoid the possibility of finding ourselves up to the neck in a flood of pathos and tears. Now obviously, Robbie, it is not going to be as easy as I imply by my brief summary and no doubt the end project will be far removed from that of my suggestions here today, but we have to begin somewhere and we can easily change or build as we go. You see, whichever way we play it, this type of show is bound to awaken those suppressed or half forgotten emotions deep within people, so whilst on one hand we don't want to discourage this, we do have to make sure that we get the balance just right. I also suggest that the filmed victory celebrations which we already have prepared be seriously reviewed and trimmed to fall in line with the delicacy of this intended show, for, as you pointed out earlier, one man's victory is only ever achieved at the expense of another man's defeat.'

'Thank you, Ned, when it comes to subtlety and nuance you are the master. Now, as Ned here has intimated we need to build on these proposals, so has anyone any further points they would like to add? You, Alan: then do by all means carry on.'

'Well, Robbie, the frequent scenery changes to cover the proposed ideas suggested even this far will, I fear, be beyond our own people in house skills. For, as you are aware, our lads are top rate when it comes to designing and building sets, but to deal with the fast scenery changes necessary for this type of show, we would need experienced scene shifters.'

'I think we can get over that quite easily, either by contracting in such skills, or alternatively by pre-recording these mini-plays and back-projecting them on stage. I am sure we can easily overcome the problem, Alan. Anyone else with a problem? Ah, you, Gregg, do by all means please carry on.'

'It's not so much a problem but another suggestion, Robbie.'

'Carry on, please do, Gregg.'

'It concerns the finale of our intended show, Robbie, but in particular the music with which to end it. You may remember in your initial review, you suggested that camaraderie was one of many ideals you saw as being essential to any proposals we had to offer concerning this last programme of the series. Well, might I suggest, we should end the show with the song "Lilli Marlene", for perhaps, more than any other song, it does in its way represent that which is implicit in the word camaraderie.'

'Gregg, we have hardly got off of the ground with your first idea and already you are talking about the finale. So, with due respect, may I suggest we deal with your suggestion some other time, for I am sure the finale is the least of our problems at the moment.

Gregg was not about to let the matter drop.

'Surely, Robbie, in view of what has been said so far, the selection of suitable music for the show is going to be one of our hardest tasks. This being the case, shouldn't it be one of our first priorities, for surely, once we have settled on the type of songs we are going to use, wouldn't the rest of the programme fall more easily into place?'

'He has a very good point there, Robbie,' Peter, having sat quietly for some while, interjected.

'All right, why this particular song and why as the final number?'

'Well, first, Robbie, from what I can make out, the song has always been a favourite with the people on both sides of what was the great divide. It has the right words and melody to unite an audience and I think as a finale, it will encourage the most reluctant of singers to sing along with the final choruses of it.'

'But is the song suitable for its intended purposes?' Ned enquired. 'After all, is it not about a lady of the night, a lady of question, whose major preoccupation seems to have been picking up soldiers as they left their barracks?'

'I have heard this view expressed before, Ned, and I can only ask if you are familiar with all the words of the song?'

'To be truthful, no, Gregg, apart that is from the opening lines which, if I recall correctly, say something about a woman waiting beside a barrack gate. Now it might be just my natural naivety, or perhaps even my down right rotten mind, but loitering with or without intent does suggest to me a rather questionable pastime.'

'I will do my best to remember that, the next time I see you waiting at the bus stop, Ned,' Alan interjected.

The brief moments of joviality subsided and Gregg continued.

'I suggest Ned, that your recollections of the song have been influenced by its association with a well known actress, for whenever she sang it she was always dressed in a black slinky gown with a provocative slit up its side. Whereas, of course, the song has very strong sentimental overtones and is much more about endearment than it is about seduction.'

'I did say that my knowledge of the song was limited, Gregg, and I am sure you would not have suggested it without thinking the idea through first, but why the finale and not perhaps elsewhere in the show?'

'Well, as I have already pointed out, the song did have a great deal of appeal to people on both sides of the conflict and inherent within its words there is this message of nostalgic regret, hope for the future and the desire for reunion. You see, following on from Robbie's brief at the beginning of our meeting, the song does seem to fit the occasion rather well. So much so, I think that it will add impact to the finish of the evening's events. It will, I am sure, leave those who view the occasion with a renewed sense of consciousness, and hopefully, it will encourage this feeling of unity amongst both the audience and the viewers who see the show, which, as far as I can see, sums up our reasons for having it.'

'Speaking for myself, you could be right, Gregg. After all, twenty-five years of peace deserves recognition and by inviting people from all over Europe to join in the show as you suggest, who knows, it might even help us to achieve peace for the next twenty-five years. What say you, Robbie?'

'Well, I am certainly in tune with your observations, Ned, equally as much as I am with Gregg's persuasive ideas, but I am beginning to wonder, Gregg, if perhaps you might be going a little over the top with this sentiment thing of yours. You see, both Margaret and Ned here have, in their own individual ways, pointed out that the war was not contested within a framework of congeniality and ethical niceties; it was a bloody war and even at times a barbaric one. So why, especially when you yourself lost your own father because of it, do I get the feeling that you are trying to influence us towards a show that avoids the reality of war and concentrates only on the sentiment arising out it?'

'I am not aware that I was, Robbie; after all, I have only been responding to your initial request, at least that is how I see it.'

'Don't get me wrong, Gregg; I am totally satisfied with your input this far. It is just that, fascinated as I am by your apparent sensitivity and understanding towards others, I wonder if you have in some way overdosed on their sentiment?'

'I don't think so, Robbie, I have merely listened to the factual experiences of different people who were involved in the war, found their stories extremely interesting and, in view of your initial remarks, allied them to what you yourself had in mind for this last programme of ours. I suppose I might have assumed that other people, like myself, would also enjoy listening to these personal stories about the war, but that doesn't mean that I am easily convinced by all that I have been told.'

'But from what I gather, quite a few of these stories do concern people who were once considered as our enemy, so what I am saying is, these stories you have collected, they are not about any personal view you may have concerning the politics of war?'

'Not at all. You see I, like most people of my age, never knew the violence of war, only a few after-effects of it, so I have neither the desire nor the reason to carry the burden of prejudice felt or advocated by some because of it. I just think that these stories are worth telling, for they are about real people, real events, even real emotions. I suppose the point I am trying to make, Robbie, is, it was you who suggested that our other twenty-five programmes of the series all demonstrated the cold reality of war, but take little or no account of the many untold personal moments of those who either individually or collectively carried out these dangerous but necessary tasks.'

'You are quite right, Gregg, but I purposely posed the questions, just to make sure that we are all thinking along the same lines.'

'Well, just in case you were beginning to think otherwise, I have no personal hang-ups or particular bias to express, neither do I suggest that our proposed last programme should be steeped in a quagmire of self indulged pity or pathos. But if we really are to translate some of these true life stories into mini-plays, then we should deliberately try to involve the viewer in all the emotions experienced by those whose stories we tell. Now, perhaps I should also point out that some of the stories I see as possible mini-plays are to say the least extremely funny, so it won't be doom and gloom all the way. That is, providing you endorse these views and proceed along the lines we have already discussed.'

'Well, if your sense of comedy is as astute as your sense of drama, Gregg, then you have without question my endorsement. What say you, Ned?'

'I agree with much of that which has been said, Robbie, for as you may recall, I did myself touch upon the challenge we face in achieving this necessary balance 'twixt laughter and tears.'

'Yes you did, which to me makes this idea of Gregg's even more exciting. Now perhaps with your approval and Gregg's imagination, I suggest we let him tell us how he sees this last act of his developing?'

'Why not, Robbie?'

'Well, what can I say, as I am without either the experience or the qualifications to justify such an invitation. I can only propose that we conclude the programme along the same lines as Ned suggested we begin it, but naturally, in the reverse manner.'

'Come, come, Gregg, I am sure you can do better than that; after all, you have already shown that you have quite a creative flair for ideas.'

'All right, let us assume for a moment that the penultimate act has just ended, the curtains have come down and the auditorium is once again fully lit. We might possibly have just listened to a couple of short speeches by a war time General from each side of the conflict.

'So, following Ned's ideas, and remembering a skit on the song I once saw, we hear again the sound of a distant siren, but this time it tells us all is clear. The muted sound of a mouth organ can just be heard as the lights fade and the curtains rise. Then perhaps, sitting at the back of a darkened stage, a spotlight picks out a lone German soldier dressed in full battledress; he is hauntingly playing the music of the song "Lilli Marlene". As the first chorus ends, he is left in a half-light and another spot comes on to show a lone woman front stage. I see her dressed in a black trench coat with its collar turned up. A handbag hangs at her side, with its strap looped over one shoulder and upon her head, tilting down to one side of her face, she has a beret. We could, I suppose, have a street lamp behind her somewhere; this would help support the illusion engendered by the words of the song. Then perhaps, returning to the act itself, the soldier starts to play the tune again as the woman first begins to hum the melody before she starts to plaintively sing it. The song ends and after a moment's pause the orchestra takes up the melody, very quietly at first, then through improvisation into the strident and louder rhythm of march time. The woman joins in with the orchestra to sing the song again, as the dancers, already suggested by

Ned here, come on stage to join the scene. Well, Robbie, I can only suggest that the orchestra then repeats the melody as the singer encourages the audience to join in for one or two choruses, before the final curtain lowers and the show comes to an end.'

'Well, I must admit, as a finale it does have that certain something and I agree, it does seem to direct one's mind objectively towards a central theme for the rest of the show. What say you, Ned?'

'I haven't any doubts about it at all, Robbie; it has considerable merit and it does summarise all that you initially asked for. It also provides us with an ideal ending to what looks like being a very unique series. That aside, I am, to say the least, a little curious as to why your harmonica-playing soldier should be German, Gregg, and not perhaps French, or even British, not that I have any personal bias on the subject, you understand.'

'Well, Ned, it is even more curious to me how you seem to have put your finger on a preconceived notion I appear to have and for which I can offer no specific explanation, other than by saying I believe it should be a German soldier. Now, why I am so convinced about this I don't know; perhaps it is simply a part of my childhood catching up with me.'

'Your childhood, Gregg, what has that to do with it?' Robbie enquired.

'Well, as you can no doubt appreciate, I was only a lad when my father was killed in the war, but from what my mother has told me, it would appear that he learned the song when he was first abroad. Needless to say, my mother, being quite a good pianist, soon picked up the tune from him, so naturally I, as a music-mad seven-year-old, soon found myself singing it.'

'But I don't think the song came to be generally known until late in the war, so when was it you first heard the song, Gregg?'

'I can only think that it must have been about 1942.'

'So where was your father stationed when he was abroad?'

'He first served with the Eighth Army in the desert, before returning to England for further training. Then, back in this country, he was stationed in Berkshire for some time, before again going off to France on D-Day. But of course, he sometimes had a few days' leave between those periods abroad, although it was on his first leave after returning from the desert that my mother learned the song.'

'So why this association between the song and a German soldier?'

'I really cannot say, Robbie, except perhaps, that my father had also brought home a battered German helmet, which for want of a better place to keep it was always left hanging from one of the hooks in the coat cupboard. So I can only think that, somehow in my mind, the song and the helmet have in some way become linked together as one. I do, however, feel as if the song has always haunted me, for every time I hear it, I find myself immersed in a whole kaleidoscope of inextricable and uncanny feelings.'

'Did your mother ever explain how your father came to know the song, Gregg?'

'Only that he had heard it when he was in the desert and that he and his mates would often sing it as they marched along. The strange thing is, that apparently the German soldiers also used it for the same purpose, which is another thing that has always intrigued me.'

'Yes, it is thought-provoking, I agree.' Ned was obviously still pondering the point as he spoke. 'I wonder how it came to be that both German and British troops shared, as it were, this affection for the same song, especially at the same time. I don't suppose your mother ever shed any light on this particular point, did she, Gregg?'

'No, although I did ask her about it at one time, but as she explained, "I had more important things to do in those days than spend my time delving into the origins of a song." Nevertheless, I know it to be a fact, for several of my German contacts have since confirmed it, some of whom actually served in the desert around the same time as my father.'

Ned, who had been quietly contemplating the matter further, spoke.

'Well, if nothing more, it does go to show how it is, at times, easier to recognise irony than explain it. For even within our limited time here this morning, we have on more than one occasion seen how the intervention of this illusory thing we call fate has somehow woven its interlinking web of association through so many different people's lives.'

'Gentlemen,' Robbie interjected. 'May I interrupt this philosophical interlude by suggesting we ourselves have further fateful interventions to make with this show of ours, so if we can return to reality, can I put another problem before you. We have settled on the theme for our show and we know that it will appeal to the older-type audience, so do we have a singer for this finale who, like the audience, would have aged with the passing of time, or do we have a younger singer?'

'Can I make a point, Robbie?'

'By all means, Peter.'

'If the idea of this show is to transport our viewers' minds back over the years, we have to put ourselves in their place and see the world through their eyes, as it was then, so I feel that a young singer is called for.'

'What say you, Ned?'

'I am inclined to agree with Peter.'

'You, Gregg?'

'Yes, Robbie, it has to be a young singer and may I suggest she has to be someone who not only has the right voice, but also has that essential innocent appeal.'

'You seem to have come up with another of your tall orders, Gregg. Who, may I ask, in these days of your average pop singer, could put the song over in the same way as someone like Marlene Dietrich, for instance?'

'This is the actress I had in mind earlier, Robbie. Now, whilst I have only ever seen a short film clip of her singing the song, her performance in that was primarily as an actress, not as a singer. Obviously her act was quite unique in a seductive sort of way, but I can't help feeling her slinky rendering of the song was out of keeping with the sentiment implied in the words of it. I also happen to think that it was this performance of hers that has helped to foster the impression that the song is about a "questionable lady" as Ned here intimated earlier. No, I would hope we could find someone with a more innocent image than Dietrich, but having said that, if she happens to have the presence and professionalism of Dietrich, then no one could ask for more.'

'That's easier said than done, Gregg, for at the moment I can't think of any singer suitable for the task, unless, of course, you or someone else can come up with a name to fit the bill?'

The request acted like a switch turning on an abrupt silence, as most of those present thought over the question and searched for answers. There was the odd suggestion of a name or two, but these failed to generate any favourable responses from others around the table, so Robbie, realising that there were no immediate nominees, broke the silence.

'I had the feeling that this was not going to be an easy problem to solve.'

'Well, I purposely avoided sticking my oar in, Robbie, but I do have a prospect in mind. However, before I name her, may I ask that you give my suggestion some thought before you reject her out of hand.'

'Of course, Gregg, but she can't be that bad, can she?'

'No, not in my opinion, but I do know how you feel about modern singers. However, I think Lorrett Lorren would fit the bill quite nicely.'

Robbie was as good as his word and waited some minutes before speaking.

'Well, my first reaction is, of course, that she is just a pop singer and from several articles I have read recently, she is not even highly thought of as such. But I have to admit that maybe I am a little bit prejudiced and predisposed to classical rather than modern music. However, she is a very attractive woman, albeit she is slightly older than perhaps Peter here may have had in mind, but the lady's singing ability is another thing. So sorry, Gregg, I feel she would not be suitable for the type of show that we have in mind.'

'I think that's a bit unfair, Robbie.' Margaret, having been silent for some time, was not going to let his remarks go unchallenged. 'I heard this lady sing on the radio some time ago and I think that she has a lovely voice, but it was quite apparent to me at the time that it is not her singing that is in question here, but more the type of material she has been using.'

'Precisely, Margaret, I couldn't agree with you more, for whilst she is a comparative newcomer to the musical scene, I personally think that given the right material and the right guidance, Lorrett Lorren has all the qualities to make it to the top, so I see her as the ideal lady for our show.'

'OK, Gregg, for the time being let me just say that I cannot understand what both you and Margaret see in the lady, but let me suggest that providing you can arrange it, we will audition her along with others, then we can best judge her singing ability. But whoever we take on for this role, it is more than likely that they may be needed for other numbers in the show, so make this perfectly clear to Miss Lorren, or whoever we interview, before we invite them to audition.

'Now, my watch tells me we are well into our lunchtime and as we need to continue with this meeting later, perhaps we could return in one and a half hours' time, if that is all right with you all, and thank you.'

Gregg had just stood up and was about to move towards the door when Robbie touched him on the arm.

'Gregg, hold on a moment, and Ned, could you spare me another few minutes. I have something further to say to you both.'

Robbie waited until the others had left the room before inviting the two of them to sit down again.

'Now, first, I would like to thank you, Gregg, for your ideas here this morning, but at the same time compliment you on the detailed research and investigative work you have undertaken for this series of programmes, over the last eighteen months or so. I am sure that I have your support on this, Ned.'

'It goes without saying, Robbie. I see Gregg's efforts as being really worthwhile, and I would like to add that it is also very nice to have him in our team.'

'One can't be any fairer than that. Now, Gregg, starting tomorrow, I would like you to sift through all the material you have. Discuss the merits of each potential mini-play with Ned here and together, try to outline the format of the show in general. Obviously, once this is under control, you can nip off to Europe again and endeavour to liaise with the people whose stories we hope to use. I will let you know about dates, facilities and people numbers as soon as I get an approving nod from upstairs. Now, you will no doubt complete most of your remaining research and liaison work well before our final programme due date and sooner than start you on our next proposed project, I would suggest a few months' tutorial under Ned's wing. This will give you a chance to get a better feel for production and at the same time allow you to fully exploit your research experiences along with those items that are best suited for use in the show. How does this idea strike you, Gregg?'

'What can I say, Robbie, other than that I am over the moon about it.'

'Are you quite happy about my suggestions, Ned?'

'Certainly, Robbie, I have no doubt that Gregg and I will be able to work together very well.'

'That's excellent, which brings me to the point, Ned, where I would also like to thank you for your wise and discerning overview of all that has been said here this morning. Your past theatre and stage experience has on every occasion before been a great asset to this company and I am sure that it will prove to be so again with this show we now aim to put on. Now, might I suggest you both join me for lunch?'

Chapter Two

It was the first day of June 1970. The sky was cloudless and the sun's warmth combined with the ambient temperature of the railway carriages had created a repressive and uncomfortable atmosphere for travellers journeying on the Sussex bound train outward from its London terminal.

Gregg, alone in the carriage, sat back in his seat beside the lowered window of the door, where the incoming draught was tormenting his newspaper into annoying shapes, finally forcing him to discontinue reading it. He tussled with it as one would with a multi-folded map, patiently trying to return it to its original shape and form before defeatedly giving up the task and placing it on the seat beside him. As his hand released the paper he noticed an item at the bottom of an unread page, compelling him to pick it up again. It said:

'The proposed personal appearance of Miss Lorrett Lorren at the London Centurion Club has been cancelled, owing to her recent misfortune.'

The article then continued to give further details before concluding:

'Miss Lorren is said to be still quite ill after collapsing on stage at the end of her recent successful television appearance. Her manager, Mr Martin Efford, informed our reporter that it may be some time before Miss Lorren would again be fit enough to return to public life.'

Gregg's eyes moved slowly away from the paper and for some minutes stared into space, oblivious of reason and void of energy. At thirty-two years of age he was showing the stress of a man some years his senior and to anyone who knew him, he did appear to be uncharacteristically tired and sallow faced. He had himself recently recognised his less than normal enthusiasm for things and begun to wonder whether it was attributable to overwork. But he had never really considered his occupation as work: more perhaps, as a time consuming activity that gave pleasure and satisfaction to his every day.

He had himself previously foreseen the eventual end to the project, which had occupied him since his employment with the company first began, but he was unable to reconcile this change of circumstance with the sense of despondency he was now experiencing.

There was bound to be this feeling of anti-climax, he thought, for he was now really a part of the show business world and as such, he would have to learn how to come to terms with this feeling of loss each time a project or show came to an end. So was it this, that made him feel as he did? Or was it the shock that he had experienced some three weeks earlier when, right at the end of the show, Lorrett had suddenly collapsed on stage. It was, after all, something that no one had expected and it had affected him rather badly, but he still couldn't understand why some newspapers had over dramatised the incident and had in one case, even implied a sense of tragedy about it. How and why could it have happened? he had asked himself time and time again. Was it indirectly his fault, by suggesting Lorrett for the show in the first place? Had the show subjected this comparatively inexperienced young woman to stresses she had not encountered as a performer before?

He could find no single answer to pacify his dilemma as he sprawled somewhat clumsily over the seat of the carriage, unaware of the pleasant countryside that was rapidly spreading out of view beside him.

As a youth, Gregg Jefferson had been fortunate enough to achieve quite reasonable progress through college and eventually on to university, where he had studied philosophy and languages, German and French being the subjects he most favoured. Having gained his degree, he had felt content enough to settle down for a few years as a reporter with a small town newspaper; this was only to be until he considered himself better equipped for a greater challenge. This was the position he now held as a research executive with a commercial television company, which fortuitously had provided him with both the opportunity and the reason to be currently revelling in some degree of personal success. But instead of feeling elated over this, he felt despondent; instead of feeling confident, he felt insecure, for now, apart from the ever present worries he had over Lorrett, there was this question of his future.

He knew that he still had his job, together with the satisfaction of this newly acquired reputation for his part in the show's success, but was this enough, he asked himself, for wouldn't this reputation now prove to be bigger than his ability to maintain it?

Whether it was the sudden realisation that the train had stopped or just the noise of slamming doors that jolted him back to reality, Gregg had no idea, but that he had arrived at his destination was now quite clear. He slowly rose to his feet, picked up his briefcase and alighted from the train. Crashing the heavy wooden door of the carriage behind him, he stepped onto the platform, hesitated for a moment, then made his way towards the ticket hall of the station. A tall lean man, in light grey uniform and hat to match, approached him.

'Excuse me, sir, are you Mr Jefferson?' he asked.

'Yes, I am, and you are no doubt Mr Moffit's chauffeur.'

'Yes, sir, so would you like to follow me, the car is parked just outside?'

Gregg was ushered into the rear seat of a nearby car and the chauffeur took up his position in the driving seat, removed his hat and placed it down beside him before starting the car and moving off.

It was only matter of minutes before the small country station, with its companionable cluster of houses, became lost from view. The car slowly passed through village and lane, allowing Gregg for the first time both to acknowledge and to enjoy the beauty of the countryside around him.

The last time he had spoken to Lorrett had been on the night of the show and only then for brief periods between her performances. He had intended to see and congratulate her once the show was over, but the only thing he could do was to stand and watch as she was carried away unconscious to a nearby hospital. He had visited the hospital the next day, hoping that he might be allowed to see her, but whilst the rotund matron was polite enough to explain that there had been no change in her condition, she had also been firm enough to suggest that any further visits would be pointless whilst Lorrett remained in her present state. It was to be some three days later when he was told that she had been transferred from the hospital to a private nursing home in Sussex, towards which he was now heading.

It had taken some fifteen minutes to cover the journey from the station to the heavily wooded lane along which the car was now travelling. From his position in the rear seat of the car, he could see two wrought iron gates and a large imposing red brick building on rising ground beyond. The car came to a stop just in front of the gates and two sharp blips on the car's horn brought a gatekeeper from a hut partly hidden in the trees to one side. The man obviously recognised the car and its driver, for without hesitation he opened the gates to allow the vehicle through. The grounds were surrounded by a high wall, within which a stony driveway stretched and twisted for some half a mile, before terminating at a wide parking area in front of a very large house.

The chauffeur stopped the car beside the wide Georgian entrance to the house. Moving from his seat he left the vehicle and opened the rear nearside door to allow his passenger out.

'If you go through there, sir, you will see the reception on your left as you go in. They are expecting you.'

'Thank you.' Gregg nodded his appreciation and walked into the building.

'Good morning, would you be Mr Jefferson?'

A young woman in a clean white starched overall had appeared from a side door near to the area marked reception.

'Yes, that is so and I have . . .'

'An appointment with our Mr Moffit.' The woman had again pre-empted his words. 'Would you like to take a seat for a minute or two, whilst I inform him that you have arrived?'

'I am quite happy to stand, thank you.'

Gregg moved over towards a large arched window that looked out onto an expanse of well maintained lawns, converging pathways and an extensive thicket to one side of the house. At first their oddity didn't register, but then he realised that the few people he could see seemed just to saunter aimlessly about from here to there without any particular objective in view. It was only then that he realised that the place was in fact a mental home. He was still contemplating the fact as the young woman came up from behind him and spoke.

'Would you care to follow me, Mr Jefferson?'

He turned and followed his courier from the large hallway down a long highly polished corridor, realising as he did that, unseen from the front of the house, the property had been extensively developed and expanded to the rear of the original building, where interconnecting covered walkways linked several other isolated buildings together.

The woman stopped at a door, holding up her hand in a pausing gesture to Gregg. She knocked and awaited a reply before entering, inviting him to follow. They entered and he instinctively held back, allowing the woman to approach a man in the centre of the room.

There were three men in the room, one of whom Gregg recognised as Lorrett's manager, Martin Efford. Another was seated in one of the several armchairs arranged together in the distant corner of the room and the third, a tall broad man, made his way towards him, after thanking the receptionist and opening the door for her as she left.

'Ah . . . Mr Jefferson; I am John Moffit and I am pleased to meet you. Thank you so much for coming all this way to see us. You know Mr Efford, I believe, so may I introduce you to our senior consultant, Dr Linley.'

The doctor had risen from his seat as the introductions began and was beside John Moffit with his hand held out in greeting, just at the precise moment his name was mentioned. Gregg shook the hands of both men before renewing his acquaintanceship with Martin Efford.

'Now, Mr Jefferson.'

'Gregg, if that's all right with you.'

'Certainly, Gregg it will be and please call me John. Now, as I was about to suggest, Dr Linley and I, in my capacity as a psychiatrist, seem to have a common interest with you and Martin here: namely, our Miss Lorren. Now, quite naturally, you most probably feel an immediate need to question me about her problem and perhaps even her progress so far. But may I beg your tolerance and ask, would you leave such questioning until later, when you will no doubt appreciate more fully why I make this request. Now, we have some coffee and biscuits here, so may I suggest we have it while it is still hot.'

'That will be most acceptable, John, thank you.'

Typically, as with most first meetings, the conversation touched upon the weather for some minutes, before the doctor casually enquired.

'Have you been this way before, Gregg?'

'Yes, I have driven through Sussex many times over the years, but I have heard it said that there are none so blind as those that drive too fast to see, so perhaps this is the first time that I have really seen enough of the county to appreciate the beauty and tranquillity of a place like this.'

'Well, of course, this is precisely the reason for our presence here, for peace and quietness is at times beneficial, if not essential, for many of our patients.'

'These patients, doctor, from the few I saw roaming around the grounds just now, they do seem to be quite a remote lot.'

'Well, I can't say I have heard them described in those terms before, but certainly it does sum up the reactions of many of our inmates here. After all, this is not simply a nursing home. It is in fact a retreat for selected patients who for one reason or another have a mental condition which, with time, we hope to resolve. This is why we have a degree of security around the place, which I am sure you must have noticed as you entered the grounds just now.'

'Yes, I was a little surprised at the height of both the gates and the wall, but perhaps the thing that struck me as being really odd was the woman I could see trotting along the path nearby. If she had been dressed in something other than the heavy topcoat and large straw hat she was wearing and without the loaded carrier bag she was holding, I wouldn't, perhaps, have given her another thought. But after hearing what you have just said, I can only assume that she must be one of your patients here.'

'Yes, that is Mrs Gold, one of our saddest cases. I am afraid there is very little we can do for her and in truth it is beyond our understanding how she manages to stay alive.'

'I am not certain I follow you. From what I saw, I would have thought she was quite healthy considering her age.'

'Physically, of course, she has to be, but it is her mind that drives her. You see, she trots around the inner periphery of that wall throughout its entire length. The wall itself encompasses the whole of the original estate and the distance around it is over five miles in length. Now, she often does this circuit several times a day, sometime jogging for periods in excess of four to five hours, regardless of the weather. What is more, we do at times have great difficulty trying to persuade her to stop.'

'Are you saying she keeps that up all the time?'

'Generally speaking, yes, apart from the occasional rest she has whilst emptying out the entire contents of that bag she carries. Then she carefully and methodically puts each item back in the bag again, before continuing on her way.'

'Isn't there something that can be done for her condition?'

'Only sedate her, which we have to do at times, but naturally, whilst this does prevent her from continuing with her marathon, we cannot just go on pumping drugs into her system all the time. You see, this perpetual motion syndrome, as we call it, is brought about by her state of mind. She seems to have a fixation that she must get there, but we have yet to find out where "there" is. She has, with certain exceptions, carried out this patrol for some years and statistically, the energy she burns up in one day is perhaps equivalent to what you or I may use in a week.'

Gregg looked a trifle dumbfounded as he turned to John Moffit. 'We don't have a problem like this with Lorrett, do we?'

'No, not quite, but we do have a problem, a problem that we feel may only be solved by first discovering as much as we can about Miss Lorren's background. This is why we asked if you would come down here for the day. You see, we need every bit of information we can get on the lady and since you seem to have known Miss Lorren quite well, we hoped that you might be able to provide us with some answers.'

Gregg was about to say something as John Moffit spoke.

'Excuse me butting in on you, but if you have finished your coffee, may I suggest that we make ourselves comfortable in the armchairs over by the window there, then we can discuss the matter more fully, for it is going to take a little time, I am afraid.'

As the four men moved across the room, the visitor had a clearer view of the high wall that followed the contours of the undulating grassland surrounding the house and its outbuildings.

'Now, let me again thank you for your time here today, which I hope has not inconvenienced the authority that employs you.'

'There is no worry there, John; it so happens that this is the first day of several weeks' leave I have due to me. Unfortunately I haven't had the time to take them before now because of the pressure of work.'

'Don't go and overdo it, Gregg, for some of our patients only found their way here because of the stress caused through overdoing things. However, let me start by outlining our progress this far, albeit you may quite justifiably consider the word progress as being somewhat of an exaggeration at this point in time. Nevertheless, we have at least recognised certain possible causes for Miss Lorren's condition. You see, when she was first checked out by the ambulance people who attended her that night at the television theatre, it was thought she had merely fainted, but by the time they had reached the hospital some ten minutes later, it was found to be something more complex than that. For after several specialists had examined her, it was realised that she was in fact totally oblivious of who she was or where she was. So over the next three days or so, the staff at the hospital carried out a whole series of tests and examinations including x-rays, blood tests and other routine inspections, but they could find no apparent medical reason for her predicament.

'It so happened, that as a consultant to that and two other hospitals in the area, I was at the hospital the day after Miss Lorren's admission, so understandably, I found myself involved in her case after being asked to have a look at her. Well, the outcome of my involvement that day was to get Miss Lorren transferred down to the home here, where we proceeded to make further examinations. This was, of course, based upon the premise that we might discover something the hospital had inadvertently missed. Needless to say, like our friends at the hospital, we also failed to find anything obviously wrong with her. Thus, in view of these findings, the doctor, myself and other medical staff within the home here all mutually concluded that if we were to find an answer to Miss Lorren's problem, we would first have to know a lot more about her as a person.

'So it was, just over a week ago now, that we decided to carry out some research into her past. You see, we have a vague idea as to what might be wrong with Miss Lorren, but we need to find the cause. Unfortunately, in some cases, this can only be found within the labyrinths of the patient's mind, but, as I have explained, in Miss Lorren's case, we are unable to communicate with her in any way. However, I was to meet Martin here and through him, I have since been able to talk over the phone with your boss Robbie Peters. He, in turn, has since sent me copy minutes of several meetings you and your team had prior to the show, which of course was now some three weeks ago. Now, whilst these papers give us a very good insight into how the show developed, they do not provide us with a moment to moment account of the show itself. This is why we asked you down for the day, for these are the details that only you can provide, especially as you seem to have been the inspiration behind this highly successful event. So, Gregg, may I begin by asking you first about your association with Miss Lorren: were you acquaintances, friends, or what?'

'I suppose we are just good friends more than anything else, John, although having said that, I admit to finding her a very attractive person.'

'That's both natural and understandable, for she is a very beautiful young woman, so perhaps if you would, could you give us a brief run down on how you came to meet and things like that?'

'Well, having those minutes of the meetings you tell me Robbie sent you, you must already know how Lorrett came to be considered for her part in the show. Subsequently, it was left to me to make all the initial enquiries. So my first contact with her was by telephone and this was to arrange a meeting whereby we could discuss the possibility of her involvement in greater detail. So, to be sure of a relaxed and informal meeting, I invited Lorrett out for an evening meal. This first meeting took place about a year ago and whether it was out of enthusiasm or sheer trepidation, I don't know, but I did rather hog the conversation for most of that first evening. Fortunately my verbal over-indulgence appeared to pass unnoticed, albeit, in my own defence, it was necessary for me to explain all the essential details of the proposed show. Such things as Robbie's request that she was to audition for the part along with others, the necessary contractual obligations that the authority expects from its clients, and everything like that.

'The outcome of this very pleasant evening, was that in principle, Lorrett agreed to do the show and was quite happy with the contract terms. I was then to be introduced to Martin here the next day, who, as you already know, looks after her interests and any bookings that may come her way. Then it was to be several weeks before I was to see Lorrett again and only then when it was necessary for me to confirm her acceptance and discuss further details about her proposed participation in the show.

'Again I took her for a meal, but as most of the formal detail was soon dealt with, we were both happy to share the rest of the evening together. We danced, we talked, and over the next three to four hours I came to know a little bit more about her as a singer, quite a bit more about her disappointments as a divorcee, but hardly anything about her as a person.'

'That's a rather ominous remark, Gregg; could you be a little more specific?' Dr Linley enquired.

'Yes, of course. Well, as you no doubt already know, much of my work is of an investigative nature, so not only do I get a great deal of pleasure from what I do, but I have also, over the years, become a rather good listener. Now, the only reason I tell you this is because normally I usually get to know people quite quickly. But this was not to be the case with Lorrett, for she has, so far, been the exception to the rule. You see, I have always felt that she has, quite unintentionally, a kind of highly developed cut-off mechanism which for some reason always comes into operation whenever a conversation appears to be coming a little too personal for her.'

'Another profound remark, but please do continue.'

Gregg was beginning to realise that both Dr Linley and John seemed to be clinging to his every word.

'Well, I am not sure what it is, but on occasions, I have found her to be rather distant, perhaps even at times otherwise preoccupied. You see, it seems as if she either loses her power of concentration for a moment, or perhaps she somehow becomes lost in her own little world. I have to say that at first I thought she was simply bored with what I was saying, but this was usually contradicted by her enthusiasm whenever the show was mentioned. If you really want my honest opinion of Lorrett, then I believe that she is an extremely reserved person, but perhaps, in more direct terms, I can't help thinking she is at times one of life's loners.'

'This is the sort of detail we need, but precisely what is it that makes you conclude as you do, Gregg?'

'Well, John, I have seen her on some three or four occasions since our first meeting and of course it follows that we have had several conversations at various times. Understandably, however, those conversations were not always about the show, in fact there were times when they touched upon, albeit quite vaguely, certain other aspects of both our lives. But Lorrett had this knack of either diverting a conversation or cutting it short in some way, if by chance it became a little too personal for her. For example, without any prompting from me, she seemed quite happy to tell me about her broken marriage and her subsequent divorce, even admitting her sense of failure because of the marriage breakdown. But as careful as I was in questioning her further on the subject, she just could not bring herself to answer some of my questions, or give any explanation for her reluctance to do so.

'On another occasion, she mentioned her mother and spoke of her with affection and kindness, yet at our next meeting, my impression of her as a loving daughter was soon shattered, for she went on to casually mention in passing that she had neither seen or spoken to her mother for some years. Yet from what I can gather, her mother only lives a short distance away from London. You see, I always had the feeling that she initiated topics of conversation without first thinking them through. Subsequently this inevitably meant that there were times when personal questions were bound to come up and generally, these were the type of questions she preferred not to answer. So, to avoid doing so, she would either cut the conversation short or tactfully turn it round in some subtle way.'

'I can certainly see how you became confused over the situation, Gregg, but what you have just told me does open up other possible avenues of enquiry concerning her present state of mind. But please continue, and I am sorry if I keep interrupting you.'

'That's all right, John. I was only going to tell you how Lorrett's reserve showed itself at our last meeting, just prior to the show.'

'Please carry on, I am interested in anything you have to say.'

'Well, we were discussing certain final arrangements concerning the show, when I suddenly realised she seemed to be miles away; then, quite out of the blue, she reached across and touching my hand quietly said that she hoped we could go on seeing each other once the show was over. I was of course taken back and was about to respond, when a look came over her face that suggested she was regretting what she had just said, so she then re-phrased her remark. "What I am trying to say, Gregg, is that I value your friendship and wish to thank you for all the help you have given me, and perhaps, hopefully, our paths will cross again in the future." You see, John, she seemed to have this need to either qualify or nullify certain remarks that she made and I admit I found this quite disconcerting.'

'I can understand your dilemma. But let me ask you, did you ever meet her husband?'

'No, because from what I can make out, they split up long before I came onto the scene and as I have already pointed out, Lorrett was not the best of communicators when it came down to personal matters.'

'I have to agree with you, Gregg.' Martin had joined the discussion for the first time. 'I have been her agent for some while and it seems as if I know less about her than you do. But of one thing I am sure, that thanks to you and your team, I believe she now has a marvellous future in front of her.'

'After the performance she gave that evening, Martin, I have to agree with you, but at the moment, I am beginning to wonder if your prediction has any real chance of coming true.'

'Which brings us to a suitable pause and my next question, Gregg. Could you give the doctor and myself a run-down on the events of that evening, for I can't help but feel that this show of yours has in some way become the catalyst in Miss Lorren's condition.'

'Did you not see it on the television, then, John?'

'No, unfortunately both Dr Linley and I were at one of our meetings. I have of course been told about it since and I did see extracts from it on the programme where they review specific television events of the week. But that review was rather brief and somewhat lacking in content. What we are really looking for is something more than just the superficiality of the show; it is much deeper than that. You see, something happened that evening which appears to have either triggered or caused Miss Lorren's condition. Now, whatever it was, we first have to identify it before we can try to understand it; then and only then can we do our best to resolve it. So could you give us your account of the events leading up to the show and perhaps even some insight into the actual show itself?'

'By all means, John. Well, as you no doubt know, the show was a great success, proof of which came by way of the different press articles that seemed to compete against each other for new superlatives in praise of the event and its producers. As to the actual planning and preparation of the show, well, much of this is best described by the paperwork my boss Robbie has already sent you. The show itself, however, is not that easy to summarise, for being backstage whilst a show is in progress is like being on a fairground roundabout. Things happen so erratically and so fast, that it becomes impossible to take them all in, but I will do my best to recall as much as I can for you.'

Gregg began by relating the sequence of events from the first idea up to the show itself. He explained the extreme lengths the team had gone to in commissioning artistes, musicians and extras for the event and then went on to describe the amount of detail to design and build the props necessary to capture the feel and presence of wartime. He continued by outlining some of the events that had taken place on the anniversary evening, just three weeks earlier, and ended his resumé as if he had completed his task.

'Well, as concise and clear as that was, Gregg, it is not of much use to us; you see, what we are looking for is more the substance of the evening, or the mood if you will. Let me explain. If our understanding of Miss Lorren's problem so far is right, and the doctor and I have no reason to believe otherwise, then something dramatic happened that night, something which appears to have had a catastrophic effect upon Miss Lorren's mind. What that something was, or how it came about, raises questions to which we have no answers, so we are left searching for some elusive unknown cause. It might easily have been something that was passed over as being irrelevant at the time, but whatever it was, it was enough to upset Miss Lorren's normal equilibrium. So let me ask you about the acts you mentioned, or more specifically, the effects of them on the audience. Did they go down well with the people gathered there, were the audience receptive, were they appreciative? These are the sort of things we are looking for. You see, from what you have told us this far, you must have picked up much of the overall response to the show that evening.'

'I can see what you are getting at now, John, and yes, there was an indescribable unity and happiness in the audience there that night and this became apparent early on in the evening. In fact, everyone there had been in high spirits right from the moment they arrived, but this elation was even more noticeable after the first mini-play of the show.'

'OK, let's start from there. Would you run through it for us?'

'Yes, I will, John, but you did mention earlier that Robbie had sent you copy minutes of our meetings. This being the case you must have already read about the incident at Monte Cassino. Well, it was this event that was to be our first mini-play of the evening.'

'Are you referring to the story about the German soldier, what was his name? Oh yes, Kerkner, wasn't it?'

'Yes, that's the one.'

'I do remember it, but if my memory serves me right you apparently had not been able to locate the British Tommy at the time.'

'Ah! you obviously only have the minutes of the meetings covering our early planning sessions; well, it was not until some time later that I was able to track down the Tommy and thus bring him and Kerkner together at the end of our mini-play depicting their story.'

'All right, tell us everything that you can about the play, how it was presented, its effects upon the people there that evening, in fact any detail you remember, whether you see it as being relevant or not.'

'If you are looking for total detail, John, it would be rather pointless if I were to tell you about the play without first giving you some insight into the type of man this Tommy fellow turned out to be. For I think it is essential to understand the man, if you are to fully appreciate the unique factors which brought about the unusual situation in the first place.'

'I am listening, Gregg.'

'Well, to begin with, finding the Tommy was no easy task, but when I did eventually set my eyes on him for the first time, I was convinced that he was not the person I had been searching for; you see, he was a vicar. Well, it turned out that he was in fact the right man, but he had only become ordained into the church since his demob from the forces after the war. I explained who I was and then went on to ask him about the story Kerkner had related to me. Naturally, he remembered the incident very well and agreed that Kerkner had described it exactly as it had happened. I was, however, soon to realise that this was yet another situation that was to demonstrate the many twists and turns of fate in war, for according to the vicar, who I will continue to call Tommy, that night on Monte Cassino was to be but one of the many steps on his own personal road to Damascus.'

'Are you saying that the incident had the same profound effect on him as it did on this chappie, Kerkner?' the doctor enquired.

'Yes, but not quite in the same way. You see, our Tommy had already gone through a similar experience in the desert some time prior to that evening and it was that which had indirectly helped to create the unusual situation between Kerkner and him that night on Monte Cassino. Perhaps it would be best if I tell you the story as the Tommy related it to me, for he went on to say:

' "I was a teacher before the war and a part-time member of the Territorial Army, so, understandably, I was one of the first to be called up soon after war was declared. Then, after completing my training, I became attached to a well known infantry regiment. After spending some time in England, my regiment was shipped out to North Africa where immediately we became embroiled in a great deal of fighting, but I was eventually to end up with the Eighth Army in the desert. There, under Monty, we were to consolidate our positions in preparation for the final push against Rommel. Now, I only tell you this because, as strange as it may seem, that final push against Rommel was not only to bring about a change in the eventual outcome of the war, it was also to bring about a dramatic change in my own personal outlook on life. So much so, that had I not experienced that change then my meeting with Kerkner that night on Monte might easily have been a different story."

'Well, John, the Tommy went on to tell me the story of how he was forced by circumstance to face up to what he had become and how it was only because of this re-awakening in his own life that he was able to find compassion for his enemy that night on Monte Cassino.'

'Whilst I suspect this has no bearing on Miss Lorren's problem, I am now intrigued to know what it was that brought about this change in your Tommy fellow.'

'As you say, John, it has no bearing on Lorrett, but it is a fascinating story just the same, for he went on to say:

' "Because of all the fighting I had been involved in before the big push against Rommel, I had regretfully become hardened to both the sight and the sound of death and regretfully, I had shown no remorse for the enemy. But it happened that one day we were street-fighting our way through the lanes and alleyways of a small desert town, where each house and structure concealed its share of enemy defenders. I had myself, without realising it, somehow become separated from the rest of my platoon, so I was cautiously edging my way along an alleyway, the end of which led into a small square. From my position, I could see the barrel of an enemy machine gun poking out of an upper window in front of me, where without respite, it was splattering its lethal fire at our lads on the other side of the square. Ever conscious of the danger, I carefully eased my way forward with my back tight against the wall of nearby buildings, making for the entrance of the property that housed this weapon and its crew. Well, I was within a yard of the entrance, ready to move forward and enter, when a young German soldier suddenly rushed out of the doorway and past me without realising I was there. He stopped and turned with his back towards me, then took up a stance in the direction of the square before bringing his automatic weapon up to fire. He fired a single burst at someone across the square, then, for some unknown reason, he took a couple of steps backwards, half turning in my direction as he did.

' "It was only then that he noticed me for the first time and in the panic to complete his turn and regain his momentary loss of balance, he had given me those vital seconds of advantage with which to swing back my rifle and lunge my bayonet into his gut. But at that precise moment, something inexplicably strange came over me, for without conscious reason or intent, I didn't bayonet him. Instead, I merely brought the butt of my rifle gently round and up under his chin. To this day I have never understood how or why, but it seemed as if both my body and my mind had for that single moment been taken over by a force stronger than my own. However, just as I was about to turn into the open doorway I heard a loud explosion above me and, ironically, I found myself flat on the ground only a matter of inches away from my prostrate victim. Fortunately I was not hurt, but it was some seconds before I was able to take control of my senses and to realise that the room above me, with its machine gun and crew, was now totally destroyed. As I got to my feet and started to wipe the dust from my face I realised how lucky I had been, for had I not been delayed by the affray with my nearby companion, I would have been inside that building when the explosion occurred. Without stopping to ponder the point further, I went to pick up my rifle from the ground and as I did, I noticed that my companion appeared to be coming round. It was then I realised that I must have only knocked him out. Unfortunately for me, his automatic weapon was beside him, but again, in those brief moments of cursing my stupidity for not killing him earlier, another strange thing happened. For from his lying position on the ground, my victim with the bloody mouth knowingly looked up and gently smiled at me, then, carefully moving his hand away from his gun, he put up his thumb in a gesture of companionship. I couldn't believe my eyes and at first I couldn't understand his reasoning, but by this one simple act, he had touched my conscience and found my soul, for from that moment on, I was never to be the same person again.

' "So it was, that in those brief moments of self recognition, all I could do to express myself was to return his thumbs-up gesture, cautiously bend down to pick up my rifle and with a friendly wave goodbye, run off to catch up with the rest of my platoon. By the next day we had taken the town, where we were to spend a further three days rounding up prisoners, burying the dead and consolidating our positions before preparing to move off again. Throughout those few days of comparative quiet, I tried to find the young German lad amongst the hundreds of other prisoners we had captured, but failed. Inevitably, however, I couldn't get him out of my mind. I couldn't forget his face, but, most of all, I couldn't forget the feeling that we had, each in our own way, been privy to a very rare experience. Such were my feelings at that time, that I felt guilty to be amongst the living, yet relieved at not being amongst the dead or the dying; I was confronted with my past but unable to see my future. But perhaps foremost in my mind in those few days were the circumstances that had changed me from a man into a savage, for I could no longer masquerade in my cloak of pretence by simply shutting my eyes to what I had become, for in truth I had, by my aggression, disqualified myself from the human race.

' "So perhaps you can see now, Gregg, the nature and conscience of the man who was eventually to find his way across the desert, onto the beaches of Sicily, be involved in the landings at Salerno and then ultimately, quietly be lying stomach down beside a large projecting rock near the top of Monte Cassino. Which brings me to my explanation of the events that night and the change that had come over me since that incident with the young German soldier. You see, throughout all of those campaigns I have just mentioned, I never again knowingly hurt or killed another human being. To avoid doing so, I would go through the motions of combat, but I would always fire away from living targets or aim at the ground well in front of them.

' "My one dread was, however, that I would again have to face a situation similar to that which I had already experienced in the desert. But as good fortune would have it the problem did not arise, until, that is, the night of my destined meeting with our now mutual acquaintance Kerkner, when at first, I thought that history was about to repeat itself. Looking back now, I am sure that there was a sense of destiny in the air that night, for the purpose of the patrol, which was to culminate in that meeting, was in itself unusual. You see, whether it was by statutory convention or merely unwritten agreement I don't know, but certain towns, cities or areas of historic beauty such as Florence, Rome and possibly the monastery at Monte Cassino, were deemed to be protected sites and as such, were left untouched by the missiles of war. Now, generally speaking, this arrangement was honoured, but it was believed by the Allies that German troops were using the high ground around the monastery for purposes that were in contradiction to this accord, for there were times when German soldiers had been seen in the locality. So it was that as dusk fell, I, along with eight others of our platoon, was sent off to reconnoitre the area up and around the monastery, with the view to confirm or dispel any doubt as to an enemy presence there. We first worked our way forward to the base of the high ground and then split up, each having been allocated a point on the mount where we would take up our positions. Mine was to be beside this large projecting rock on the far side of the mount, just a short distance down from the summit. Well, it must have taken me over an hour to carefully work my way up to the rock for, understandably, I had to avoid the risk of becoming seen against the moonlit skyline. But having reached my designated spot, I settled myself down under the leading lower edge of the rock, so that I could get a clear view of the courtyard wall and upper part of the monastery beyond.

' "Now, we had been told before we left on the venture that our artillery was to remain silent until our return, so you can imagine my surprise when suddenly our guns opened up. But it wasn't so much surprise as total disbelief when, as the guns began firing, I saw this German soldier hop over the low wall above and begin to slide down the rough terrain on his backside towards me. The fact that he was forced to stop for a moment some two metres away from the rock gave me enough time to quickly sum up the situation and to suppress an overpowering temptation to burst out laughing. You see, the reason he had stopped in mid-slide was because his crutch had somehow come into contact with something sticking out of the ground and I could see by his face that he wasn't too pleased with the encounter. However, in those few seconds between the suppressed emotions of laughter and fear, there was just enough light to see that his rifle had no cartridge case or bayonet attached and of course, it wasn't until some time later that he was to realise that I was there. So you see, I was in the advantageous position of knowing that he could do very little to hurt me and I had no desire or reason to hurt him.

' "Well, I think you know the rest, Gregg, except perhaps that the only reason I am able to tell you this story today is because I was fortunate enough to pick up a stray bullet in my shoulder the very next day whilst out on another patrol. I say fortunate, because the rest of my platoon, with the exception of two others, were all killed whilst on that same patrol, so, sadly, they still remain there, buried in the ground that they fought for. But thanks to God, you tell me that after all these years, I am to have the profound experience of seeing again this stranger whose face I shall always remember and whose fear I shall never forget. But why is it that I suddenly find myself becoming relieved of a burden I have carried since those far off days of war? Is it because I have always known that Kerkner and I would one day meet again, or is it that I am at last able to come to terms with my past?"

'Well, John, that was Tommy's account of the incident and our interpretation of it on stage consisted of a set designed to simulate the location and two actors acting out the incident as it happened that night on Monte Cassino. Before the mini-play began, a newsreel clip of old film showing British troops in action was back-projected on stage, whilst a narrator gave a brief account of the circumstances leading up to the event, telling Tommy's story as I have just told you. By arrangement we had positioned Kerkner and Tommy well apart from each other amongst the audience and at the right moment, they were discreetly ushered through different exits to opposite sides back-stage. As the mini-play came to its end, the two of them were brought together front stage for the first time after all those years and from that moment on the atmosphere was beyond description. There was this kind of serene elation about the audience that one felt they could touch; there was cheering, there were tears and a large number of the audience were on their feet clapping their hearts out. There were others who preferred to remain inconspicuously seated, either because they had been overcome by the emotion of the event, or because they had reason to remember similar situations in their own lives. Well, it was a good ten minutes before we could continue with the final surprise we had up our sleeve, for we had been able to trace and track down that young German soldier, whose act of friendship had changed our Tommy's life.'

'My God, Gregg, what an event, what an experience, it is almost impossible to contemplate. For, just sitting here as I am now, I can feel the tension that must have been there that evening and for the first time appreciate the effect it must have had on those who saw the show that night. I am bound to say, however, you were without a doubt playing with fire that night, Gregg, albeit it seems as if you and your team did their best to limit the possible risk from such a soul-searching exercise.'

'Your remarks imply that by putting such a show together, we had not contemplated the possible effects it could have on either the audience or those participating in it, John. So let me assure you that the show and the intention behind it was no hit or miss affair, it was meticulously planned and very carefully considered down to the last detail before putting each of these mini-plays together and portraying them on stage. So at no time did we cross that very fine line that exists between drama and trauma.'

'I was not suggesting the show itself was psychologically damaging in any way, although it does seem at the moment that it had some indirect effect on Miss Lorren, but I am saying that, perhaps without realising it, your show seems to have had all the potential to have developed into a spectacle of mass hysteria. Fortunately the theme of the show was based upon mercy, love and compassion, which generally are all unifying emotions and which no doubt did unite the minds of anyone who saw the show that night, hence the audience's reaction you described earlier. But that same hysteria at, for instance, a political meeting could quite easily end in violence, or at a religious revival meeting, in hundreds of converts. You see, as a psychiatrist, I meet people every day of my life who, for one reason or another, could quite easily become highly agitated or completely irrational if subjected to an intensity of emotion such as you have just described. So my remarks about the potential volatility of the show were not specifically intended as criticism, but more as an observation of the possible dangers in stirring up people's emotions. For no matter how one chooses to say it, you and the team could have easily been faced with some unexpected problems that night. Fortunately this was not to be the case, so I can only conclude by saying that I have every admiration for your team's handling of what is ostensibly an extremely delicate subject. But let me proceed further and ask: did you put on other plays that evening similar in theme to the one you have just described?'

'Well, in total we put on four short plays, John. One of these was like Kerkner's and Tommy's story; the other two, whilst based upon the central principle of uniting people with their past, were of a comical nature and as such turned out to be extremely funny and again, they were well received by the audience there that night.'

'Would you briefly run through one of the funnier plays for us?'

'Certainly. Perhaps the second one of these was the most amusing. This concerned a number of British prisoners of war who were held in captivity by the Italians high up in the hills of northern Italy. The camp, which by design was quite remote, had been purpose built in a large clearing cut out of a dense forest area. Like other such camps, it consisted of a compact hutted area, the guards and administrative quarters, two surveillance towers, and the normal peripheral rolled barbed wire barrier which had been taken up to the edge of the forest surrounding the site. On the outer side of this barrier, a narrow track had been worn by the Italian sentries whose job was to patrol the entire length of the track and ensure that there were no attempts to break out. At two points along this track, there was a sentry box which had been backed up against the barbed wire barrier surrounding the camp.

'The incident, which was re-enacted on stage, came about because the Italian camp commander had, as a punishment, cut off the supply of firewood to the prisoners' huts at a time when the weather was severe and the temperature was below zero. So some of the innovative inmates, whose hut was positioned near to the wire barrier and in line with one of the sentry's huts, decided that it was time to do something about the situation. Now, it would appear that each of the prisoners' huts had its own unique collection of useful knick-knacks, which had either been unethically acquired or simply purloined, depending upon the current owner's own personal view of things.

'Well, from what I gathered, apart from the many other bits of equipment they owned, such as a small distillery, a home made collapsible ladder and other such items, they had an highly valued length of strong rope. So a plan was put together whereby two prisoners were to waylay and occupy the duty sentry at a point on his route where his sentry box was obscured from sight by adjacent trees. Then, on a given signal from a nearby lookout, the box was to be surreptitiously hauled over the barbed wire before quickly being removed from sight, where it was to be chopped up and eventually used as fuel. I was also told that, by this time in the war, the Italian soldiers in general had become more than disillusioned with their lot and were often quite happy to fraternise with their prisoners and even occasionally exchange possessions. So any opportunity for a chat over the barbed wire became something of a relief to them as they trod their repetitive route back and forth along the lonely outer track. Well, John, on a given signal from the discreetly placed observers, the rope was first looped, then thrown over the wire barrier so that it lasso'd the main body of the sentry box just below its roof line. Then, with the combined effort of several inmates, the loop was tightened and the box was silently and quickly pulled over the barbed wire barrier before being sawn through into three handy sections and smartly disappearing into the nearby hut.

'I was told by the instigator of this plan, whom I met for the first time some nine months before the show, that apart from the pleasure of a warm hut that night, there was the extra benefit of watching the antics of a half drunk sentry, who had returned to find his sentry box was no longer there. You see, John, the sentry had been only too pleased to share and enjoy both the cigarettes and the home made hooch he had been offered.'

'What a wonderfully humorous situation. I would have loved to have seen it. Tell me, did you again use actors for this play?' Dr Linley enquired.

'No; in fact, we managed to find all the lads who were actually involved in the original incident, so we put them in uniform and let them re-enact the event in front of the television cameras on stage. We did again, however, use a narrator to describe the plan and the event as it took place, but the Italian sentry watched the re-enactment from the wings so that he could be presented to the lads on stage at the end of the play.'

'So you were also able to find this Italian chappie after all those years?'

'Yes, John, but this was one of the easier bits of research, for I was given his name by the lads long before the show took place and fortunately they also remembered the name of the village in Italy where he came from.'

'I should think it was hilarious when they all came together afterwards.'

'Extremely so, John, especially when the lads ceremoniously presented Mario, that was the sentry's name, with the sentry box used in the show, which intentionally was a replica in size and colour of the original. You see, I had purposely avoided telling Mario the precise reason for his proposed appearance on television; I had merely told him that it was related to an incident in the war that had indirectly involved him. So he was left in the dark as to the exact reason for his presence there that night and he was still unaware of it as he stood in the wings watching the lads on stage go through the motions of stealing the sentry box. Needless to say, once Mario was brought on stage we couldn't stop him laughing, for, as he said, "As I watched, it gradually all came back to me, but I couldn't understand how the box could have been hidden in the camp all that time and how it was now there on stage in front of me."

'Well, Mario then went on to tell us how the loss of the box that evening some twenty-seven years earlier had become a topic of conversation amongst his fellow guards for months after the event. But the funniest part was that, even after the show, he was still convinced that the box we had made for the event was in fact the one he had lost all those years before.'

Both the doctor and John were still chuckling to themselves as Gregg completed his review.

'Well, they say that the truth is stranger than fiction and in this incident, it was obviously a great deal funnier. Now tell me, Gregg, did most of the show evolve around these individual playlets?' John enquired.

'Oh no, I suppose in all they represented some forty per cent of the show's duration; the rest of the programme consisted of a mixture of other acts, mainly visual because of the nature of our cosmopolitan audience, then there were the dancers, the big band numbers and of course the singers.'

'Was Miss Lorren involved in any other part of the show, apart from the finale, that is?'

'Oh yes, in fact it was she who helped to glue the whole show together and give it that essential international sparkle and flavour.'

'So was the show televised live throughout Europe as hoped for?'

'Not entirely; it did go out live and most of the main countries did participate in the venture and here again, there was nothing else but praise for the show's entertainment value and delicate presentation.'

'Good. Well, I think that both Dr Linley and I have now the full measure of what went on that night and from what you have said it was obviously a highly emotional and relevant evening's entertainment, both for the people there and for everyone else who saw it on television. Now back to Miss Lorren, and let me ask: in what other ways was she involved with the show?'

'Well, in the planning stages it was intended that she would sing two songs about halfway through the programme, but owing to her popularity on the evening, she did in fact sing an additional song, all grouped together just prior to the pre-arranged interval we had organised. Then she sang another number midway between the interval and the finale.'

'Were all the songs sung in English that evening, or were there other singers apart from Miss Lorren?'

'We did have two other singers from the Continent in the show, but Lorrett also sang her songs in a mixture of English, French and German.'

'Did her midway performance go smoothly; by that, I mean, did she show any sign of excessive tension at all?'

'No, Doctor, if anything she appeared to enjoy every moment of it and she handled the situation like a veteran, so much so that at the end of it, we had to wait a considerable time for the applause to stop.'

'Let us move on to the grand finale, in fact to the point where Miss Lorren collapsed, and Gregg, could I ask you to think carefully about everything you saw and heard as you stood in the wings watching her perform. Take your time and try to recall if there was anything that struck you as being out of context with your expectations of the scene, or inconsistent with Miss Lorren's normal poise or demeanour.'

'I will do my best, John, but it did all happen over three weeks ago now and time does have the knack of eroding one's memory. However, the penultimate act had come to an end and the speeches that followed were finally concluded. Then the lights in the auditorium began to dim and at the same time, the distant sound of an all-clear siren could be heard.'

Gregg then went on to explain how the curtains slowly went up to expose a darkened stage and a lone German soldier quietly playing a harmonica. He then described how, after hearing the first chorus of the song

'Lilli Marlene', the spotlight was cut above the soldier and another came on to show Lorrett, as she, in turn, stood quietly humming the opening bars of the song. He then continued with his resumé, by giving a word by word account of Lorrett's performance that night, now some three weeks in the past.

'As she finished humming the first verses, she then began slowly to half speak and half sing the words of the song. Well, such was her performance, that I personally felt as if I was the only one there. So much so, that whilst there were over a thousand people in the auditorium that night, their silence as she sang was quite unbelievable. Then as she came to the end of the song for the first time, she paused before beginning to sing it again, but this time she sang it in German, still in accompaniment with the harmonica and still within that prevailing and inexplicable silence. You see, one could virtually feel the uncanny empathy that had built up between the audience and Lorrett that night; in fact, as she finished the song for the second time, she lowered her head as if in prayer and the audience did nothing more than remain perfectly still. It was only as Lorrett lifted her head some seconds later, that everyone began to clap. Then they clapped, and continued clapping until eventually the orchestra had to interrupt the ovation and with a change of tempo to march time, began to play the melody again. Lorrett took up the song once more, but the previous submissiveness in her voice was now gone, for this time she sang it with a feeling of defiance and determination. People began to tap out the rhythm of the music with their feet, others were on their feet clapping out the time as small groups of people, symbolically dressed in the uniforms of different nations, gradually congregated on stage. The song ended; Lorrett moved a little further forward and with tremulous humility thanked her audience first in English, then German, and finally in French; she then invited them to join her in the final chorus. Then, as the main lights came on, I moved back from the wings to get a better view of the audience out front, but little did I realise at that moment that I was sharing with them one of the most emotional experiences of my life. People were scattered all about the place, some were standing on their seats, others had left their seats and were mock marching along the aisles in time with the music.

'I could see hefty men embracing each other, whilst others without embarrassment or care sat wiping tears from their faces. I saw two or three white-belted ambulance men moving here and there, tending to odd people who had without a doubt been overcome by the tremendous impact of the show, for there was an indescribable unity there that night. Now, feeling as I did, I cannot remember my exact reaction when at the end of the communal singing I saw Lorrett first embrace, then collapse into the arms of, the German harmonica player. For whilst it was planned that he should come forward to meet Lorrett at the end of her song, her collapse wasn't a part of it. Fortunately the audience must have viewed the situation as if it had been intended, for the curtain fell quite naturally to end the show without spoiling any of the elation the event had created. Subsequently, the on-stage panic to deal with Lorrett's problem was not seen by the audience. Our only difficulty was the inevitable non-stop clapping and encores calling for Lorrett's return on stage. So as soon as she was put on a stretcher and wheeled away, the curtain was taken up and someone explained how Lorrett had fainted due to exhaustion. Then the orchestra, realising the problem, quickly took up the melody again and the audience joined in and sang along with it. This was to continue for some minutes before it was decided that the show had to end and the final curtain was brought down.

'Now, thinking back on the show as I have been doing, I have to admit to a degree of personal satisfaction with that finale, for, with the exception of Lorrett's collapse, it came over exactly as I had envisaged it, and in some funny way it has satisfied a yearning I have always had since my childhood days.'

'Well, thank you for that very detailed review, Gregg, but naturally it does raise further points, which I would now like to clear up. For instance, you said that Miss Lorren sang parts of her songs in either German or French, so am I to assume she was primed for this by learning the translation parrot fashion?'

'No, she can speak both languages, albeit her French is a little rusty and needs perfecting, but her German is quite fluent. I have to say that I was surprised over this, when I learned about it at one of our early auditions. You see, after we had become convinced she was the right person for the show, I asked her if she would be prepared to learn parts of selected songs in German and French. Well, she did no more than to answer my question in German and added some extra comment in French. I was to learn later that she had in fact lived in Germany as a child and English, German and on the odd occasion French, were spoken in the home. She also told me that she had studied German at school. So, do you see this as being relevant then?'

The question came as the doctor and John were silently facing each other across the room, both with a quizzical look upon their faces, so it was some moments before John turned his head and responded to the question.

'Possibly Gregg; if nothing more, there could be a connection between Miss Lorren's early life and her last act on stage that night, but her vague and less obvious association with the French language fascinates me more at this point in time.' John paused hesitatingly.

'On your arrival here today, Gregg, I asked if you would delay any questions you had concerning Miss Lorren's health. My reason for this was because I didn't want to influence your thoughts, observations or responses to me, when questioned. But I think perhaps now is the right time for me to tell you as much as Dr Linley and myself know about Miss Lorren's problem. You see, we are fairly confident that she is suffering from a very unusual form of amnesia and this has in some way affected her nervous system. In fact, it appears to have left a part of her mind locked into some type of psychic void, thus preventing her from communicating with, or responding to, the world around her.

'Now, usually this condition can be brought about by injury, disease, traumatic shock, or simply fatigue of the brain, and its effect is such, that the patient has consciousness with sensation, but no understanding. In other words, a patient will react to contact, but fail to understand the reason for it; thus, they can no longer relate to, or equate with, normal stimuli. To expand on this analysis, one might compare it to the mysticism of something like Yoga, where a Guru might say that the mind can be disciplined into and out of a state of deep meditation thereby isolating it away from influences of the body and thus freeing it to function in a void, where both greater perception and understanding can be achieved. As to one's belief in such matters, this is not relevant, but it does help us to explain the effects of the problem, although anyone with Miss Lorren's condition cannot simply discipline their mind into, or out of, it. However, it is possible that the condition can with rest, or conversely, in some cases, with specific external stimuli, return to normality, but this generally depends on the initial cause of the problem. In Miss Lorren's case, we have no evidence to suggest damage to the brain caused by either disease or injury, but we do seem to be gathering sufficient information to suggest that the problem could have been brought about by excessive mental strain or fatigue, probably compounded by a sudden shock. This is why, Gregg, I needed to hear what you had to say concerning this show of yours first. You see, if you had been told these details earlier, they could easily have influenced either your answers to me, or the manner in which you gave them. This may have resulted in the possible loss of very important detail, but as it happens, most of what you have said this far does seem to help us towards a better understanding of Miss Lorren's problem.'

'So it is possible that Lorrett's participation in the show did in fact prove to be too much for her?'

'No, I don't think so; after all, you yourself implied earlier that she appeared to enjoy giving her performance. But of course, I am ever conscious of the fact that an artiste's performance may only represent a part of the extensive mental and physical preparation necessary to achieve what their inner egos demand of them. So, if anything, it is this self inflicted discipline that takes its toll on people and all too often we are faced with the individual who doesn't know when to stop chasing this elusive dream we call perfection. This may or may not have happened in Miss Lorren's case, although particularly in view of the highly sensitised nature of the show itself, it might have some bearing on her condition. But I am beginning to think that the cause or reason for Miss Lorren's problem is firmly rooted in her past and that the show and her involvement in it merely became the judge and jury of her predicament. However, theorising, so they say, doesn't buy the baby a new hat, so let me return to another problem that we now seem to have. For since your disclosure that Miss Lorren sang some of her songs in French, I think I should tell you about a little incident that happened some ten days ago, for it is possible that you might be able to help us with it.'

'I would only be too pleased to help if I can.'

'I am sure you would, but bear with me, whilst I explain.'

'Of course, John.'

'Let me first tell you about some of the things we do here. You see, we have, with time and experience, developed and established a whole range of diagnostic equipment, procedures and tests, where certain primary causes and cures for specific mental problems can within reason be recognised fairly quickly. But for much of the time, our endeavours to solve patients' problems only come about through the use of persistent and innovative experimentation.

'So in cases such as Miss Lorren's where there is no evidence to suggest physical damage, where on the face of it everything appears normal and where we are unable to communicate directly with the patient, we have to revert to either experimentation or historic analysis for inspiration. We jokingly call this our CASE procedure, our own acronym for Clutching At Straws Experimentation; however, the investigative work that this often involves is far removed from the flippancy that the title suggests. Now, it was just over a week ago, that one of our nursing staff noticed that Miss Lorren, who has consistently remained silent since her arrival here, occasionally broke her silence whilst she was sleeping. Obviously, we were delighted that some change appeared to be taking place, so in came our CASE procedure and we decided to set up some equipment to record any sound she made whilst sleeping. Now we carried out these tests over a period of five nights, but unfortunately much of that which was recorded consisted mainly of disjointed garbled noises. But just on the one occasion she did speak a few words, but they were in French. So we asked one of the staff here to see if they could make any sense of it, but their knowledge of the language is rather limited, so we are still left in the dark as to exactly what was said, or whether there is any intelligible significance to it. So, Gregg, we wondered if we were to play it back to you, whether you would see if you can make anything of it for us?'

'I will do my best, but how long does it go on for? you see, you did say that the experiment covered the period of some five nights.'

'Ah, yes, I forgot to explain that we set up the recorder with a voice-activated circuit in conjunction with the microphone; subsequently it only switched on and recorded when anything was said. Furthermore, since then we have edited this down to just over ten minutes of actual recorded information.'

'Thank goodness for that; for a moment there I was working out how I could get a pair of pyjamas and a toothbrush together, but if it's only ten minutes I don't have to worry, so let us hear what we are about to hear, shall we?'

The whirl of the motor from a rather antiquated tape recorder interrupted only by the spasmodic and feeble meanderings of Lorrett's voice, occupied all without exception before it was turned off and the three men sat quietly waiting for Gregg to look up from the piece of paper he had been making notes on.

'What can I say, except most of it is nothing more than mutterings. There are a few words however, which, providing you give licence for an element of conjecture, I interpret as love, time and possibly hope, forget and met. Apart from that, I don't for one moment suggest I understand anything she said. But there is one thing which does seem to be more than a little coincidental, that is the rhyming of the two words forget and met and the gap between their delivery; it is as if she was mumbling some kind of poem. But beyond that, John, your guess is as valid as mine.'

'Not to worry, it is as much as I expected and it serves no purpose to pursue the matter further at the moment. So let me come back to that crucial moment of Miss Lorren's collapse and ask, was her embrace of the German soldier at the end of her performance planned?'

'Now you have come to mention it, John, I don't think it was, unless there were some last minute changes made by Ned or Robbie whilst I was not there. At the rehearsals I saw, it was intended that the soldier was to come forward from backstage and Lorrett was to give him a surprised look, before linking arms with him, then turning to face the audience. The object of this was to show, as it were, the reunion of two people after many years of separation, visibly suggesting to those watching that the waiting implied within the words of the song was now over.'

'So Miss Lorren and this man taking the part of the German soldier had acted out this gesture before at rehearsals.'

'No, John, they hadn't. Lorrett had of course gone through the motions on previous occasions, but the man who took the part of the soldier in the show was an actor who had been employed just for the evening. You see, he was engaged mainly for his ability to play the harmonica, and the final action, being as simple as it was, did not warrant the need for rehearsal.'

'So we are saying that this man and Miss Lorren had never met before.'

'As far as I know, John, they were complete strangers, but of course they might have met previously; after all, I didn't know Lorrett that well.'

'That's fair comment, so why then did Miss Lorren embrace him?'

'Well, until a few minutes ago I hadn't given the matter much thought, John, but you are quite right, there is a contradiction here. Thinking about it still further now: as Lorrett turned to face this man she really did appear to show genuine surprise, then her arms went round his neck as if she was about to embrace him. But before she could complete the move, her legs seemed to give way under her and her body leaned heavily against him as she slithered through his arms to the floor.'

'Right, Gregg, now perhaps we are getting somewhere; this seems to be the something I have been looking for. Tell me what was the man's reaction to the situation; did he for instance appear highly concerned?'

'I wouldn't say excessively so; naturally he was completely taken back by the incident, although he was soon down on his knees trying to be of some assistance and of course he was concerned, but I would say, not in the same way as perhaps a relative or a loved one would have been.'

'You met this man before the show, I assume.'

'Yes, Doctor, but only briefly. My boss Robbie introduced him to me some months ago.'

'Would Miss Lorren have been around at the time?'

'Oh no, we met him at the theatre where he was working.'

'Gregg, you said that Miss Lorren had lived in Germany when she was young; did she ever say where in Germany, or what age she was when she left for this country?'

'No, John, but you have to remember, she was not the best of talkers and really, the times that we ever spent together were comparatively few.'

'How did other people take to her? I mean, was she generally well liked, did she get on with other people all right?'

'Yes, I think everyone I know saw her as being a very lovely person and, don't get me wrong, I thought so too. It was just that somehow we didn't quite gel together, but this could have been my fault as well as Lorrett's.'

'Returning to this actor in the German uniform that night: was he quite a reasonable looking chap, I mean, he wasn't sinister looking or anything like that?' The doctor was obviously still unconvinced about something.

Gregg, recognising it, picked up his brief case and searched out a batch of photographs.

'Judge for yourself, Doctor, here is a photograph of him taken by one of the press men before the show that night.'

'Oh yes, he has quite a pleasant face, a face that is more likely to please than to frighten.' The doctor passed the photograph to John, smiling as he did.

'Well, like you, Doctor, I can see no reason for thinking that this fellow's face might have some relevance to Miss Lorren's collapse that night. So are we trying to find something that just isn't there? Unless there is some association between the uniform and Miss Lorren's childhood past.'

'John, I can't see the uniform has anything to do with it for Lorrett had come into contact with other men in German uniforms in the latter stages of rehearsal and she had no problem then.'

'That seems to put paid to that possibility, so unless there is something else we haven't thought of it looks as if her collapse at that precise moment was nothing more than coincidental, unless you have any other ideas, Doctor?'

'Well, there is the possibility, John, that it came about through a combination of things rather than any one.'

'Even if that is the case, we are still left with the same question why, so perhaps it's best if we leave the matter to rest for a while.' John stopped to look at his watch before continuing. 'Well, having reached this impasse, this seems like the ideal time to toddle up to the canteen to see what concoctions our chef has for us today. Gregg, you will join us for a bite to eat, won't you?'

'I would be happy to, and thank you for the invitation.'

The four men, having selected their choice from the varied display of food presented, sat at a table in the corner away from the drone of conversation coming from around the large central and other adjacent tables. As the first mouthful of food quelled the pangs of hunger, the hitherto silence of the group was broken and the conversation began to flow again.

'Do you know, Gregg, I can't stop laughing to myself over the story you told us about Mario and his long lost sentry box; in fact, the more I think about it the funnier it seems. Tell me, you said you knew of many other funny incidents like that one, were they all just as amusing?'

'Well, it does depend on your sense of humour, John, but certainly, since beginning my research, I have learned of quite a few war-time situations which were either comical or downright hilarious, albeit in some cases, the comedy only emerged out of an otherwise moment of tragedy.

'For instance, I was told the story about a rather rotund middle aged lady called Millie, who, throughout the war, lived in one of those old Victorian terraced houses in the east end of London and had, like most other people in the big cities, experienced her fair share of the bombing. The house, in keeping with the majority of these slum dwellings, had an outside loo which had been built onto the back of the property, more as an addition to it than a part of it. Of course, any compulsion to use it was made via the back yard and in view of any neighbours who happened to be out in their own yards at the time. Well, it would appear that on one particular day in 1945, the lady in question had just composed herself on the board covered shelf in her loo, when without warning, a German V2 rocket came down and exploded not very far away from the house. A friend and near neighbour, who incidently told me the story, lived in the house directly backing onto Millie's and on hearing the explosion, rushed out into her own back yard to see, who in her words, "had got it this time". She then went on to explain what had happened:

' "As I went out of my back door, I could see where the cloud of dust and dirt was settling and I realised as luck would have it, that the rocket had landed on some spare ground at the end of our street. The blast had done quite a bit of roof and window damage to some of the houses, including some minor damage to my own. There were also one or two people who had been slightly injured by falling glass or other debris. Well, after finding out that I could do nothing to help in any way, I turned to go back indoors and as I did, I suddenly noticed my friend Millie sitting as it were transfixed on her loo. It was only then that I realised that the blast had knocked down all the walls around her, except one section that supported the overhead cast iron cistern and chain. At first I thought she was dead, for she was as motionless and silent as a contemplating statue, with her larger than life bloomers still draped around her ankles and feet. So expecting the worst and as quickly as I was able, I clambered clumsily over the low dividing fence between our two gardens. Then, as I finally cleared it and turned, Millie suddenly burst out laughing in such a loud and enduring way, that for a moment I thought she had gone mad. As I found my way over the debris around, her laughing seemed to get louder and the more concerned I became, the more she appeared to laugh. Well, after reaching her, she calmed down enough to tell me through further bouts of giggling, the reason for her outburst. 'Mary,' she said, 'I've had three lots of jollop from me doctor for me blocked bowels and they haven't moved a thing, but that bloody explosion has worked wonders and what a relief. The only thing now is, I bet the bleeding landlord will blame me for knocking down his loo.' " '

'How funny and how typical of cockney humour under duress. But of course, it was this reactionary humour and courage, coming as it did from ordinary people such as Millie, that kept up the morale of the nation in those difficult times. It also gave rise to this fantastic *esprit de corps* that was to develop amongst people from all walks of life, throughout those war years.'

'Yes, you are quite right, John, and from my understanding of it, most of the people who experienced that unity still remember it as being something that they had never experienced in their lives before. Furthermore, it was not always confined to one's countrymen or allies, for I am sure, that even without speaking that night on Monte, Kerkner and Tommy were only able to find their real selves by finding each other.'

'Yes, it is quite a strange old world. However, at the moment the most important part of that world to us seems to be the lovely Miss Lorren. So, gentlemen, if you have all finished your feasting, may I suggest we shift ourselves elsewhere and continue with the problem at hand.'

The four men eased themselves from their seats and moved towards the door of the canteen.

'John, may I ask whether I can see Lorrett while I am here?'

'Strange as it may seem, you are progressing in her direction now, Gregg, for the doctor and I had previously agreed to such an exercise. You see, we would like to observe her reactions upon seeing you again. After all, with a little bit of luck, your good looks and charm, plus perhaps a soupçon of fate, may just bring her out of her shell. This will then kill two birds with one stone. You see, I have always had this self-imposed obligation to the doctor here, for he continues to hope that some day we will be lucky enough both to diagnose and to solve one of our patient's problems in just a few hours, instead of the time it normally takes.'

'Are you back on my hobby horse again, John? That's the worst of these psychiatrists, Gregg, they won't easily let go once they have latched onto someone's foibles.'

'Please, Doctor, not in front of our guests here.'

Martin and Gregg looked smilingly at each other, conscious of the odd bouts of comical rapport that occasionally seemed to surface and fade between the two very likable and dedicated characters.

'John, I don't suppose you have made any contact with Lorrett's mother to see if she could shed any light on her daughter's problem?'

'I have spoken to her over the phone, although it was not in any way enlightening.'

'I would have thought she might have been able to give you some idea as to Lorrett's early life and perhaps even put her finger on a possible cause for her current state of health.'

'I did try to talk with her about the points you make, Gregg, but apart from telling us that Miss Lorren had been a fit and normal child she was, to say the least, not very co-operative.'

'Has the mother been down to see Lorrett at the home here?'

'No, but then I did not suggest she should; furthermore, I have the feeling she would have rejected the idea if I had. To be frank, I am inclined towards the opinion that perhaps both mother and daughter are one of a kind; either that, or a past family upset has taken its toll on their relationship.'

'What about Lorrett's ex-husband, has any contact been made with him?'

'Yes, but here again, whilst he was reasonably helpful, he had nothing positive to offer other than confirming the void that appears to exist between mother and daughter. All in all, Gregg, we have had very little help up to the time of your arrival here today, but thanks to you I am now beginning to feel we have at least made some progress.'

The group had talked their way from the canteen, down two flights of stairs, along a corridor and out of a large door to the rear of the building. From here a covered walkway projected off in two directions, each distantly terminating at the entrance of a similarly designed and constructed red brick building. The four men, led by John, turned right and walked some hundred yards before arriving at the entrance of the wing marked 'Female'. The doctor took out a bunch of keys from his white coat pocket to open a door, allowing all to pass through before turning to relock it. The procedure was repeated before passing through another door giving access to a room that Gregg took to be the recreational area. It was large and spacious with a series of tables end to end down the centre of the room and a number of upright chairs arranged around them. Most of the remaining area was cluttered by a host of tatty mixed style armchairs, settees and well used pouffes. There were some fifty or more women within the room and whilst it had obviously been cleaned frequently, the inevitable lingering drift of human frailty seem to prevail over the underlying, but less detectable, smell of polished floors.

There were a group of women around the far end table, upon which there were a variety of wools, cottons and other miscellaneous materials.

A well built masculine woman emerged from the group and made her way forward.

'Good afternoon, Doctor, have you come to see Miss Lorren?'

'Yes, providing it's convenient, Sister.'

'Yes, of course.'

The two housemen with Martin to one side continued talking to the sister as Gregg stood back taking in the scene. It had only been a matter of minutes since his entry into the room, but already he was experiencing a sense of despondency and nausea at some of the sights around him. There were several inmates huddled asleep in armchairs as others drifted aimlessly about the ward in ill fitting and well worn slippers. In one corner of the room, his eyes settled on an old withered woman, bent with her head drooped over her body, as dribble seeped from her mouth and settled on her apron-covered lap. Another figure, which by comparison to many of the others there seemed normal, sat constantly stirring an empty bowl with a large wooden spoon. In an attempt to avoid the inevitability of further shock, Gregg tried to concentrate his attention on some old blankets spread across a nearby easy chair, only to realise gradually that he was looking at another woman, whose body had twisted and contorted beyond description. As he tried to replace his inner feelings of repulsion with those of compassion, he was reminded of his days as a young man at university and his introduction to the philosophical works of the poet Omar-Khayyam, who, comparing his maker to a potter, questioned why some pots were destined to be perfect and others incomplete or obscenely distorted. Gregg was pondering that very same question as a voice interrupted his thoughts. It was John. 'Over here, Gregg.'

Gregg moved forward, following the three men and the sister to the far end of the room. At first he couldn't see her, for she was partly concealed behind the activities of others around her, then Lorrett was there, seated quietly and majestically in an upright chair in front of him. His hands began to tremble and his legs weakened a little as her fascinating eyes stared past him without purpose or recognition, but even so, there was still a warmth about her that seemed to touch the inner depths of his feelings.

'Well, Gregg, there she is, still unaware of us and the world around her. Is she to remain this way, or can we open the door that shut out her reality?'

'Speaking for myself, I would do everything possible to help open the door, John, but what can I do other than admit to my own inadequacy?'

'I just may be able to supply an answer to that remark later, but are you at least a little happier now that you have seen her?'

'Well, as happy as one could be under the circumstances, but would she not be better off in a private room on her own?'

'Are you saying that she should not be here amongst some of our more serious cases?'

'Not in so many words, but I do feel that her condition is not compatible with most of the other people here.'

'It may outwardly appear that way, Gregg, but in common with most of the other patients here, it is Miss Lorren's mind that is the problem and any physical differences you see between them stems either from age or from the degree of mental degeneration that has taken place, nothing else. But the reason we are keeping her here for a while is because, as I mentioned earlier, sometimes external stimuli can help to initiate recovery. Now, would you approach her and take hold of her hand; we would just like to see if there is any reaction from her.'

Gregg sat down in a seat beside Lorrett before somewhat cautiously taking her right hand in his. Her face was ashen white, unmasked as it was by the make-up that he had become accustomed to, but the subtle oriental slant of her eyes still expressed a spiritual truth that he was unable to define. She was receptive to both his touch and his movement, but lost in her ability to understand whose hand she felt or whose face she saw. He placed his other hand over hers, completely cupping it between his own, subconsciously willing her to respond to his touch, but all to no avail.

'All right, Gregg, I am afraid there was no reaction.'

He placed her hand gently down on her lap and stood up to rejoin the others who had been studying her every move.

'It was worth a try, but obviously this is not the day for miracles.'

'How do you feel about the situation now, Gregg?' The doctor posed the question as they made their way back to the interview room.

'Confused, concerned and, yes, despondent, doctor, for I cannot come to terms with this extreme feeling of despair, having now seen Lorrett and all those other poor souls suffering as they are.'

'Your despair is generally unwarranted, Gregg, for most of our inmates are for much of their time without comprehension as to their condition, their surroundings, or even the pain that you probably assume they must be enduring. Furthermore, many of them enjoy sustained periods of normality when often their unseen talents surface for all to appreciate.'

The visitor turned his head sideways as if to seek further detail.

'I am not sure if I am with you, Doctor.'

'Did you see that large oil painting on the wall inside that room?'

'Yes, I did.'

'Well, the old lady sitting at the table stirring her empty pot did that; mind you, it was in some of her more lucid moments.'

'I would have never thought it possible, such detail.'

'Oh yes, Gregg,' John interposed. 'We have all sorts of brilliance here; for instance, one of our patients was once a well known opera singer who in her prime had performed in many of the world's most renowned opera houses. Another was a past Olympic gold medallist, and if you were to visit a particular London art gallery on a regular basis, it is more than likely you would see one or two other paintings bearing the same signature as the one you saw hanging in that room just now. It may also surprise you to know that teams of our inmates compete against outside teams in various sporting activities. This, at times, is not entirely without its problems, but the important thing is that our patients are not passed over or cast aside in any way.'

The group had reached the interview room and had all made themselves comfortable in the easy chairs they had left some hour or so earlier.

'Well, gentlemen, we appear to have exhausted all there was to discuss here today, so perhaps it's time to summarise what we have so far.'

From the moment of introduction, John had shown himself to be both precise and articulate by the way he tended quickly to separate the wheat from the chaff in any conversation. He now obviously felt this need again to consolidate his findings and sum up what had been said.

'Well, thanks to Gregg's presence here today, we can confidently say we have identified certain facets of Miss Lorren's life that could in the long term prove to be relevant to her current state of mind. We know, for instance, that she has at times in recent years had the tendency to be reserved if not withdrawn. But this doesn't appear to be characteristically normal, for, as we know, she more than adequately demonstrated her naturally outgoing personality on the night of the show. Her sleeping appointments with the French language, however, seem to be of little or no relevance at the moment, so perhaps we should disregard them for the time being. We now know that she lived in Germany for some part of her childhood, so is there any connection between this actor fellow in the German uniform and her past, or even perhaps the possibility of a previous relationship between them?

'Was her reluctance to talk about her private life deliberately sustained to conceal something she was ashamed of, or was it simply that she was embarrassed over past mistakes and preferred to keep them to herself? Had she been depressed for some unknown reason? If so was this indirectly responsible for the stress that may have finally caused her collapse? We can, of course, continue to pile question upon question like this, but it doesn't provide us with the answers, which is why I would now like to take you up on your earlier remark, Gregg, for it implied that you would like to help Miss Lorren if you could. But before I do, I think that both the doctor and I have a confession to make to you. To be honest, we did have more than one motive in asking you down here for the day and now I think an explanation is in order. You see, in our endeavour to obtain more information on Miss Lorren, I made contact with your boss Robbie who, after a long discussion about the show, let me have a chat with your associate Ned.

'Now, my interest at the time was only in Miss Lorren, but as the conversation with your two colleagues progressed I found myself becoming increasingly spellbound by the concept of the show, the highly sensitive nature of it and the apparent goodwill and unity that came from it. But perhaps most of all, both the doctor and I found ourselves bewitched by this character who had suggested the idea for the show in the first place. We now admit, quite openly of course, that at first we wondered if he was a bit of a crank, but in our defence, we quickly rejected this possibility and decided that he had to be a psychiatrist who had himself defected to the other side. Again, we were to change our minds and we eventually concluded that he had to be a genius with a cause; but as we now know, we were wrong on all counts.

'But having now met you, I shall not endeavour to label you further or even to attempt to repeat all the good things that have been said about you; suffice it to say that you are both highly regarded and respected by your colleagues, you seem to be popular with most people you come into contact with and you come highly recommended as a researcher. So with such antecedence, the doctor and I hoped that you might help us to carry out some research into Miss Lorren's past, for the answer to her problem is somewhere out there, Gregg. You see, we have neither the time nor the ability to undertake such a task, and understandably we couldn't neglect our other patients. Furthermore, we do not have the experience to seek out personal detail from strangers who, because of the delicate nature of our enquiries, might simply refuse to give us the information we are looking for.'

'So, John, what you are saying is, that you intentionally planned to cajole this supposed crank of yours into doing some of your dirty work for you. What a crafty couple of old mind-benders you are, and what a waste of effort, because as you have gathered from my earlier remark, I was hoping that I could help in some way. So it will be a pleasure to do whatever you want of me. The only reservation I make is that I would have to ask Robbie for extended leave if I haven't concluded the work by the end of my holiday.'

'Actually, the subject did somehow crop up in my conversation with him, Gregg, and his response was simply: "It is in everyone's interest to see Miss Lorren well again, so Gregg can have as much time as it takes, but only on the condition that we have him back once he has finished, for we are not about to let him go now." So, as you can see, you are in demand and as it so happens, your research for us will in its way break new ground, for it will possibly be the first time that anyone has ever gone out to interview people solely for the purpose of finding a solution to someone's mental problem.'

'That's fine by me, John, in fact, it is always exciting to break new ground, providing you can accept the possibility that I might also make new blunders; so, to minimise this risk, have you any suggestions to offer?'

'No, not specifically, but perhaps I should point out that this research will not be quite the same as that you undertook for the show; people's reaction to you may be less receptive. This is understandable, of course, because you just might be infringing their privacy and to them, this could possibly prove to be extremely personal, highly embarrassing, or perhaps even downright sacrosanct. In contradiction to this, even if you find them willing to talk, you may have to conclude that there was greater relevance in what they didn't say than in what they did say. The point I make, Gregg, is, words alone can often cloud or misrepresent reality, for people sometimes only tell you what they think you want to hear, whereas any tell-tale signs of hesitancy, reluctance or refusal on their part may tell you more than their words ever will.'

'I hear what you are saying, John, for I have experienced this myself, but I have to admit that I have never consciously thought about it before.'

'Perhaps that is the secret of your success, Gregg, for your own communicative skills do come over as being both spontaneous and natural, which is no doubt why people find you easy to talk to and generally are always happy to respond to your questioning. Now, is there anything you need from us before you begin?'

'Two things, John. The first is, will you let me have as much information as possible on those people you think I should see, then I can follow up any additional leads from there.'

'Yes, I will ensure that such detail will be ready for you by the time you leave here today. And your other requirement, Gregg?'

'Well, it's not quite as simple as the first, I am afraid, John. You see, I still have this feeling that I am partly responsible for Lorrett's condition, so I have to ask, do you think that her collapse would have still occurred if she had not been in the show?'

'Who can say, Gregg; the evidence suggests that she had been heading for a breakdown for some time, but as to how or where this would have manifested itself other than in the way it did, is purely a matter of conjecture. Having said that, I am now quite convinced that the show was at least in some way instrumental in bringing about Miss Lorren's collapse, if nothing more, but how, is the question that puzzles me.'

'John, whilst I am fully aware of the emotional content of our show, I still don't see it as being mind-blowing in the way you seem to suggest.'

'Until your meeting here with us today, you had no reason to consider the possible long term implications of that night, for from you and your team's point of view, the show's success was enough to justify its end. But it did at times have its strong subliminal moments, so it could quite easily have had a detrimental effect on some people. However, if it does nothing more than help you to come to terms with your conscience, I think it best if we review exactly what it was that made the show, such a show.

'From what I can gather, you spent about two years prior to the show that night, collecting the information and collating the anecdotal material necessary to produce a series of some twenty-five programmes about the war. So your involvement in this obviously brought you into contact with a large number of people from this and other countries across the continent. Well, through the process of questioning, some were to tell of their personal experiences in the war. Thus the subconscious seeds for your idea were sown and naturally, as soon as you suggested the idea to Robbie, he quite happily agreed to consider your proposals.

'Now, let us look at exactly what happened. Your research was by definition specific, for it concentrated on people who some twenty-odd years earlier had experienced the whole spectrum of human emotion, fear, trauma, sadness and, as you have shown, even the comedy that can come with war. But time and maturity had calmed what in youth had been their arrogance, their defiance and their aggression, and your interest in them as a television researcher gave them, perhaps for the first time in their lives, a chance to talk about themselves and their experiences.

'Now, this unintentional selection process was, by circumstance, to cream off from an international society in general, a unique number of people who, irrespective of their previous differences, all had something in common with each other. They had all experienced a tragic war. You then sought out men and women from ex-services clubs and other such institutions throughout the UK and Europe, who, together with your selected guests, were to become your audience.

'So, at the invitation of the authority that employs you, they were all brought to London, expenses paid, ready to attend this unusual show. Now, from what I have been given to understand, these people arrived in London on the day prior to the evening of the show and were housed in a number of different hotels. Then before the evening's events the next day, they were wined and dined on a lavish menu of food and drink, all again at your company's expense. After completing their meal, they were transported to the inner sanctum of your television theatre, where they settled down ready for the evening's events. Let us stop the clock there for a moment and attempt to capture the mood there that night. You see, within the comparatively confined space of the theatre that night, you had assembled together a large number of ordinary people who, in anticipation of the evening's events, were all, no doubt, in a highly elated frame of mind.

'They were, I am sure, in their own way, all feeling extremely proud and privileged to have been invited to such an event and, perhaps quite understandably, were all in a receptive and friendly mood, for they were there to celebrate a very special coming together. Forgotten no doubt were most of their past prejudices, faded no doubt were their past sorrows, and what remained was this prevailing sense of understanding and goodwill towards all who shared with them this common experience.

'It was quite probably the first time that many of them within that theatre, or even those viewing the programme in their homes, had ever shared such an experience before. It was to be, as I believe you suggested to Robbie, a reunion, but not just a reunion with past acquaintances. It was to be a reunion of like minded and like feeling people who were in reality strangers, but who by selection had become kindred spirits, and of course, it was no coincidence that the entertainment that they were about to see was based upon this same emotional theme. So the show began, followed soon after by the mini-play involving Kerkner and Tommy, which when acted out in front of this highly perceptive audience was to have the inevitable results. You yourself have already described, how people were on their feet at the end of each act, clapping, cheering and, in general, besotted by the wave of emotion that had overcome them and one doesn't need to wonder why. You see, Gregg, that night, you were playing their song, you were inside their minds, you were touching their hearts. That night, that show, will, I am sure, be remembered by your audience and the millions of viewers who saw it for a long time to come, because it went beyond the realms of just good entertainment and became a totally moving and uplifting experience.

'So, Gregg, do you propose feeling responsible for those influences your show may have had on other people apart from Miss Lorren? Of course not, it would be too silly to contemplate, so forget this guilt feeling and concentrate your mind on helping us to find the key to Miss Lorren's problem, then we can all share the pleasure of hearing her sing.'

'I take your point, John.'

'Good. Now I would like you, if you would, to let me have frequent reports of your activities, and please bear in mind that in every probability, we are looking for detail which may have been passed over as being insignificant at the time it occurred. A childhood fall, a trauma, an upset or perhaps even a personal failure that has never been forgotten. It is this type of detail we are looking for, Gregg, for it is possible that within these undisclosed or unnoticed moments of her life, there is a clue as to her current state of health and if we can find it, we may then hopefully find both the reason for and the answer to her problem.'

'I'm with you, John, and I shall keep you informed of each and every detail.'

'We somehow thought you would, Gregg; now might I suggest an unorthodox conclusion to this meeting.'

John left his seat and walked across the room to a small cabinet. He opened the door and took out a bottle of whisky and four glasses, placing them on a small tray. He returned and poured out the whisky.

'Gregg, you came as a stranger, but I hope you leave as a friend, which would then make Miss Lorren a new found friend of both the doctor and myself. So with your permission I will dispense with the formalities of our profession and propose a toast to Lorrett and her future.'

Chapter Three

A teak-covered portable radio was relaying early morning music as Gregg went about preparing his breakfast. The centrally located flat he leased in London was compact but spacious, for the furnishings had been discreetly selected to allow comfort without congestion. Emphasis had been placed upon a clear cut image for the decor, enhanced only by the deep maroon colour theme of the upholstered seats, settee and other various items placed throughout the flat.

Gregg, at thirty-two years of age, was a bachelor, the status of which he accepted more than enjoyed, for his desire to marry had been suppressed by a past experience of disillusionment. Since then, he had found it preferable to touch only the surface of feminine relationships, thus avoiding any of the complications that might possibly lead to a further emotional commitment on his behalf. But a recent contradiction to this cocooned independence was Lorrett, who for some reason seemed to be constantly in his thoughts. He had convinced himself, at first, that this was due to the show and his involvement with it, but now he justified his continued interest in her by seeing himself as a courier on the road to her recovery. Naturally, he recognised that she was a very attractive woman, but he preferred to believe that this was entirely incidental to his interest in her as a friend, a friend who simply needed his help at this particular time.

He had spent some two days mentally reviewing and considering his recent meeting with John Moffitt and he was now determined to pursue the link, if there was one, between Lorrett's past and her present state of mind. Throughout this period, he had contacted a number of people by telephone, some of whom had been involved in the hiring of staff for the one night show that had taken place some weeks earlier.

Gregg, having finished his breakfast, cleared the table of dirty crockery which he quickly rinsed under a running tap and placed on the draining board to dry. He slipped on his jacket, felt for keys in one of his pockets, then made for the door. Stepping out into the narrow cobbled street of the mews, he hesitated for a moment to admire the tubs of flowers arranged somewhat regimentally in front of the small row of terraced houses. His hand went forward to unlock his car door. Bending into a half leaning position, he reached into the car and withdrew a cloth before cleaning off traffic film from the windscreen, then, easing himself into the driving seat, he slowly drove away.

The theatre was not immediately apparent, for its frontage was not significantly different to the many other wharfside buildings that lined the street backing onto the river. It was to be, therefore, some minutes before he noticed an obscure sign directing people to the main entrance of the premises and to a car park at the rear of the building. Having locked his car, he could see a safety exit to one side of the theatre where a door had been left open, so he made his way through it, only to be confronted with another pair of centre-opening doors further in. Quietly he pushed at the drop bar to one of the doors, then hesitantly stepped into the dimly lit surroundings beyond and onto the plush soft carpeting of the theatre's unlit interior. After carefully closing the door behind him he stood for a moment, allowing his eyes to get used to the darkness. As he turned, he could see the backs of four figures silhouetted against the brilliance of a well lit stage in front of him. They were sitting in seats some six rows back from the leading edge of the stage, watching the rehearsal of four performers as they acted out the final lines of what he took to be a rather amusing farce.

He eased himself into one of the seats at the side of the aisle, conscious of his intrusion into the rehearsal that was taking place, and prepared to wait for an opportune moment at which to approach the men seated in front of him. Movement upon the stage went on for some ten minutes before a man appeared from the wings to take up his timely entrance into the play being rehearsed. Gregg immediately recognised the face as that of the actor he had come to see and mused again at the leg-pulling remarks between John Moffitt and the doctor at their recent meeting. He was, as the photograph had shown, a good looking man with clear cut features, blue eyes, blond hair and a physique that appealed rather than rejected.

Gregg sat for some twenty minutes immersed in the activity of those on stage, until one of the men in the forward seats clapped just once to catch their attention.

'Right. Thank you. Would you take an hour's break; you all seem to have the problem under control. We'll have a final run through at twelve.'

The four men were conferring amongst themselves as Gregg sidled down the aisle to where they sat.

'Excuse me interrupting you. I have an appointment to see Mr Dantry; is it all right if I go backstage to see him?'

The four stopped talking and turned their heads in his direction, then one of them spoke.

'Yes, by all means, but may I ask first who you are?'

'My name is Jefferson, Gregg Jefferson that is.'

'Oh yes, Jimmy did mention that you were coming along to see him. You will no doubt find him in the props room backstage: up those steps over there, and turn left just behind the curtain. Incidentally, may I congratulate you on that fantastic show your people put on; it was very enjoyable.'

'Thank you, it is very nice of you to say so.'

Gregg passed through one of the rows of seats towards the hubbub of conversation taking place out of sight somewhere in the wings, up the steps and onto the edge of the stage. One or two people turned to face him as he emerged from the maze of thick velvet curtains and someone spoke.

'Ah, Gregg, I was just about to go front of the house to see if you had arrived, but obviously you have managed to find me. It's nice to see you again; how are you?'

'Very well, thank you, and I am sorry if I am a little early.'

'Not at all; in fact you have timed it just right. Now, what is it I can do to help? For your conversation with our receptionist the other day did suggest that is why you wanted to see me.'

'Well, before I begin, could we find a spot a little more private, Jimmy?'

'Yes, by all means. Will my dressing room be all right?'

'Excellent. I shan't keep you long.'

'Oh! that's all right, we have an hour's grace before our next rehearsal, so make yourself at home.'

Jimmy had cleared a pile of clothes from a stool within the room and invited his visitor to sit down, then, after moving an old tea chest away from a side wall, he seated himself on it. 'So how can I help, Gregg?'

'Quite simply, by answering some questions, as long as you don't mind, Jimmy.'

'I don't mind at all, providing I have the answers to give.'

'Good; so may I first ask whether you knew Miss Lorren prior to the evening of our show?'

'No, we had never met before. To be honest with you, I hadn't even heard of her until that night. Of course, I will never be able to say that again, in view of both her brilliant performance and the unfortunate way it came to an end. May I ask how she is, for I have read various newspaper reports which seem to suggest she may never be quite the same again.'

'Well, certainly there has been no change in her condition, but the press does tend to exaggerate these things. It would be true to say, however, that at the moment the doctors are somewhat baffled by her condition. This is why I am here, looking for any detail that might help them.'

'If there is anything I can do to assist in any way, please just say the word.'

'That's very kind of you, Jimmy, and perhaps at the moment the only way you could help is by having a chat with John Moffitt at the home; he is the psychiatrist who is looking after Miss Lorren.'

'No problem; if you let me have his phone number before you go I will give him a ring and arrange a meeting if necessary.'

'Good, that helps. Now, can you in any way recall those few seconds prior to her collapse on stage that night? I mean, was there anything that struck you as being strange about her, her poise for instance, her facial expressions, perhaps, or anything like that.'

'Well, of course, the whole situation was strange in that sense, Gregg; after all, it is not every day that someone finds himself trying to support a collapsing woman, especially on a stage at that precise moment of her performance. If it had been planned, the timing could not have been better or the impact greater and there was no one more surprised than me when it happened. So what can I say, except perhaps that it was an experience I would have preferred to have missed. But I think I shall always remember Miss Lorren's face when she turned to face me for the first time that night. It was as if I were some kind of ghost, or perhaps the image of someone who had suddenly come back from the dead.'

'You mean, she seemed fearful, scared or something like that?'

'Partly, but initially it was much more a look of uncertainty, a look that suggested disbelief and expressed confusion. Of course, fear and surprise may have also come into it for her face seemed to describe all of these emotions separately and together at the same time. Then it changed and took on a rather fatuous stare before her eyes closed, she began to sway, then fell forward into my arms as I gently lowered her to the floor.'

'So, are you saying that she appeared to go into a state of shock upon seeing you for the first time?'

'Yes, I suppose that's right, but I don't usually have that effect on people, so I cannot account for her reaction.'

'Not to worry, Jimmy; I know how difficult it is to recapture such fleeting moments, especially in the case of accidents and the like. However, let me thank you again for seeing me and, with your permission, I would like to keep you in mind for any possible work that might come up in the future.'

'That would be appreciated, Gregg, and it has been nice seeing you again.'

The conversation with Jimmy had been as expected, necessary but unfruitful. It was, nevertheless, satisfying to know that there had been no previous friendship between the actor and Lorrett prior to the show that night. Gregg knew that the task he had undertaken was not going to be easy, for he had learnt from his past experiences that research was much more about persistence than perspicacity, and that the old adage of leaving no stone unturned was still the best approach to the task he now had in front of him. He was never more conscious of this basic rule than now, as he drove his car along the Embankment away from the theatre.

Having negotiated his car through the confusing pattern of intersections at Hyde Park Corner, he turned into the park, made his way towards Marble Arch, and then headed off in the direction of Maida Vale. It was here where he hoped to find something specific by way of answers to the many questions floating around in his head. Was her bad marriage the key to Lorrett's problem? he asked himself. Was her ex-husband the cause of the marriage breakdown and perhaps indirectly responsible for the predicament she was now in? Gregg drove his car into a parking bay, confident that just across the road from where he stood he would find both Lorrett's ex-husband Grant Stevens and perhaps some consolation for his ever recurring doubts.

There was nothing to indicate that the building in front of him was a sound recording studio, no bell or knocker on the front door with which to request entry and no sense of pleasure that one might expect to get when approaching a structure with such a well defined heritage. Instead, there was a grubby piece of paper graphically directing callers to one side of the building, where steps, leading down to an entrance below street level, brought a visitor face to face with a sign saying 'enter'.

Gregg passed through the door, under a low ceilinged entrance and into a space that, with effort, soon became recognisable as a reception area. Its dark mauve-coloured interior did nothing to counter the claustrophobic feeling he was experiencing, as he waited a response to his tap on the partition in front of him. A small hatch panel in the partition slid open.

'Yes, can I help you?'

One of the four spotlights within the area shed just enough light onto the face of the young woman framed within the aperture of the hatch.

'I would like to see your Mr Stevens, if I may.'

'I am sorry; he's busy on the floor at the moment.'

She giggled to herself before re-phrasing her remark.

'On the recording floor, that is. He's doing a take.'

Gregg felt sure he knew what she meant. 'I would like to wait, if I may.'

'Yes, that's all right, but who shall I say wants him when he is free?'

There was no time to reply, for at that moment a man entered the office through a rear door. 'Who's that, Mary?' he enquired.

'Someone to see Mr Stevens.'

The man left the office and within a matter of seconds came through a gap to one side of the partition into the reception area. 'Can I help you at all? Mr Stevens is tied up with a recording session at the moment.'

'No, not really; you see my visit is by way of being a personal matter.'

'Are you a friend of Grant's, then?'

'No. It's just that I know his ex-wife, and she is the reason for my visit.'

'Wait a minute, aren't you the chappie who was involved with that television show some weeks ago?'

'Yes, Gregg Jefferson's the name.'

'I am pleased to meet you, Gregg, I am Stuart Bailey. I remember seeing your picture in one of the show-biz mags. You might as well come through and wait, that's as long as you don't mind seeing how the other half works.'

'Thank you, Mr Bailey.'

'Please, can we forget the mister, call me Stuart, everyone else does. Now, would you care to follow me.'

The man turned inward towards the door through which he had come, and Gregg followed closely behind. They passed the young typist who had greeted him, and proceeded along a corridor and into another small anteroom. Stuart pointed to a red light glowing on the wall. 'A warning that they are still recording; could you go quietly until we reach the can.'

Gregg, not knowing what his guide meant, followed him without a sound. After taking a few more steps, they passed behind a thick curtain, through another door then into a brightly lit room. The room was some twelve feet long by about eight feet wide. It was aluminium clad throughout, with a plate glass window extending completely down one side. Adjacent to the window was a large desk carrying hundreds of switches, knobs, slider controls and lights. A man on a stool sat altering the array of gadgets as he looked through the window in front of him; a strap over his head and down one side of his face supported a pair of headphones and a small throat microphone.

'It's OK now, Gregg, you can speak. This, as you can see by the aluminium cladding, is what we call the can, obviously built like this to make it soundproof, and here we have the main control panel. This regulates all the sources of sound coming in from out front, where, as you can see, all the activity is going on at the moment.'

The visitor, looking through the window, could see the agitated movements of some twenty or so musicians playing their instruments; this struck him as being rather amusing, in view of the lack of sound coming from them. Stuart, reading his visitor's thoughts, leant over the shoulder of the man seated on the stool, and moved a slider control upwards. As he did, music from the hitherto silent instruments came through speakers mounted on a panel above them. He then reset the control back to its neutral position.

'Have you done any sound recording?' Stuart enquired.

'Not professionally and, looking at all this gear, I don't think I should try.'

'Oh, it's quite easy, once you know what to do. This board controls up to thirty separate microphone inputs, some of which, as you can see, are being used at the moment and the red bank of sliders are for ceiling mounted microphones at the dead end of our studio.'

'Dead end?' Gregg queried.

'Yes; you can see that for some distance the low ceiling continues. This is where sound soon becomes dampened, that's why we call it the dead end. Beyond that, which you cannot see from here, the ceiling is considerably higher, purposely designed to avoid damping; this is the live end of the studio where you can see the band is now playing. It would appear as if Grant has nearly finished. That's him over to one side, balancing the individual sound levels throughout the studio. He is in fact preparing and presenting the sounds of each instrument for Ted here to put on tape.'

'It's quite fascinating, Stuart. What are you actually producing at the moment?'

'We're doing the final touches of some big band music that is to end up as a long play record. It should be a good disc.'

The music had stopped; the man sitting at the control desk took off his headphones, placed them on the panel and turned to face Stuart and his visitor.

'This is Ted, our chief engineer.' Stuart made the introductions.

The two men shook hands just before the door to the can opened and Grant Stevens came in.

'Did you get that final treble lift, Ted?'

'Yes, Grant, it was just right.'

'Grant, I don't know whether you have met, this is Gregg Jefferson. You may remember he handled your ex's part in that fantastic show on television recently.'

'No, we haven't met but pleased to see you, man. What can I do for you?' he enquired.

'I wonder if I can take a little of your time and ask you a few personal questions?'

The other two men still in the room realised that they could be in the way and started towards the door.

'We'll leave you to it, Grant; we'll be having a coffee, OK?'

'Yes, that's all right, Stuart. By the way, you can tell the band our next session will be at two, so they might as well go and have some cookies. Now, Gregg, sit you down and let's see if I can help you with what you want to know.'

'It's about Lorrett. You know, of course, she is in a nursing home for people with mental problems; well, I am trying to help her out of that situation and to do so I need some answers from you.'

'I have already told the headshrinker what he wanted to know, isn't that enough?'

'No, not really; in fact, John Moffitt seemed to think there was probably some reluctance on your part even to talk about Lorrett. You see, I don't think you fully realise how critical her situation is, for in truth her entire future is at stake. So I am looking for anything that may have possibly been the reason for Lorrett's present state of mind.'

'Well, her state of mind, if that's what you call it, existed long before I did. In fact, it was her state of mind that now makes me her ex-husband.'

'No doubt what you say is true, but weren't there many other reasons as well? More desirable reasons, like other women?'

'Well, of course there were other women, but what is a man to do? If there's no food in your own larder, you have to eat out, don't you?'

Gregg began to feel a little agitated. 'Look Grant, I'm not here to moralise over what you do or don't do, but I have a professional interest in the lady and I don't want to see her left in her current state of isolation for the rest of her life.'

'I'm sorry, Gregg, but I do get a little high when it comes to Lorrett, for you have to realise that in my stupid way I loved the girl. The only difference is that she didn't love me.'

'What makes you so convinced about that?'

'Well, it was only a matter of a few months after we married that she seemed to find some sort of pleasure in taking digs at me, then we got to the situation where she seemed to disapprove of almost everything I did, until one day, she upped and told me straight that she didn't love me.'

'Can you trust me enough to tell me the whole story, Grant? That is, your side of it, failings and all. I assure you, it is only in Lorrett's interest.'

'OK, let me take it from the roots. I first met Lorrett just over four years ago, that was when she came here to cut a disc. It was her first and she was extremely nervous, for she was, of course, quite fresh to the game. Her agent had brought her along to do a demo pop number for one of the record companies and, to say the least, she was lost. Anyway, I summed up the situation and nursed her through the take; mind you, it wasn't easy. We cooked the song about thirty times before ending up with a clean cut and by the time we had finished, I was over the top for her. I did eventually manage to persuade her out for a meal one evening and that's where it all began.'

'So was it purely a sexual thing on your part?'

'No, man, that's the funny thing, I just didn't try it. Somehow I just wanted her legit. I just wanted to marry her and as you now know, that's what happened.'

'Did she herself show much enthusiasm over the prospect of marriage?'

'Well, she didn't exactly jump over the moon. Looking back at it now, I guess I assumed that she felt the same way as I did. However, I was forced to conclude in the end that Lorrett was just one of those negative types.'

'Negative types, I am not certain I understand what you mean?'

'Well, there are plenty of people who never say yes and never say no; they just move with the tide. I guess Lorrett's one of them. She always seemed aloof from, and unconcerned with, most of the things that went on around her, until, that is, she was herself directly affected. Like at the recording session. Then she goes all soft and appealing on you.'

'Are you saying she was withdrawn?'

'Yes, in a way. You see she never showed much emotion over anything. She always appeared as if she had left her real self behind somewhere. Of course, she has this fantastic beauty to compensate for this flaw in her character and I suppose it was this beauty that confused me.'

'Grant, can I ask you how your sexual relations turned out?'

'As I said, I did eventually begin to eat out. You see it wasn't that she turned me down, it's just that somehow I felt she didn't dig the action. As a matter of fact, someone once told me they used a brothel in Alexandria and this character said that the dames there often used to sing and smoke whilst operating. Well, in some ways the action with Lorrett was similar. She just didn't seem to participate and I'm a community man myself. I like to do things together, do you see what I mean?'

'Yes, I get the picture. How long did the marriage last?'

'About a year, then we separated and she got her divorce within the following year. Of course, I admitted adultery which made it easier.'

'Did you ever meet her mother?'

'Just the once, it was about a month after we were married. We were passing through Reading at the time, that's where the old girl lives, and on the spur of the moment Lorrett decided to drop in and see her. However, we only stayed for about fifteen minutes.'

'Was there any particular reason for that?'

'Well, I knew that Lorrett hadn't seen her mother for some years although I never did find out why she didn't visit her. Anyway I understood a little more after we'd made the call.'

'And the reason for this better understanding?'

'Well, they just couldn't communicate with each other; in fact it was an embarrassment just being there watching the scene. Now, whose fault it was, I don't know, but neither of them had anything to say. It seemed to me that they were both striving to find words that avoided any mention of the past and this made it impossible for either of them to relax and talk freely. The old girl went through the ritual of making us all a cup of tea, then we sat down in a kind of semi-silence whilst we drank it. Of course, they talked of such things as the weather and how nice the garden was, but they both seemed to avoid any conversation that touched upon personal matters. Anyway, in the end I suggested that if we stayed too long we would be late for our appointment, so we left and, believe me, I was glad to get away from there for the atmosphere was as cold as rigor mortis.'

'Did Lorrett tell her mother she was married?'

'No, and what's more her mother didn't even enquire, yet she must have noticed the ring on her finger.'

'After you left the house, did you ask Lorrett about her mother?'

'Yes, I did, but she was as tight as a clam, so obviously, there must have been some sort of a problem between them for a long time, and I feel sure it had something to do with Lorrett leaving home when she was in her early twenties.'

'So you have never really known the reason for this stand-off between them?'

'No, Lorrett wouldn't ever talk about it.'

'Has she a father?'

'No, apparently he died when she was eighteen.'

'Did you, in the time you were together, find Lorrett depressive, unbearable or neurotic in any way?'

'No, not really; in general we got on reasonably well. Of course, we weren't always in each other's pockets, for we both had our individual commitments, but we didn't row or anything like that.'

'This disc she cut, did it do much good?'

'Well, it was played a few times on the radio and a few thousand copies of it were sold, but it never really made it beyond that. Of course, we didn't know then what we know now.'

'I'm not with you.'

'It's obvious she was being put into the wrong greenhouse; pop music wasn't her scene. You should know for, from what I've been given to understand, it was you who put her on the right track.'

'That is partly true, but I still don't follow your reasoning.'

'Her manager, he was giving her the wrong material, and from what I can make out, it was you who encouraged her to sing those ballads on the night of the show, isn't that so?'

'Yes, I and my colleagues all felt that this was more her type of music.'

'There you are, then, she's never going to look back now, she's on the road to the top.' Grant hesitated for a moment. 'Hey! that's not really so, is it?'

'At the moment, no.'

'Do you know something, I've just realised how badly her situation has hit me. This thing with Lorrett, I mean, I'm just beginning to see now how selfish I have been. I'm sorry, I've been talking as if I am not concerned about her, which I am. I realise now that whilst I may not be what's good for her, I don't want Lorrett to miss out on the chance of future happiness and success.'

'And to get that, we have still to find the source of her problem, or she will be forgotten with the passing of time.'

'No, that mustn't be, Gregg, that mustn't be, especially now after her fantastic performance that night.'

'You feel it was that good, Grant?'

'Well, you have to appreciate that I am no impresario, but being tied up with music as I am, you soon learn to recognise the commercial viability of either a certain sound or an individual performer. Now, I know that Lorrett has this ability to give of herself to an audience and can quite naturally sing straight from the heart. This is something that is rarely experienced today, but even I never realised that she had this quality until I saw her on television that night, then it hit me like a bomb, especially after that "Lilli Marlene" number. Believe me, Gregg, I was genuinely in tears by the time she finished that number and I can't ever remember being moved like that before.'

'Grant, I think that in view of all you have said, you cannot take all the blame yourself for what has happened, because I'm beginning to get the impression that Lorrett wasn't herself even before she met you. In fact, I think you hit the nail on the head when you suggested that she had left her real self behind somewhere. But for now, you have told me all I need to know, apart from one other point. I have only ever known her as Lorrett. I know her proper surname is Webster, but what is her off stage christian name?'

'Lorraine, Gregg. I believe it was from this that the first part of her stage name was devised.'

It had been a week to the day, since Gregg had made his pilgrimage to the nursing home and now, as he sat in his sports car driving towards Reading, he was mentally reviewing his previous telephone conversations with those who had known Lorrett before he had met her. It certainly seemed as if she was quite different from the normal number of women he had met before, but she did have this tendency to avoid sustained relationships with people in general. Was she really one of life's loners, he wondered; did her fantastic beauty conceal the heart of an automaton, or was there somewhere, beneath that attractive façade, a lonely and desiring young woman just waiting to get out. She had, after all, expressed herself both lovingly and emotionally to her audience that night of the show; she had also reached out to touch him on one occasion, he recalled, so was it, he thought, that she had somehow withdrawn into her own protective self? There was the possibility, of course, that she, being as beautiful as she was, had grown tired of men who had pursued her with only one thing in mind. But then, this didn't quite ring true either, for according to one or two of her female friends, she had at times acted in a similar fashion towards them.

Gregg entered the town of Reading, still baffled by his own doubts yet still as hopeful as ever. It took him some time to find the road in which Mrs Webster lived, eventually locating it on the outskirts of the town where the density of red bricked houses gradually thinned out to reveal an approaching countryside. He drove slowly down the road, looking carefully at each house as he went, inwardly cursing the local authority that had allowed some residents simply to name their houses without numbering them. He first noticed a woman hoeing in her front garden, then the house name he had been looking for. He drove his car onto a grass verge in front of some trees, locked the doors and passed between some entwined foliage and onto a long path that led down to the front of the house.

'Excuse me.'

The woman, engrossed in what she was doing and with her back towards him, hadn't noticed her visitor walk down the path.

'Good afternoon, are you Mrs Webster?'

The woman slowly stood upright from her half-bent stance. 'Yes, I am.' She looked quizzically at her visitor.

'My name is Jefferson, Gregg Jefferson.'

'Oh yes! and what can I do for you, Mr Jefferson?'

'It's about your daughter, Mrs . . .' Gregg didn't have time to finish his remark before being cut short.

'She doesn't live here, she lives in London. I'm sorry I can't help you.'

'Mrs Webster, I haven't come to see your daughter, I've come to see you about your daughter.'

'I'm sorry, Mr Jefferson, I'm afraid I can't help you.' She stressed her point vehemently for the second time.

'Can't or won't, Mrs Webster?'

The woman preened herself with a look of defiance. 'Young man, I don't know who you are, or why you are here and I certainly don't like your manner, so would you kindly leave.'

'Yes, if that is what you wish, Mrs Webster, but before I do, I would just like to say that I cannot understand your attitude. However, there seems to be little point in trying, for I don't suppose that even the Almighty could approach you in your present frame of mind.' Gregg turned and started to walk back up the path towards his vehicle.

'Young man, . . . er, Mr Jefferson,' the woman called after him.

'Yes?' He turned half expectantly.

'Are you an authority on the capabilities of the Almighty?'

'No, far from it, Mrs Webster, but I do seem to recall that consideration and kindness towards others is in some way associated with such an ideal, which is somewhat contrary to the feelings you appear to have towards your daughter.'

'Mr Jefferson, who and what are you?'

'I come only as a friend of Lorrett, your daughter, for, as you already know, she is in need of some help at this time.'

'Well first, Mr Jefferson, my daughter's name is Lorraine not Lorrett. However, whilst I can see that your intentions are good, your judgement seems to be a little inaccurate. You see, I would have thought that Lorraine needs nobody, so are you now trying to suggest that she needs me?'

'Yes, I am sure she does, and whilst I am not in a position to judge, I would have thought she has always needed you. After all, is it possible for any human being to be totally complete within themselves?'

'No, Mr Jefferson I don't suppose it is, but how can one be expected to understand the feelings of others if they are not prepared to communicate with you in any way? But since your words appear to have a critical tone about them, I am not without love for my daughter and perhaps the only way I can convince you of this, would be by suggesting you come into the house, where a cup of tea may possibly help to smooth out some of these obvious differences between us.'

Gregg sat in a comfortable armchair sipping his tea, whilst the middle-aged Mrs Webster perched herself on a stool to one side of a table.

'Now, Mr Jefferson.'

'May I suggest Gregg, Mrs Webster.'

'Well, all right, Gregg it is. Now, perhaps first you would kindly explain to me how this daughter of mine needs my help.'

'Mrs Webster, let me tell you first how I find myself involved in your life, then perhaps you may understand my motives for being here.'

He ran through a brief account of his short relationship with Lorrett and how he felt that he was, to some degree, instrumental in bringing about her current condition. He touched upon her dissolved marriage along with other aspects of her life, purposely avoiding his recent interview and discussion with Grant Stevens.

'Well, as it seems that your efforts are entirely out of concern for another human being, perhaps I should be prepared to hear you out.'

'Thank you, Mrs Webster; I am sure that it will be in your interest in the long term, so will you now allow me to ask you some further questions?'

'Yes, all right, but there is a limit as to how far I'm prepared to go.'

'That is understandable, but my most difficult question is perhaps my first. You see, from your reaction so far, I get the impression that there has been a rift between you and your daughter for some time. May I ask what brought this about?'

'I'm sorry, that is one question I would prefer not to answer. It is after all a personal matter.'

He realised that this was one interview that was not going to be easy, yet the woman's outright refusal to answer his question made him even more determined to find the answer.

'Yes, I understand Mrs Webster.' Gregg decided to avoid the point for a while longer. 'Do you mind telling me about Lorrett when she was young? For instance, was she a happy child? Was she prone to illness in any way? But more importantly, was she a wanted child?'

'Strange as it may seem to you at this moment, she was a very happy child. She naturally had many of the illnesses of childhood in common with others but nothing serious. She was well loved by my husband, myself and her very many friends and in those days, she always had a smile on her face and a song in her heart.'

'So she sang even when she was young, Mrs Webster?'

'Yes, she belonged to a church choir, then when she was fourteen she joined a local choral society. I never thought, however, that she would end up as a professional singer, but she did always love music even as a baby.'

'Am I right in believing that she spent the first years of her life in Germany?'

'Well, in Germany, then France until she was about five years of age.'

'You obviously lived in Germany at the time then?'

'Yes, you see, my husband was in the forces in the war; in fact he was an officer in intelligence. He went across from England soon after D-Day and continued through into Germany.'

'What exactly did he do?'

'He was an interrogator. His job was to seek out people such as quislings and the like who had committed war crimes under the German occupation.'

'Were you in the ATS or WAAF then?'

'Oh no, I was a civilian living in England throughout the war and I joined my husband in Germany soon after the war ended.'

Gregg was immediately aware of a contradiction in what she had said, for Mrs Webster in her more relaxed frame of mind had left herself open to further explanation. Should he tackle her on the point or should he leave it for a more opportune moment? He decided to wait.

'Lorrett speaks German quite fluently, Mrs Webster, I suppose she must have picked up some of this as a child?'

'Yes, perhaps a little, but my husband spoke both German and French; that is why he was with an intelligence unit.'

'Well, it may interest you to know that your daughter's knowledge of languages has helped her considerably towards a successful future. That is, provided we find a solution to her current problem, which I believe you already know about.'

'Yes, I do, and you need to understand, I have no wish to hurt Lorraine, because contrary to what you may think, I love her equally as much today as I did when she was young.'

'Have you the courage to prove your love then, Mrs Webster?'

'Yes, if I need to, why?'

Gregg decided it was time to challenge the lady over her previous remark.

'Mrs Webster, Lorraine, or Lorrett as I know her, is, as far as I understand, now over twenty-six years of age. This means that she was born before the end of the war. You have told me that your husband went across to France just after D-Day and that you joined him in Germany just after the end of the war. Now, if my calculations are right, D-Day being as it was at the beginning of June 1944 and the end of the war coming as it did in May 1945, there seems to be a gap of some eleven months which doesn't tie up somehow.' Gregg avoided pursuing the point too forcefully and said nothing further.

An embarrassing silence followed. Gregg wondered how the rather strong willed Mrs Webster would react as he sat looking inquiringly into her eyes, hoping that his timing was right. One moment there had been a determined and resolute lady defending her pride, then, as if all control had gone, tears started to flow gently over her cheeks. Gregg waited a few moments before getting up from his chair and moving over to where she sat. He put his arms across the woman's shoulder and spoke. 'I did say a few moments ago that I come to you as a friend, a friend to both Lorrett and yourself. Won't you accept me as such and tell me all of the facts?'

The restrained flow of silent tears turned to sobs of pent-up emotion.

Gregg waited before gently squeezing her shoulder with his hand.

'We are going to solve this problem between us, aren't we?'

The now despairing lady nodded her head in an agreeing gesture, trying at the same time to contain the flood of tears with the end of her apron.

Gregg reached into his top coat pocket to pull out a clean white handkerchief.

'You know,' he said, 'I am of the opinion that if you are going to do anything in life, do it once, but do it big, so come on and cry it out; it will make you feel so much better afterwards.'

She lifted her head and smiled at him bravely through her tears.

Pouring the second cup of tea had given the now noticeably softened lady time to regain her dignity and Gregg waited patiently for her to break the silence.

She spoke slowly and softly. 'Perhaps I had better start from the beginning.'

'If you feel up to it now, do so, but please remember I am here to help you in any way I can.'

'I can see that now, Gregg. My husband and I were married before the war in 1938 and we were very happy together. Unfortunately, like many men, he was called up for the forces in 1941, but as luck would have it, he remained in this country until he went across with the invasion forces a few days after D-Day. We both loved and wanted to have children, but it was not until some time after our marriage that I found out that I was unable to conceive. We talked about adoption but felt that owing to the uncertainty of war, it was better to wait. Then my husband went off to France and, as I have already told you, I joined him some two months after the war.

'My first week in Germany was spent putting some sort of home together. You see, we were given married quarters, not that they were in any way palatial, you understand. Nevertheless, it was lovely to have some form of home in which we could share our lives again. The first two weeks flew past, and in the third week after my arrival I was to have perhaps the loveliest surprise of my life. It started when my husband came home very early one day. "Jessie," he said, "I want you to leave what you are doing; put a coat on, I'm taking you off somewhere special."

'That was my husband, always happiest when he knew I was happy and always so tantalisingly full of surprises. Anyway, I did what he asked and although my curiosity got the better of me I knew there was no point in questioning him for he wasn't about to tell me where we were going. Because of his rank, my husband had the permanent use of a jeep and this was to be the first opportunity I had to view my new surroundings since arriving in the country some three weeks earlier. I can even see it now, the way the vehicle bounced from pot-hole to pot-hole through street after street of utter devastation. I can still see the distress and torment upon the faces of those people I saw living, or more accurately just existing, amidst the rubble and remains of what once had been a beautiful centre of civilisation. I felt both terribly sad and angered at the same time for I could see no sense of logic in the destruction about me. I remember that at one point, I even began to shake with anger, so much so that all that I wanted to do was to stop the jeep and try to help those poor wretches in some way. But what could I have done, for apart from the sympathy I had for them, I had nothing else to give.

'It was some forty minutes before we drove into the grounds of what I soon realised was a hospital and my imagination began to work overtime as I tried to fathom out why we were there. I was then lifted out of the vehicle's seat by my husband who took my hand and led me speedily inside. We passed down a corridor congested with wounded and sick people on either side, through a large hall and into a hospital ward. Even then I didn't know what was happening, until my husband tugged me into position at the side of a child's cot, looked at me and said, 'Well, Jessie, is she nice enough to be our daughter?'

Mrs Webster paused in contemplation and Gregg realised she was living those moments over again.

'Well, Gregg, that child in the cot was Lorraine and that's how she was born to us. I shall never forget that day and since then we both gave her as much love as any child could have and, to be absolutely fair, she returned that love with every fibre of her being. That was, of course, until our world came to an end some six years ago.'

'Was that when she left home and went to live in London?'

'Yes, and now, upon reflection, it was really my fault that it all happened.'

Gregg could see that Mrs Webster was at last prepared to free herself from her pent-up past. Was this the same distress that the daughter shared, was this the beginning of Lorrett's gradual mental decline? he wondered. Mrs Webster continued with her explanation.

'You see, my husband finished his commission with the army some five years after the end of the war, then we all came back to England and settled down in this house. Well, he eventually became a partner in a local insurance business and Lorraine was to grow up and blossom into a lovely young woman. We were, you see, a very united and happy family. But, looking back, I think our troubles really started about a year after my husband's death. Lorraine was nineteen at the time. She had met a young man at a musical concert and over the period of the next year or so, she had grown very fond of him. Well, they were to become quite inseparable and had decided to get married on her twenty-first birthday. This was to be where our problems began. You see, my mistake was, I had intentionally never told Lorraine that she had been adopted, for I had always felt that there was less danger to her happiness in ignorance than there was in her knowing the truth. However, I was wrong and she has never been able to fully understand why I did what I did.'

'Mrs Webster, I personally can't see that you were wrong. What surprises me more, and what I can't easily understand, is why such knowledge appears to have affected Lorrett so deeply. After all, it was quite a major step to leave her home and everything you had shared together for all those years.'

'That is how I saw it at the time, Gregg, but since then I have realised how wrong I was.'

'I still cannot see why; after all, it was a valid judgement on your part.'

'Yes, it was, but she was quite a sensitive young woman and perhaps she saw it as a betrayal of my confidence in her at the time. I am sure now, it was both the discovery of her adoption and the anxiety that came with it that forced her into making several wrong decisions at that time.'

'So, were there other problems as well?'

'No, not especially, it was just the way she appeared to make large mountains out of things which I saw as comparative molehills. It really all started when she had to produce details of her birth and her birth certificate, in preparation for her marriage. You see, we never had a birth certificate as such, all we had was something similar, but this only gave the briefest of details about us as adoptive parents and the little that was known of her as a child. It had nothing about her place of birth, no information as to the name of her real mother or father and naturally, no actual birth date or other details like that.'

'So this so called document was quite unusual, then?'

'Well, by today's standard, certainly, Gregg, but you have to realise that we adopted Lorraine in Germany at the end of a devastating war. The administration of the country, like everything else at the time, was in a state of chaos and there were very few civic buildings left in which to deal with such problems. The German forces had, of course, all surrendered, so there was hardly anyone available for civilian employment. The hospitals were full to over-flowing with the wounded and dying and there were literally hundreds of abandoned or parentless children to look after. So, yes, whilst it was an authentic document issued by a recognised official at the time, its lack of detail did quite naturally give rise to a great deal of doubt and confusion on Lorraine's part. As a result of this I was forced to tell her of her adoption just as I have now told you.'

'I understand the difficulty you must have had, but I still cannot see why she should continue to feel as you suggest, for all this time.'

'There is an answer, Gregg, albeit not a simple one. You see, from the lack of evidence on the so called birth certificate we had, I think she latched on to the possibility that she might have been the bastard offspring of a casual and unhealthy wartime liaison. She then must have convinced herself that there was some sort of obscene trace in her make up, so she decided not to go through with her marriage. Of course, my neglect in not telling her sooner about her adoption made me the cause of her predicament and subsequently the recipient of her blame. I feel she now realises her mistake, but the gap between us seems to be beyond repair.'

'Didn't her young man at the time try to convince her against her decision not to marry?'

'Yes, he did at first, but Lorraine was so sure that she was right, that the young man ended up agreeing with her and perhaps, even a little thankful for his release. After all, at that age relationships between boy and girl are often quite fragile, so they can at times be easily knocked off course. But it also has to be said that a healthy and pure upbringing can, at times, bring about an instant dislike of anything that is suspect or tainted in any way.'

'What happened to the young man, Mrs Webster?'

'He went abroad to work some six months after the break up; it was to Italy, I believe. Lorraine, of course, left home only two weeks after she challenged me over her birth.'

'So was it really love she had for this young man?'

'Yes, I think so, but of course he could have been the subconscious replacement for her father's love and possibly, if her father had been alive, things may not have turned out quite as they did.'

'May I ask what your husband died of?'

'It was a blood clot to the heart, suspected to have been the result of a small wound he received some months before the end of the war.'

Gregg didn't need to ask whether she missed him, for the answer was written over her face.

'It's a strange thing, isn't it, that we have two people both in their own way loving and sincere, both really thinking as much of each other as they do of themselves and yet ending up poles apart merely because of the inability to compromise with each other. Mrs Webster, the only error that you and Lorrett seem to have made was to allow your pride to overrule your heart.'

'Yes, no doubt you're right, but I could have done nothing to stop Lorraine thinking the way she did. After all, she was entitled to wonder over her birth and perhaps question my reasons for concealing the truth.'

'I feel sure that many people faced with the same problem have to consider how, or even if, they should tell their child they are adopted. One thing is certain: this error, if error it be, must not be left to decay into further sadness and bitterness. Together we must try to right what is wrong.'

Mrs Webster bent silently forward to touch his hand. 'Thank you so much, Gregg, thank you.'

'If you want to thank me, Mrs Webster, what about a nice fresh cup of tea? I've left this one to get cold whilst listening to your tall stories.'

He smiled and joked away what, to him, was an embarrassing moment. Whilst the lady was out of the room Gregg mulled over the conversation that had taken place so far. Certainly, from Mrs Webster's account of things, it was highly probable that Lorrett's condition came about as a direct result of this family quarrel. There was certainly enough substance in the knowledge of her adoption to have jolted a young woman's security.

But, he repeatedly asked himself, was the impact of suddenly finding out that she was an adopted child enough eventually to bring about Lorrett's current condition? He was beginning to think not. He tried to put himself in her place and to understand the reason for breaking her association with the man she loved. He also found it difficult to believe the motive, that made this young inexperienced woman leave the security of a comfortable home and venture into the potential isolation of a big city like London. The more he thought over the subject, the more he became convinced he still had a long way to go and that there was quite a bit more detail to be coaxed out of Mrs Webster.

'Here we are, Gregg, a nice hot cup of tea, given with pleasure rather than irritation this time, and perhaps you can forgive a silly middle-aged woman for having a little too much pride.'

'There is nothing to forgive, Mrs Webster. We both have to look forward to tomorrow, for there has to be a new tomorrow for you and Lorrett. Now, would you mind if I ask some further questions?'

'Of course not, I'm all right now; please go ahead.'

'Well, you remember just a little while ago you challenged me over my remark about the Almighty and a little later you mentioned that Lorrett had been in a church choir, so may I ask, did she have an extremely religious upbringing?'

'No, Gregg. We started off by sending her to Sunday School but we never insisted on anything further than that. However, by her own choice she found that she wanted to continue with her church activities. It was there, within this association, that her desire to sing was encouraged and, of course, she did really have a lovely voice. Mind you, at that time, it was mostly religious works that she sang.'

'So you wouldn't say that she had been subjected to an overdose of religious indoctrination, then?'

'No, definitely not.'

'You mentioned that your husband was called up in the early years of the war; why was he not de-mobbed like most others at the end of the war?'

'Well, yes, he was due for de-mob at the end of 1945, but he was asked to sign on for a short term engagement because of his work. You see, he was an essential witness in many of the trials that were to follow later.'

'I understand. Now I wonder, can you ever remember Lorrett having any major accident or even perhaps being frightened as a child?'

'Nothing comes to mind; there were naturally several little childish ailments and accidents but nothing too traumatic, you understand.'

Gregg was silent for a few moments, obviously thinking things over in his mind. 'Lorrett must have been about a year old when you adopted her then?'

'Yes, it was believed so, but we never did know her date of birth.'

'As a mother, would you have thought it possible that a baby of that age could have been frightened by something which was only to show itself later on in life?'

'I really can't answer that question, Gregg, but I wouldn't have thought so.'

'I am trying to consider the possibility that Lorrett may have been frightened in her early childhood days before you adopted her.'

'Well, it is quite possible. After all, she was at that time living in a country that was being incessantly pounded with the many devastating components of war. But would she have been the happy child that we knew? Wouldn't she have been a morose or perhaps a pathetic child instead of the happy little creature that she was?'

'That's a very good point. Were you ever given any clue as to who Lorrett's real parents might have been, or for instance, any other details relating to that first year of her life?'

'No, Gregg, and I can see it is obviously still quite hard for you to really understand things as they were in those days. Let me try to tell you about those early post war months in Germany, then you can perhaps see how difficult it was, for it is not easy to envisage those times if you've never experienced the chaos that is war. Well, as I have already said, we were given married quarters, which in fact was a small house amongst other properties on the outskirts of Hamburg. Now, as you may or may not know, much of Hamburg had been flattened by the Allied bombing, but the hospital we drove to that day was situated in a small country village some thirty kilometres from the city centre. Being quite isolated, it hadn't been touched by the bombing; this was no doubt why it was used to house the hundreds of children who had either been abandoned or had been orphaned by the pillage of war. Needless to say it was packed to the extreme, not just with children, but with many of the wounded civilians from the city. Furthermore, there were hundreds of people milling around outside the hospital, all waiting and hoping to be accepted in. They were very emotional times, Gregg, for the despondency on people's faces was indescribable. There were the crippled, the lame, the young, the old, all desperately short of warm clothing, all with those gaunt faces of hunger that seemed to stare into one's conscience as they silently looked at you. It was a terrible sight to see and even worse to experience, for it didn't seem possible that one part of our civilisation could have done this to another. Any statement attempting to justify the suggestion that these poor souls had reaped what they deserved, could in no way equate with the horrific conclusions that they had to bear. But of course, life went on and as time slowly passed, people gradually emerged from the unseen sewers and tunnels beneath the ruins, dirty, weary and often hardly strong enough to scratch out their needs for survival from the depravity that surrounded them.

'The hospital, which incidentally was called Kindorf Hospital in those days, was where, after adopting Lorraine, I was to spend much of my free time whilst my husband was away working. You see, after getting to know some of the people there, I used to go back to help out because of the staff shortages. Anyway, after my husband had finalised all the arrangements, the adoption procedure was dealt with at the hospital by some kind of official who, so we were told, came from Hamburg. Thinking about it since, we never really knew who he was exactly, or whether he had the full authority to carry out such a procedure. But we were given the certificate as proof of the adoption and, bearing in mind the situation as it was then, it all seemed to be dealt with in a reasonably orthodox way. I suppose it is possible, of course, that the depleted German bureaucracy, such as it was at that time, were either so hard pressed or even so demoralised by their defeat that they cut corners or ignored certain official procedures, but how were we to know? It also has to be remembered that the German people at the time were still under military control and were, to say the least, all short of food, so they themselves were in no position to take on other mouths to feed. Well, as you can gather, Gregg, our adoption of Lorraine was a very unusual occurrence at the time, especially when you consider that there were literally thousands of unclaimed and unwanted children that had to be cared for. You see, at one time, Hitler had openly encouraged women to give birth to children for the state to bring up. These so called Aryan children were generally the illegitimate offspring of German soldiers and free living women and they would, in the earlier years, have been cossetted and educated by the state for the state. But many of them were released onto the streets or into institutions once the invasion began.'

'So what you are saying to me is, in view of all this, it is highly probable that Lorrett could have been one of these children.'

'Yes, Gregg, but neither my husband nor myself had ever talked about those times in front of Lorraine and so she never knew of her German origins until she saw that certificate.'

'But having seen it and having learned German at school, as she obviously did, she must have also learned something about the history of the country and even some of the things that happened in the war. So perhaps she added two and two together and concluded that she was in fact one of these bastard children.'

'Yes, and as far as we were able to make out at the time, she might well have been. But after seeing the certificate, Lorraine just withdrew into herself and would not talk about it further. You see, I always knew that one day she was bound to find out about her adoption, but I had hoped that as a young woman she would have been better equipped to cope with the facts, but as I have already said, I was wrong.'

'Yes, I can see now how unfortunate that was. In fairness to Lorrett, though, once she had become aware of her possible illegitimacy, you can begin to understand how she might have felt. But who was it that told you about Lorrett's origins in those days?'

'Well, as I have already explained, I helped out at the hospital for some time after that first visit, so I became very friendly with many of the nurses and staff there, one of whom I have corresponded with over the years. Well, it was she who told me.'

'So, knowing then that Lorrett could quite easily have been one of these illegitimate children, you still went ahead with the adoption.'

'Yes, but in fact, like you, I did ask a lot of questions before doing so, although in truth, nothing, simply nothing, would have stopped me from adopting her, Gregg. You see, when my husband took me into the ward that day and I picked up baby Lorraine for the very first time, something quite strange happened to me.'

'Strange, you say, Mrs Webster, in precisely what way?'

'I am little reluctant to talk about it really, Gregg; you see, my husband never believed it at the time and perhaps even to this day, I still have difficulty in coming to terms with it myself.'

'You can tell me, can't you; after all, it may have some bearing on Lorrett's problem.'

'I don't think so, but I will tell you. You see, as soon as I saw Lorraine in her cot that day, all I wanted to do was to pick her up and hug her. So I did exactly that, then, just as I put my cheek to hers, I heard a mature woman's voice say, "This was intended to be." Now it goes without saying that at that age she couldn't even talk, let alone express such a profound remark, but I knew then that yes, it was intended to be. Of course, it is all so insanely impossible to believe, but Gregg, it did happen and those words did come from her, not from my mind, not from anyone else nearby, but from that beautiful and adoring young baby.'

'It is very difficult to believe, I must say, but for some unknown reason I do believe it. Why, I cannot explain. But in an attempt to come back to reality, was Lorraine her name when you saw her that first time?'

'No, Gregg, she just had a nickname, so we decided that as she was born to us from the moment we saw her, we should begin as if she had been our own child and that was the name we gave her.'

'Going back a bit, you said you had a friend with whom you communicated over the years; where did you write to exactly?'

'The hospital I mentioned earlier, but I haven't had any letters from her since my last letter some two years ago, in which she mentioned that she had been promoted to Matron. So whether she has been posted to another hospital or not, I cannot say.'

'Would you mind me knowing her name?'

'Mrs Wals, but in those days she was known as Johanna Schultze.'

'At the moment that seems to be it, except perhaps, to go back to Lorrett's young man. Was he a local lad?'

'Was and still is, I believe, Gregg. You see, he returned from Italy and, so I am given to understand, he still lives with his parents.'

Gregg looked at his watch. 'Oh dear, nearly six o'clock, I should be off.'

'I was going to cook myself an evening meal; would you like to stay and have something with me?'

'No, that's very kind of you but . . .' He hesitated. 'Look I have a better idea. I shall take you out for a meal, then perhaps I can get to know more about the mother of a lovely daughter I have the good fortune to know.'

'Well, if you insist, but won't it make it late for you? Unless of course you stay here overnight. You could sleep in the spare room, which was Lorraine's old room; you will find it very comfortable.'

He gave it some thought for a moment. 'I happily accept your invitation and thank you. Thinking about it, I could then call upon Lorrett's young man in the morning; it might just add something to what you have already said.'

'He may not be there, of course, Gregg, but if he is, remember that he is not her young man any more. I wouldn't want you to find yourself in an embarrassing situation over something that happened a long time ago.'

'That's nice of you to think like that, so thank you and now, my dear Mrs Webster, may I have the pleasure of your company and take you to dine?'

'By all means, Mr Jefferson, providing we can agree not to involve the Almighty in any way.'

It was eight a.m. as Gregg opened his eyes. A bright ray of sunlight pierced the narrow gap between the floral curtains of the bedroom and, from somewhere below, he could hear the rattle of cups on saucers. He eased himself from the extremely comfortable single bed and for some moments sat poised on the side of it taking in his surroundings.

There was, he realised, a feminine feel about the room, with its delicate pastel coloured furnishings and accessories, but also an atmosphere, a detectable presence which he couldn't quite explain, yet was happy to experience. A presence that suggested his visit was not altogether accidental; so was it that, by his visiting the mother, he was now able to feel a greater affinity with Lorrett the daughter? He couldn't say.

He shared an enjoyable breakfast with his hostess and prepared himself to say his tentative farewells, assuring Mrs Webster that, come what may, he would be back to continue with the friendship that he now felt they shared.

It was ten o'clock in the morning as Gregg waited at the front door of a house in a quiet tree-lined street some half a mile away from the home of the lady he had just left. He rang the bell and waited.

'Good morning, I'm sorry to bother you but are you Mr Durrant?' Gregg realised immediately that he was not speaking to the person he had come to see, for this was a much older man.

'Yes,' the man answered.

'Then it must be your son I'm looking for, Malcolm Durrant.'

'Yes, that is my son. May I ask who you are and why you wish to see him?'

'My name is Gregg Jefferson. Your son doesn't know me, but I would like to have a few words with him if possible. It is about a private matter.'

'You had better come in, Mr Jefferson; Malcolm is just having his breakfast. You are lucky to find him at home.'

The caller was shown into a front room reminiscent of the Victorian parlours that were, in the past, often only used for visitors or on special festive occasions.

Mr Durrant senior moved in front of his visitor to switch on both bars of an electric fire. 'Would you like to sit down, Mr Jefferson, I'll get young Malcolm for you.'

There were a few minutes of waiting before a mystified look appeared round the half opened door.

'I'm sorry,' the young man said, 'I don't think I know you.'

'You are quite right, Mr Durrant, we haven't met before, but my name is Gregg Jefferson. I wonder if you would be kind enough to spare me a few minutes of your time.'

'Well, er . . . yes, but I cannot spend long with you, for I have a twelve o'clock plane to catch at Heathrow.'

Gregg gave an explanation for the visit and apologised for interrupting his privacy. The young man was reluctant to talk at first but after several general questions were put to him he became less guarded and more prepared to talk about his past association with Lorrett.

'Malcolm, looking back, do you feel you were really in love at that time?'

'Yes, I think so. It was perhaps a rather immature love, but then, maybe the innocence of one's first love is the only form of true love. After all, our thoughts and habits do become a little tarnished with the passing of time.'

'Very true, Malcolm, but do you have any regrets over your decision not to marry Lorrett?'

'I don't know whether regret is the right word. Put it this way, it could have restricted my chances of advancement if I had married her but no doubt, there would have been many other compensations. It was not my decision to cancel the wedding, however, it was hers.'

'About that decision, Malcolm. Do you think it made sense to withdraw from the marriage arrangements merely because she found out she was adopted?'

'No, I couldn't see her reason for the decision at that time, but in fairness, I wasn't in her shoes. All I can say is, rightly or wrongly she was convinced that she should not marry and I eventually had to conclude that if her beliefs were stronger than her love, then it was perhaps, after all, the right thing not to marry.'

'Did you, by chance, happen to see her on the television recently?'

'Yes, fortunately I was home that evening. She was fantastic and I have to admit that some of those moments we had shared together came back to me again.'

'Would you, if you had the chance, like to take up from where you left off with Lorrett? I'm sorry, but I haven't got used to thinking of her as Lorraine.'

'That's a difficult question, Mr Jefferson, I just don't know. I can only say that I have never married and that I have never felt the same about any other woman since.'

'Malcolm, when you have the time, would you be prepared to visit the nursing home and possibly see Lorrett?'

'Yes, I would be quite happy to do so providing the doctors looking after her think it is the right thing to do.'

'I feel sure it is, Malcolm, and if you care to take this card, perhaps you would be kind enough to ring Mr Moffitt prior to your anticipated visit. Now, since I have delayed you and I'm going to London, may I drop you at the airport?'

'That's very nice of you, Mr Jefferson, but would you like a cup of coffee before we move off?'

'That would be most enjoyable, and please call me Gregg.'

Chapter Four

The flight had been calm and uneventful and as the plane circled over Hamburg, Gregg could see how the land had been cut away by the outflow of the river. He was reminded of an article he had once read, which explained how the city had been built on stilts and now, as the glistening sunlight picked out the multitude of inter-connecting waterways below, he could see why it had often been compared with Venice in Italy.

The journey had allowed him time to reflect upon the last fourteen days since his interview with John Moffitt and the doctor. He had, as promised, forwarded his written report to them, covering his first three interviews. In it, he had suggested that the meetings had posed as many questions as they had answered, for there were now one or two further avenues of enquiry that demanded his research. The report ended by informing his newly found friends that he was about to pursue these new lines of enquiry, by visiting Germany.

His arrival and dispatch away from the airport had been quick and efficient, helped as it was by the taxi driver who obligingly carried his case and, upon request, recommended a hotel near to the city centre. After arriving at the hotel, the driver agreed to return within the hour and take Gregg for his planned visit to the Kindorf Hospital.

There was just enough time to unpack the things from his case and have a wash and tidy up before the internal telephone rang and a woman's voice informed him that his taxi had returned.

As the vehicle wove its way through the streets and lanes of Hamburg, Gregg found it hard to believe that this was the same place that Mrs Webster had described to him only a few days ago, for it was no longer a mass of rubble, it was again a proud and thriving city.

It was not long before the congested streets and compact houses of the city gave way to the approaching countryside with its more satisfying scent of field and foliage.

Gregg had booked on an early flight out of London intentionally to make the most of his first day, for it was a part of Germany that he had never visited before. Sitting comfortably back in the rear seat of the car, he reflected on his recent meeting with Lorrett's adoptive mother and found it quite difficult to understand how two very nice people such as they could have become divided by such a comparatively minor detail.

The tall, lean, smartly dressed driver, realising that his fare was a stranger to the vicinity, occasionally broke the silence to point out particular sites of historic significance along the way, but apart from the odd response or two, Gregg was content to enjoy the ride without the need for creative conversation.

As they approached and passed through the village, the only vehicles to be seen were those parked on some ground in front of a large stone-faced building lying well back from the road. As the driver slowed the car down to turn off the road, Gregg could see a sign showing it to be the Kindorf Hospital. He paid off the driver and thanked him for his polite and efficient manner and walked up a flight of wide stone steps under a large suspended sign showing the directions of different departments within the hospital and into the main entrance area. There was an immediate feeling of calm about the place, broken only by the discreet sound of background music that appeared to seep out from the walls and ceilings of the building. He casually made his way up to the reception desk.

'Can I help you, sir?' A woman had moved away from a distant table and now faced him across the counter.

'I am enquiring after a Mrs Johanna Wals. I was given to understand that she is a matron here.'

'Mrs Wals, you say; I don't know of anyone by that name myself, but if you will excuse me I will go and ask someone else; you see I am fairly new to this job and I am not familiar with everyone here yet.'

Gregg nodded his appreciation, then turned and stood with his back against the counter to watch others, as they scanned the mass of information on the overhead sign board, just beyond the ever opening and closing entrance doors.

'I understand you are looking for Mrs Wals.' Another woman had replaced his first contact behind the counter.

'Yes, I am, and are you able to help me?'

'Only by telling you that Mrs Wals retired owing to ill-health some time ago, so can I assist you in some way?'

'Unfortunately not; you see my reason for wanting to speak with the lady is of a personal nature, unless, of course, you happen to know where she lives. It is rather important that I see her.'

The woman was able to tell him that the former matron was still living locally and went on to explain how he could find her property at the far end of the village, some ten minutes' walk away.

He knocked at the cottage door and waited. There was the rustle of clothes behind the door before it opened, then a short plump woman stood unsteadily in front of him. She spoke to him in provincial German:

'Yes, young man?'

'Hallo, my name is Gregg Jefferson, would you be Mrs Wals?'

'Yes, I am, but I don't know you, should I?'

'No, Mrs Wals, we haven't met before, but I am pleased I now have the opportunity to remedy that failure.' Gregg went on to give a brief explanation for his presence, but it wasn't until he mentioned the name of Mrs Webster that he found himself inside the cottage and being asked if he would like some coffee.

'I am sorry to hear of your illness, Mrs Wals; was it this that prevented you from writing to Mrs Webster? You see, she did mention that she hadn't heard from you for some time and thought perhaps that you might have moved. But she did speak of you with warm affection.'

'It wasn't that I was unable to write, it was just that my illness had made me lethargic and incapable of sustained concentration, but as I am now feeling better, I will write to her again soon.'

Gregg spent some time telling the ruddy cheeked lady of his association with Lorrett, the show and his link with Mrs Webster the mother, before continuing to explain the incident that had brought him to Germany. He carefully touched upon the rather delicate situation between Mrs Webster and the daughter, conscious of the fact that whilst he preferred to avoid unnecessary chit-chat, Mrs Wals had obviously been starved of news from Mrs Webster for some considerable time. The demure and placid Mrs Wals was receptive to any information he had to offer, so it was with some ease that Gregg was able to change his role from that of an informer to that of an enquirer and thus, get back to the point of his visit.

'I assume you still have clear recollections of those times that you, Mrs Webster and the infant Lorrett, spent together at the end of the war.'

'Oh yes, how could I forget those days. They were, you see, extremely difficult but wonderfully rewarding times, for my friendship with the family is something I have always treasured. This may sound strange to you now, Mr Jefferson, in view of the conflict that had previously existed between our two nations, but ordinary people don't start wars, they are just left to suffer them.'

'I have no hesitation in agreeing with you there, Mrs Wals, but let me digress and ask you about those days, or more specifically about baby Lorrett in those days. For I am given to understand that you knew quite a bit about her, before you ever knew of Mrs Webster.'

'Yes, I did, for of course I was the one who had to take charge of her when she was first brought into the hospital. All the other nurses, you see, were busy dealing with the injured from an air raid on the city that night.'

'I am sorry, I don't quite understand.'

'The baby was crying rather loudly when she was brought in that night; the doctor wasn't able to pacify her, you see.'

'So, had this doctor been tending to the child before passing it over to you, or was it he who actually brought the baby into the hospital?'

'He brought her in that night; but, of course, I didn't recognise him at first, for he had been crying and he was trying not to show his face too much.'

'So you also knew this doctor, then?'

'Yes, I had seen him around the wards on a few occasions, but naturally, as a trainee nurse, I hadn't ever spoken to him or worked under him at all.'

'But from what you say, he did appear to work at the hospital.'

'Well, he did and he didn't; he only appeared to be there on odd occasions, mainly after some of the bigger air raids on the city, or when we had a large casualty list. You see he was really a military doctor at the barracks hospital some forty kilometres from here on the other side of Hamburg.'

'So he obviously wasn't on the permanent staff of the hospital?'

'Well, I am not certain, but I feel sure there were times when I never saw him for months on end, then he would suddenly reappear. I think there must have been some arrangement whereby the hospital could call on military assistance when it was needed, for we often had different army doctors working there. I suppose, at times, there were not enough resident doctors at the hospital to cope with ever increasing numbers of casualties.'

'You wouldn't happen to remember his name after all this time, would you?'

'Oh yes, he was always known to the staff as Doctor Kraske, but of course he held an officer's rank in the army.'

'It's quite apparent that time has not clouded your memory, Mrs Wals.'

'That is perhaps understandable, for the subject was discussed quite a bit before Mrs Webster adopted the child.'

'So could you give me some indication of what actually happened the night this doctor fellow passed the baby over to you?'

'Well, at the time, I was making my way through the foyer of the hospital to the ambulance outside, when in rushed the doctor with this child in his arms. He must have seen my uniform, so he immediately came over to me and without any initial explanation, passed the child along with its bedding over to me. He told me to take the baby and put her in the ward along with the other destitute children already being cared for at the hospital. He then instructed me to inform the head administrator that the child had been made an orphan that night and that he would return as soon as he was able to sort out the details; he then left in the same hurried way that he had arrived.'

'So there was no mention of the dead parents or child's name then.'

'No, but I assumed that such detail was to be discussed upon his return.'

'Did you happen to see the doctor when he returned?'

'I don't think he ever did return, for when the baby was adopted by Mrs Webster, I had to sign a document to verify his statement to me, that the child was in fact an orphan.'

'I don't suppose you ever saw this doctor at the hospital, once the war was over?'

'No, that night was the last I saw of him. Of course the Allies took over the hospital within a couple of weeks after peace came and if he is still alive, he could of course be anywhere now. You see, people were so transient in those days that it was nearly impossible to keep up with all of their comings and goings.'

'You said earlier that he was stationed at a barracks not far from here; would you happen to know where they were?'

'Oh yes, in fact they are still there, but naturally they are now occupied by the combined forces of NATO. I knew the spot quite well in my young days for as nurses we used to look forward to the monthly dances that were held at the barracks. As a matter of interest, I still know one or two of the staff who work there.'

'Do you mean people who were stationed there during the war?'

'No, one of them is an American officer who is in charge of the military hospital within the barracks and the other, who is a friend of mine, works as a civilian in one of the offices.'

'Without meaning to be impolite, Mrs Wals, are you on friendly terms with the American officer, or is he just someone you know as a colleague?'

Mrs Wals could see that her visitor was obviously hoping that some form of introduction might be forthcoming.

'Why is it that I have the feeling that you are going to ask me his name and perhaps even want me to show you where the barracks are?'

He smiled. 'Are you something of a thought reader as well as being a very understanding lady?'

'No, merely a very interested party, Mr Jefferson. Now, how long do you think you will be in Germany?'

'That's hard to say, but possibly a week to ten days.'

'Would the use of a car help you at all? I have one in the garage which since my illness has hardly been used and you are welcome to borrow it.'

'Well, that would certainly be most helpful, and thank you.'

'Now, I cannot go on calling you Mr Jefferson so can we dispense with formalities and please call me Johanna.'

Gregg sat in the seat of the vehicle gradually adjusting himself to driving on the right side of the road and half listening to the rather fragile Mrs Wals beside him as she recalled various incidents of the times she had shared with Mrs Webster and the family. She mentioned briefly her own husband, his demise and how they had no children of their own, confident that in Gregg she had found a compassionate listening ear. The journey across country bordered the outskirts of Hamburg and either by chance or design, his passenger made a point of directing him along a road where a line of terraced houses stood back amid some trees.

'That's where Mr and Mrs Webster had their married quarters. She often used to leave the baby in her pram just out on that grass patch there in front of the house.' Mrs Wals pointed to the property as she spoke.

Gregg hadn't said much, for his attention had been divided between his rather talkative companion and his concentration on the road in front of him. But in a rare moment of silence he managed to squeeze in a question that he had been waiting to ask.

'Did the doctor give any indication of the baby's age that night?'

'No, you see, as I have already mentioned, he seemed to be in a hurry and the exchange of the child was all over in a matter of seconds. But the staff at the time thought that she was about ten to twelve months of age.'

'So there was no mention of the baby's name as the doctor passed the child over to you?'

'That same question was put to me the next day and in truth I wasn't sure then and I cannot be sure now, for as he approached me that night he did mumble something to me, but what it was I really don't know. But whatever it was he said, I thought a name like Heidi came into it. You see there were so many confused and shocked people milling about near the hospital entrances that night, many of them vying for my attention, that I was never sure whether he did or did not mention the child by name.'

'How far is it to the barracks now, Mrs Wals?'

'If you turn down that lane you can see on the left, the entrance is about two kilometres from there.'

The car jerked and bounced its way over various pot-holes in the road before coming to a halt opposite two large wooden gates supported on each side by two heavily bricked piers. Projecting off from these supporting piers a high wall disappeared into the distance on either side. An armed guard in the re-styled uniform of the modern German army stood to one side of the gates.

'Providing I can arrange it, would you like to meet the American officer I mentioned to you earlier? It's a chance but if he is here and he is prepared to see us, he may be able to give you the answers to any question you might have relating to the staff here just prior to the end of the war.'

'I wasn't going to ask, but having considered the possibility, yes, it would save me a lot of trouble if you could.'

'Good. I'll see if they will allow us in without an appointment.'

Mrs Wals moved awkwardly out of the car and across the narrow lane to speak to the sentry on duty. A few minutes later she returned and sank back into her seat.

'We have to drive through and pull over by the guard room just over there.'

As she spoke, one of the gates was released from its fixing and swung back. Gregg drove in, parked the car on a space to one side and looked across at his passenger for further instructions.

'We have to wait here until someone comes out of the guard room.'

Once beyond the high wall surrounding the site, the vast area covered by the barracks could be seen, with its mixture of old and new buildings, a large parade ground and acres of fields rolling away to one side where hundreds of newly varnished tanks, armoured cars and other transport vehicles were parked.

A head popped through the open window beside Gregg. The man, a corporal in the military police, requested that they leave the car and follow him. Gregg took the arm of his doddering companion and followed the soldier along a pathway between a line of prefabricated huts, past two tall water towers and into a modern administrative building. The interest in his surroundings as they sat waiting denied him seeing the arrival of a tall good looking officer in American army air force uniform.

'Johanna, how are you? It's so nice to see you again.'

Mrs Wals and the American put their arms around each other in an embrace before standing back to face each other with a silent look of friendly togetherness. 'Hank, I would like you to meet Mr Jefferson. He is a friend of an old friend of mine, Mrs Webster.'

'Mrs Webster; don't I know that name from somewhere?'

'You may do, Hank, for you did meet her once at the hospital but that was a long time ago.'

'I can't recall the occasion. However, I'm pleased to meet you, Mr Jefferson. So what brings you to these parts and what is more important, how are you these days, my old Burner?'

'Hank, Hank, we are in company.' The surprised Johanna coyly put her hand on the American's arm in an attempt to dampen his joking remark.

'Oh, I'm sorry, old buddy.' Hank turned to face Gregg. 'That's my leg-pulling name for Johanna here.' The American realised further explanation was necessary. 'It goes back to our early days together when Johanna here was a probationary nurse at Kindorf Hospital.'

An obviously embarrassed Mrs Wals tried to stop any further comment on the subject, but Hank continued with his explanation.

'You see, Mr Jefferson.'

'Can we make that Gregg?'

'Yeh, sure, Gregg. Well, the nickname Burner comes from way back near to the end of the war when our boys moved in on Kindorf Hospital. It was Jo here who at the time was given the job of cleaning off a corpse with methylated spirit, or something like that. The poor guy had died from his injuries which had been covered with large areas of sticky-taped field dressings. Well, he had to be cleaned and spruced up for burial and this was Jo's job. It was unfortunate that at the time there was no power on at the hospital, so the work had to be carried out by the light of hurricane lamps and large candles. Anyway, not thinking, Jo here had covered the body quite liberally with this high octane cleaner and without realising it she held one of the lighted candles nearby so she could see what she was doing. Well I will leave you to imagine the rest, but you can see how Jo here got the name and why at times we used to pull her leg about it.'

Gregg smiled politely, but whilst he realised the story was obviously true, he failed to see any humour in either the tale or the need to perpetuate it.

'Now that's enough, Hank, you'll have Gregg here thinking I'm some sort of maniac.'

'Oh, Jo, I'm only laughing with you and not at you. Don't forget in some ways they were happy days, weren't they. Anyway, now you are here, what can I do for you?'

Mrs Wals explained the reason for calling in on the spur of the moment and concluded her remarks by asking a question.

'Would you happen to know if there are any records still kept here from the war days, medical records, files and things like that. You see, we are looking for some information on a German officer.'

'Well, I just don't know, but I guess there must be for we have never destroyed anything as far as I know. Tell me what you want and I will see what I can do for you.'

Gregg interjected, 'What I would like if at all possible, is some information on a German officer who was stationed here at the barracks hospital for some part of the war. Apparently he was a medical officer and according to Johanna here, his name was Kraske. I am trying to find out where he is now.'

'Excuse me a moment.' Hank left his two visitors to catch the eye of a passing soldier. The soldier stopped and casually saluted.

A few minutes later Hank returned to where his visitors were standing.

'Right, while we are waiting I suggest we go and have a nice friendly drink at the canteen.'

The three had sat for some fifteen minutes enjoying mutual conversation when a mess steward approached their table.

'Excuse me, sir, I understand you are waiting for this.'

'Yes, thank you, soldier.'

Hank took the envelope marked 'confidential' off the tray the steward was holding and, dismissing him, opened it, then smiled.

'Well, I think this is what you wanted. It looks as if your man was one Dr Weiner Kraske, Medical Officer with the Ninth Panzer Division until late 1946. Now presumably just plain Dr Kraske who, according to these rather old official records, lives in the town of Rüdesheim on the Rhine.'

Hank had copied details from the records onto a piece of paper and passed them to his visitor.

'That's marvellous, thank you, you do seem to have an efficient staff here.'

'All things considered, they're not a bad bunch of lads; mind you, there's nothing like an unusual task to stimulate enthusiasm. However, it's the end result that counts, isn't it?'

'It certainly is and thank you again for your help.' Gregg slipped the piece of paper bearing the details into his wallet and settled down to share the next ten minutes of conversation with his host and Mrs Wals.

The return journey back to the ex-matron's home was quicker than Gregg had anticipated. He saw the lady into the house and they sat with a cup of coffee, discussing his intended plans.

'Now, are you sure that you have no need for the car?' he asked.

'Of course I'm sure and as I've already said you are welcome to stay here at any time whilst you are in our country. I shall always be delighted to have your company.'

Gregg thanked the very pleasant Mrs Wals for all her help and told her he would return, possibly within the next few days, then drove back to his hotel in Hamburg, quite satisfied with his first day of enquiry.

The small town of Rüdesheim showed none of the scars of war or any signs of the essential rebuilding programmes that so many other towns had been subjected to. Its many crooked narrow streets were a pleasure to the eye but obviously a nightmare to any delivery driver who found the need to unload or collect goods from the shops or offices housed within its centre. The journey from Hamburg along the autobahn had given more scope for speed than for contemplation and as Gregg manoeuvred the bouncy Citroën car between the gable-ended houses and the turret designed fascias, the enchanting rococo and Gothic style buildings seemed to unite as one with the suggestion that he was welcome. It was mid afternoon as he parked the car, stopped the engine and stretched his legs. His persistent enthusiasm demanded that he should forego the brief rest he had promised himself after the long drive and he was about to leave the car when something previously unconsidered occurred to him. Supposing the good doctor he had come all this way to see had no personal knowledge of the child he had taken to Kindorf hospital that night; supposing the poor fellow was dead, or perhaps had something to hide and refused to talk about it.

It was not normally his style to consider defeat but as Gregg sat quietly mulling over his thoughts he was beginning to recognise the possibility that his journey might have been in vain. His thoughts wandered off in several directions, considering other alternatives, contemplating other options, before quickly returning to its logical beginnings and answering his own doubts. If the doctor had no personal knowledge of the child, how could he know it had been orphaned? Why, according to Mrs Wals, had the doctor been crying that night, and didn't she say that he had briefly mentioned a name just before he passed the child over to her?

It was a once again self-assured Gregg that locked his car, made some enquiries from a passer-by and stepped off into the direction of Grabenstrasse.

He turned into the narrow street and began searching for the number. The very old beamed property was near to the end of the road and on a panel beside the heavy wooden door a polished brass plate showed it to be the residence of Dr and Mrs W. Kraske. He paused to control his rather rapid breathing before ringing the bell and waiting. There was the creaking of boards underfoot from within the passage before the door opened and a tall, upright but heavily paunched man stood before him.

'Excuse me, would you be Dr Weiner Kraske?'

'Yes, I am.'

'My name is Jefferson, Gregg Jefferson. I am sorry to interrupt you but I have travelled from England in the hope of meeting you. So I wonder if

I may take a little of your time to discuss a matter of considerable importance to me, a matter which I also believe indirectly concerns you and more particularly an incident in your past.'

'My past, young man; I don't see that as being any of your business.'

'Dr Kraske, I am here in an attempt to help someone who needs all the help they can get. Now, I can understand if it is not convenient at the moment, but I would hope that you could suggest a time suitable to you so that we could talk.'

'Well, if you insist,' the doctor replied. 'But can we make it some other time, for I was just about to go for my afternoon walk?'

'By all means, Doctor, but providing you have no objection, I would be happy to walk along with you and talk as we go.'

'That would be satisfactory Mr . . . ?'

'Jefferson.'

'Would you wait. I shall only be a few minutes.'

The doctor turned and went back down the passage of his home, leaving the front door half open as he did. A short period elapsed before he reappeared, now complete with a jacket to match the tweed trousers he wore, the bottoms of which had been wrapped around his legs and secured by brown leather leggings and matching boots. He carried a walking stick which was obviously not used to further the squire-like image that encompassed him, but to assist him with the obvious disability of a badly injured leg. The two men started back in the direction from which Gregg had come.

'I hope you like walking, Mr Jefferson; you see, I need to do a couple of hours a day to prevent further muscle deterioration in my gammy leg.'

'Did your injury come about by an accident, Dr Kraske?'

'Oh no, I've lived with this for about twenty-eight years now. In fact, I really can't even remember what it was like to be without the problem.'

'That suggests it could be an injury from the war then.'

'Yes, unfortunately I was wounded early on in the war; but still, that was a long time ago and it doesn't pay to dwell on such matters. Now, this discussion you would like to have mystifies me. What is it all about?'

'A child, Dr Kraske; to be more specific, a child that you apparently took to the Kindorf Hospital some time before the end of hostilities between our two countries.'

'Go on, Mr Jefferson.'

'Well, I have been given to understand that you found this child in

Hamburg one night whilst an air-raid was in progress and according to my informant, you delivered the child to Kindorf Hospital, suggesting it was an orphan.'

'Who was this informant of yours, Mr Jefferson?'

'A certain woman who is now a Mrs Wals, but who, at the time, was a nurse by the name of Johanna Schultze.'

'I don't recall the name.'

'But you do remember the incident, Doctor?'

'Mr Jefferson, before we go any further with this conversation I should say I am not prepared to answer questions *carte blanche* from a total stranger without first knowing the reason for them.'

'I can fully understand that, Doctor, so perhaps you would allow me to explain. I am here in Germany to research into the background of a young woman who, according to her doctors, appears to be suffering from a mental condition that has unfortunately culminated in her total loss of memory and an inability to communicate. After subjecting the lady in question to a whole range of examinations, all of which proved negative, it was suggested by the gentlemen in charge that the problem might indirectly have stemmed from a trauma experienced in early childhood.'

'Am I to take it that the woman that you refer to and the child are both one and the same?'

'Yes, Dr Kraske, and perhaps you can now see the reason for my presence here and why I am attempting to find out as much as I can about her early childhood.'

There was quite a noticeable period of silence as the doctor tried to summon up a suitable response to what he had just heard. Gregg was happy to wait, for the doctor's hesitancy seemed to confirm that his journey had not been in vain.

'Well, Mr Jefferson, I'm prepared to answer your first question, for I do remember the incident very well; in fact it's hardly something I will ever forget. But I don't think that I am prepared to go much beyond that.'

'Do you have something to fear, then, Doctor?'

'Certainly not, Mr Jefferson, and I rather resent you thinking in those terms.'

'I am sorry for that impertinence, but I am sure that as a doctor you would do everything possible to help someone in need of your care, and in my own way I am only attempting to do the same thing. I do acknowledge, however, that I probably lack the tact or finesse to handle such an intention in the same way that someone with your experience would.'

'I am sure that is not true, Mr Jefferson, but you do need to appreciate that one's shame and regret over incidents in the past are not the most pleasurable topics for discussion, especially with a stranger. For by your presence here today, it seems that my past has now returned to haunt me.'

Gregg wondered what it was that the doctor was ashamed of; was it that Lorrett was his child?

'No, Mr Jefferson, it's not what you might be thinking; it was not my child, although I would have carried with pride the accusation of fatherhood had it been so. The child was an orphan, as I distinctly recall telling the young nurse at the time. Now, a question for you: if this child we are talking about is in fact the one I took to the hospital that night, is she merely being treated in your country or does she normally live there?'

'She lives there, Doctor, and your question, together with that earlier remark of yours concerning fatherhood, seems to imply that you might have more than just a fleeting interest in her. If that is the case, I suggest you would be very proud of her if you were to see her today.'

'I would? Then perhaps you will enlighten me further, Mr Jefferson?'

'By all means, but first let me ask you another question. Did you by chance see the last of a series of programmes about the war on television recently? It was transmitted from the UK and relayed throughout Germany and much of Europe.'

'Yes, I did, and I have to say what a wonderful series it was, especially that last programme.'

'Well, Doctor, the young lady who . . .' Gregg wasn't allowed to continue.

'No, it can't be, it can't. Were you about to tell me that the singer of that "Lilli Marlene" number is the child . . .'

The doctor suddenly stopped in mid sentence and looked as if he was about to stumble, his face drained of all colour as he paused to catch his breath before erratically continuing with his unfinished question.

'The child, the child we have been discussing and the singer in that show, were you about to tell me they are one and the same? They are, aren't they? That was young Ellie, that was my Ellie, wasn't it?'

'Yes, I believe she is the child you took to the hospital that night all those years ago, Doctor. Her real name is Lorraine Webster and her stage name Lorrett Lorren, but you mentioned the name of Ellie.'

Gregg remembered how Mrs Wals had thought the child's name could have been Heidi or something like it and he now realised how close she had been.

'Yes, it was Ellie, Ellie Mollen, the name of both the child and her mother.'

The doctor no longer found the need for reserve.

'I can see now why I had an uncanny feeling as I sat and watched her on the television that night, for there was something about her that I couldn't explain. It was as if her mother was with me again and now I can see the reason, for they are one and the same. My God! how wonderful, how wonderful; little Ellie is alive and I have found her after all these years.'

The hitherto outwardly defiant doctor was now showing further signs of distress for he had taken a clean white handkerchief from his pocket to soak up the flood of tears rolling down his face.

Shocked as he was, the doctor was forced to sit on a low wall near to where he had stopped, whilst Gregg stood quietly beside him with one hand on his shoulder, waiting patiently for him to speak again.

'I am sorry, Mr Jefferson, so sorry for my rather unmanly display, but these last few moments have jolted me back to a time when, like now, I was immersed in a whole ferment of emotion. Now, like a child, I sit here stumbling over words, not knowing what to say concerning my regret, my guilt, but most of all my happiness at finding that Ellie, my Ellie, lives on in her daughter. I just cannot begin to express the joy that you have brought to me today, Mr Jefferson, but please may I call you Gregg and as a friend would you call me Weiner.' The doctor put his trembling hand forward and in clasping it Gregg felt a sense of relief, knowing that he had at least overcome his first major obstacle.

'Can I suggest that we go over there.' Weiner pointed his stick at a shop across the road where a sign showed it to be a beer and wine bar. 'I usually stop off there for a glass of wine after my walk each day, but today I shall have to forgo my walk for, try as I will, I cannot stop shaking.'

Gregg took the arm of the doctor as they moved across the street and into the heavily panelled interior of the wine bar. There were already a number of older men sitting at some of the tables as the doctor and his new found friend entered. The group politely passed the time of day to the doctor and his companion who in turn acknowledged and returned the greeting.

'Shall we sit over there?' Weiner ushered his guest across to a corner of the room beside the window. They settled into their chairs just in time for the owner of the premises to appear at the table.

'Good afternoon, Herr Doktor, how are you this day?' Weiner half rose from his seat, putting out his hand to shake that of the owner's. 'Herr Smitz, I would like you to meet a friend of mine from England, Mr Jefferson.'

'I am pleased to meet with you, Mr Jefferson. Now, what can I get you, gentlemen, or will it be the usual for you, Herr Doktor?'

'No, I think today is a day for celebration, so perhaps we should welcome our guest here with one of your selected vintages.'

'That will be my pleasure.'

The proprietor, immaculately dressed in black pin-striped trousers, a white shirt, black waistcoat and tie and with a clean white apron around his waist, retreated from the shop into a rear room. It was some minutes before he re-appeared with two glasses and a bottle of his best German wine. He carefully poured an amount into a glass, passed it to the doctor and stood back waiting to receive his approval.

'Wunderbar, mein Herr, wunderbar.'

The proprietor, half-bent in a subservient fashion, smiled and after filling both glasses returned to his bar at the rear of the shop.

'As you say, Weiner, wunderbar; it is a magnificent wine.'

'That is good; I am so glad you like it. Now, let me apologise again for my behaviour and may I suggest that we now continue with our conversation, for there is so much I want to know and obviously so much we have to talk over. For instance, how did you become involved with Ellie, or perhaps it would be easier if I call her Lor . . . rett, if that is how you say it?'

'Yes, that is correct, Weiner. But perhaps it is best if I first tell you how I was to meet Lorrett and the circumstances that eventually led up to our association as friends. This, then, will help you to understand the reason I have undertaken this rather unusual task and how I come to be here now, enjoying this excellent wine with you.'

Gregg began by giving an account of his association with Lorrett and the show as Weiner, still with the occasional tear in his eyes, sat quietly listening to his every word. Throughout the fifteen or so minutes it took to complete the review, Weiner had, without his visitor's notice and with very little awareness of his own action, continued to share the remaining contents of the wine bottle between them. As Gregg finished, Weiner, with a gesture, called over the proprietor to their table.

'Herr Smitz, your wine is perfection but unless it's my eyes, your bottles seem to be getting smaller: not enough in them, I feel, to satisfy the thirsts of my friend and me, so perhaps we should have another.'

'I don't think I should have any more, Weiner, otherwise I will be, as your countrymen say, totally kaput.'

The laughter lines around the doctor's eyes became evident as he smiled.

'Come, come, you must have another glass or two, my friend; it is not every day that two strangers become friends within such a short space of time.'

'Well, all right, Weiner, providing I can now have some answers from you.'

'As many as you like, my friend.'

'Weiner, not knowing the kind of relationship that you shared with the child and her mother, but bearing in mind your remarks on how you felt that night as you watched Lorrett on the television, there seems to have been quite a strong bond between the three of you, perhaps even more particularly between you and the mother. You see, I get the impression that somewhere along the way you lost both the child and the mother and that you have never really stopped mourning their loss.'

'Well, inevitably, sharing, as I did at that time, my life with someone who could only be described as a beautiful human being, it is understandable that I still have many nostalgic recollections of those times and, yes, I do still often feel Ellie the mother so near to me. If this is what you see as mourning, so be it, but it is something much deeper than that, Gregg, something beyond either the triviality or the complexity of normal human relationships. For if you had experienced just a day with Ellie the mother, you too would now be sharing with me the total joy of having known her and the feeling that she is still here, for she was a very beautiful person.'

Gregg began to ask himself whether his new found friend was blessed with an over fertile imagination, for he couldn't help but feel that Weiner's association with his past seemed to be somewhat unreal, or perhaps even a little unnatural.

'By the look on your face, Gregg, I can see some further explanation is necessary. You see, Ellie Mollen, the mother of your Lorrett, was not just another woman, she was someone who in her own humble way was to stand out as a rarity amidst the predictable norm of most others around her. A human being with the qualities of a real human being, a woman that touched my life and many other lives in a way that no other person had ever done before or since. To have known Ellie was to live an experience that was both exhilarating and uplifting, an experience that one would never want to forget, and as I sat watching your show that night every detail of the time we shared together all those years ago came flooding back to me. You see, I had avidly followed the previous twenty-five programmes of the series and expected the last programme to be, as it were, a summary of what had gone before. So you can imagine my delight when it turned out to be this wonderfully nostalgic reunion show. As far as I am concerned, the whole programme that night was without question a very moving experience, just as my life with Ellie had been. Then, when this unknown singer came on to sing her first numbers, I was immediately transported back in time to those years of war. One of the songs she sang was that lovely French song "La Vie en Rose". Then of course there was the finale, where she sang her final song with that same emotional feeling as someone else I had once known; what was more, she was actually singing her song.

'You see, Gregg, as I sat watching this young unknown singer on your programme that night, her voice assumed the identity of someone I had once known a long time ago. It was a voice that, in some inexplicable way, was to touch the innermost depths of my feelings, a voice that reminded me in no uncertain terms that I had lived through this same experience once before in my life. I had felt this love and warmth within me for someone who was not just a beautiful singer, but also a very wonderful person. It was as if my life had suddenly returned to that period in wartime, when I was surrounded by much of that which was bad in the world, but through my association with this singer, Lorrett's mother, I was only able to see all that was good in it.

'Now you might think, Gregg, that this all sounds a little far-fetched or perhaps even incredible, for in a strange sort of way, it is, and that is also how I feel about your presence here today. You see, it is as if I have been waiting all of these years for something like this to happen.'

'Weiner, I have to admit that at the moment I don't fully understand all you are saying, but let me ask you about the song, for you implied that it was Ellie the mother's song; what exactly did you mean by that?'

'It is a song that I personally attributed to her, partly because of its association with our first meeting, but more particularly, because of the way it was to bond us together then and the way it seems to be continuing to do so now. But to understand this in any real way, I would have to tell you about that period in my life and I wouldn't want to inflict that on you.'

'It so happens, Weiner, I do need to hear more; but first another question. From what I gather so far, it is obvious that you knew both the mother and the child quite well, so can you ever remember the mother telling you of any accident or frightening incident that Lorrett may have had as a baby?'

'As far as it is possible to recall, there was no such incident. If there had been, however, I would have certainly been aware of it at the time. Was this the type of thing you were expecting to find, then?'

'Yes, hopefully, for so far I have covered most other aspects of her life and found very little that could be seen as a possible cause of her condition.'

'Well, the wine may have impaired my judgement a little, Gregg, but I am wondering if Lorrett's problem may stem from something much less obvious than the obvious. Something which until now I have never stopped to consider. It concerns an incident that happened in 1944, and a letter I received from Ellie, the mother, at the same time. Both the incident and the letter mystified me then and have continued to do so ever since. But perhaps, at the moment, the letter seems to have greater relevance, for I am wondering now whether it might hold the clue to Lorrett's problem?'

'What was so mysterious about the letter then, Weiner?'

'If I were to tell you what was in that letter, without explaining why I received it and why it was written, you would be none the wiser, Gregg. For it is only now, in these moments of quiet review, that I am beginning to see how both the confusing composition of the letter and the possible intention behind it seem to be coming together. It is perhaps like an apparition; you don't actually see anything, yet you are conscious of something being there. You are unable to describe or explain it, yet you know there has to be a reason for it. Now, if Lorrett's problem is in some way related to that event, then I shall have to try and tell you the full story, for it is possible that, with hindsight, I might just recall or recognise something that I have either forgotten or failed to consider until now.'

'Well, as I have already said, Weiner, I am a good listener.'

'I think you might have to be, Gregg, for it is in its way a very unusual story. As a young man, I trained to become a doctor in Munich, but took up practice here in Rüdesheim, after my studies and final exams were completed.

'You see, I was soon to be married and as my wife came from this area I was quite content to set up my practice here, in 1937. Well, we were fortunate, for here we were cushioned from many of the nefarious activities of the Third Reich, but inevitably, it wasn't long before I found myself directed into the forces. So it was that in 1939 I was drafted into the army and eventually became a Medical Officer serving with the Ninth Panzer Division. Now I don't know whether you are aware of it or not, but both the Ninth and the Eleventh Panzer divisions had a very good reputation in those days. For suffice it to say that they both played a major role in our quick advance through Europe. I was part of that advance; in fact, I was with a mobile hospital unit dealing with the wounded. Then in late 1941 I was shipped across to Libya, where, under Rommel, we were eventually to fight our way to a point on the map in the Western Desert called El Alamein. This was where I became wounded. Well, because of the nature of my wound, I was sent back to our main barracks and military hospital just outside Hamburg which, in those days, was called Stronheim Barracks. It was here that many of the Panzer Divisions were trained and in fact, because of its location near to the port of Hamburg, it was also a transit camp for troops either being despatched to, or returning from, various parts of the globe. The wound I received was fortunately only in one leg, but it was enough to get me medically down-graded away from active service. Well, after some two months or so as a patient within the hospital, I was fit again to continue my work as a doctor and, as good fortune would have it, a position as Medical Officer within that same hospital became available. Now, as I look back, this was to be the first of many steps that were ultimately going to direct my life towards this meeting of ours here today.

'You told me earlier, Gregg, that you had been to those same barracks just recently so you will realise that they are just a few miles from the outskirts of the town. Anyway, I became established within the barracks in late 1942 and found myself involved in a very busy life. My work covered such things as medicals for the soldiers entering and leaving the camp, inoculations and, understandably, care of the wounded who like myself had been returned to the base hospital for either major surgery or psychological rehabilitation. For those first few months I was to find myself working extremely long hours with hardly any rest, so I had little or no time for any leisure activities. I suppose my story really began one evening when, for the first time, I was able to summon up enough energy to attend a function that was being put on in the Officer's Mess. I decided to attend it mainly for the break, for in truth I found I had little in common with many of my fellow officers who were, I am afraid, infatuated by the power and success of their dear Führer. Well, we and the invited guests sat down to a meal in the traditional style of officers under the Third Reich. For there was always, you see, this Wagnerian sense of protocol with its silverware, its cut glass, its rituals and all the other paraphernalia that were a part and parcel of the elitist German officer class. After dinner, a section of the regimental band played popular music of the times whilst the officers and their ladies, many of whom were nothing more than mistresses or high class call girls, danced or drank the next hour or so away. It must have been about eleven p.m. that I decided to return to my quarters and was just about to leave when the orderly officer of the day stood up to make an announcement.

' "Ladies and gentlemen, we have by way of entertainment this evening a young lady with a beautiful voice and, might I add, a beautiful personality to match. So for your pleasure may I present the lovely Miss Ellie Mollen." '

'That was how I saw Ellie the mother for the first time and for the next hour or so I stood at the bar, mesmerised by the personality of this beautiful woman and completely elated by the sound of her voice. She sang with so much feeling that I felt as if I was there close to her. You see, she had this presence about her, this . . . how would you say it?'

' "Aura", is that the word you're looking for, Weiner?'

'Yes, yes, an aura, that is it. It was, as you say, like an unseen aura that I felt I could touch, even though I was removed from her by the distance between us. I can't recall all the songs she sang that night but I do remember one of them as being "Auf Wiedersehen", then, like your Lorrett on television, she sang "La Vie en Rose" in French. She was loudly applauded at the end of each song and it was quite plain to see that everyone there adored her. To end her performance, she then went on to sing what to me became her song; that song was "Lilli Marlene" and it was here that my obsession for both the singer and the song began. It was something I will never forget, for until that night I had very little time for cabaret signers, but when Ellie sang it was like being gently wrapped in a blanket of fine silk. You see, the clarity of her voice and the deliberation of her words had a way of personalising itself with all who listened and I am sure that everyone in the mess that night felt as if she was singing for them alone. It was song that came from the soul and touched the soul.'

It was some seconds before Gregg could bring himself to speak.

'Weiner, I'm still a little confused over this reference of yours that it was her song.'

'I'm afraid you will have to be a bit patient and bear with me, Gregg, because the explanation is not a simple one.'

'I'll try, Weiner, but you can understand that I need to ask questions.'

'Of course, I would be the same. However, as I was saying, the experience of hearing Ellie sing had moved me so much, that as I returned to my quarters that night I felt relieved of much of my previous tension and somehow rejuvenated by the events of the whole evening. Well, the hectic life within the hospital went on and even began to increase, as our armies became involved on other fronts. It was under this momentum of long hours and constant pressure that we were to be subjected to two further problems. The second of these, which was the bombing of Hamburg, did not come until some time later, but when it did, it was to give rise to a demand for our help in non-military hospitals, hence the reason why I occasionally helped out at the Kindorf Hospital. The first problem, however, was much more subtle and yet, if not checked at the time, it could have had a devastating effect on our forces within the barracks and indirectly on our overall combat strength in the field. It was VD.

'Of course, it is easy to understand how those virile young men, trained to the peak of their fitness and faced with the probability of their own early demise, found either the immediate reason or the need to satisfy their new found manhood with the opposite sex. But all too often, youthful impetuosity has a way of creating problems that others are left to deal with, and VD is one such problem.

'Thus, from the number of men that were found to have one or other of these diseases, we realised that the situation was getting out of hand and, inevitably, some form of immediate action was necessary. So at a meeting of the medical staff within the barracks, it was agreed that the most obvious course open to us was first to try and locate the main sources of the disease, then to treat both the recipients and the benefactors of these liaisons. With this in mind, I and my fellow doctors began questioning soldiers who came before us and we found that most of those infected had contacted it from one of three different sources of infection.

'Two of these sources were back street brothels in Hamburg and the third appeared to be the women who, without my knowledge at the time, apparently hung about outside the gates of the barracks, solely for the purpose of picking up soldiers. These were more than anything free and easy good time girls. As a result of our findings, we concluded that the only hope we had of containing this problem was to act swiftly and effectively. So the whole of the other ranks in the barracks were paraded and given an infection check, told of the dangers of VD and then verbally warned that under army regulations they could be charged with personal neglect if they continued to expose themselves to unnecessary risk. Once the treatment of those found to have been infected was completed, the Waffen SS were given the task of raiding the brothels and bringing before us the women who earned their living from prostitution. These, too, were promptly given a medical check and those that were cleared were released, whilst those that were infected were kept in medical detention until they had completed a course of treatment. Then came the round-up of the women who regularly hung around the camp outside and this was planned for a Friday night, when most of the troops received their pay. Such were the arrangements, that I was to be on duty to check out these girls as they were brought in, so that the innocent amongst them could be released without too much embarrassment, for obviously they were not all tarred with the same brush.

'Well, Gregg, that evening I sat waiting in my office and at about seven p.m., two army lorries drew up outside with some twenty or so women aboard; these were taken into an outer waiting room and watched over by three or four SS guards. Then, one by one, they were shown into my office, where I was first to ascertain, as much as it was possible to do so, whether they were just good time girls, or the genuine girlfriends of soldiers stationed at the camp.

'If I had any doubts about them, I would pass them through to a colleague of mine in the next room, who gave them a physical check to confirm one way or the other. I don't think I will ever forget that evening, for I can recall how I had seen all of the girls except one and was sitting at my desk, completing some paperwork on the previous girl I had just interviewed, when the door opened and what I took to be my last client was ushered into the room. I didn't look up immediately, for I was still writing, then I slowly lifted up my head to face the woman standing there. In that brief moment I was completely taken back, for the very beautiful woman before me was no other than the singer I had seen that night in the Officer's Mess, Ellie Mollen.'

Weiner hesitated for some moments, obviously reliving a part of his past life, before he described the conversation as it had taken place.

' "Oh, I'm sorry, Miss Mollen, I don't know who you are looking for but it would appear that you have come into the wrong room."

' "Herr Doktor," she said, "it pleases me that you know my name, but I believe that it is you who is looking for me, for it seems that it was your idea to have me arrested and brought here along with the other girls."

'Well, Gregg, I suddenly realised that Ellie must have been picked up outside the gates, but I hardly felt that she was one of the people I was after.'

Weiner continued to relate the conversation as it happened that night.

' "Miss Mollen, there seems to have been some mistake; the only ladies who have been brought in here tonight are those who regularly hang about outside the barracks with the intention of picking up our soldiers, and it is obvious to me that you are not one of them."

' "But Herr Doktor, I am one of those ladies and I do hang about outside your gates; furthermore, I do at times pick up soldiers."

'I can still hear her defiance now, Gregg; it was as if she was challenging and baiting me at the same time, then waiting with some satisfaction to study my reaction before continuing to gently chastise me.

' "So Herr Doktor, I am afraid you will have to take my word for this, but contrary to what you may think, I am not one of your good time girls and to satisfy any professional doubt you may have, I am a virgin, so I have not hired myself out to any of your young soldiers and I have no intention of doing so."

'You can appreciate my surprise at such candour and virtuous defiance, Gregg. On the one hand she admitted picking up men and yet on the other confirmed in no uncertain terms that she was pure. I was at a loss to understand why this beautiful woman with so much talent appeared to succumb to this practice and I certainly didn't know what to say next, I let her go without further questioning and without subjecting her to a medical check. Gregg, I have never in my life been so completely knocked off balance as I was that evening and what is more, I knew then that I had a love for this woman. I was eventually to find out that this love was not like that I had for my wife, but something so totally and indescribably different. A love that was completely fulfilled merely by being in her presence. A love that was based upon the total respect and adoration of someone who, because of what she was and what she did, justifiably deserved such adoration. You see, she came into my life as an enigma, she was herself an enigma and, sadly, she was to die leaving a further enigma. Even to this day I cannot find the words to describe her fantastic presence, her compassion and kindness, or the joy I was to reap in my future years at having had the good fortune just to have known her.'

Gregg sat silently dazed by what he had just heard, and he was glad that the doctor himself remained quiet and distant for some minutes.

It was Weiner who broke the silence as he took out a watch from his waistcoat pocket. 'My goodness, Gregg, do you realise the time, it looks to me as if I will have to forget my walk today, especially as I now feel incapable of taking another step.'

Weiner called the proprietor of the bar over and asked for his bill.

'Herr Doktor, would you allow me to welcome you and your guest by accepting the wine with my compliments, for it is always a pleasure to see you.'

'My dear Herr Smitz, I do have some difficulty with accepting gifts or gratuities, but on this occasion I will thank you for your generosity and accept on the condition that, when my guest and I next return, you will do us the honour of joining us at my expense. Now, may I wish you good day, Herr Smitz.'

'Good day, Herr Doktor, good day, Herr Jefferson.'

Both men found their way out of the premises into the fresh breeze of late afternoon and hesitantly turned to re-trace their way back to Weiner's home. Gregg, holding on to the arm of the doctor, was suddenly to find himself at a standstill whilst Weiner hesitated over something he was about to say.

'Do you know, Gregg, I can't remember feeling like this for a long time. Isn't it strange, you came into my life just a short time ago and yet I feel I've known you all my life. For your presence here today has given me a renewed sense of purpose. A purpose with which to fill my limited tomorrows, a purpose that excites me and one that I feel has to go on.'

'I think I know what you mean, Weiner; it is as if two people who would normally have no chance of ever meeting, have been slowly manipulated by circumstance to complete something that until now has remained incomplete.'

'I think that just about sums it up, Gregg.'

'Did you make your journey here by car today, Gregg?'

'Yes, I have it parked on a plot some two streets away. Do you think it will be all right to leave it there until I find myself a suitable hotel?'

'I think I know the spot and I am sure it will be safe enough. But I was going to suggest that you stay with me whilst you are here for I have plenty of room and I would welcome your company. I can easily get my housekeeper to prepare a room for you and then perhaps we can share some further reminiscences and bottles of wine together.'

'That's most hospitable of you, Weiner, and thank you, but please, if I am to stay with you, you must allow me to pay my way.'

'I wouldn't think of it, Gregg, you will be my guest. But you can supply the odd bottle of wine or two if you like, providing and only providing that you don't encourage me to drink too much, as you have this afternoon.'

'I will try to avoid it, Weiner.'

Gregg was shown to his room by Mrs Kipros the housekeeper who at the same time filled a large jug with hot water and placed it beside a wash bowl on a nearby stand. After unwrapping a new bar of soap, she searched in a landing cupboard outside and returned with two white fluffy towels. Putting them down beside the stand, she then left the room, gently closing the door behind her.

Gregg took advantage of the somewhat Victorian facilities and had a refreshing wash and brush up before finally treading his way carefully down the old oak stairs to the lounge-cum-dining room below. Weiner was sitting comfortably in a high backed armchair beside a glowing log fire. His face was flustered and his eyes were dazed as he looked across at Gregg with a wide mischievous smile that told its own story.

'Ah Gregg, excuse the fire, for it does get cold here in the evenings. Now, sit you down there, dinner is on its way.'

'Yes, I can smell the enticing flavours, Weiner, and I thank you for inviting me into your home.'

'Your company is my pleasure, for much of my time is spent alone since I lost my wife.'

'How long have you been on your own?'

'It was in nineteen sixty-five that she died, that's, what, just over five years ago now and life has never been quite the same since. I have to say I do miss her, for we did have a very happy marriage.'

'Can I ask you a rather personal question, Weiner?'

'I can't see why not.'

'Having spoken of your love for Ellie, how did you reconcile this with the love you had for your wife?'

'I didn't need to. Of course, I have to admit that in the early days of my friendship with Ellie I was unable to rationalise my feelings towards her, but as I continue with my story after we have had our meal, you will begin to understand how this compromise was made for me. You see, I found that I could love and be loved by someone other than my wife without destroying the bond of loyalty and trust that I and my wife shared together. In truth, both my marriage and my life have been enriched simply because Ellie was there for those few precious moments in time. Now, let's eat, shall we?'

The plump and homely Mrs Kipros who had been out of the room preparing the meal had brought it through in piping hot tureens before serving it out and taking up what was obviously her seat at the table. It wasn't until some hour or so after they had finished the meal that Weiner and Gregg found themselves alone and sitting comfortably opposite each other beside the open grated fire. In the mutually perceived silence which followed Gregg noticed a photograph on a nearby shelf showing his friend in German officer's uniform with an attractively dressed woman beside him.

'I see you were looking at that photograph, Gregg. Just in case you are thinking otherwise, it is my wife there beside me, not Ellie. It so happens that I don't have a photograph of Ellie, which is something I have always regretted. Now, I hope you enjoyed your meal, albeit somewhat removed from your own countrymen's favourite fish and chips; however, can I suggest a brandy and perhaps a cigar?'

'That would be very nice, providing that by doing so, I am not again influencing you to drink too much, Weiner.'

'Well, you are, but fortunately I am not the complaining type.'

Both were smiling as the host half filled two goblets with brandy and then settled back into his chair, still drawing on the unlit meerschaum pipe hanging from the corner of his mouth.

'I suppose I had better return to my story, otherwise you will begin to think that it was only the wine that was talking this afternoon.'

'Well, I was myself beginning to wonder whether I had dreamt away the afternoon, Weiner, for at the moment I am finding it extremely difficult to register, let alone believe, all that you have told me this far.'

'I know and I can understand your conflict, for I too have the need to question my own beliefs at times, but everything I have told you and all that I am about to tell you is actually how it was; no frills, no old man's fantasies, just hard to believe reality.'

'I hope my remark didn't offend you, Weiner, it is just that at the moment I feel as if I am involved in something that I have no control over, something that seems to have a momentum of its own.'

'Oh, I don't think you are merely an involuntary participant in all of this, Gregg. If anything, I am beginning to see you as perhaps a destined mediator more than a passive bystander. But I shall not say anything more than that at the moment, otherwise you might begin to question my sanity, so perhaps it is best if I continue with my story.

'Now, where were we? Oh yes, I had just finished telling you how I let Ellie go without giving her a medical that evening. Well, naturally that brief interlude we had shared puzzled me for days after and, having an inquisitive streak in me, I decided to make some discreet enquiries into how she came to be at the mess that night. It soon became known to me that she sang regularly at a night club in Hamburg which many of my fellow officers frequented. It would appear that one of these officers had invited her to sing for us at the mess, hence my first sight of Ellie and the awakening of my male ego. So I decided to visit the club myself and I anxiously waited for the first opportunity to take a night off.

'Germany at that time, Gregg, was generally short of luxury commodities although it still had most of the essentials such as food, clothing and footwear, but austerity was nowhere to be seen at the club that night. I remember that I entered and after waiting for a few moments I was shown to a table that edged up to the uncarpeted area of the floor where both the dancing and the cabaret took place. I had naturally gone alone, but within the first five minutes I found myself talking to an attractive female hostess who had planted herself on a chair at my table. I found no reason to reject her company, although I knew there would be a price to pay. It was, however, better than being on my own and before I had realised it, I had spent a pleasant couple of hours dancing and chatting to my interesting and interested companion. Throughout that period, as we sat drinking champagne or gliding our way around the floor, I couldn't help but notice four soldiers at a table on the other side of the floor to ours. The thing that struck me most about them was their extravagance, for the champagne flowed like water and they seemed to order quite liberally from the rather expensive menu. If they had been four of my fellow officers and not simply privates, I wouldn't have given the matter another thought, but as it was, I was left wondering how they could afford such a night out.

'This question was still on my mind as the cabaret began, first with a dance routine, followed by other odd acts, until ultimately there came the announcement for which I had been waiting. A man in evening dress faced the audience and spoke. "Ladies and gentlemen, we are proud to have discovered, we are proud to know and we have pride in presenting to you, our own Ellie Mollen."

'I had wondered beforehand, Gregg, whether I was going to be disappointed at hearing Ellie sing for the second time, but I soon realised my fears were unfounded, for again I found myself totally obsessed by both the singer and the song. There were cries of "encore, encore," from the patrons as she finished each number for, without question, she really did have the ethos of a star. But I think the most emotional part for me that evening was when, at the end of her last song, Ellie bowed and, withdrawing from the centre of the floor, she walked over to these four soldiers sitting at the table opposite. As she did, two of them stood up with some difficulty whilst the other two remained seated. Ellie then went round the table kissing them on their cheeks and putting her arms affectionately around each one of them in turn. A spotlight had been turned on to her and it was only then that I noticed that the soldiers had all been wounded in one way or another; in fact, one of them I recognised as being a patient of mine from the barracks hospital. I didn't quite understand the situation, but it seemed to me as if these four young men were having some form of celebration. But this didn't answer all my doubts, for I still couldn't deduce how they could afford such lavishness on their pay as private soldiers, or why Ellie had done what she did. Still in a quandary over what I had seen, I called the waiter over and asked for my bill. I was then just about to take out my wallet, ready to pay the account, when he stopped me.

' "Mein Herr, I am to tell you that your evening here is on the house, with the compliments of the management."

'You can no doubt appreciate my embarrassment by this surprise gesture of kindness, for it wasn't as if I had been a regular visitor to the club, so all that I could do was to ask the waiter to thank the management on my behalf and leave both him and my friendly hostess a rather large tip.

'That free evening was to remain a mystery to me for some days, until, that was, I had the time to talk with my patient, the wounded soldier I had seen at the club that night. I first had a chat with him about his wounds, his future and other personal details like that, then I casually touched upon his visit to the club. It was then that I was able to suggest that the club was perhaps a little expensive and ask him if he had also found it so. Well, I was soon to have the answer, for he went on to say,

' "We didn't have to pay, sir, Miss Mollen arranged and took care of it all."

'I then naturally asked him whether the lady in question was a personal friend of his, or of one of the other three soldiers.'

' "No, sir; you see, she often takes different soldiers to the club."

'You can imagine how I felt, Gregg, for upon further questioning it turned out that Ellie did, at times, actually wait outside the barrack gates to pick up soldiers. But, contrary to my confused belief, this was only so that she could take them to the club for a completely free evening's entertainment. I was to learn later that these soldiers were usually men who had been wounded but who, by the nature of their wounds, were reasonably mobile. So I then began to ask myself if my own free meal that night had also been instigated by this same source of generosity, and if so, why?

'My brain was numbed by a surfeit of unanswered questions, but I was at least beginning to see the reason for Ellie's pretended indignation that evening in my office. For, as I was eventually to find out, her portrayal of a self-righteous lady had been purposely staged just for me. That was Ellie, a bewitching and beautiful woman, whose childlike sense of feminine mischief always came to the surface whenever she was in doubt or under duress in some way.

'Well, Gregg, before my formal introduction to Ellie, I was to discover that she had an arrangement with the management to reserve a particular table at the club exclusively for the use of these wounded visitors. The owner of the club had also given Ellie an old car which had been adapted to transport her disabled guests to and from the camp. Then I later realised that she had also put on a couple of shows for the troops at the barracks and, naturally, they had also been a great success. But I suppose the thing that fascinated me most in those early days, was how Ellie managed to share her life with so many susceptible and lonely young men, yet retain that enviable bloom of dignity and innocence that she always had. You see, it wasn't until some time later that I realised, people simply loved her for what she was and what she did. Looking back now, it is easy to understand why, for she was always there when anyone needed help or sympathy and she never seemed to disapprove of people or attempt to judge them in any way. She also had this uncanny knack of being able to pre-empt what you were about to say, or at times, even know what you were actually thinking. I am sure now that most of those who knew Ellie in those days saw her as being someone who was above and beyond their normal expectancy of people and that, whilst they might not have outwardly shown it, they all, I feel, loved and respected her for simply being herself.

'Of the many things I was to learn about Ellie in those early days, I was not to know then that she was soon to become my most honoured friend. My discovery that she had been behind my free evening at the club that night and my formal introduction to her came as a complete surprise to me, but then, Ellie was always full of surprises. I can recall that evening even to this day, for without prior thought or intent, I suddenly felt this overpowering need to get away from the camp and take a walk in the fresh night air. I remember, I had just passed the sentry at the gates and turned into the lane beside the barracks, when I saw this figure of a lone woman waiting in the darkness just a few metres in front of me.

'Within the limited light I could just see that she was wearing a long leather coat which came down to her knees and a beret on her head. In my somewhat vague frame of mind and the comparative darkness of the night nothing registered at first, but as I looked again, she had moved slightly into the limited light from a nearby street lamp that lit up one side of her face and the reflective surface of her shiny black coat. It was only then as she turned to walk towards me that I could see it was Ellie.

' "Herr Doktor, I somehow knew that you would leave the barracks tonight which is why I have taken the opportunity to pick you up. You may recall I admitted to you that picking up soldiers was a habit of mine!"

'She had done it again, Gregg; she had for the second time knocked me off balance and found me wanting for words. She then put her arm through mine and started to slowly walk me away from the camp.

'"Doctor Kraske, or may I call you Weiner? You have been on my conscience since my unreasonable attitude towards you that night in your office. So perhaps you would allow me to apologise, for I didn't fully appreciate at the time either the urgency or the need for the unpalatable duty you had to carry out. Since that evening I have made certain enquiries about you which show you to be a highly respected officer and an understanding gentleman. But may I also suggest that, from the look on your face tonight, you are also a very tired man. You see, I have, without you realising it, over the past month or so noticed an ever increasing strain upon your face; this was even more obvious to me the night you visited the club and that is why I decided to meet with you tonight. For I hoped that you would allow me to give you something in return for your never ceasing care towards those unfortunate men you help to heal. That something is my friendship and deepest affection.

'"You see, my dear Weiner, even as distant strangers I knew we were to become united as friends, for I am sure that we both felt that immediate bond that was there between us that night in the Officers' Mess. Now, as I walk near to you, that feeling is even more intense and I know that what we are about to share together was intended to be."

'Well, Gregg, that was it, that was the gift that she had, this ability to pre-empt people's feelings, thoughts and, at times, their intentions. Coupled with this was that inexplicable radiance she bore, which somehow seemed to unite itself with everyone who came into contact with her.

'It was as if she could make you feel totally complete within yourself, as I did from that point of introduction. I once heard it said of a man, that he walked with God. I think that statement was intended to imply that through his own devotion to others he had himself found total happiness. If that was so, then Ellie too shared this same privilege, and throughout the months ahead I was myself able to find that same total happiness by sharing a part of my life with this remarkable woman.

'It would appear that she originally came from another part of Germany, where, at twenty years of age, she fell in love with a young man from her own home town. This was about late '39 but soon her love, as she referred to him, was like myself drafted into the army, and posted to Stronheim Barracks for training. Apparently all was well to begin with, for they were then able to correspond with each other for some year or so, but by the end of 1940, some months had elapsed without any letters from him. So, owing to this lack of news, she decided to leave the comfort of her home and travel to Hamburg in the hope of finding him. Then, as a tentative measure, she set herself up in a couple of furnished rooms at the top of a three storey house and found herself a waitress job at the club. This meant her working from late evening to early morning, which of course suited her, for it allowed her time in the day to pursue her plan. You see, her hope was to locate her young man and then set up home near to him for as long as possible, but she was unaware at the time that he had in fact been posted to an unknown theatre of war some months earlier. I was later to find out that Hans, that was her boy friend's name, was unable to write at first, then by the time he was able to do so, Ellie had left home. Thus the twist of irony had made its first of many appearances. It was, in fact, her explanation for staying in Hamburg after realising that Hans was no longer there, that gave me my first insight into this rare gift of extrasensory perception that Ellie had, for she said,

' "When I came to this area for the first time, Weiner, I knew that Hans had been here, for I felt his presence everywhere and, since I don't know where he is now, I shall remain here within this nearness to him until such time that we can be united again."

'You see, Gregg, she really did feel that because Hans had been stationed at the barracks for a while, he had left behind him this lingering persona, as she described it. Again you will find this extremely hard to believe, as I did at first, and whilst I still cannot explain the phenomenon, I'm sure that to her it was something that was as natural as breathing. She also went on to suggest that whilst she remained conscious of this persona around her she knew that Hans was alive and well.

'So now perhaps you are beginning to see, Gregg, how I, even with all my experience as a doctor, have never understood the nature or extent of this fantastic gift that Ellie had, but then she herself never spoke of it or acted in any way that suggested she was aware of it. Now, whether this was in some way related to her unusual humanist ideals and her ongoing dedication to others I shall never know, but, suffice to say, I wish I did.'

Weiner leaned forward in his chair to poke the now ashen logs of the fire and in the brief moment of re-kindling, dancing patterns of light lit up the darkened beams and whitened walls of the room.

'Now, how about a nice whisky, Gregg?'

'Yes please, Weiner, that would be most enjoyable.'

Weiner moved over to the other side of the room to pour the drinks, and as he did so he looked at his watch.

'Do you realise it is eleven o'clock already? Would you like to go to bed now or shall I go on?'

'Oh, definitely go on, Weiner. I have to know the rest of this story before I put my head on that pillow tonight.'

'That's good and, believe me, I am quite happy to continue with it.'

After passing the drink to his obviously comfortable visitor, the doctor returned to his seat, settled down and slowly drank the contents of his glass before speaking again.

'Right, now to continue with the story. Well, Ellie told me how she first became a camp girl, as we used to call them. She explained that initially she would hang around outside the barrack gates, simply to enquire from any passing soldier whether Hans was still stationed at the barracks. She was soon to realise, however, that the barracks were mainly used for training only and that once trained, the crews were posted off to active service units throughout our occupied territories or theatres of war. So, concluding quite rightly that Hans must have had been posted to such a unit before her arrival in Hamburg, she began to direct her enquiries towards those soldiers who had obviously been wounded. She had soon come to realise, you see, that most of the wounded stationed at the barracks had been returned from active service units to the base hospital. So, quite understandably, she thought that possibly one of them might by chance have known Hans prior to his arrival back at the barracks. However, after some insistence on my part, she then went on to tell me how she began caring for the wounded.

' "I was waiting at the gate one evening," she said, "when I could see a soldier on crutches slowly making his way towards the gates. He eventually managed to make it to where I was standing and it was only then that I could see the sadness and the look of despair upon the young soldier boy's face. Suddenly I became aware of my own selfishness, for I realised that in my endeavour to find Hans, I had ignored the personal pain and anguish of the many others I had previously bothered by my questioning, and immediately I felt this overpowering desire to compensate for my past neglect and lack of consideration. So I approached him and asked whether

I could help in any way, but he just looked at me without saying a word, so I then took his arm and asked him where was he going.

' " 'Nowhere in particular, Miss, I just needed to get away from the mass of uniforms everywhere, for I keep seeing them as shadows of my dead friends lying there beside me." '

'In fact, Gregg, I was to learn later from the man himself, whose name was Anton, that he had actually left his quarters that night with the intention of committing suicide. But he apparently had no idea what it was that made him focus onto those distant barrack gates and undertake the long and arduous walk towards them, for, as he tried to explain, he just felt this compelling need to distance himself from others around him so that he could quietly end his life. But I have often asked myself, was it just that, or was it something else that directed him towards those distant gates and into the safety of Ellie's compassion that night?

'I know, Gregg, you are either thinking that I have been blessed with an over sized imagination or that I have lost contact with the real world around me, but hear me out before you go making too many wild conclusions.

'Well, apparently without a second thought, Ellie hired a taxi and took this soldier to the club, where she was due for work later that evening. The other half of this story was told to me sometime later by the owner of the club, Herr Cramer, who, incidentally, was to become a great friend of mine and who I was eventually to know as Gunter. He told me how Ellie had brought this soldier into the club that night and asked if he could be allowed to sit at one of the tables to watch the show. She apparently then went on to suggest that the soldier should be given anything he wanted, the cost of which was to be stopped from her wages as a waitress, until she had paid for it. Gunter went on to explain how normally, private soldiers in uniform were not allowed in the club, and that he himself wasn't normally in the habit of considering such requests from members of his staff. But as he said, "Faced with the persuasive and compassionate tenderness of this lovely young lady and with the torment of war showing on this young man's face, I could do nothing more than agree to her request and give the soldier the best in the house."

'Gunter continued by telling me how the best that evening, both for him and for the soldier, was yet to come. For it would appear that after the cabaret had finished that night, the band went on to play a slow dance number. Well, as they played, someone from somewhere in the darkened club started singing the words of the song. Well, according to Gunter, it wasn't long before people stopped what they were doing, just to listen to this lovely voice from the darkness. It was at that point that one of Gunter's staff had the good sense to direct a spotlight onto the area and Gunter then went on to tell me what happened next.

' "As the light came on, I could see that it was Ellie, my waitress, she was sitting at the table beside this soldier chappie, with her arms across it holding both of his hands. In her eyes, there was an expression of warmth and gratitude, as she quietly seemed to dedicate the words of the song to this obviously battle scarred young man.

' "The song ended and the clapping began as an obviously embarrassed waitress picked up her serving tray from the table with its pile of used crockery and glasses, ready to disappear into the kitchen. I did no more than immediately to move across towards her, take the tray from her hands and encourage Ellie onto the floor to sing something else for her obviously enthusiastic audience. She chose the song 'Lilli Marlene' and Weiner, you can imagine what happened, the clientele went mad with delight and I had lost my heart to her, her voice and her lovely ways."

'You can now see the effect she had on people, Gregg. Well, Gunter went on to tell me that from that night on Ellie became their resident singer and in return she was given a very good wage and allowed to bring up to six soldiers a week to the club for a free evening's food, drink and entertainment. Apparently the news of this concession soon became known to the regular patrons and over the next three months or so to many other people around Hamburg. Such was the impact of both Ellie's singing and this magnanimous gesture of Gunter's that the club was soon to become packed out every night and as Gunter himself said, "Suddenly, the recognition I had been seeking and had never been able to achieve since I opened the place was there and it was Ellie who had made it all possible."

'This was Ellie, and she never changed. She simply explained away this concern she had for people by suggesting that she found so much happiness from life and living herself that she wanted to share it with others, especially those who needed her help or understanding.'

Weiner attempted to stretch his defective leg before picking up his tobacco pouch from the floor beside him. He slowly filled and lit his pipe before finally comforting himself back into his chair.

Gregg, taking advantage of the quiet period, sat silently in thought, content to wait on Weiner's decision to continue with his story.

'I could tell you many more stories of Ellie's personal consideration for others, Gregg, but for now let me follow through with the main text of my life with her. As the days went by I found that any spare time I had was taken up by helping Ellie to organise these visits to the club for some of the wounded under my care. Then we were able to arrange one or two shows in the wards at the barracks hospital for the benefit of those who were bedridden because of their wounds. So life was hectic, tragic and, because of the increased bombing, often quite dangerous, but it was at the same time so highly charged with personal satisfaction that I have never felt so much at peace with myself as I did in that time of war.

'Many was the night that Ellie and I spent in some dark dank basement sheltering from falling missiles, fated as they were to change the pattern of some people's lives for ever. But any fear that might have surfaced on the faces of those that shared our shelter was soon quelled by the song and laughter that Ellie imparted on all around her. Even under such duress I never once saw anything about her that annoyed me, repulsed me, or made me change my view of her, in fact, if anything, my feelings towards her were compounded day upon day because of this ever present happiness I found in her company. But I was ever conscious of the possibility that like Pagliacci's clown Tonio, she had concealed behind her smile a yearning loneliness that cried out for fulfilment. In my own ineffectual way I did my best to take her mind off her own personal fears by seeking out different things I could do to help her. This also gave me an opportunity to help compensate her for her undying efforts towards others and her kindness towards me. I did eventually have a key to her flat and I would go there as often as I could whilst she was working, to do one or two odd chores for her. Looking back on all those wonderful times, I think my greatest excitement and pleasure came when suddenly I found that I could do something quite special for Ellie.

'Like most things in those times it came about quite unexpectedly and again it was more by irony than by plan. It was in the first days of August 1943 that, by way of routine, I was checking out the fitness of some twenty men who, because of your RAF, found themselves temporarily housed within the barracks. They were tank crews who were apparently being transferred from active service on the Russian front to another army group stationed near to the French coast, when the train in which they were travelling was forced to stop some twenty kilometres from the centre of Hamburg.

'You see, in the last days of July the RAF had bombed and devastated the docks and much of the industrial heart of the city, so much so that all rail traffic had been halted, which subsequently meant that the train had to be cleared of its passengers until such time that the lines could be repaired. So as a temporary measure, these tank crews were brought into the barracks and, as a part of our routine, all military personnel posted to or away from the camp had to have a brief medical check up. Hence I had the job of checking out these twenty soldiers on the day they arrived.

'Well, I had seen four of them and in came the next. As he walked into the room, the first thing I noticed was that he had a strawberry birthmark on his left cheek. Nothing clicked to start with, then after that first initial impression, I nearly fell of my chair with excitement. I was still unsure, for his face wasn't quite like that of the photograph that Ellie kept on her sideboard within the flat. But as he sat down in front of me, I was more or less convinced that it was Ellie's young man. I asked him for his army record book and as he passed it to me, my eyes went straight to the name and it was, as I had thought, Hans. Well, Gregg, I managed to contain myself and decided that I should at least question him before disclosing my knowledge of Ellie. So I carried out my medical check on him and in the process asked him about his experiences on the Russian front.

'In this way, I was able to carefully lead into questions of a more personal nature and ask him if he was married. Of course I already knew the answer, but it allowed me to follow up his response, by asking him if he had a girl friend. He told me that he was no longer certain, for having had no letters from her for some considerable time, he wondered whether something had happened to her or if she no longer cared. Well, as he was so obviously concerned about her, I consoled him by suggesting that it was quite natural for men away from home always to fear the worst, especially if they were not getting regular mail from their loved ones.

'However, as I continued talking to him, I found myself working on a plan to bring Ellie and this young man together again. So, on the excuse that I had to check over some details relating to his fitness, I asked him to return to see me later that same evening, when, hopefully, I would have an answer to the query at hand. My first impressions of Hans told me that he was a very nice young man, but I could see by the look on his face that he was not too pleased with me at the time, for without my knowledge then, he had apparently made prior arrangements with his friends to spend their first night of freedom out on the town.

'Well, I dealt with the remainder of the group and then set about arranging with Gunter, the club owner, what I had in mind. He was, of course, as excited as I was about my proposed plan, so much so that he said that he would lay on something special to celebrate their reunion at the club that night. Of course, it was agreed that in the event of another air-raid, the plan would have to be delayed, but fortunately as things turned out, this was not to be the case and that evening was to be one of the most memorable of my life.

'Come nine that evening, I was busying myself in my office when Hans knocked and at my invitation came into the room. He was smartly dressed and I got the impression that he expected the interview was only going to be short-lived. So, after suggesting that he sit down, I apologised for messing up his evening and I went on to explain that the query I had raised about his fitness earlier had since been solved. I then touched again on the subject of his experiences at the front and in the conversation that followed, I suggested that in compensation for spoiling his evening and with the view to meeting someone who was keen to write an article about his experiences, he should join me for an evening at the club.

'So, with mixed feelings of guilt and pleasure over my methods of persuasion, we arrived at the club some thirty minutes later. As I vacated the car I invited my guest to follow me and we entered the club to meet Gunter, who was already standing there in anticipation of our arrival. I winked at him as I introduced my companion and, like a true thespian, he acted out his part of the plot by leading us to a table under the balcony area some distance away from the dance floor. The position had been agreed at the time of my earlier telephone conversation with Gunter, for the table, being back behind other tables and out of direct view from the dance floor, was ideally positioned to spring our surprise on both Hans and Ellie.

'Well, the scene was set and the only thing I had to worry about was making sure that Hans didn't have too much to drink, but I need not have worried for he quite obviously had his priorities right, as he tucked into the food he had selected from the menu.

'I explained to Hans that my writer friend would not arrive until some time after the cabaret and then, in an attempt to get to know him better and perhaps cautiously feeling somewhat protective towards Ellie, I questioned him about his life before being drafted into the army. I was to find out that Hans loved music and had begun playing the piano when he was only six years of age. His father had apparently died when he was ten, but with encouragement from his mother, he continued to pursue this interest until he was called up for the forces. From my conversation with him, I was soon able to gain some insight into the comparatively short period of time that he and Ellie had shared together prior to his enlistment into the army. It wasn't long, therefore, before I could see how compatible he and Ellie were as a couple and how her obvious love for this young man was so easily understandable.

'So it was more out of a sense of admiration than of patronage that I asked Hans to forego the formality of my rank and to call me Weiner. It was then that the conversation began to change from a previously sterile exchange of words to topics of warmth and interest in each other as companions of war. Thus, our enthusiasm for continued conversation was only to be interrupted when I heard the announcement that the cabaret was about to start, for this was a signal for me to begin playing out my part of the plan. I was, of course, aware that as soon as Hans saw Ellie, I might have to find a way to calm him until the show was over, but this was something I was prepared for and could only deal with as it happened. You see, I was hoping to prevent Hans from hearing the announcer mention her name as he introduced her, so I had to be careful how I handled the situation.

'Well, the normal supporting acts came and went and then it was time for the master of ceremonies to introduce Ellie. So at that critical moment, I distracted my guest with another question, which of course he naturally answered and in so doing, it took his attention nicely away from the show and subsequently Ellie's entrance onto the floor. He was still facing me when Ellie began to sing, then, on completing what he had to say, he casually turned his head to watch the rest of the show and I just sat back to study his reaction.

'By the movements of his head, I could tell that he couldn't believe his eyes, then after the first few moments of watching he began twisting about on his seat, for he was obviously trying to think of a way to let her know that he was there. He then turned to face me and, with surprise written all over his face, quietly but excitedly said:

' "Weiner, that is the young lady I told you about, the lady singing, that is my young lady!"

'He looked at me as if he expected me to be taken back by what he had said, but I just sat there expressionless for a few moments, then, when I could not contain myself any longer, I smiled at him.

'It was a matter of seconds before he latched on to the possibility that I might have had something to do with the situation, but I could tell that he was still conscious of my position as an officer and unsure about the reason for my smile, so I then decided to explain away his confusion. I first mentioned that Ellie was still as fond of him as she had always been and that she was the mystery writer he had come here to meet. I then suggested he had no need to worry about attracting her attention, for the evening had been planned this way and that there was no fear of him losing her this time.

'Well, Ellie finished her last song and remained silently standing there whilst the usual applause continued, then Gunter walked onto the floor and, taking Ellie's hand, waited for the applause to die down before speaking.

' "Ladies and gentlemen, I am sure that by now you are all fully aware of the gift we have here in Ellie Mollen. I am also sure, as many of our wounded soldiers at the barracks would confirm, that in this lady we have all found a love and compassion that goes beyond our comprehension and our own inadequacy to equal it. Thus, perhaps, in my position, you too would find it difficult to summon up the words that might just adequately express the gratitude, the admiration and the respect that I am sure we all have for this very lovely young lady.

' "But tonight ladies and gentlemen, I have the feeling that my friend Weiner Kraske and I have, in the most human of terms, found a way to compensate our Ellie for all that she has given to us. So if I could have the spotlight on please."

'From our table in the subdued light of the seating area, Gregg, I could see Ellie's face as she tried to understand what Gunter was talking about, for the spotlight had at first been purposely directed at a spot some distance away from our table. So Ellie couldn't see us until Gunter, leading her by the hand, worked his way between the tables in front of ours and the spotlight was redirected on to our table. It was obvious that she was totally shaken at first, for she hesitantly held back for some seconds before rushing forward to greet Hans, as he stood up beside his chair. I shall have to leave you to imagine the tears of joy that were shed between them, Gregg, and I have to say they were not alone.

'Well, Gunter went back to the dance floor, explained the situation to the patrons there, and informed them that free champagne was being provided to toast the couple's future. The band began to play her song "Lilli Marlene" and then the event really took off. I don't know what came over everyone, but suddenly they had all forgotten their fears and went mad with joy. At one point I made my way to the table where Ellie and Hans were sitting and after a hug from both of them, I suggested that Hans' posting to France would have to be postponed for a week, because he was suffering from battle fatigue. I also suggested that, as the other men from his unit all appeared to have the same condition, they too were to be sent home for a week.

'Then, Gregg, after we packed the couple off home, Gunter, Anton, myself and several of my fellow officers, all drank our way through a whole range of mind-blowing intoxicants, every glass of which was raised in the couple's honour, before disappearing down those very happy throats.

'Throughout the next few days, I was to see Ellie twice, and on both occasions there was a radiance about her and Hans that spilled over from them. Hans embarrassed me by repeatedly thanking me for looking after Ellie and at the same time making it possible for them to be together.

'Gunter opened the club on the Sunday night that it was normally closed and some two hundred guests were invited from the barracks to the most fantastic and hilarious party I have ever experienced. It was champagne all the way and there was the most varied selection of food I have ever seen. How this was achieved I shall never know, but I think that it was a little more than coincidental that the officer in charge of catering at the camp happened to be one of the guests there that night. It was to be Hans' and Ellie's evening, for if they were toasted once they were toasted a hundred times, but the most significant thing about that evening was the fantastic comradeship that prevailed between everyone there. It was as if Ellie had spread her influence amongst them, for everyone seemed to share in that happiness which she herself always effused.

'Looking back, I'm so glad, oh God, I am so glad, that it was possible to give them this week of complete happiness, for without knowing it then, this one week was to be the total extent of their lifetime together.

'Well, Hans, together with the other nineteen men, duly returned to the barracks on the appointed morning, for I was able to pull a few strings and arrange passes and travel vouchers for the rest of his companions, so they too had those few precious days at home. Then they were dispatched off to their new posting in France and we were left to cope with the sadness of departing friends. Ellie was a little subdued for about a week, but gradually the colour returned to her cheeks and the effervescent smile to her face, so it wasn't long before she was again sharing the many burdens of those she came into contact with.

'Giving you just a brief summary of those times and outlining the more relevant incidents as I have done, Gregg, you need to realise that I didn't see Ellie every day, but like my wife she was always there in my thoughts. I tell you this because in war, one begins and ends each day with this ever present feeling of uncertainty, for each occurrence or event appears to present itself spontaneously and without invitation at your door, leaving you with no other alternative but to react or respond in much the same way.

'There were, of course, the odd occasions when, by reason of a particular event, one might just find enough time to step aside from this ongoing momentum and think about one's own life, one's own hopes and one's own future. Well, the Christmas of 1943 was one such time and it was to be on the Christmas Eve of that year that I was to share with Ellie one of the most profound and memorable experiences of my life. We had both hoped that Hans might have managed to get some leave, but it wasn't to be, so we, along with Gunter, his wife, Anton and just a few of Gunter's friends, had spent a quiet and pleasant Christmas Eve dining at Gunter's flat over the club. Fortunately there was no enemy air activity or gunfire, in fact nothing to contradict the stillness and peace that is Christmas, and as we walked back to Ellie's flat late that night, even the motionless silhouettes of the bombed buildings seemed to suggest that it really was a Holy night.

'On arriving at the flat, we were both content to relax and enjoy the tranquillity of a forgotten silence that both sought and found our recognition. Ellie was obviously not ready for bed, just as I was not ready for the drive back to camp, so we each sat in an armchair, quietly contemplating our thoughts and our hopes and, perhaps both trying to recapture those elusive half remembered dreams of Christmases gone by. I suppose we must have sat there without a word between us for some fifteen minutes before I realised that Ellie was looking across at me. I was about to say something when she moved forward in her chair, reached out to put her hand gently over mine, then quietly said:

' "Do you know, Weiner, I can't help thinking how lucky I have been, for not only do I have Hans in my life, I also have you. Weiner, I want you to understand that whilst I don't think of you in exactly the same way as I do Hans, I have to tell you that I do have a great love for you. It is a different love from that I have for Hans; it is a love that is born out of the respect I have for you, a love that makes no demands and expects no returns, a love that is complete and has been so since I first saw you. It has to go no further than my need to express it and your need to know it, for any change beyond that would only spoil the elation and wonder of it. But, my dear friend, if the influences of time and circumstance had in some way been reversed, I would have loved you in the same way as I now do Hans."

'Gregg, can you imagine how I felt, sitting there in that room listening to what she was saying. My throat was dry and I could feel the pulse of my heart pumping away in my neck. I couldn't swallow, I couldn't speak, for paramount in my mind was the tenderness of her hand on mine and this inexplicable benevolence that seemed to radiate from all around her. The boarded up windows, the broken sections of ceiling in the flat, the carnage of squandered life that, like candles, had become extinguished before my eyes, were all there to remind me that death was but a whisper away, but there was a glory within me that night that perhaps only eternity could describe.'

Gregg moved uncomfortably about in his chair trying to find words that might convey his understanding. There were none; he just found himself stranded on an island of silence with no one there to prompt him.

'I can see by your face that you are as mute now as I was that night, Gregg, but Ellie was not expecting a response, for she went on to say:

' "Weiner, please don't say anything, you have no need to for I am aware that you feel exactly as I do and I know that your wife has a wonderful husband in you. The reason I tell you this now is that Hans and I both share this admiration for you and the work that you do and we both realised in the very short time we spent together that you are as important to our lives as our child will be. Yes, Weiner, I am going to have a baby and if it's a boy, we both want to name him after you."

'As you can see, Gregg, irony had made another of its appearances and again I was reeling under the impact of further emotional confusion. I wanted to run away from my embarrassment but at the same time I felt like jumping with joy at the prospect of a new life, but Ellie hadn't finished.

' "Weiner," she said, "If I am fortunate enough to bring this child into the world but unfortunate enough to die after it is born, would you do everything you can for it, would you help it to find the happiness that you have fashioned for me?"

'How would you have answered, Gregg? What could I have said to satisfy her doubts at that moment; how could I explain that it was she who had spread so much happiness, not I. The only thing I could do was to try and pacify her fears by telling her that whilst I lived so should her hopes and desires live, but that she, Hans and the unborn child would go forward to enjoy the future with the same happiness they had shared in the past. Well, it was in early May of 1944 that the child was born and both mother and child were fit and well. So, Gregg, the baby, who was one day to become your Lorrett, turned out to be a very beautiful blue eyed angel who was to bring immediate delight to Ellie, myself and the few others that had shared the anticipation and hopes of the event prior to the birth.

'Well, the baby was to bring back the smiles on many a face in those otherwise dark days, for by that time, people were beginning to show the signs of despondency that were characteristically symptomatic of a defeated and broken nation. You see, the people, many of whom were just surviving amid the city's ruins, had been faced with our defeats in the desert, North Africa and Italy and were by then beginning to see the prospect of our total defeat on the Russian front. Food was in short supply, their pleasures were few and far between and, on a more parochial note, the club was only open for business on the Friday and Saturday night of each week.

'Yet even within the depressed atmosphere of those times, the child was to be one of the happiest and most contented I have known. That it wasn't a boy did disappoint Ellie at first, for, as I have said, they had hoped to name him after me. However, she was soon able to come to terms with the status quo and, to help counter her disappointment a little, I suggested that perhaps as a compromise, she would allow me to name the child. Ellie happily agreed to the suggestion and naturally followed up her excitement by asking me if I already had a name in mind. Of course, there could be only one name for the child as far as I was concerned and that was her mother's. She was perhaps a little reluctant to accept my suggestion at first, but eventually she agreed. So, Gregg, the child became another Ellie Mollen, until such time as their intended marriage, when of course the child would have taken the father's surname of Schirmer. As a bachelor, Gregg, you may find it difficult to understand, but I was a surrogate father to your Lorrett for the first eight months of her life. Any moment I had to spare, I would find my way to the flat, nurse or play with her and at all times love her. But little did I know then of the tragedy and sadness that were waiting to appear from behind one of life's hidden sign posts, for time and destiny had chosen their moment of collusion.

'Since that one week together in August '43, Ellie's hopes that Hans might get some leave had been dashed to the ground on three different occasions. She wrote to him frequently and he replied by return when he was able, but any attempts to follow through with his expectations of leave were cancelled each time by the jittery commanders in control of our defences around the French coast. This, of course, was understandable, for by that time in the war, most of us were aware of the British and American threat to launch their second front, and the most disconcerting part of this expectation was the waiting. So everyone shared the trepidation and fear of the unknown and, as you are no doubt aware, it was in the June of that year 1944 that the invasion began. Naturally, this was a worrying time for both Ellie and me, for we knew that Hans was stationed in the area of the landings and was inevitably bound to get caught up in the fighting. She had sent Hans a letter in the May, telling him that they had a daughter and she had received a letter back by return; but sadly, this was to be the last she would ever hear from him. As those desperate months went by, everyone lived in hope of a turn around in the situation, but it wasn't to be. Then in the September of that year, your airborne forces were to drop out of the sky at Arnhem in an endeavour to take their first steps onto German soil. Our own losses in both manpower and armoured equipment, were on the increase; this meant that even untrained troops from the barracks were being dispatched to the front with tanks that were outdated, misused, or totally unreliable. Looking back at the situation now, it is easy to see how impossible it was to avoid the inevitable cloud of tragedy that was about to affect the lives of so many people and which, in the early days of December 1944, was to cast its everlasting shadow over mine.

'I will never forget that day. It was 7th December 1944 and like the day it was destined to be, there was an uncanny threat about the darkened sky over Hamburg. I had been on duty since early morning and without any food in my stomach or the time to stop for a brief rest, I was feeling quite tired and hungry by late afternoon, but the thought of spending the evening with the two Ellies spurred me on to finish all I had left to do.

'Ellie was, of course, at home for much of the time since having the child and only worked at the club on the nights it was open. There hadn't, quite fortunately, been any major air raids on the city for some time, albeit a part of the cadre stationed at the camp still spent much of their time helping the depleted civilian services to repair the roads and knock down the remnants of any remaining dangerous buildings. Do you know, Gregg, I can still see myself now, leaving the barracks in that Mercedes staff car that I used. I can remember that, as I left the camp behind me, I was to recognise the familiar flashes of intermittent light appearing on the clear, uncluttered and darkened skyline some fifty or so kilometres away. They came of course, from distant ack-ack guns firing at enemy aircraft over their territory, warning me that any minute I could expect our local sirens to sound off. Well, they did, soon enough, so I increased my speed to get to the flat as quickly as possible. It must have been some twenty minutes later that I arrived at the house in which Ellie had the top flat, I parked my car on the nearby cleared bomb site, mounted the half a dozen steps that led to the front door and pressed on the bell to her flat. After waiting for a response and failing to get it, I searched for the key that Ellie had given me. In view of the imminence of an air-raid, I entered the house and went straight down the narrow stairs inside the building to the basement area, expecting to see Ellie there, along with the other families that all used the basement area as a shelter.

'After quickly scanning the faces of those already in the shelter, I realised that Ellie was not amongst them, so, being a little concerned, I ran up the stairs to her flat at the top of the house, tapped on the door, just in case she was feeding the baby, then went in.

'As I entered, I could see young Ellie in her cot by the sideboard, kicking her legs, moving her head and chuckling to herself as babies do, I went towards her and put my finger in her hand, calling out Ellie's name as I did, but there was no reply. I called her name again but there was still no reply, so, in a questioning state of mind, I waited for a second or two before pushing open her bedroom door and going in.

'To my shock and dismay, Gregg, there, fully clothed, lying on the bed in front of me, was Ellie, absolutely motionless and with a face as white as a sheet. I rushed over to her, touched first her forehead and then her face; she was warm but I couldn't make her respond to my gentle shaking. My hand went instinctively to her arm to check her pulse, but there was none, she was dead. I went quickly through all the rituals of resuscitation many times over, but nothing I could do was going to bring her back.

'I must have sat on the end of her bed for some minutes, shaking like a leaf as my body passed through a state of violent shock. Tears were streaming down my face and a tidal wave of blood was rushing through my head. I hadn't noticed the letter on the edge of her dressing table at first, but as my tears gradually subsided, I could see the corner of this envelope pointing at me, like a dagger to my heart, and I knew then that her death had been self-administered. It was the rumble of distant gunfire that brought me out of my initial state of despair and returned me to the reality of my situation and that of the child lying there in the next room. I got up from the bed and quickly looked into the room, just to assure myself that the baby was all right; fortunately she was still happily gurgling away to herself and obviously quite unperturbed by the distant gunfire. With at least some relief I returned to the bedroom, sat down on the bed and opened the envelope with my name in large letters written across it.'

Weiner moved uncomfortably in his chair, leaned forward and took two pieces of folded paper from a shelf beside him.

'These are the actual pieces of paper that came in the envelope I found beside Ellie that night. One is the letter I have already spoken of; the other, which is just as intriguing, I will show you later. But first let me read you the letter.

'It begins, "My dearest and greatest friend Weiner," then goes on as follows: "I am sure that as you begin to read this letter your hands will be shaking as mine are, writing it. Stop for a moment, Weiner, and in that moment, remember all the happiness that we have shared together.

' "Don't jump to the wrong conclusions or make hasty judgements, for you will with time understand why it was intended to be, my dear, dear friend. You see, it has happened, Weiner, for this morning, an unknown hand turned off the source of life from the body of my dear Hans, where, how, or why, I know not. But the radiance of him, that has been with me since our first meeting, has left me, so I must again search to find him.

' "Please Weiner, try not to question or find reason, just accept that because I die, our daughter will live to find and treasure, through you, the happiness and joy of life that we have known.

' "So, my dear Weiner, whilst there are tears in my eyes and regrets in my heart as I leave you, I find some comfort in knowing that we have already discussed all you have meant to me, to Hans and to Ellie our lovely daughter. I do not leave you, therefore, with words unsaid or hopes unfulfilled, just with a love and gratitude for that wonderful period in our lives that we were destined to share together.

' "So I simply say *au revoir*, Weiner, because you will, I know, unite us all again one day. Until then, bless you, my friend. Your lady of the lamplight, Ellie Mollen." '

Weiner sat holding the letter in his trembling hand, silently contemplating its content, before leaning across and passing it to his companion.

'There you are, Gregg, read it for yourself; that is a part of my history.'

The doctor was only too pleased to wait silently for his visitor, as he read and re-read the letter, but it was to be some minutes before Gregg lifted his head and with a baffled look of disbelief, returned it to its owner.

'What can I say, Weiner, for obviously all of this must have come as quite a shock to you, but it is a lovely letter. However, I fail to see at the moment how either the incident or the letter has anything to do with Lorrett's problem. If you still think that there is some connection, then I shall need many more answers from you, for to me, much of that letter is somewhat surreal and even a little beyond my interpretation. You see, I keep finding the need to pinch myself, just to make sure that I am here and not lost in some fantasy world. So I have to ask, Weiner, was Ellie of sound mind, when she wrote that letter?'

'I can understand your dilemma, Gregg, and answers you will have, but I think you need to know all the facts first, before raising such a question, for, contrary to what you suggest, I am sure Ellie's mind was as normal as yours or mine that night. You see, there are some things in life that are beyond the realms of normal understanding, but our inability to understand them or our reticence to recognise them does not invalidate them.

'But like you, as I sat on the end of Ellie's bed that night, I read that letter over several times and, again like you, I couldn't take it all in. So I quickly looked at this other piece of paper in the hope that it might help me towards a better understanding of why, but, as you will see later, it does nothing to clarify her reasoning or quell one's confusion.

'Try, if you can, to imagine the situation and then put yourself in my position, Gregg. There I was, in a severe state of shock, sitting on a bed with my dearest friend dead beside me. The words of that letter spinning around in my head, the possibility of an impending air-raid and a child in the next room, whose future depended upon my ability to find an immediate solution to a very desperate situation. What was I to do with the child, where could I leave her, knowing that she would be safe from the devastation around us and cared for until such a time that I was able to return and look after her?

'My first reaction was to leave her with Gunter's wife at the club, but I soon realised the danger in that. Then I considered going absent without leave and taking her home to my wife, but again, I was to foresee the many complications of such a plan. Then, just as I decided to ask one of the other families living in the house to look after her for a day or so, I thought of the Kindorf Hospital, where I knew they had all the facilities to house orphans and refugees. So, without further hesitation, I went back into the living room and quickly lifted the child out of her cot, together with her mattress and blankets, ready to take her down to the car. At that moment, I suddenly felt an overpowering desire to see Ellie the mother for the last time, so sooner than attempt to put the child back into its cot, I hastily laid her down on the floor beside it, knowing that it was only to be a matter of seconds before I was to pick her up again. I returned to the bedroom and without any reserve I went over to Ellie, kissed her on the forehead, then stood back for a moment to ponder the tranquil beauty of her face. It was then, just as I was about to leave the bedroom, that a nearby ack-ack gun went off, creating such a deafening noise that it shook the whole of the building. As it went off, I heard something drop to the floor in the next room, so I quickly rushed through to see if the child was all right.

'Fortunately, she did not appear to be hurt in any way, but it was a near miss, for one of the items Ellie had kept on her sideboard had fallen and smashed on the floor not far away from the child's face. Well, I quickly bent down to pick her up and as I lifted the mattress on which she was lying, she suddenly burst into tears. Thinking that perhaps she had been hurt in a way that I hadn't noticed at first, I quickly checked her over, but I could find nothing to account for this sudden outburst of tears. So, satisfying myself that there was nothing physically wrong with her, I speedily took her down and laid her into the back of the car.

'Now, Gregg, the only question that arises out of the incident, is why she was to continue sobbing right up to the time that I left her at the hospital some hour or so later, for she had no obvious injury and this sustained crying was inconsistent with her normally happy disposition. This, as far as I know, was the only time the child ever showed any signs of trauma and whilst I concur that the gun incident might easily have frightened her, I hardly feel that she was in any way damaged by it for, as I have said, she did not start to cry until I picked her up.

'Well, as I drove away from the house that night the flashes of gunfire over the city had luckily cleared the streets of vehicles and people, so I was able to reach the comparative safety of the open countryside quite quickly. Once out into the country and away from the prospect of falling missiles, I stopped the car and nursed the child on my lap for some time, but any hope of pacifying her soon became a lost cause. After putting her back in the car and settling myself behind the steering wheel, the impact of everything that had happened that day suddenly hit me and I found myself engulfed in a wave of self pity, utter loneliness and total despondency. If there was ever a time in my life when I needed to question my own sanity, it was then, for I couldn't rid my mind of the fact that I was never to see Ellie the mother again.

'I must have driven into the grounds of Kindorf hospital some forty minutes later, where a whole host of ambulances and people conjured up a scene of chaotic disorder. As I passed through the entrance, I noticed a young probationary nurse, who I now know to be your Mrs Wals. Recognising as I did the need to appear vague and impartial about the handover of the child, I used the authority of my rank and profession to persuade this obviously inexperienced young nurse to accept the child without too many awkward questions being asked. I put the baby in her arms, told her that she was an orphan and instructed her to take the child and have it put into care with the others at the hospital. You see, Gregg, knowing that the wards were full to overflowing, if those in charge had become aware of my association with young Ellie and the mother in any way, they would have insisted that I made alternative arrangements. I suppose it was not quite gallant of me to don the mask of anonymity and to leave abruptly without further explanation to the young nurse, but what else could I have done?

'In view of my experiences that night, it was perhaps no surprise to me that on reaching the bottom of the steps outside the hospital I suddenly felt as if I was about to faint. So I held onto the guide rail and carefully lowered myself down onto one of the steps. My only recollection of the incident came as I felt the cool calm of someone's hand wiping my forehead with a dampened cloth. It was the hand of another nurse who I knew quite well, so, thanking her and then rejecting any need for further concern, I remained quietly sitting there contemplating my life as a distant siren sounded its monotone all clear.

'In what must have been only a matter of minutes, I saw again those times I shared with Ellie and I was to realise that within the brief period of one hour I had lost three people that I loved: Ellie the mother, Ellie the daughter and, if that letter you have just read is to be believed, Hans the father.

'The loss of young Ellie that night, however, was only intended to be a temporary measure, for as I had driven her to the hospital I had planned to return and collect her within the next few days. I had, you see, decided that as soon as time allowed, I would take her to my own home and leave her with my wife until such time as I was free to pursue my intention, which, subject of course to my wife's agreement, was to adopt the child.

'After regaining my dignity, I picked myself up from the spot where I had rested, returned to my car and headed towards Hamburg, knowing that the first thing I had to face was the unpleasant task of reporting Ellie's suicide and arranging for the collection of her body. As I made my way towards the city, I again found myself mulling over the past. I was reminded of all the young men who had been sent off to war, with the confidence and bravado of youth written all over their young faces. I reflected upon the extreme changes on many such faces when, with the aftermath of battle behind them, some had been sent back with missing limbs, tormented minds, or the prospect of a future that had no future. I thought about the destroyed fabric of our beautiful cities and the madmen who in their lust for power had with ignominy created the circumstances for both my meeting with Ellie and my parting from her.

'Well, I was eventually to enter the city via several diversions and was about to turn into the road where Ellie's flat was situated, when I found my path blocked by bricks and masonry. I backed up and drove my car into an off street parking bay, locked the doors and made my way hurriedly down the road towards the flat. It was only then that I realised that my momentary fear for Ellie's safety was foolishly misplaced, because, of course, she was already dead. You see, Gregg, fate had played a double hand. For the house and flat I had left only some two hours earlier was nothing more than a pile of rubble, just an abstract brick and dust memorial to someone who had been touched by death twice in one night.

'The area was swarming with firemen, wardens and soldiers from the camp, all clawing away at the ruins in an attempt to locate and recover anyone beneath the high piled debris. I stood back, waiting to see if I could render any assistance, conscious of how fate, in all its irony, had in its way confirmed Ellie's own preconceived destiny, but had excluded both myself and the child from its devious deliberations. As I stood there, totally void of understanding and shaking with emotion, a young soldier came over to me, saluted, then told me that they had found Ellie's body under the debris and asked if I wanted to see it? I obviously couldn't say no and as he led me across the debris I was to realise that he, along with everyone else there, must have taken it for granted that Ellie had died as a result of the air raid. As I looked down at her blackened and damaged body, I decided that there was nothing to be gained by correcting false assumptions or by reporting her death as a suicide, so until now, Gregg, no one else has ever known how Ellie died that night. Well, I instructed the soldier to organise some transport and have the body taken to our mortuary back at the barracks, so that I could arrange for her burial. It was only then, as I was thanking him for his efforts, that he casually mentioned how unfortunate it was that the club had also been destroyed that night.

'So, in a dazed state of disbelief, I made my way through the alleyways to where it had once stood. From the information I could gather, some twenty or more bodies had already been recovered, but those searching believed there were many more still trapped under the masonry and Gunter was thought to be one of them. Again I waited around for some time, but come the early hours of the morning, and knowing that I was soon to be on duty, I left and made my way back to the barracks hospital. On my arrival, I went into the mortuary to ensure that the soldier had followed my instructions and then, in an emotionally wrung out state, I sought my bed.

'The next morning, after pondering over the events of the previous day, I realised that I had to come to terms with my situation, to appease my inevitable tendency for self pity and attempt to tidy up the many loose ends that circumstance had left me. So as soon as I began my duties, I called a few officers together, explained the situation to them, and discussed the necessary arrangements to give Ellie a decent burial. It was decided that we should use one of the coffins normally kept for military purposes for Ellie's body and two of our army ordnance estate cars to transport the coffin and any of my fellow officers who might wish to attend the funeral. We then went on to arrange for a plot at a nearby cemetery and to deal with any personal floral tributes that those at the meeting might wish to make. I was to spend the rest of that day dealing with the formalities of death and attempting to sort out the injuries of others who had unfortunately felt the effects of the previous night's bombing. But as much as I tried to make further enquires, there was no news of Gunter.

'It was early morning on the third day after Ellie's death when I found myself in the mortuary with several other officers, ready to move the coffin from its makeshift stand and put it into our improvised hearse. Four of the officers present took up the coffin between them, then we carefully made our way down and out onto the edge of the parade ground. As we slid the coffin onto the map reading table at the back of the first vehicle, I could see a number of troops assembling for what I took to be their normal early morning parade, but I was not consciously aware of the other army vehicles parked some distance behind us. Then, without any further thought, I and the four other officers seated ourselves in the second vehicle ready to move off. It was only then, as the soldiers on parade were brought to attention, ordered to slope arms and began their march towards us, that I realised that something quite moving was about to take place.

'I looked across at one of my companions in the hope of an explanation.

' "Instructions from the camp Commandant, Weiner: the men are to join the cortège and follow us to the cemetery." It would appear that the news of Miss Mollen's demise spread quickly around the barracks and there was a queue of other ranks requesting permission to attend the funeral. From what I can make out, the Commandant made the point that if he was to attend, why shouldn't others who wished to, do so.'

'So, Gregg, the marching men followed behind our vehicle towards the gates of the barracks. Bringing up the rear were several cars and two troop-carrying vehicles, each of the latter with a number of mobile wounded from the barracks hospital.

'The whole event was to be extremely moving, but perhaps the most poignant moment for me was as our vehicle reached and passed slowly out of the gates. The two duty sentries, both wearing black arm bands and dressed in full ceremonial uniform, stood to attention, presented arms and lowered their heads in respect, as the coffin passed by them. Then, as each of the officers in charge of the different squadrons of marching men went past the gates and out into the lane, they turned their heads and saluted the spot where Ellie often waited to pick up her soldier boys. On arrival at the cemetery, the troops formed into two columns along an avenue where the burial was to take place. They were brought to attention as I, being nominated for the task, said a few words over the grave. The coffin was lowered into the ground and some two or three hundred men stood in silence as a mechanical digger filled in the grave. As the last shovelful of earth was ceremoniously hand spread over the surface of the grave, one of the wounded soldiers still under our care at the hospital walked out from the front column of men and proudly placed a simple white cross at the head of the grave: on it, the words, "Our Beloved Ellie Mollen".

'Standing to one side of the grave with my back to the troops in line behind me, I could see, through the mist of my suppressed tears, the monolithic symbols of other people's sadness all around me, but the one simple cross of dedication to Ellie stood out and above all that day, just as Ellie had done in life. That was it, Gregg, that was how I found and lost Ellie the mother and on our arrival back to the camp that same day, we were informed that most of us at the barracks were to be posted to our depleted active service units at the front within the next twenty-four hours. I, together with other medical staff, were to leave late that same night and by the afternoon of the next day we were to find ourselves dealing with the mass of wounded brought into our mobile emergency unit some ten miles behind an ever retreating front line. Then, in January of 1945, our unit with its complement of military personnel was to suddenly find itself cut off and captured by your advancing forces. We were, of course, subjected to the inevitable rituals of interrogation that came with captivity, but within a few days my life was to continue in much the same way as it was before, dealing with the German wounded who, like myself, had suddenly found themselves prisoners of war.

'I was to be treated with both respect and civility by your people and until the August of 1946, which, you may recall, was more than a year after the end of the war, I shared with them all the wonders of new equipment and the congeniality of the British sense of humour. Of the many things I worried about as a prisoner of war, such as my wife and how she was coping, I was constantly reminded of my hope and failure to return to Kindorf hospital and collect young Ellie, for of course I realised that the longer I was held captive, the less chance I had of claiming her back. But the day for my release did eventually come and I made my way home here, where for some days I did my best to settle down to the life that my wife and I had planned, all those years before.

'My wife, of course, knew about Ellie, Hans and the child, for I had always kept her informed either by letter or by word of mouth when on the rare occasions I had some leave. But owing to my capture she knew nothing of Ellie's death or of my hope to adopt the child, for I felt the matter had to be discussed on a personal basis rather than through the unreliable mailing services at that time. So after the first few days at home, I told my wife of the events that led up to taking the baby to Kindorf hospital and of my hope to collect and eventually adopt her. We then talked over the prospect of adoption and finally agreed that it was something we both wanted to do, but it was only then that I realised our hopes were never to come to fruition. You see, as I explained to you earlier, Gregg, in my devious endeavour to avoid any assumed or stated connection with young Ellie as I passed her over as an orphan that night, I tried to appear detached from any personal feeling toward her and concerned only in the way that any doctor would be. Well, in my panic to find a safe haven for young Ellie, I had failed to think my intention through properly and by neglecting to do so I had inadvertently destroyed any chances I had of finding her again. For I had not stopped to consider that, as an orphan without a name, she would have become classed as a displaced person and naturally given a new name. This meant that I had no way to identify her and therefore no way of ever finding her again unless I could actually see her in person.

'So my return to Kindorf hospital in the September of 1946 was simply founded on hope, but this proved to be of no worth, for I was to return home two days later realising that there was nothing more that I could do and totally convinced that I would never see young Ellie again. The hospital had, of course, been taken over by the Allies in 1945 and all the unclaimed children that were there had over some months been farmed out to an undefined number of children's homes throughout Germany, other parts of Europe and in a couple of cases, so I was told, to homes in the USA.

'I wasn't to know until now, of course, that the child had been adopted by your Mrs Webster in 1945 and that your Mrs Wals was to remember both the incident and my name after all this time. The irony is that I did try to find Mrs Wals when I went back to Kindorf in 1946. But again, I had no name to go by, I could only vaguely remember what she looked like and many of the people I had once known at the hospital had been replaced by Allied personnel. Of course I know now that even if I had found her, it would have been too late to have changed anything. But perhaps all is not lost, for I am now wondering whether my intentions at that time were destined not to succeed and if I have at last been given the first and only opportunity to keep that promise I made to Ellie the mother, all those years ago.'

'Are you suggesting, Weiner, that my somewhat flippant remark to you earlier, intimating that we were destined to meet, could in fact be true and that you personally now feel you have to act in some way to resolve Lorrett's problem?'

'It is beginning to look like it, Gregg, but for the life of me I cannot see what I have to do to make it possible, although I do keep returning to the point I made earlier, when I suggested the possibility of a clue in that letter of Ellie's. You see, I feel that there must be something of a hidden intention behind the words of that letter. As you say, it is as if I have to act in some way, to actually bring about the solution to Lorrett's problem. This is why I am sure that the letter has more relevance today than it had all those years ago.'

'Well, the wording of the letter is somewhat ambiguous. For instance, you were never able to confirm whether Hans did die at the time suggested by Ellie in the letter and from the way that it reads, it seems that there was no evidence at the time she wrote it to justify either her conclusion or her subsequent act of suicide. So perhaps she really wasn't quite normal at the time she wrote it, Weiner.'

'I have already expressed my view on that, Gregg, but I do agree that her reasons for doing what she did could only have been based upon her belief that Hans had died and not on any factual evidence.'

'That is my point, Weiner, so was this in keeping with the character of this loving and compassionate woman you have been telling me about?

For what kind of woman is it that could leave a child on her own and open to the fortunes of chance as Ellie did that night when she took her own life?'

'Well, that is a valid view, Gregg, but only if one is dealing with the conventional logic of normal human beings. As I have tried to show you, Ellie was no ordinary person, for she was both perceptively and actively different to most other people. Let me take up one of the points she made in that letter, a point which you seem to have missed and which serves to prove that she was receptive to premonitory experiences. A point that not only suggests a stable state of mind, but also confirms her ability to prophesy or anticipate events long before they actually happened. You will recall for instance that in her letter she said, "Because I die, our daughter will live." Well, from your silence, Gregg, you have obviously missed the point that this prophesy did in fact come true less than three hours after she penned that letter, for if I hadn't have been forced into action by her demise, both the two Ellies and I would no doubt have perished in the building that night, just as all the other occupants did.'

'But that could have been coincidental, Weiner; after all, if Ellie really did anticipate this particular event, wouldn't she have insisted that you should all vacate the premises to avoid such a preconceived notion?'

'A good point, Gregg, but if this gift of Ellie's to anticipate a situation came by the way of a premonition, then any such experience might only foretell the inevitable outcome of an event and not the circumstances leading up to it.'

'So what you seem to be suggesting, Weiner, is that her suicide and the content of that letter were all a part of some preconceived plan to protect her daughter and that this thing we call chance or coincidence, simply does not enter into it. If that is so, how could Ellie have been sure that you would in fact turn up at her flat that night, especially at that crucial time, unless you are going to suggest that she waited to see your car arrive before carrying out her act of suicide.'

'Not arrive, Gregg, but leaving the barracks quite possibly, for it was only then that I could be sure that nothing was about to change my plans. Ellie incidentally, had been dead for some fifteen minutes when I found her, so she couldn't have waited to see my car before doing what she did. But again, I have to suggest that she instinctively knew that I was on my way to her flat and so the question of chance didn't come into it. Of course, I accept that chance plays its part in many people's lives, including my own, for it was only by chance that I stayed to watch the show in the mess that evening, when I was to see Ellie for the first time. But it certainly wasn't chance that brought about our first meeting outside the gates that night some time after. For you may remember Ellie's first words to me that night were, "I knew somehow you would leave the barracks tonight, Weiner, which is why I have taken this opportunity to pick you up." Then there were the two other remarks she made a little later: "You see, Weiner, even as distant strangers I knew we were to become united as friends," and "I know that what we are about to share together was intended." I think you will agree that these remarks contradict any suggestion that our meeting was one of pure chance, Gregg, for they do in fact show that Ellie must have had prior knowledge of both our meeting and our future friendship together. If you can accept this as being so, then it becomes easier to understand why, for instance, the details surrounding her death most probably happened the way I have suggested they did.'

'I still find this all very hard to believe, Weiner.'

'I can see that by your face, but it is equally difficult for me to supply documented proof of this gift that Ellie had, for the phenomenon is hard to identify, harder to understand and even harder to prove. But I am now totally convinced that somewhere in my past, hidden from either my sight or my mind, there is both the reason for and the answer to Lorrett's problem.'

'I can only hope you are right, Weiner, for it is, as you say, this lack of proof that still leaves me unconvinced of your belief that there is this connection between your past and Lorrett's future. But please bear with me and let me return to the matter of this clue you spoke of: what were you referring to, exactly?'

'Well, I am still unable to explain it fully, but because of your arrival here and your subsequent questioning over certain details of my past, I can see that some of the points made in Ellie's letter make a lot more sense to me today than they ever did before. You see, her letter, as you may recall, suggested that with time I would both understand her reasoning and would in some way help her daughter to find the happiness that she and I once enjoyed together. She also ended her letter, you remember, by suggesting that I would in some way unite us all again. Now perhaps, even after all this time, these points could turn out to be true, if I was able to help solve the problem with Lorrett, then ultimately meet up with her.'

'I can see the point you are making, Weiner, but that still wouldn't totally complete Ellie's prediction, for you cannot unite the living with the dead.'

'In body, no, but in spirit, yes, for if a solution to Lorrett's problem can be found, she would eventually learn to know and love her real mother through us and this would, in principle at least, unite the three of us again.'

'Well, I go along with that part of your theory, Weiner, but even if I accept the premise that Ellie had this gift, I still can't believe that it is in some way linked with events that have taken place twenty-five years later. I suppose what I am really saying is, I want to be convinced and perhaps I could easily be so, if just one of the points in Ellie's letter could be proved. Going back to her death, how did she take her life that night?'

'I never had the time to confirm my visual diagnosis for the reasons I have already explained to you, but I feel sure it was cyanide poisoning.'

'Would that have been easy to obtain then?'

'No, not easy, but phials of it were issued to certain military personnel in case they were captured, but how Ellie obtained it, I shall never know.'

'Another point that puzzles me is why Ellie didn't move nearer to Hans when he took up his new posting near the French coast.'

'She did contemplate doing so at first, but Hans put paid to the idea in one of his letters to her, for sensibly there was the threat of the invasion and of course she was expecting the baby, so quite rightly she stayed put.'

'Now, perhaps a question I have been wanting to ask you since our introduction, Weiner. Seeing Lorrett on television as you did that night, would you say that she has grown to resemble her mother in any way?'

'How strange, for it is only now as you raise the question that I realise how much alike they really must be, for I am now finding it difficult to separate my impression of one from that of the other. Yes, the more I think about it, Lorrett is very much like her mother and she certainly has a lovely singing voice like her. So was this the reason why I felt so near to Ellie the mother, as I sat watching your wonderful programme that night?'

'The very question that has been on my mind since the beginning of our conversation, Weiner, so does this not suggest that fantasy and reality can easily become one and the same to someone who has lived with so many memories of the past, as you have done?'

'Well, as I said at the beginning of my story, everything I have told you is actually how it happened, apart from the elements of conjecture I have put forward to substantiate some of my reasoning. Of course, I can understand how difficult it must be for you to believe it all, and perhaps even see how you might think that it is all just fantasy, but I am still personally convinced that Lorrett's problem is in some way linked to the past, so unlike you I am not looking for proof, simply an answer.'

'Weiner, don't mistake my inability to believe, for downright disbelief is not as simple as that. It is just that if there is a link between your past and Lorrett's return to normality, it is of no use unless we can find out what it is. But sooner than continue along these lines, let me return to my earlier question at the beginning of our conversation and ask again, why "Ellie's song?" For were you in fact intimating that she actually wrote it, or that she was in some way the inspiration behind it, for from what you have told me, her life at times did parody the words of the song?'

'No to both of those questions, Gregg, but I do agree that the song did have a great deal of influence on her life, perhaps even more that I shall ever know. But to avoid any further debate on another contentious issue, let me tell you the facts about the song and the effect it seems to have had on so many of our lives, including, it would appear, your own. You see, it was in the early stages of the war, as our forces pushed their way through France and the Low Countries, that the song seemed to be on everybody's lips, but it was not a new song, for it had been around in Germany for some time. Now, how its world-wide popularity came about, I shall come to in a minute, for had there been no war, the song might have just remained another archive piece. Well, like myself, many of those troops who had first fought in France were eventually shipped across to Libya to join up with Rommel's divisions in the desert, so it is easy to see how the song soon spread amongst those troops already there.

'Now, such was the way of things in those early days of war in the desert, that at first, contact with your troops mainly came by way of intermittent skirmishes rather than by long drawn out battles. Thus there were periods of comparative inactivity, when our two opposing armies would face each other across a silent stretch of open desert. On these occasions, our radio people would often broadcast propaganda programmes in English, in the hope of demoralising your forces of the Eighth Army. Well, sentimental music was an essential part of this process and one of the songs used to promote this intention was "Lilli Marlene", which, of course, could awaken the emotional sentiment in the most ardent of fighting men, especially as they were far away from home. Inevitably, these broadcasts were to increase further the popularity of the song amongst our own troops but, without my knowledge at the time, they also served to spread and extend the song's popularity to your lads in the Eighth Army.

'For the reason you now know, I was to be returned to the barracks in Hamburg some two months before Monty's break out at El Alamein, which is the point not only where my story began but also where my lifetime's fascination with the song began. Now, the explanation you have been waiting for, Gregg. You recall I told you that I personally attributed the song to Ellie, because of its association with our first meeting. Now whilst this was true, it is only a part of the truth. You see, it wasn't until I opened the envelope containing the letter and this other piece of paper that I realised how, in fact, her life had in many ways, mirrored both the words and the sentiment of the song. For as the song suggests, she did often wait "Under the lamplight by the barrack gates". This, you recall, was also where I met her formally for the first time and the reason I saw her as "My lady of the lamplight". But the most intriguing part of this association concerns this piece of paper, which you haven't yet seen, for written on it is a poem. Read it, Gregg, for I would like to hear what you have to say about it.'

It was a matter of minutes before Gregg again looked across at his companion in a way that sought an explanation, rather than offered one.

'What can I say, Weiner? Again I am confused, for it appears that the words of this poem have been taken from the words of the "Lilli Marlene" song, which puts the questions, why? and did Ellie write it?'

'I was hoping you might suggest a possible solution to this conundrum yourself, but as you haven't, it looks as if I have to suggest yet another of those explanations which will again challenge your belief. However, what else do you see on that piece of paper?'

'Just the figures nine oblique sixteen at the top of the page. Have they some relevance then, Weiner?'

'Yes; they are in fact a date which suggests that the poem could have been written in the September of 1916, which of course was during the great war and not the last war. Furthermore, if I were to tell you that this in fact appears to be true, you can see how Ellie could not have written that poem. But you can see how perhaps the poem might have been the inspiration behind her song. Now, it was this fascinating anomaly that was eventually to push me into researching the origins of both the poem and the song in 1964, although I wasn't able to complete this research until after my wife died in 1965.

'I suppose the idea to undertake this research really began when I first obtained the sheet music of the song and I was able to confirm that it was of German origin and that it had been written by two of my fellow countrymen. After a number of telephone conversations and a great deal of travel, I was eventually able to establish that the song was composed in the thirties and, from what I could make out, it seems that the words of the song were inspired by the original of that poem that Ellie left me. So I have always assumed that someone between the two wars must have copied the poem I have here from a book or some other publication and then given it to Ellie, for when comparing it with Ellie's letter, it is easy to see that it is not her writing.

'However, to continue, I was eventually able to build up a picture of how the song began its delayed rise to fame and popularity and how in so doing, it was to become one of those unique random occurrences that was destined to have an unaccountable and unpredictable effect on so many people's lives. You see, it would appear that the original poem was written by a soldier in the trenches sometime in 1916. I was unable to find out the name of the poet, but the sheet of music I had purchased gave me the two German composers' names, one of whom, so I was told, wrote the music and the other the lyrics.

'Now let me return to the beginning of my explanation, when I briefly mentioned how the song began its rise to popularity, for it was not all that well known in Germany before the war. In fact, it wasn't really until our forces invaded Czechoslovakia, prior to the declaration of war between our two countries, that the song actually became to be more widely known by the German people and this came about in a very strange way. It would appear that after entering Prague, our forces set up a radio station there and, having no available source of recorded music to hand, they sent out a team of men to commandeer the stock of several record shops in the capital. According to my informant, amongst the records collected was a rare original copy of the song "Lilli Marlene", sung by Lala Andersen. So it is, of course, easy to see how, with only a limited selection of records to choose from, this one record was to be used quite frequently and how, because of its frequent use, it was to become very popular with our troops occupying the country at that time.

'So it was, that in the early stages of the war between our two countries, many of those troops that had initially been used to take Czechoslovakia were withdrawn to join other divisions that had already begun their move into France and the Low Countries. Well, naturally, the melody travelled with them and soon the song's hitherto limited popularity spread and became a favourite with most of our troops at that time. Then, as I have already explained, many of those men were eventually transported across to North Africa or the Western Desert. So you can see how the song spread throughout Europe and across the Middle East, but the most fascinating part of this unseen evolution for me, was how it by-passed the barriers of war and became a favourite with your people and then with the people of other countries around the world.

'I suppose it was the song's international popularity that had always intrigued me the most, so much so that after my wife died, I found myself travelling to London to keep an appointment with a gentleman I came to know as Peter. He was, in fact, the head of a well known music publishing company and had himself written a number of songs in the thirties and forties. Well, with the help of one of your policemen, I found myself climbing the stairs of a rather old building in an area, which for reasons unknown to me then, your people called Tin Pan Alley. After my introduction to Peter, he organised some coffee before I settled down to learn of the simple twist of fate that had turned a hitherto national song into an international evergreen.

'It apparently all happened in the early years of the war, when London was being subjected to our persistent bombing raids on the capital. You see, although Peter worked in London, his home was in Berkshire, so he always made a point of leaving his office for home early each afternoon so as to avoid getting caught up in the nightly bombing.

'From what I was to gather, this chance event took place whilst Peter and a band leader friend of his were enjoying a quiet drink in their local village pub. It would appear that some time after their arrival, a number of British soldiers came into the bar and as the evening went on these lads, who by that time were a little well lubricated, began to sing and one of the items from their repertoire was "Lilli Marlene". Apparently it was their limited singing ability and their half hearted attempt to sing the song in German, that first drew Peter's attention both to the song and to the fact that neither he nor his friend had heard it before. So after treating the lads to one or two rounds of drinks, he asked about the song. The explanation given was, of course, that they had initially picked it up from our propaganda broadcasts in the desert and it had, in their words, become "their song".

'One of the soldiers then went on to tell how he had learned the German words of the song from an old record he had and, after some persuasion, told the story of how he had come by the record. He then went on to explain how his battalion had been involved in the capture of a small desert town and in the process, how he and his mates had had the job of removing a number of our troops from a heavily fortified building. From what I could make out, having dealt with the problem they went on to search the building and clear it of any suspect traps or booby devices and it was whilst he was carrying out this task that he noticed the record still spinning on a record player in one of the rooms.

'So this young soldier, being a collector of souvenirs, decided he would keep the record and, after wrapping it carefully in something soft, he put it in his back pack and returned to his less discriminating role as a soldier. Inevitably, Peter, realising that the song had further potential, asked if he still had the record and if so, might he see and perhaps borrow it for a few days. No sooner the request than the action and the soldier left the pub there and then to return some thirty minutes later with the record in his hand. Well, to cut a long story short, it wasn't long before Peter realised the potential of the song and that in principle it could, with certain minor changes, be published and sold in the UK and abroad. He then went on to tell me that the soldier, on loaning him the record, asked if he would look after it until he returned to recover it after the war, but sadly he never returned, for apparently, like its previous owner, he was also killed in action.

'Well, prior to thanking Peter for his time and departing that day, I was actually shown the record that he had kept for all those years and as it was passed to me, I couldn't help but feel a tremendous sense of privilege to be handling what was, in effect, an object of historical significance and a symbol of some considerable relevance to many people's lives.

'So, Gregg, this was how the song's international debut began and, for your interest, I have two copies of sheet music here. One is the original version of the song, which you will see names the two German composers; the other is the British version, which has the same two composers' names, but additionally the name of an English gentleman. It can also be seen that by comparing these, you will notice that both the words and the music have been scored somewhat differently.

'Now, I am not going to suggest that this enchanting story of the song's development had any direct relationship with Ellie's life in those days of war, but without a doubt, it was to influence her libido in some subconscious or subliminal way. So much so, that in many ways her life did in fact emulate the words and spirit of the song for, like the song, her presence could stir up a whole range of emotional and ideological feelings even in the most uncaring of people.'

'So are you saying that Ellie actually came to symbolise the empathy and love that is inherent within the words of the song?'

'Yes, in a way, but perhaps I am more particularly suggesting that both the song and Ellie were manifestly products of their time, as perhaps your Mr Churchill was. It was as if this association between Ellie and the song and the song and Ellie, had in some way been destined to blossom and bloom at the same time. For although Ellie could personify and capture the mood of any song that she sang, when she sang "Lilli Marlene" it was as if she, the song and the moment had all been made for each other.'

'Well, Weiner, I can certainly say that this meeting of ours has turned out to be something of an experience for me and I must compliment you on a fine piece of research, for I know how difficult it can be to pierce the cosmetic coating that often covers the most simple fact. It is however, quite strange to think that if you had researched Ellie's background immediately after the war, as you obviously did the song many years later, I might not be sitting here now in the early hours of a summer's morning trying to tell myself that there has to be a link between you and her daughter's future.'

'Well, I am, of course, sorry that I have been unable to totally convince you of my beliefs, Gregg, and I have myself long regretted my early failure to find out more about Ellie's background, her parents and all the other things that I should have done at that time. But believe me, after the anxiety and trauma of the war, those highly emotional and dramatic times I shared with Ellie and my time in captivity, I tried not to look back over my shoulder. I suppose, if I am honest about it, I was so emotionally torn apart over my failure to find the child when I returned from Hamburg in 1946 that since then I have never been able to face up to the prospect of returning to the city, or all that it meant to me in those years of war.'

'Weiner, you have no reason or need to apologise to me, after all fate wasn't always on your side, but as a matter of interest, could there have been some specific reason why Ellie put that copy of the poem in with her letter to you that night?'

'I just don't know, Gregg, for I have never understood how the poem came to be written on that piece of paper in the first place, how it came to be in Ellie's hands, or why she put it in with her suicide letter to me; what makes you ask?'

'Oh, it is only something that came to me as I was thinking about your man Peter and the song. You remember how I told you I met John Moffitt and Dr Linley at the mental home where Lorrett is being cared for. But I never mentioned to you that whilst I was there, they asked me to try and interpret some taped recordings of Lorrett. The outcome of this was that the few words she appeared to say, which incidently were in French and were not very clear, seemed to come from a poem. Now obviously, there could be no connection between this and Ellie's poem, which you now have, but it does show how, perhaps, Lorrett has a lot in common with her real mother and even how their lives seem to have followed similar paths.'

'Well, of course, this probably has something to do with heredity, but were you expecting me to comment on the point in some other way?'

'No, Weiner, I was merely thinking out loud, for as I have already said, I had Peter and the song's history on my mind, but there was something I wanted to ask you and I cannot think what it was, now.'

'Was it something to do with the way the song became popular?'

'Yes, that's it, Weiner, now I remember. Going back to your research for a minute, did this Peter fellow give you any other information on the soldiers he met in the pub that night? For instance, I gather they had not long returned from the desert, but did he tell you anything else about them?'

'Only that they were men who had seen a great deal of action and who, because of their combat experience, had been sent back to the UK to train others in preparation for the eventual second front landings in France.'

'So he didn't mention the name of their regiment?'

'No, he just told me that some of them belonged to one of the Highland regiments, but from the impression I gained, they were not all from the same regiment. Why do you ask?'

'Well, my own father might easily have been one of those soldiers in the pub that night, for he too returned from the desert to the UK around about that time and, if my memory serves me correctly, I think that he was also stationed somewhere in Berkshire.'

'How strange.'

'Yes, it is, but it is perhaps even more strange, that it was he who introduced my mother to the song on his return from abroad, hence the reason for my own affinity with it since my early childhood days. Perhaps you can see now how it was this early fondness for the song that made me suggest it to my boss as a suitable number for the finale of the show and how I was able to convince him that Lorrett was the ideal person to sing it. But now, more relevantly, comes the question, was it my father who actually told your man Peter about the song that night all those years ago and even perhaps, was it he that loaned him the record?'

'Well, what a strange turn of events. So who is it now that suddenly finds himself confronted with an inexplicable sequence of happenings that go beyond simple explanation or easy understanding? Perhaps you can now see, Gregg, how at times I have been forced to believe in the incredible rather than the logical and how the influences of circumstance can sometimes change one's views or cloud one's judgement.'

'Well, I certainly have to recognise that there is something quite strange about Peter's story and my father, Weiner, and I am beginning to see how both of our lives have now come full circle, simply because of our meeting. But how does one tag, or label if you will, the cause and effect of these events if we remove chance and coincidence from the equation?'

'Are you asking me, if so why, for is it always necessary to catalogue things, Gregg, can't we just accept them without a label?'

'I suppose we could, but again I was really thinking out loud or perhaps even questioning my own reasoning. For do I now accept all of these occurrences in our lives as being merely the natural progression of things, or should I see them as a sequence of incidents that this thing called fate has carefully arranged to ensure Lorrett's ultimate recovery? This, above all else, is why I would have liked to have seen something other than that letter, to have proven the existence of this otherwise hypothetical link between our meeting here today, those years of war and Lorrett's problem.'

'Well, there is no hope of that, Gregg, but I am sure that if you could just forget this obsession of yours to always find logical answers to less than logical occurrences, you might one day accept that we are not always the masters of our own destiny.'

'Well, perhaps now is the right time for me to make one or two decisions without the help of our friend destiny, for I feel that I have come to the end of my research. You see, other than that point you made about baby Lorrett's crying session that night, there is little else in your story that could be seen to have any relevance to her current problem and as you have already dismissed that incident as being of no significance, there seems to be nothing else that I can do.'

'So you still cannot believe that Ellie foresaw the danger to all of our lives that night?'

'No, I am sorry, Weiner, but I have to say that I am more inclined towards the belief that the destruction of Ellie's house after you and the child had left was purely coincidental and not related to what you see as a prophecy within her letter.'

'Then do you feel that your time here has been wasted?'

'Not at all, Weiner. I have found a new and very special friend, I have through your past and your subtle innuendos learned something about myself, but most of all I have enjoyed hearing about your life and sharing your company. You see, like you, I really do want to believe that there is some kind of link between the past and the present and if just one of those points made in Ellie's letter could be shown to be true, then no one would be more pleased than I.'

'Would you like me to tell you more about Ellie and those times?'

'I don't think that's necessary. You see, I have no difficulty in accepting that Ellie as a person did stand out as being someone quite unique. I can also see how her unselfish acts of kindness, stimulated as they were out of this ongoing compassion for others, made her a very rare human being indeed. But whilst I can appreciate that she was, without a doubt, loved and admired by those who knew her, I do find it very difficult to accept the premise that she could read people's minds, redirect them in some way and even, perhaps, see into the future.'

'So where does that leave you, Gregg?'

'Disappointed, naturally, worried for Lorrett's sake, certainly, and feeling somewhat of a failure, most definitely. My only hope now is that John will find some other way in which to solve her problem.'

'What will be your next move?'

'Well, first I have to write out a full report on everything we have discussed, thought over or even rejected, then send it off to John Moffit and his associate. I shall have to ring Mrs Wals to make sure that she does not need the car, for it was she who very kindly let me have the use of it. Then, I am not sure, but I might spend some further time in this area. You see, I am in fact supposed to be on holiday and from what I have seen of this spot so far, it would be a shame to waste such a golden opportunity to see more of it.'

'So you will stay on here for a few more days then?'

'When you say here, Weiner, do you mean here in Rüdesheim?'

'Yes, but also here in my home.'

'I was thinking of finding myself a local hotel, for I have no wish to outstay my welcome.'

'My invitation on your arrival, Gregg, was for you to stay here for as long as you like, now and at any other time you may happen to be in the area. So, provided you would like to stay, you don't mind my housekeeper's cooking and you agree that we call on our friend Herr Smitz again, then so be it.'

'That would be most acceptable to me, Weiner, and thank you. Perhaps also, if you have the time, you might like to join me and show me around the area?'

'That will be my pleasure. Now, I wonder if I could ask something of you.'

'Why not?'

'Well, you obviously have to return the car to Mrs Wals at some time and I wondered if you would take me along with you. You see, somehow my previous reluctance to return to Hamburg now seems somewhat foolish, especially in view of the changes that must have taken place after all of these years, so I think I can now face those remnants of my past that may still remain, without becoming too emotional over them.'

'It goes without saying that you are more than welcome and of course, if you wish, I can introduce you to Mrs Wals. I will also be paying another visit to the barracks, so, provided you feel you can cope with it you could also accompany me there.'

'I will have to think about that, Gregg, but why, may I ask, do you have to return to the barracks, for from your remarks a few moments ago I thought you had come to the end of your investigation?'

'Well, I have to satisfy this insatiable curiosity of mine, for to me, every question has to have an answer and at the moment, I am tormented by a recurring question that keeps spinning around in my head.'

'May I ask what that is?'

'I hardly feel you need to.'

'So am I to take it that you are not a total disbeliever after all?'

'Now who is the one that's attempting to put labels on things, Weiner?'

Chapter Five

Weiner pointed to a distant road sign. 'That should be the turn off for Mainz, Gregg.'

'So are we then heading towards Wiesbaden?'

'Yes, this will take us a little out of our way, but the scenery is worth it; we can pick up the road to Wiesbaden, Hannover and Hamburg further on.'

Gregg turned the car into the direction suggested by his friendly guide, then relaxed back into what seemed to be a mutually agreed period of silence. It had only been some six days since his initial introduction to the doctor, but as he sat with his elbow resting upon the ledge of the car door, contemplating the events of the last days, he felt as if it had been a whole life time ago.

'You are not having doubts over your decision to return to Hamburg with me, are you, Weiner?'

'None whatsoever, but I am feeling the after effects of last night, for I think we did rather push the boat out, so to speak.'

'If you insist on making such an observation, I would suggest that in your case, it was something more than a simple boat you were pushing out.'

'Well, perhaps I did have a little too much to drink, but what a fantastic night it turned out to be. Do you know, it was the first time I have ever seen Herr Smitz drunk and I have to say, he is great company once he lets himself go. I don't think I have seen anything quite so funny as the moment he took off his bar clothes to put on those shorts and that disgusting old pair of ex army boots he had. But the bit that tickled me more than anything, was when he put those two bunches of grapes into that old bowl and started to tread them down. Then to see the other old boys take off their shoes and socks to join in: well, that completed the scene as far as I was concerned, from then on, I just couldn't stop myself laughing. It was you that started him off on that track, by asking him to explain the different processes of wine making, I think that because of his lack of English and his rather intoxicated state, he decided that actions were better than words.'

'It was not all down to me, Weiner; you were the one who went and found the old bowl and began stamping your feet up and down.'

'Well, no matter how it began, it was a great evening. Incidently did you manage to make the phone call to your psychiatrist friend John Moffit?'

'Yes, Herr Smitz let me use the phone in his back office, before all that hullabaloo with the grapes began. By the way, John has received that report of mine and he is still studying it.'

'Did he think my story about Ellie was so unbelievable, and did he feel it could have some connection with Lorrett's problem?'

'No, he made no specific comment on it, but, surprisingly to me, he did not discount it in any way either, in fact, he did suggest that he had come up against a similar problem once before in his career. He also mentioned that whilst there had been no major change in Lorrett's condition she does appear to be mumbling to herself quite a bit more.'

'That sounds a little more hopeful; perhaps this could be the first sign of a gradual break-out from that isolated world of hers.'

'I only hope so. Incidently, John did congratulate us on the quality of the report we sent him and hopes that some time in the future he is going to have the pleasure of meeting you. Oh yes, before I forget, he also asked if he could have your phone number, that is of course provided you don't mind, for he might need to contact you over the report at some time.'

'That was very nice of him to mention our possible meeting and of course you can let him have my number; after all, I am family now, am I not?'

'From what you have told me, Weiner, you have always been and I do get a great deal of comfort in knowing you have Lorrett's interests at heart.'

'I don't have to tell you that is how it would have been if I had found her at the end of the war, although now, the more I think about the possibility of meeting her as a grown woman the more it worries me, for it will be a very strange experience, seeing her again after all these years.'

'Well, that's provided a solution to her problem can be found, Weiner.'

'Oh yes, there has to be an answer to it, there just has to be.'

'Weiner, I have purposely avoided any further discussion on Ellie or Lorrett for the last few days, but having spent so much time compiling that report for John Moffit, I now find there are quite a few more questions I need to ask you. For instance, when you took baby Lorrett to the hospital that night you emphasised the point that she was an orphan; now, whilst I can appreciate your reasons for saying what you did, was it not wrong to do so? For if Hans did survive, he would have gone through some sort of hell, trying to find out exactly what had happened to both Ellie and the child after the war.'

'I did, myself, think about this a great deal whilst I was held in captivity, and for some good time after I might add, but as I have already said, there were no other options open to me at the time. But knowing Ellie as I did, nothing will shake my belief that she instinctively knew of Hans' death as she sat down to pen that letter and then, sadly, commit suicide.'

'Another point, Weiner: as you were telling me about your life with Ellie, you described her as being somewhat of an enigma, suggesting perhaps that there were times when you found it difficult to fully understand both her and some of the things that she did. So, by your own words, you were saying that she had an elusive personality and yet, you have no qualms in believing that she was really gifted in some special way.'

'No qualms at all, Gregg, for whilst it would be difficult to define her character, I have no doubts about this extra-sensory gift that she had.'

'Well, one thing is certain, I am inspired by your consistency, Weiner, but let me ask you something else. You did, at one stage of your story, use an example to suggest that Ellie walked with God, so was she in fact quite a religious lady?'

'This depends upon one's point of view, for I am sure that many people would have associated her care and consideration for others as being the act of someone with strong religious beliefs, but Ellie never saw herself as anything other than a simple humanist. You see, she felt that she was only in harmony with her real self when she was helping others. But I know what you are thinking, for I did myself raise this question of beliefs with her once for, like you, I tried to understand her ideals in some envious way. Now, whilst I am sure that Ellie's reply to me was never intended to be philosophically clever, it did inevitably leave me with the belief that she had somehow inherited an inner wisdom, from someone before her, for her words were, "Weiner, whichever way we turn, we are confronted with the wonder and beauty of nature all around us, but beneath its apparent innocence, there is a primitive violence that insists on the perpetuity of death for its continued survival, so does a believer base their faith on the beauty or the violence?" Faced with such contradictions, why should I even try to believe? No, I prefer to find my contentment and love in those that have in some way become the victims of nature's suffering, for in them I can find an understanding and a purpose that is both tangible and real.'

'I see what you mean, Weiner. It does make you think, especially coming as it did from someone so young. Is it that war, with its inevitable tendency for disaster, tends to heighten one's senses and extend one's sympathies? Sorry, I was just thinking and talking out loud, so let me return to my questioning and ask, in view of Ellie's popularity and her subsequent death, how did you explain away the child's disappearance to your fellow officers in those last days at the barracks?'

'Well, as far as I can recall, the subject only came up once or twice and on those occasions, I merely answered any enquiry with the minimum of facts. But of course, most of those still at the camp were too preoccupied with their own worries and fears at the time, so I suppose they never gave the subject too much thought. By the way, look out for the sign Hannover; if my memory serves me right, it should be about a mile or so along this road; we will have to turn left there.'

'I will keep my eyes open for it. Now, another rather personal question. You admitted at one stage that you had to rationalise your feelings towards Ellie, which suggests that at times it was not that easy, so how did you handle the conflict between your adoration for her on the one hand and your need for necessary restraint on the other?'

'I don't think I ever needed to, for, you recall, Ellie made it quite clear that night in my office that she was a one-man woman and, as you now know, Hans was that man. You see, ours was an intuitively perceived love, Gregg, it was, as Ellie said, "a love that was born out of the respect we had for each other", and it didn't need to go any further. I know that as a bachelor you may find this all too difficult to understand, but as it was an unconsummated love, I have never had to deny it, regret it, or even feel guilty over it. Furthermore, it was a love that will continue to embrace me for the rest of my life, just as it has always done throughout these past years.'

As Gregg looked up through the car's interior mirror, he could see that Weiner's eyes were again moistened a little more than normal.

'Weiner, did your association with Ellie affect your wife in any way, for, as you have said, she did know of Ellie's presence and obviously she must have had some doubts as to the depth of feeling that existed between you?'

'Oh yes, my wife knew of the bond that was there between Ellie and me, but she was also aware of the love and loyalty I had towards her. She was, after all, a very perceptive woman in her own right and this was borne out by her immediate acceptance of my suggestion to try and adopt young Ellie. So she never felt threatened in any way and of course Ellie the mother was no *femme fatale*, albeit she was a very beautiful woman and had all of the necessary allure to have been one, if she had so chosen. You see, in spite of all her lovely ways, her sense of feminine mischief and her natural outward going personality, Ellie was never flirtatious; in fact, to the contrary, for she always had this mystical air of feminine vulnerability about her. It was perhaps this above all else that somehow seemed to epitomise outwardly the person within, for she really was a wonderful and beautiful young woman.'

'Well, Weiner, no one could say that you haven't been honest with me and I now fully understand why you feel as you do, but again, isn't it strange that if you had not been wounded at that particular moment in time, we most probably wouldn't be here as we are now.'

'Believe me, I have myself on many occasions over the years been ever conscious and grateful of this fact, even though at times the pain from my wound has been as hard to bear as the loss of those three people that once shared my life.'

'You never said how you came by the wound, Weiner.'

'Well, our mobile hospital unit and quarters were some twenty kilometres behind our forward lines facing El Alamein and at times, quite naturally, we were subjected to artillery fire from your lads in the Eighth Army. It was a piece of shrapnel from one of these shells that cut through the calf of my leg and severed the bone. It was thought at the time that the whole leg would eventually have to come off; that is why I was returned to Hamburg. Now, even in spite of the pain and suffering I have had from the leg over the years, I have to look back with gratitude, for had it not been for the devious and impalpable twists of this thing we call fate, I would never have shared that part of my life with Ellie.'

'A small price to pay, you think. Now, perhaps my last question, at least for the moment. It concerns the first meeting you had with Ellie outside the gates that time. You recall, you spoke as if, without reason or intent, you suddenly found the need to walk out of the barracks that night, suggesting perhaps, that Ellie was in some way willing you towards her. Is this what you really believe?'

'I can see you are wearing that doubting Thomas mask again, Gregg, so let me say, it is not what I believe, it is what I know. Now, sooner than have another debate about this gift that Ellie had, let me tell you about an incident that happened between Ellie and me in those days, then you will perhaps see what I mean. It all came about because Ellie was due to keep an appointment some distance away from Hamburg on a particular Sunday in 1943. This meant that she had to make a journey by car, so she asked one of her waitress friends if she would like to accompany her. Now, I really had no need to be working at the hospital on that particular Sunday, but feeling a little restless I decided to go in and catch up with some paper work that had been piling up on my desk. Well, I was alone in my office plodding away at the various pieces of paper, when for some unknown reason I began to feel concerned over Ellie. Now, don't ask me why, but I stopped what I was doing and just sat there staring at the telephone, thinking that perhaps something might have happened to her. How long I sat there, I don't know, but suddenly the telephone began ringing and, without stopping to reason, I half heartedly picked up the handset and spoke my name.

' "Weiner, it's Ellie here. I don't know why, but I just felt this compelling need to phone you, are you all right?"

' "Yes, Ellie, I am quite all right and thank you for phoning me." Well, Gregg, the line then went silent and I spent the next ten minutes or so wondering how it was that she knew I was in my office, and trying to convince myself that I hadn't just dreamt up that call. I was to learn some days later from the waitress who had gone along with Ellie that day, exactly what had happened. It would appear that they were driving along a main road some forty miles from Hamburg when, without any warning, Ellie suddenly turned the car off the road and down a narrow lane. Her friend asked her why the change of direction and Ellie simply mentioned that she had to phone me and that there was a phone box at the bottom of the lane. Well, upon questioning Ellie after she had made the call, the friend found out that Ellie had never been anywhere near the place or even the area, before and yet, as her friend pointed out, she knew exactly where that phone box was situated even before she had turned the car off the main road. So perhaps you can now see how on both the night of my first meeting with Ellie and again on that Sunday, my own consciousness had in some way been inexplicably interlinked with that of Ellie's.'

'Do you happen to have any use for this doubting Thomas mask of mine, Weiner; you see, I don't feel comfortable in it any more.'

'I am not surprised at your decision to dispose of it, Gregg; it never suited you in the first place. Now, since it was you that cajoled me into returning to my mysterious past, what plans have you in mind for our visit? Bearing in mind that tomorrow happens to be another one of those Sundays and military personnel are often thin on the ground on such days.'

'I hadn't thought of that. Yes, you are quite right; I don't suppose Hank will be there on a Sunday. Perhaps we should book into a hotel on the outskirts of the city for the night, then tomorrow morning we can call in on Mrs Wals. I am sure that you and she will have a lot to talk over.'

'Can I add to that suggestion, Gregg?'

'Why not? After all, it is your life we are researching.'

'I was wondering if we could visit the cemetery where Ellie is buried while we are here.'

'Is that wise, Weiner, especially after all this time? Don't you think that it could prove to be too emotionally upsetting for you? You see, speaking for myself, I have no objection to your suggestion and it would be a pleasure to take you there, but shouldn't we just leave that part of your past frozen in time, as it has been for these past twenty-odd years?'

'Gregg, within the last few minutes or so you have heard the story of how Ellie reached out across time and space to contact me that day. Now I think it is time for me to return the compliment, don't you agree?'

'Why not, Weiner, after all I am beginning to get a much clearer view of things since I have got rid of that damn silly mask I was wearing.'

'That was very nice of Johanna. I did not expect her to prepare that midday lunch for us, but it was certainly most acceptable.'

'Yes, she is a very nice lady and you two seemed to get on quite well together; in fact a stranger might easily have thought that you had known each other for years, especially as she was prepared to tell you that story about the corpse.'

'Well, naturally, nurses, just like doctors, do have to face up to some rather weird and wonderful experiences throughout their careers. I know, because I have often found myself caught up in a situation which either made me want to burst out crying, or conversely, burst out laughing. Fortunately, one learns to cope with such situations and of course, just occasionally, one sees the odd miracle or two.'

'What, genuine miracles, Weiner?'

'I don't quite know how one differentiates between miracles, Gregg, but I think I can see what you mean. What I speak of are of course those unexpected things that happen in life which are not in accordance with the usual course of events and which in general act for the good of something rather than to its detriment.'

'Does one come to mind?'

'Well, yes; at least, I think it was a miracle. It was something that happened to one of your RAF pilots during the war, whom, incidentally, I met at the time and have had the pleasure of meeting on two other occasions since. You see, the spot where it took place was in fact just a few kilometres away from the barracks and I was there when he was brought into the hospital for a check over, just after he had been captured by our patrols. He was the pilot of a badly damaged aircraft who had been forced to bale out at something like 10,000 feet, but his parachute had failed to open.

'Well, apparently, whilst he was hurtling down towards the ground and death was rushing up to greet him, he was unaware that, fortuitously, below him, an old farmer was leading his horse and cart towards a nearby inn. Again fortuitously, the cart happened to be piled high with hay and as the pilot chappie said to me afterwards, "It would have been rather rude of me if I hadn't have joined the old boy for a few snifters after he had been so accommodating, wouldn't it?" You see, the farmer was so surprised by the incident that after finding him in the middle of his haycart, he invited his unexpected guest to join him for a drink and that was where our patrol found him an hour or so later.'

'There is a rather tawdry British remark that quite succinctly describes that kind of luck, Weiner, but I don't think I will mention it here. Now, if I remember rightly, this is the road that Mrs Wals and I took the day we met Hank at the barracks. You did say the cemetery was not far away from the barracks, didn't you?'

'As far as I can remember, it was about five kilometres further on, but there have been so many changes that I cannot recognise where we are at the moment. However, there were always plenty of signs to point the way in the old days, so perhaps we might see one of them in a minute or two.'

The car had been driven up to the edge of a kerb and was parked some hundred metres away from the entrance to the cemetery.

'Now, are you sure you want to go in, Weiner?'

'No, not completely, although I feel I should; do you mind coming in with me?'

'Not in the slightest, but I cannot help feeling that we may have some difficulty finding the spot where she is buried; after all, it was quite a long time ago now.'

Gregg had driven in through the opened gates and, being unsure of his surroundings, stopped the vehicle near some buildings to one side.

'I think that building there is the chapel and the one nearer to us the original keeper's lodge, but things have changed a little since I was here.'

'It is obviously a very large cemetery. You don't happen to recall in which direction you turned when you came into the site that day?'

'No, but I remember the actual grave was on the side of a hill and over there to the right is where the ground rises, so perhaps it is up there.'

Gregg, having switched off the engine, was just about to re-start it when a uniformed keeper appeared at the side of the car window.

'Can I help you in some way?'

'We were hoping to find a particular grave, mein Herr, but we are not quite sure where to begin.'

'Is it of a recent burial?'

'No, it is a war time grave.'

'Oh, you are going to have a problem then. You see, there are well over four thousand war graves in this cemetery alone and many of them are unmarked, so I don't quite know how to advise you. I don't suppose you happen to have the registered plot number of the grave?'

'071244/4.'

'Ah, you will find that up there, in the fourth avenue of remembrance. If you drive your car up to the beginning of the avenue you will see a car park beside a coffee bar there, but you will have to walk up the remainder of the way. The plot is somewhere about five hundred metres up on the right hand side.'

'Thank you, mein Herr, that is most helpful of you.'

Gregg started up the engine and moved off. 'How the heck were you able to come straight out with that plot number like that, Weiner, have you got it written down or something?'

'No, in fact that was a rather strange experience. You see, as soon as that keeper mentioned the word plot, I was again standing there at the graveside as I was all of those years ago. I could see again that young wounded soldier sticking that wooden cross into the ground, and I suddenly remembered how at the time my eyes had become mesmerised by this short stick poking out of the ground beside him. On it, of course, was the plot number.'

'Weiner, for a moment there, I was beginning to wonder whether it is you that has this sixth sense and not Ellie.'

'Oh no, if it was anything other than just a momentary flash-back, I would have seen a doctor about it years ago.'

The two companions began to laugh at the flippancy of the remark, but was it really the remark, Gregg wondered, or was it that laughter can at times express one's feelings much more profoundly than tears.

'Well, Weiner, we have certainly come more than the five hundred metres; do you think the keeper has made a mistake?'

'He might have done, for I have looked at every grave with a cross on it, so I am sure I couldn't have missed it.'

'Wait a minute, Weiner, what has happened to our thinking? After all, we can't expect an exposed piece of wood to still be here after all this time, so surely the cross you spoke of must have rotted away by now. I think that perhaps we should be looking for an overgrown or unkept plot.'

'Yes, how stupid, this is the problem when you get something locked into your brain, you tend not to think how time can change things. I did see an overgrown plot some way back there and, as far as I can recall, it was more like the location I had in my mind.'

'So, let's go and have a look, shall we?'

'I think this has to be it, it certainly has that feeling of familiarity about it, but it has no plot number.'

'I will leave you alone for a few minutes, Weiner.'

Ever conscious of the need to allow his friend time for personal reflection, Gregg moved across to the other side of the pathway and began casually browsing at some of the other headstones implanted there. Scattered amid the sunlit trees and flower covered graves, there were others, who seemed to be either silently attending plots, or simply reminiscing within the peace of their surroundings. He waited for some minutes before stepping back to the side of the pathway where Weiner was standing, only to find further interest in the messages on those graves near to him. As he casually scanned the dates and detail of the closely packed headstones, he suddenly found his eyes alerted by a name, but it was some moments before he realised its relevance.

'Weiner.' The doctor turned his head to face his companion some metres away from him.

'Would you mind coming here for a moment?'

Weiner turned and moved down the slope towards his friend. He was standing in front of a beautifully carved marble headstone with a peripheral border and plinth of carved onyx. The inscription was different from that which Weiner had described, for the dedication read, 'Dear Ellie, you have passed beyond our sight, but not our minds.' Below this, it showed that the monument had been commissioned and erected in 1946 by members of the Ninth Panzer Division.

It took some minutes for Weiner to clear the emotion from his throat, but even then he was somehow lost for words.

'I just don't know what to say, Gregg.'

'Why try, Weiner, your silence says it all.'

They both stood admiring the graceful design of the headstone, each in his own way trying to understand what the other might be thinking.

'Weiner, at least at the time this was erected, there were obviously quite a few people who cared; furthermore, by the look of those comparatively fresh flowers, someone still continues to do so. I am also wondering who might have put that Iron Cross medal behind that vase, or is it normal practice in Germany to put personal tokens on graves?'

'I wouldn't say normal, but, yes, some people do it; more importantly, someone, as you say, obviously still cares.'

After waiting some minutes, Gregg put his hand on the doctor's shoulder.

'Come on, my friend, let us see if we can find out who this person is.'

The two men slowly found their way down the stony slope of the pathway and back towards the car.

'That was quick, couldn't you find it?' The keeper was standing in the sun outside his lodge as they approached him.

'Yes, we found it, thank you, although we were not expecting to see such a monument as that. As a matter of interest, were you working here at the time it was installed?'

'No, it was there before I came here, which is a little over twenty years ago now.'

'We noticed that there are reasonably fresh flowers on the grave. Is this a part of a service that you people provide?'

'No, no, but that particular grave usually has quite a lot of flowers on it; you see, so many people come here to see it.'

'When you say many, have you any idea of how many?'

'Not exactly, but over the years, I must have had some two hundred people ask me where the grave is located, many of whom had travelled quite a long way to see it. Some were obviously families, but generally most of the visitors have been gentlemen on their own. Then, of course, there are those who come back regularly, perhaps two or three times a year.'

The two friends looked at each other. 'These people must have known Ellie in the old days, Weiner.'

Gregg turned to face his informant again. 'I don't suppose you would know who it was that recently replenished those flowers on the grave?'

'No, I couldn't say definitely, mein Herr, but it is more than likely that it was our two regular Sunday visitors who put them there. In fact, they usually turn up in their black Mercedes round about this time.'

'When you say they, I assume you mean a man and a woman?'

'No, two men; they have been coming here most Sundays for a number of years now.'

Gregg took out some paper money from his pocket and, passing it to the keeper, thanked him for his help.

'Well, Weiner, what do you make of that? It seems as if we might be in luck and, speaking for myself, I think we should wait to see if these gentlemen return again today.'

'I agree, although I am not so sure we can put it down to luck, but whoever they are, they certainly seem to be dedicated people. Now I am beginning to wonder precisely how long they have been coming here.'

'Well, I am sure that, like me, you are only too eager to find out as much as you can about them, and I don't know why, but I get the feeling that they might turn out to be a couple of officers from your old regiment.

I don't know whether you noticed, but there are several benches along each of the avenues, and there was one just a little further up the slope past Ellie's grave. I suggest we go and sit up there, to see if these chappies turn up today, for I am quite intrigued by all of this.'

'It is slightly unsettling as well, I might add.'

'That is the beauty of research work; you see, there is always this element of expectancy about it.'

The seat was one of many around the site, all given by families or friends in memory of those who had since departed. The plaque on the seat where Gregg and his companion sat was dedicated to a family of six who had all died in an air raid in 1943. Gregg was again reminded of Weiner's observation that, had it not been for Ellie's letter, he too might easily have become just another name, on another plaque, on another seat.

'Gregg, the inscription on Ellie's headstone suggests that quite a few people subscribed to it, so I wonder who it was that organised it all. You see, I would have thought that after we had all been posted to the front in '44, there would have been very few troops left at the barracks.'

'Well, it was certainly no cheap item, Weiner, so perhaps there is some kind of regimental old comrades' association somewhere in the area; but hopefully, if these two fellows turn up, we should be able to find out all that we want to know, so be patient, my friend.'

A lull in the conversation, the sun's warmth and the rather oversized meal that Johanna Wals had given him had made Gregg a little drowsy, so stretching back into the seat with his legs fully extended out in front of him, he was quite happy to close his eyes and doze off for a while.

'Strange, isn't it; a little over a week ago I would have rejected outright any suggestion of visiting this place, Gregg, yet here I am and somehow it all seems right. It is as if I have suddenly become relieved of a burden that I have been carrying for much of my life.'

Weiner turned his head, unaware that his words had fallen on deaf ears.

Not wishing to disturb his companion, he returned to the vigil of watching out for their expected visitors. He was able to see the cars in the parking area at the bottom of the slope and it wasn't long before a large black Mercedes glided into position to join them.

Gregg felt an open hand gently squeeze his knee.

'A large Mercedes car has pulled into the car park.'

Rubbing his eyes and shaking his head a little, Gregg leaned forward to get a clearer view of the car park below. Two men had left the car and were making their way across the carriageway and onto the pathway where it joined the road. The younger of the two walked with a stick, the other, a heavily built and older man, was wearing a black Homburg hat; both were dressed in dark suits with white shirts and black ties. A pair of horn-rimmed sun glasses concealed much of the older man's face, as he, looking more hesitant than his companion, held on to the younger man's arm for support before tackling the gently rising slope.

'Weiner, they look as if they are the men we are expecting. Try not to make your interest in them too obvious, for we had best ensure first that they are here to attend Ellie's grave.'

'Well, the younger man is carrying a bag and a large bunch of flowers, so they are certainly here to decorate someone's grave.'

The moments of silent waiting were broken only by the slow but rhythmic crunching of stones underfoot as Gregg and Weiner watched the two approaching figures out of the corner of their eyes.

'Gregg, I think I know the face of the younger one.'

'Who is he then, Weiner?'

'I can't put a name to him at the moment, but I am sure I know the face from somewhere.' Weiner spoke in soft tones, conscious that the men who were now facing Ellie's grave might be able to hear what he was saying.

The younger of the two men unwrapped the bunch of flowers he had been carrying and, bending forward, carefully arranged them in the terracotta vase on top of the plinth.

When he had rejoined his companion on the pathway, they both stood facing the headstone, as the older of the two removed his hat and remained silently still for some seconds.

Again Gregg felt the hand clasping his knee.

'I know the other man, Gregg, it's Herr Cramer.' Weiner instinctively started to get up from his seat as Gregg, catching hold of his coat sleeve, attempted to hold him back.

'Wait a moment, Weiner, don't rush it, just leave them for a few minutes. This Herr Cramer fellow, wasn't he the club owner you call Gunter?'

'Yes, Weiner whispered. 'You remember, I said I never knew what had happened to him that night his club was demolished and at the time I thought he must have been killed.'

'Well, whilst he is obviously very much alive, I think I should warn you that he might now be blind.'

'Blind, Gregg?'

'Yes, I think so, for from what I can see of his eyes behind those dark glasses, it appears as if they have no movement.'

'My God, poor fellow.'

The younger man again took hold of the other's arm and started to move off slowly down the hill. Weiner in his excitement rose quickly from his seat and made off after them, calling 'Mein Herr!' as he did. Gregg followed behind until the two men had stopped and turned to face the voice that had called them. Within a matter of seconds, all four men faced each other on the path.

'You will excuse me, but you are Herr Cramer, are you not?'

Weiner had turned slightly towards the older man as he spoke.

'Yes I am, but please would you identify yourself for I cannot see you.'

'Gunter, you may not remember me, but I am Doctor Kraske, Weiner Kraske.'

'No, no, you can't be, not Weiner, I thought . . .'

'Yes, Gunter, Weiner from all those years ago.'

For a moment or two, there had been a gap of separation between them, then, with the flurry of lost affection, they embraced each other in a hug as the tears ran down their faces.

'Thank God, you are alive, my dear Weiner, what can I say? Twenty-six years ago you passed out of my life and now you are here. Weiner, my old friend, where have you been, where did you come from after all this time?'

It seemed like an age before they broke away from the embrace and stood there in silence with their hands locked together in friendship.

'Weiner, why now and not before? Where have you been all this time? No, no, don't try to answer for a moment; let me instead ask if you remember my partner here?'

'I know the face, but I am unable to place it at the moment, Gunter.'

'It is Anton, Anton Fuller, he was the first soldier that Ellie brought to the club that night, don't you remember, the night that Ellie first sang for us. My God, what a lovely voice she had and what a lovely person she was.'

'So, like me you have never forgotten her, Gunter, but please let me first remedy my failure. I am so sorry, Anton, I just couldn't conjure up your name, how could I forget it, but how wonderful it is to see you again.'

The two men shook hands, then, after releasing their grips, briefly placed the palms of their hands on each other's shoulders.

'Gunter, my friend here is from England, so may I introduce him to you. His name is Jefferson, but he prefers to be known as just Gregg. It is he who has led me back to you and Anton here today.'

It was only a matter of minutes before the introductions were over and Anton, realising that they all had so much to talk about, suggested they should all perhaps return to the car park where there was a cafeteria.

Gregg, with four cups of coffee on a tray, placed them down on the table just as the others had settled themselves into their seats.

'Gunter, I have so many questions to ask, but I don't know where to begin.'

'It is the same for me, Weiner, I just keep asking myself, is it really you, for as you never came back after the war, I have always assumed that you must have been killed. Now, after all these years, you are but an arm's length away from me across a table and yesterday is with us once again. Weiner, I have never forgotten you, our friendship, or that wonderful person that was so much a part of you in those days.'

'Gunter, I also thought that you were dead, for I saw your club after it was devastated that night and I was told that you were believed to be buried somewhere beneath its remains.'

'Fortunately I wasn't actually in the club when it happened, Weiner, so it was only by a twist of fate I am here today, albeit that was the night that I lost my sight.'

'So how was it, that you were away from the club at the time?'

'Well, I was there with some of the members when the siren sounded and as we had always felt that the basement was comparatively safe, some of the guests stayed on. Then, some thirty minutes after the alert sounded, there was a loud explosion and I could tell that it came from somewhere nearby. So I quickly went up to the entrance, to see where the device had landed. As it was in the direction of Ellie's flat, I put on my protective helmet and quickly made my way through the alleyways to the house. Well, as you probably know, there had been a direct hit on the house next to Ellie's so the dust cloud covering the site was still rising from the debris as I got there. There were no rescue teams in the area at the time, so, in my panic, I decided to run back to the club for some of my staff, hoping that together, we could at least begin the search for those lost under the ruins.' Gunter hesitated before continuing,

'Well, I must have only been some five hundred metres from the club, when there was this blinding flash across my eyes, but from that point on, I didn't know anything more until I regained consciousness in a hospital ward some two days later. In those moments of coming round, I could feel that both my head and my face were heavily bandaged, I could hear the movement of people around me and I could detect the smell of chloroform in my nostrils, but I could no longer see anything. In the days that followed, I was able to recollect that within the brilliance of that momentary flash, I could see this heavy wooden rafter coming through the air towards me. It must have been that which hit me and I am sure that had it not been for my helmet it would have killed me. I was eventually to learn that as I had turned into the road where the club was situated, a bomb had landed on a building nearby, wrecking several properties and killing some of my staff along with many of the guests there that night. Thankfully, the surgeons managed to save my life and, from what I was to gather, it was you who arranged for Ellie's burial. But sadly, of course, they never ever did find the body of the baby.'

Gregg was suddenly aware of the potentially delicate situation his companion was now facing for, from what Gunter had just said, it was obviously thought that the child must have been lost in the explosion that night. So would Weiner now tell his friends exactly how Ellie died and how the baby had survived, or would he leave the truth unsaid?

'Gunter, I know how you must feel, for I share the shock of that terrible night with you. You see I was there when they recovered some of the bodies and yes, I did arrange for Ellie's burial. Some three days later.'

'I heard about that from Anton here. I don't know whether you are aware of it or not, but he was one of the soldiers who attended Ellie's funeral that day.'

'No, I wasn't aware of that. So you must have followed behind in one of the vehicles that day, Anton?'

'Yes, and I am so glad that I was able to be there.'

'If I remember rightly, weren't you also the young man who told me that Ellie actually prevented you from committing suicide?'

Weiner was obviously intent on confirming the facts for Gregg's benefit.

'Yes I was, and I have been eternally grateful to her for that act of mercy ever since. You see, I never knew Ellie until that night and to this day, I have never been able to understand how she was able to read my mind and save me from myself. But she did, so that first meeting is something that I shall never forget, for it was to change my life in so many ways. This is just one of the reasons why Gunter and I visit the cemetery every week, for we have never forgotten Ellie or all that she meant to us in those days of war.'

'It seems, Gunter, that all three of us owe our lives to Ellie in one way or another, for if you hadn't left your club that night you probably wouldn't be sitting here now.'

'How right you are. I have always realised that had it not been for my thoughts of Ellie, I would probably have stayed in the club after hearing the explosion that night. But I am not sure I understand how Ellie was able to save you, Weiner.'

Gregg could see by his companion's face that he was now caught up in an embarrassing situation, so would Weiner now have to say how Ellie actually died that night?'

'Gunter, there is a lot I have to tell you, much of which I never knew myself until recently meeting my friend Gregg here. So be patient with me, for you will soon know all there is to know. But one thing is certain, we have all in our own ways known and loved dear Ellie.'

'How true, Weiner. That is why Ellie's grave has come to symbolise that wonderful spirit of togetherness that was always there with us in those days of war. So is it that in some strange way, she has again been the reason behind our meeting here today, just as she was all those years ago, and is it that even in death she is still able to unite people?'

'This is not the first time that such a remark has been made, but I will not go into that at the moment. I can see, however, that we all have many reasons to remember her.'

'Well, without wishing to brag in any way, Weiner, I may have an advantage over you. You see, Ellie had only left the club some fifty or so minutes before I lost my sight that night, so I can still see her face clearly in my mind's eye and nothing will ever change that, for it can never age or fade with time.'

'You deserve to have such a long lasting reward, my friend, for yours has certainly been a long lasting love.'

Weiner turned again to face Anton.

'Do you also feel the same towards Ellie, Anton?'

'Very much so. You see, after that night she took me to the club for the first time, I often used to spend my evenings there, helping out in any way that I could, so Gunter and I became very great friends. I have therefore always been indebted to both Gunter and Ellie for their friendship, help and understanding. Then, after Gunter lost everything that night, including his sight, it gave me an opportunity to return just a little of that which he had shown towards me. So after the war, we reclaimed the bomb site that had once been the club, negotiated for the site of the building that used to be next door and today we have, without question, the finest restaurant, club and hotel in Hamburg.'

'So a new club has risen out of the ashes of the old one?'

'Yes, Weiner, today Gunter and I are partners. I have a family that I like to think is as much his as it is mine and we all agree in principle that none of this would have been possible if Ellie hadn't come into our lives.'

'How wonderful, another club. Is it like it was in the old days, Gunter?'

'I would hope that you will soon be able to judge that for yourself, my friend.'

'I can hardly wait, but perhaps something more relevant to me at the moment is, who was it that had that beautiful monument erected to Ellie?'

'It was really a joint effort,' Anton interjected. 'You see, after returning to the camp that afternoon of Ellie's funeral, some of the men at the barracks felt that they would like to see some kind of monument to her, so I started up a collection around the camp. By the end of the day, I had collected a fairly large sum of money and as most of the lads were to be posted to the front within the next couple of days, I was left to carry out their wishes. Well, after the war, Gunter very kindly made up the balance to pay for what is there today. It was also his suggestion that it should be as much in memory of those men of the Ninth Panzer Division who died, as it is of Ellie.'

'So how have so many people come to know about the grave, Anton?'

'Well, initially it must have become known to just a few of the lads that had subscribed to it and who had returned here to see it after the war; then the numbers must have simply grown by word of mouth. Nowadays, of course, most of the visitors that want to see the grave either stay at our hotel or visit the club before coming here to the cemetery. You see, many of them just want to reflect upon the old days and naturally, the hotel and club is where this contact with their past is best experienced.'

'I am not sure I follow you, Anton.'

'Perhaps I should let Gunter explain.'

'Weiner, the reason for Anton's remark is that once the club had been rebuilt, we both felt that its name and ideals should in some way both reflect and promote the friendship and spirit of that wonderful woman we once knew, so it was re-named the Hotel and Club Mollen.'

Weiner, leaning across the table, placed his hand over Gunter's. 'Blind though you may unfortunately be, my dear friend, you are still blessed with a vision that in some way sees beyond the mere obvious. So perhaps now is the right time for me to suggest that one day soon, your club may yet again echo to the beautiful voice of Ellie Mollen.'

'Please do not joke with me, Weiner.'

'I would not joke with you over such matters, for Ellie Mollen does live on through her daughter. Ellie's child was not lost in the bombing that night. She survived the war and, just like her mother, she has this gift of a lovely voice. So, God willing, she will one day soon fill your club with the same warmth and congeniality as her mother did in those far off days of war.'

Gregg could see that Gunter was finding it difficult to speak. His face had become flushed and he had taken off his dark glasses to wipe the moisture from around his eyes.

'I don't know what to say, I don't even know what to think, for suddenly my past is now my present. Weiner, I think it best if you were to tell me all that has happened to you over the years and why you have come here today and not before. Then perhaps, we can both come to terms with this legacy of ignorance that the war has bestowed upon us.'

'Yes, Gunter, you are right. Now is the time for a full explanation, then perhaps we shall both be a lot wiser than we are now.'

Weiner began by explaining how Gregg had come into his life, then went on to cover much of the detail that he and his new found friend had been discussing over the past few days, pointing out that their visit to the cemetery had only materialised out of a purely spontaneous suggestion since their arrival in Hamburg. He talked about Lorrett and went on to explain how he himself had seen her on television without realising she was in fact the baby he had lost all those years before. After some fifteen minutes of explanation and questioning, Weiner was about to complete his story when Anton interrupted the conversation.

'Weiner, from what you have just said I am now bound to ask, how was it that you were looking after the baby that night when Ellie was killed? For we have always thought that the baby must have died along with her mother, even though no corpse was ever found to justify such an assumption.'

It was the one question that Weiner was hoping he would not have to answer, for he felt that nothing could be gained by telling his old friends the truth about Ellie's death that night.

'I was forced to take the child to the hospital, for she had been crying and I couldn't find out what was wrong with her. This is how both the child and I survived that night, but of course I had to leave the child at the hospital and that is how I came to lose her.'

Gregg, knowing the truth about Ellie's death, somehow felt that his friend's explanation was somewhat lame and wondered how the obviously astute Anton would react to it. There was no immediate reaction from him, other than a look of doubt that seemed to spread over his face, so Weiner, feeling that he had dealt with the problem quite successfully and only too conscious of the delicate position he was in, went on to tell the rest of his story.

It was some ten minutes later that Weiner completed all he had to say without giving any explanation of how Ellie had actually died that night. It then soon became noticeable how by telling his story, it had reduced the need for further specific questioning from his old friend Gunter, for they were now quite content just to talk about the less imperative moments of their past.

Gregg, who had purposely remained quietly in the background, soon came to realise that both he and Anton were, quite unintentionally, being excluded from the inevitable flow of reminiscences being exchanged between their other two friends sitting at the table. So, waiting for the right moment, he quietly broke the silence.

'You seem to be miles away, Anton.'

'Yes, I am sorry; I was just thinking about some of the remarks that have been made in the last few minutes and how strange it is that we should meet like this after all these years.'

'Is it perhaps the feeling that you have been manipulated in some way by this thing called circumstance? For at times that is exactly how I feel.'

'Yes, possibly, but I am aware that this happens and I have at times been only too happy to go along with the tide as it were; after all, that was precisely how I felt the night I was to meet Ellie for the first time.'

'Going along with the tide is one thing, Anton, but from what Weiner has told me and from your own words earlier, it suggests to me that Ellie was capable of taking over your mind in some way?'

'I am not sure that taking it over is the right term for it, but influencing it in some way, yes.'

'Again, was that really so, or was it that because of your wound you had become somewhat depressed and perhaps understandably, a little vulnerable to the probability of auto suggestion?'

'If you are politely saying that I wasn't myself that night, that is not so. Gregg, you need to understand that the decision to end my own life came only after a great deal of logical and rational heart-searching on my part. You see, unlike a lot of the lads, I had chosen the army as a career, for being an orphan without any home I could call my own, the army was to be my life.

'But of course, once I had become wounded and had been put on administrative duties back at the barracks, I realised that I would eventually have to face the prospect of my inevitable discharge once the war was over. So, yes, I had become a little despondent, for I realised that the wound would not only end my career in the army but it would also reduce my chances of future employment. But believe me, when I left my quarters that night, I was quite rational, quite calm and ready to do what I had planned, which was to find a quiet spot in the wooded area behind our quarters and peacefully depart this life. Now, I cannot easily explain the rest of it, for having once made the decision to do what I was about to do, I suddenly felt as if my mind had become tranquillised by an indefinable peace. It was as if, in some peculiar way, my soul had become separated from my body; my personality had become detached from its carrier. It had, to all intents and purposes, been removed and then replaced by this passively all embracing contentment inside me. I have never really been able to account for everything that happened that night, but I feel sure that in those moments of tranquil oblivion I have just described to you, I had in some way, become highly receptive to the transfer, or interchange, of other thought processes. So perhaps it was that, as I began to walk along the path that night, Ellie must have seen me slowly hobbling along on my crutches. Knowing Ellie as we do now, her natural sense of compassion and consideration for others must have welled up within her and in those few brief moments, our minds must have come together as one.

'So instead of turning off the path and into the woods that night, I somehow found myself being pulled gently but firmly towards those gates and, of course, into the sanctuary of Ellie's care. I think you know the rest, Gregg, but what you may not know is that there were many other people in those days who had themselves experienced similar situations with Ellie.'

'Thank you for telling me about it, Anton; it has helped me to understand several other things that have been confusing me. But do you think that Ellie was actually aware of your intention to commit suicide before you met at the gates that night, or was it that she could more easily understand your obvious pain?'

'Again, this was something else that I was thinking about just before we began talking together. You see, after picking me up that night, Ellie took me to the club and then after a discussion with Gunter, I was seated at one of the tables so that I could watch the show. Well, from then on, different waitresses kept bringing me either food or drink, and at other times they would just come over to make sure that I was all right. So perhaps you can see now how that night was to change my life, for I was to realise for the first time that some people actually cared what happened to me. But to answer your question, Gregg, I should perhaps tell you of the conversation between Ellie and me, as she took me back in the car to the barracks that night.

' "Anton," she said, "As I saw you hobbling along the path tonight, I could tell that you were obviously in pain, but, more relevantly, it was not the pain that alarmed me, but the fact that its persistence was clouding your judgement. You see, Anton, what you had in mind could never have happened, for it was not destined to be."

'As you might gather, Gregg, as a realist, I couldn't believe what I had heard, for obviously she had in some way read my mind as one would read a book. You see, I have never met anyone with such a gift before and I had certainly never known anyone who had shown me so much kindness and consideration before. She went on to say, "Anton, everyone has their own individual destiny to fulfil, although, sadly, some have less time in which to fulfil it than others; but Anton, contrary to your earlier intention, yours is a life that was meant to survive and succeed into its late years."

'Now of course, Gregg, I am in no way suggesting my interpretation of Ellie's remark is right, neither do I suggest that what I am about to say is based on any factual insight on my part. But her words that night have always left me feeling that she herself was amongst those who, in her own words, had less time to achieve what she had in mind to do.'

'So are you saying that you think that Ellie was simply fated to die early, or that she could foresee the time when she herself would be forced to bring her own life to its end?'

'Well, up to the night she died, I had always felt that she was going to do what, according to Ellie, I was not meant to do. But of course, this must have been no more than a feeling on my part, for whilst she obviously did die young, it wasn't by her own hand.'

'And you were actually thinking about this, just prior to my first question to you some few minutes ago?'

'Yes, I was.'

'So did this arise out of something Weiner said?'

'Yes, partly, but perhaps more from what he didn't say. You see, it was very unusual for Ellie to leave her baby with anyone in those days, but, more specifically, there was something so noticeably different about Ellie herself that night. You see, as Gunter mentioned earlier, she had made a brief visit to the club that night and had left some time before the siren went off. Now, in the first place, her visit to the club was itself quite surprising, for since having the baby she rarely ventured out at night, and in the second place, she did something that was quite unusual that evening. You see, she made the point of kissing all of the staff on the cheek just before she left for home. I may, of course, have been the only one to have noticed its significance, but what with that and the apparent sadness on her face that night, I have always held the view that Ellie had come round to the club especially to say her last farewells.'

'So you are saying she knew in some way that it was to be her night of destiny?'

'Yes, but how or why I came to be convinced of it, I don't know.'

'Perhaps, Anton, like me, you make the odd mistake in deducing things at times. May I ask how you intended to bring your life to its end that time?'

'I had a phial of cyanide which I had kept after returning from the front. You see, there was always this fear of what might happen if we were ever captured by the Russians, so active service personnel were sometimes given the option to carry a phial of it, if they so wished.'

'What did you do with it once you decided not to go ahead with your plan?'

'I don't know, Gregg, I just can't remember after all this time.'

'I am sorry if I have been a bit tedious asking you these questions, Anton, for they have all rather bordered on the morose and I am sure from what Weiner has told me, life was often far from that in the old days.'

'There is no need to apologise, for it is quite understandable. You need to know as much as you can and the inevitable recall of old memories was bound to come up at such a surprise meeting as this. But you are quite right, for Gunter and I do not come here each week in sadness, we come to re-acquaint ourselves with the spirit of fun and friendship that was Ellie. In fact, you may find this hard to believe, but there have been times when both Gunter and I have walked down the slope from Ellie's grave laughing like two adolescent young men, simply because one or the other of us had suddenly remembered one of the pranks that she often used to play on us. No, Gregg, in spite of the war and all the tragedy that came with it, we were never morose. How could you be with someone like Ellie around, for she was one of the happiest and most unselfish of people that one could ever know. But any tears that we may shed in memory of Ellie today are as much for those people who never knew her, for she came and went like a single passing moment of time.'

'I am a little lost for words, Anton, but tell me, how were you able to avoid the bombing of the club that night?'

'I left some five minutes after Ellie, for I was on duty later that night.'

'Another question: did Ellie ever tell you what part of Germany she came from originally?'

'Well, let me say that, if there had been no war, I might easily have bumped into her on the street.'

'I am sorry, I am not with you.'

'All I am saying is that there was every possibility that we might have met one day, because we came from the same town. In fact, at one time, I was in lodgings only about two kilometres away from her home, but naturally I never knew that, until I went back there after the war.'

'So where was her home exactly?'

'A town called Hersbrück; it is not all that far from Nürnberg.'

'Would you happen to know the actual address?'

'I did have it at one time, but the family no longer live there, for her father is dead and the mother is in an old people's home in Nürnberg.'

'But you know that address.'

'Oh yes, for I have been there to see her on a couple of occasions and I have at times written her the odd letter or two.'

'So do you see yourself as a friend of Mrs Mollen?'

'Not really, Gregg; you see, I thought it only right that someone should tell her what had happened to Ellie, so after the war I went to see her.'

'Did you tell her that Ellie had a daughter?'

'No, because in the absence of anything factual, it was generally accepted that the baby must have died along with her mother in the bombing. I have to say, however, that in view of what I have already told you, it did strike me that there had been no mention of the child in Weiner's short graveside speech. So it was my intention at the time to ask him about the child the next time I saw him, but of course there was no next time, for he, along with most of the others, was suddenly posted off to the front that same night.'

'So, generally, you came to accept that the child had died in the bombing?'

'Yes and that was the main reason I didn't mention it to Mrs Mollen the first time I went to see her.'

'The main reason you say, so were there other reasons?'

'Well, I felt there was also very little point in mentioning that she had once had a grandchild, especially when both of its parents were dead.'

'Say again, Anton?'

'I am sorry, Gregg, I am not with you.'

'The last part of your remark, did you say that both of the child's parents were dead.'

'Yes, does that surprise you?'

'Well, if you are really telling me that Hans is dead, then yes, it does.'

'He was killed in the war, didn't you know?'

'No, Anton; in fact it is precisely this point that has brought Weiner and me back to Hamburg today. Tell me, how did you find out about Hans?'

'It was Mrs Mollen who told me when I went to see her that first time after the war. You see, after telling her that Ellie had been killed that night in the bombing and after she had time to get over the initial shock of hearing what I had to say, she seemed to find some consolation in believing that as Hans was dead, it was best that Ellie never lived to learn of it.'

'So did you ever find out exactly how or when Hans died?'

'No, I was a little reluctant to press her for further answers at that time, for she was obviously quite emotional and, to be honest with you, I never knew Hans that well, so I had no real need to find out any more than I was told.'

Gregg was obviously quite shaken, for he realised how Weiner had been so right in insisting that Hans must have died, otherwise Ellie would have never had done what she did.

'Now who is it that seems to be miles away, Gregg?'

'Sorry, Anton, but I was just thinking how the casual disclosure of something that has been of so little relevance to you has turned out to be of so much relevance to me; you see that news about Hans has hit me quite hard.'

'But you never knew him, Gregg.'

'Until my arrival in Germany some ten or more days ago, I never knew Weiner, I had never heard of Ellie and I hadn't met you or Gunter, but that doesn't mean that I haven't come to know and like you all now. But perhaps I should change the subject entirely and ask whether you would like another coffee?'

'Yes, that would be very nice.'

Gregg turned his head to face his two other companions still chatting away across the table beside him.

'Weiner, sorry to butt in, but would you both like another coffee?'

It was Gunter who replied. 'I have just been suggesting something to my dear friend Weiner here and he tells me that I have to ask you about it first, Gregg, so may I ask if you intend staying in Hamburg for a few days?'

'That was the original idea, but since speaking to Anton here, I no longer feel we need to, why do you ask?'

'Well, as you no doubt appreciate, this is a very happy day for Weiner and myself and I was hoping that you might like to stay with Anton and me at our hotel and club for a few days, then we can all celebrate this wonderful occasion in a style worthy of it.'

'What can I say, Gunter? Being a specialist in reunions myself and knowing how my friend Weiner here likes the odd glass of wine or two, I could hardly refuse even if I wanted to, so thank you and we graciously accept. But I still don't know whether you want this other coffee or not.'

Chapter Six

Gregg and his now inseparable friend Weiner stayed at the hotel as invited. It had been Gregg's intention to spend perhaps a day or so with their hosts before leaving for Nürnberg where Mrs Mollen lived, but Gunter and his partner Anton had other ideas and had influenced their guests into staying over for five days. Three of these timeless days had been spent in near continuous festivity and jollification, for, as Gunter tried to explain. 'We need the first day to drink to the past, the second day to celebrate the present and the third day to welcome in the future.'

As far as Gregg was able to recall later, it seemed as if day and night had become one, for time had passed without recognition. He could vaguely remember some of the introductions to others around him, he also realised that he must have dined quite luxuriously at times, but he had no positive recollection of either eating or sleeping throughout those first three days.

There had been no exaggeration in Anton's remark when he had suggested that the hotel and club were the finest in Hamburg for, without a doubt, the complex had been designed and built in quite an unusual style.

First impressions of the four-storeyed hotel built on the site next to the original club suggested that its design had emanated from a subtle blend of both Georgian and Teutonic influences, with its corner quoining, rusticated stucco work and wide ornate porticoed entrance. But once inside, it was impossible to avoid the obvious tendency towards Palladian style architecture, with its arches, pillars and beautifully tiled floors. The accommodation was sumptuous, enticingly comfortable and without a doubt totally convincing, for it summarised all that is synonymous with what could best be described as the ultimate in luxury.

The club, whilst quite separate from the hotel, was nevertheless built as an integral part of it, but with its own similar entrance some distance away from that of the hotel. There was, however, an inter-connecting passage at ground floor level which allowed the free flow of people between the two venues. If the hotel could quite justifiably be described as being sumptuous, then the club, without a doubt, was unashamedly ostentatious but undeniably functional. Its height when viewed from the street matched that of the hotel, but behind the false façade at fourth floor level, bushes, trees and plants grew in profusion between the pathways and patios of what was a well established roof garden. Directly below this at third floor level and styled in the period of the late twenties was a large buffet and wine bar, which in isolation from the main club area on the lower floors, satisfied the needs of those clients who preferred to dine without entertainment. The main area of the club was in the basement below street level, whilst the large dome shaped ceiling that covered it rounded off some twenty-four metres higher. A balcony at ground floor level, with its centrally housed Regency staircase leading down to the basement, had been built as the main restaurant area of the club. Its construction was similar to the balconies of many pre-war theatres, but without the fixed seating. Instead it had been terraced and furnished in such a way that it allowed patrons a clear view of the stage and dance floor below, whilst still sitting to enjoy their meal. A red carpet that covered the balcony floor had been extended to include the whole of the basement area and the lavishly decorated stairway between floors. Directly below the balcony, where its supporting pillars had been fashioned into the shape and style of Corinthian columns, there was another more intimate dining area, where dimmed lights and low ceilings enhanced the prospect of romance for those who sought it.

The overall colour scheme throughout the club was in various pastel shades of pink and green, while most of the ornamental motifs that decorated the ceilings, walls and fittings had been delicately etched with gold leaf to match the inaurate theme of the seating and other furnishings within the club. It was, Gregg concluded, a vision of both opulence and palatial grandeur, which, regretfully, he was only able fully to appreciate with hindsight and not at the time he was there. The nightly cabaret had been spectacular, the costumes exquisite and the presentation near to perfection. But as Gregg sat comfortably in the front passenger seat of the car, he couldn't help but conclude that the show itself seemed to have little or no impact on its audience. As Weiner had said, 'It was a good all round show, but it needed the presence of someone like Ellie or Lorrett to have made it a great show.'

The car was now being driven by Weiner as it sped on its way along the autobahn towards Nürnberg.

'Well, Weiner, how are you feeling now, after wallowing in these last five days of absolute self indulgence and, of course, the many other drinks that we both managed to knock back?'

'Somewhat vague, certainly quite exhausted, but also serenely contented.'

'What was your reaction at the cemetery, when you first realised that one of the two men standing in front of Ellie's grave was Gunter?'

'I don't know if I can explain it, Gregg; I know that I was shaking quite considerably, my temperature was going up and down like a yo-yo and I remember feeling quite weak at the knees. But I just could not believe it possible that Gunter was standing there just a few metres away from me, after all those years.'

'So does that suggest you are glad that you came?'

'Why not just read my face, Gregg?'

'Now don't you wish you had returned to Hamburg sooner, Weiner?'

'No, I don't think so, for until your arrival at my door there would have been little or no purpose in doing so and the chances of my meeting Gunter and Anton as we have done would have been negligible. No, I am sure that our actions have again been created by circumstance and that these moments were scheduled to occur precisely as they have. I am also now quite sure, that this research of yours will ultimately lead us to the solution we are looking for.'

'Well, I have to say, that if it hadn't been for those remarks of Anton's, we certainly wouldn't be heading towards Nürnberg now, for to be perfectly honest with you, I fully expected to find out that Hans had in fact survived the war. In fact, I think the thing that surprised me the most about his disclosure was the casual way it came out and it fascinates me to think how by wrongly phrasing my questions I might so easily have missed that vital snippet of information and wound up my research. So let's hope now that our efforts will lead us to something in the end.'

'Personally speaking, Gregg, I think they will and I am enjoying every minute of it. You see, I now think of myself as Mr Hide and you as Mr Seek, for you intentionally seem to seek out a past which I have unintentionally hidden.'

'Well, I am not unhappy with that, as long as you are not wanting to reverse the roles and take over Mr Seek's job, Weiner. But, going back a bit, did you eventually tell Anton and Gunter the truth about the way Ellie died, for I am sure that Anton at least had always instinctively felt that there was something not quite right about the circumstances surrounding her death?'

'It's funny that you should ask that, for I did find myself facing up to a number of persistent and awkward questions from him, so I decided to tell them both the truth and now I can fully understand Anton's reaction.'

'What exactly was his reaction?'

'Strangely enough, after showing them both Ellie's letter and the poem, Anton just went quiet, but I think you were right, he did have doubts about her death. But Gunter: well, he was quite taken back by the discovery, so much so that it took him some time to get over the shock of it. But he eventually came to terms with the facts, although I have to admit I did feel a little guilty over not telling him earlier. However, the conversation went on from there and I told him the reason for our presence in Hamburg after all these years. As a matter of fact, as we talked, I found myself thinking how nice it would be if we could actually find out where Hans is buried and perhaps even arrange to have his remains reburied beside those of Ellie's. I mentioned this to Gunter at the time and at first, he wasn't too keen about the idea, but he did, I must say, warm to it sometime later. Now I am wondering whether to pursue it or not.'

'It is not for me to judge, Weiner, but I would think it best if you left things as they are. After all there has to come a time when only the past can take care of the past.'

'Yes, I think that is what Gunter and I might have to conclude. But, forgetting all that for a moment, let me change the subject completely and ask you about something that came up in the conversation between us. Why is it that you have never married?'

'Yes, that does tend to turn things around rather abruptly, I must say, Weiner, and reluctant as I am to talk about myself, I could hardly not answer you, in view of your complete openness towards me. I suppose you must see me as a confirmed bachelor, or even perhaps someone who is a little odd. But I am really just someone who has never really found the right someone.'

'So you are not without interest in the ladies?'

'No, as a matter of fact I enjoy female company, but the older I get the more selective I become. There was a young woman I knew a few years ago whom I might have married, but it wasn't to be, so now I prefer to leave things as they are. But of one thing I am certain, she would never have been another Ellie.'

'Or even another Lorrett, Gregg?'

The two travelling companions glanced sideways at each other for a moment without a further word.

Weiner turned the car off the main road and began weaving his way through the now increasing flow of traffic.

'According to my calculations we should be in Nürnberg in about fifteen minutes, so do you want to find the home straight away, or do you propose having something to eat and drink first?'

'I do like to get my priorities right, and having starved ourselves for the last five days, it has to be food first, if that's all right with you?'

Weiner laughed. 'The trouble with you is that you burn up anything you eat with all that nervous energy of yours. I can see I shall have to show you how to calm down and live a little.'

'So what have we been doing for the last few days, Weiner, marking time?'

'No, but I think we could do with a lot more of it. But joking aside, I must say that this has all been such a fantastic experience for me and I am at last beginning to rid myself of the guilt I have always felt by neglecting to carry out the promise I made to Ellie.'

'I see no reason for you to feel guilty, Weiner; you may have made the odd mistake or two, but is that so bad? After, all, if there is to be a judgement day for each of us, how many of us will report to the Boss with a completely clean shirt and underpants?'

'Well that's a great worry off my mind, I must say, for I was just beginning to wonder how I was going to get my dirty washing done this week.'

'Yes, Mr Jefferson, we do have a Mrs Mollen here and whilst we are quite happy for her to have visitors, may I ask the reason for your visit? You see, we try to ensure that our residents are not subjected to too much stress.'

'I endorse your concern, Warden, but we are not in any way the bearers of bad news. We would just like to have a chat with her about her past and perhaps, more specifically, her daughter.'

'Well, I am sure that will not be too upsetting, but may I ask you to be just a little careful with her?'

'By all means, Warden.'

'That's good and thank you for your consideration. Now, if you would like to sit down a moment, I will let Mrs Mollen know you are here.'

It was some five minutes later that the Warden returned and invited them to follow her. A rather stoop shouldered, white haired old lady sat half bent in her wheelchair as her two visitors were shown into the room.

'These are the two gentlemen I spoke of, Mrs Mollen. This is Mr Jefferson and this Dr Kraske, but they would prefer it if you would know them as Gregg and Weiner. Now, will you be all right if I leave them with you?'

'Yes, and thank you, Warden.'

Her visitors, each in turn, gently shook the hand of the old lady, then presented her with the large bouquet of flowers they had purchased just prior to their arrival at the home. The Warden accepted them on Mrs Mollen's behalf, then, quietly making her way towards the door, she left the room.

The visitors drew up a chair and sat down, one on each side of the old lady's wheelchair. 'Now, you are sure you don't mind us asking you some questions about your daughter Ellie? Or, if you feel you would sooner not answer some of them, please just say so.'

To the eye, Mrs Mollen certainly showed the signs of age, but the impediment of her years had in no way destroyed the clarity of her mind.

'Young man, no doubt if you were to discuss it with your friend here, he would tell you that the greatest pleasure in life as one gets older is talking about the past. But in a home like this, we all have old age in common, so you find that there is an abundance of talkers, but very few interested listeners. The point I make is that I am only too happy to talk to you, providing that you don't ask me too many personal questions like who my earlier lovers were, or even perhaps, who my recent ones are.'

Both men laughed, but it was Weiner that responded. 'That does disappoint me a little, for I was hoping that you might not have been spoken for.'

'Well Dr Kraske, or as you prefer, Weiner, if I find that I am let down in any way by my current admirers, whoever they may be, you will be the first one I shall call. Now, what is it that you would like to know?'

It was a minute or two before Gregg was able to stop smiling and respond to the question asked.

'Just general things. For example, we both know quite a bit about Ellie whilst she was living in Hamburg, but as a matter of interest, what did she do from the time she left school until the time she left home?'

'She trained and worked in child care at a local nursery.'

'Was she always a happy and contented person?'

'Oh yes, very much so and although I say it myself, we were a very happy family. I was quite sad when she took herself off to Hamburg, for I felt as if I had lost both a daughter and a wonderful friend.'

'But that didn't cause any animosity between you.'

'No, not at all. Of course I would have preferred it if she had stayed at home, but I understood her reasoning, for it was quite obvious that she was very much in love with Hans. It is strange though, isn't it, how that little word "if" can have so much relevance to people's lives, for if Ellie had not left home she would probably still be alive today. You see, our house was fortunately unaffected by the war.'

'I think it is that same "if" that has brought us here today, Mrs Mollen, for I am told that you know a mutual friend of ours, Anton Fuller, who from what I can gather, has visited you on the odd occasion or two.'

'Yes, he has been here to see me several times and has continued to be very kind to me over the years, so much so, that I often get flowers or a basket of fruit from him via our local supplier. In fact, it was only through Anton visiting me after the war that I was to learn of Ellie's life in Hamburg and, sadly, how she was killed in a bombing raid.'

'So did he also tell you how she had devoted much of her time to soldiers who had been either wounded or mentally scarred by the twists of war?'

'Yes, but I wasn't surprised at that, for she was a radiantly receptive and compassionate young woman who always had time for, and empathy with, disadvantaged people, children and, of course, animals. You see, she had always been that little bit different even as a child, for there was never the greediness that you often find with some children and she never had tantrums or things like that. Mind you, she did have this ability to pre-empt things, so I suppose whenever she saw the possibility of conflict arising out of a situation, she instinctively kept out of the way. I have often wondered since whether this foresight of hers in later years enabled her to realise who her real mother was.'

'I am sorry, Mrs Mollen, I am not quite with you. Are you saying Ellie was not your daughter?'

'Legally she was, yes, but she was an adopted child, did you not know?'

'No, we didn't, so you are suggesting that Ellie followed in the footsteps of someone other than yourself?'

'Oh, I am sure that we, that is I and my husband, influenced her life in many ways, but of course any genetic characteristics such as those we have been talking about obviously came from her real parents.'

'Did you ever know her real parents?'

'I never knew the father, but her mother and I had been friends since our late teens.'

'Do you think you could tell us as much as you know about the mother and how it was that you came to adopt her child?'

'Yes, providing you are prepared to bear with me, for my memory is not as good as it was and I wouldn't want to bore you.'

'I can assure you we shall not get bored, Mrs Mollen.'

'Well, seeing me now, it is perhaps hard for you to believe that I was once a professional dancer. Mind you, that was not the first job I had as a young woman. Let me see now, it must have been around 1910 when I first broke into show business and that was in the chorus line of a second rate night club in Paris. I was nearly twenty years of age at the time and as I had been living at home with my parents, some distance from Paris, I had to leave home and find myself somewhere to live.

'Suffice it to say, that on the limited wage I earned at the time, this was to be just one room at the top of a large four-storeyed house in old Montmartre. The place itself was to say the least quite dilapidated, but it was somewhere to lay your head and, more essentially, it was cheap. This no doubt was the reason why it housed some thirty other people, most of whom were striving artists such as painters, sculptors and musicians.

'Having had a humble but loving upbringing, I would not normally have chosen to live there, but it had its compensations. For any despondency that might have come from living in such a place was soon placated by this ever present feeling of creative vibrancy, which somehow seemed to fill the whole house with an atmosphere of hope and youthful expectancy. I am only telling you this because, without this bond of companionship, this blend of laughter and happiness that we all seemed to gain from each other in those days, I might never have known Ellie or her mother. You see, by sharing the building with so many others as I did, there was always this underlying feeling that help was near to hand if anyone had the need to call upon it and it was this that was to bring us together as friends. The room opposite mine, across the landing, was occupied by a young girl whom I would only ever see on rare occasions. Usually this would be either as we passed on the stairs or along the passage, but wherever it was, we would always nod and say hello. Now, doing two and sometimes three shows a night, I didn't get home until the early hours of the morning, so it was perhaps understandable why I hadn't got to know my neighbour better, but things were about to change.

'I can remember the events of that night so well, for just as I was climbing the last flight of stairs to my room, there was quite a rumpus coming from my neighbour's flat. I then heard a few loud thuds, followed by a series of screams, so I started to bang on her door. Suddenly the door opened and a man came barging out of the room before speedily running off down the stairs. Without any hesitation, I went into the room only to find my young neighbour in a state of nervous shock and as white as a sheet. After I had calmed her down, she told me how she had been attacked by the man who had just made off in hurry. Well, I took her into my room, made her a hot drink and gradually, she began to tell me exactly what had happened.

'To cut a long story short, the young girl, whose name was Yvette, had only been living in Paris for about four months and like me, she had gone there to find a job in one of the clubs, as a singer. Having been unable to get an audition, she looked around for any other work that was going but, failing to find anything, she decided in desperation to try prostitution. It was, however, unfortunate that her first client was someone who had been paid by a number of other prostitutes to frighten Yvette off their patch. Well, I befriended her and suggested that if she gave up all further attempts to earn a living in that way, I would try to get her a job at the club where I danced. So it happened, that within two weeks, Yvette was put to work in the kitchens of the club and this was to be the beginning of our often distant, but consistent, friendship.

'It must have been some two years later, that I was taken on as a troupe leader at one of the top night spots in Paris, just off the Champs Elysées. Naturally, I continued to see Yvette on rare occasions, but I had a very busy life so these meetings became less frequent as time went by. Now, how it happened I don't know, but Yvette did eventually get an audition and subsequently she became very popular as a singer in many of the clubs around the Moulin Rouge area of Paris.

'Well, I managed to see her show one night and there was no doubt about it, she was a very good all round entertainer. But looking back now, I think perhaps that it was her choice of songs that gave her the eventual success that she so much wanted and not particularly her voice. You see, it wasn't a voice that had romantic appeal and yet it certainly stirred up a great deal of emotion within you. For when she sang, it was with the passion and pathos of someone who had really known the pangs of hunger and the despair of poverty, that both she and I had ourselves experienced. It was a voice that had a certain guttural quality about it, a voice that seemingly appeared to remind the bourgeoisie who frequented these clubs of their own plebeian beginnings.'

There was a knock on the door and the Warden entered the room with the flowers now arranged in a vase. In the moments of interruption Gregg pondered over what Mrs Mollen had just said, for there was this element of similarity that seemed to be emerging between the grandmother, the mother and the daughter. Did this mean that his friend Weiner was right and that there was a connection between the past and Lorrett's present condition?'

The old lady waited for the Warden to leave, then, after admiring the flowers for a moment, she again took up her story.

'Now where was I? Oh yes, I had just finished telling you about Yvette. Well, as time went by, I found myself a nicer place in which to live just off the Rue de Lafayette, for, as good fortune would have it, my income had improved quite considerably and because of my work, I was mixing with a different class of people. You see, as dancers, we were often invited out to parties or functions, some of which were quite big affairs, so you could easily find yourself talking to, or rubbing shoulders with, a contrasting and varied number of people. For instance, I did at one time have the pleasure of meeting with, and talking to, the artist Toulouse-Lautrec; on another occasion I shared an evening with some friends and a number of hopeful politicians, two of whom were to become quite famous over the years that followed.

'Even if I tried, I don't think I could describe the excitement and thrill that I felt, by just being there in Paris in those early years of my life, for if you had clawed your way up from the lowest level of society, as Yvette and I had done, you just couldn't ignore the feeling of privilege that seemed to overwhelm you from time to time.

'It was in 1912 that I first met my husband to be. He was a German who came from Hersbrück, but who at the time was working and living in Paris. He was, in fact, the manager of an international company that had its base in Germany and offices in Paris and I was introduced to him at one of his company's functions. Needless to say, we fell in love and were married in the December of that same year.

'Well, within three months of being married and due mainly to the unsettled situation that was developing prior to the 1914–18 war, my husband was called back to Germany, so I naturally gave up my job as a dancer and settled down in Hersbrück as a housewife. Yvette and I wrote to each other for about a year after that, although like Ellie, I was never one for writing letters. However, once the great war in 1914 began, there was a restriction on cross border letters, so there was little point in continuing to write. But as a regular subscriber to a show business magazine, I often came across the odd article or two where Yvette's name was mentioned, so I knew that she was still pursuing her career.

'Soon after the war ended, we began to correspond again and in early 1919, I was to receive a letter from her that was to turn my world completely upside down. You see, Yvette had become pregnant and as she wasn't married, she wrote saying that she was thinking of having an abortion. Ironically, I had myself been told that because of some irregularity, I was unable to have children, so my husband and I asked Yvette if we could adopt the child. Well, it was agreed in principle, so I went off to Paris just prior to the birth and looked after the mother until Ellie was born. Some six weeks after the birth, my husband came to see the baby before finally making up his mind about the adoption. He saw and loved her immediately, so we went ahead with our plan to adopt her.

'As the years went by, the letters from Yvette became less frequent, for she was by that time singing regularly with a band who were touring France and other European countries. She did however visit us at home on three occasions over the years. Looking back at the last time she came to see us, I remember thinking how lonely she seemed and I couldn't help but wonder whether she ever regretted giving up Ellie for she would play with her for hours on end. Thinking about it now, I am sure that, given the chance, she would have loved to have just settled down to become a wife and a mother, but alas, she never did find her Mr Right.'

Gregg and Weiner had remained silent, content to listen to the old lady's story, for it was, even without its relevance to their visit, a fascinating insight into the young life of someone who was herself something of a fascinating character. It was Gregg who opened up the conversation again.

'Thank you for telling us all that you have, Mrs Mollen. Now, you say that Yvette came to your home on some three different occasions, so obviously she saw the child each time she came, but from what I gather by your earlier remark, you never told Ellie that Yvette was her real mother.'

'No, you see we had planned to tell her that she was an adopted child when she reached fifteen, but at the time of Yvette's last visit, Ellie was only eleven years of age. I have, of course, often wondered whether I should have told Ellie that Yvette was her real mother, for sadly, Yvette died not long after that last visit to us. But I wasn't to know of it until some time after her death and even then, I only found out in an indirect way.'

'What, if any, was Ellie's reaction to Yvette when they met?'

'Well, the first time very little; we just casually told Ellie that she was her Auntie Yvette and left it at that. But on Yvette's second visit, there was quite an emotional attachment between the two of them. Now, whether it was something instinctive I don't know, but from that time on, Ellie would always be asking questions about her Auntie Yvette.'

It was Weiner who spoke next. 'So presumably you told Ellie of her adoption some years after Yvette's death, but from what you have said, she never knew that Yvette was in fact her real mother.'

'No, she was never told who her real mother was. You see, we were afraid that Ellie might turn against us if she found out that her mother had in fact been her Aunt Yvette.'

'Yes, it was a very awkward situation for you, I must say. Tell me, did you ever find out the cause of Yvette's death?'

'Yes, eventually, but I would prefer not to talk about it if you don't mind.'

'We don't mind at all, Mrs Mollen; in fact, it is very nice of you to answer any of our questions. To change the subject, can I ask whether Ellie ever wrote to you while she was in Hamburg? You see, as a military doctor stationed near Hamburg, I knew Ellie for some time throughout the war, but she rarely spoke about her home life, in those days.'

'Well, yes, she did write to me at times but, like me, she was not the most ardent of writers, so her letters were brief and generally only touched upon day to day things. She always wanted to know if everything was all right at home and things like that. You see, Ellie was inclined to be a little bit self sufficient at times, so I didn't worry too much if there were long gaps between her letters.'

But did Ellie ever tell Mrs Mollen that she had a baby, Gregg wondered. It was on his lips ready to ask, when he remembered the Warden's earlier request. He hesitated for a moment, then decided he would wait for a more suitable time to pose the question.

'Ellie's friendship with Hans, Mrs Mollen, did you approve of it?'

'Very much so. He was a very nice young man and they would have made a lovely couple had they both lived. I don't know whether you are aware of it or not, but Hans was quite a brilliant pianist and had only just finished composing his first major work before being called up for the army. I remember, at the time, it was thought that he had a great future in the world of music.'

'We had been told of his talent, but we knew nothing of his composing skills, Mrs Mollen. It is sad to hear about the loss of any life, but perhaps even more so when a life with so much talent is simply wasted in such a futile way. Did you know his parents at all?'

'Not well, for I only met his mother twice; his father, you see, had died when Hans was quite young. In fact, the first time I met his mother was just before the end of the war, when she came to tell me that Hans had been killed. She quite rightly thought, of course, that I was the best person to tell Ellie of his death and I, believing that Ellie was still in Hamburg, said I would write and tell her the bad news. Of course, neither of us knew at that time that Ellie herself had died in a bombing raid some months earlier. The only other time the mother and I met was when she picked me up in her car one day and took me to see where Hans was buried.'

'Can you remember where that was, Mrs Mollen?'

'I know that it was in a military cemetery somewhere near Münster but that is about all.'

'Did the mother ever tell you how Hans was killed?'

'No, for she was never told herself. Apparently all she had telling them of his death was a telegram saying that he had been killed in action, but she never knew where he was buried until just after the end of the war.'

Gregg was not about to lose the chance of asking the one question that had been on his mind since reading Ellie's letter. 'A difficult one now, Mrs Mollen. You wouldn't happen to know the date of his death, would you?'

'That's not difficult at all; you see, as soon as I saw his grave I mentioned the coincidence to his mother, for it was, you see, the same date as my wedding anniversary, 7th December.'

'Would that be 7th December 1944?'

'Yes, for, as his mother remarked on returning home from the cemetery that day, 'Just six months more and he would have survived the war.'

It was neither the place nor the time for Weiner to comment on what had just been said, although he was sure that his friend was now at last positively convinced of Ellie's extra-sensory powers. It was, after all, exactly as Ellie had implied in her letter and the only reason that she had taken her own life that day, but even he, Weiner, found it difficult to believe that his own long held convictions had at last proved to be true.

'You mentioned earlier, Mrs Mollen, that Ellie often anticipated things, so would you say that she was capable of predicting an event or a situation some considerable time before it actually occurred? For instance, perhaps a year or more before?'

'I don't ever recollect it going that far, but certainly at times she knew what I was about to say before I said it, or she would know that I was going somewhere before I had even thought about it myself.'

'Did you not feel that there was something unusual in that?'

'No, not really, for she was like her mother in that way. She too had this knack of pre-empting things, although, now I think about it, not to the same extent. I suppose at the time I saw it as nothing more than just one of her little characteristics, so I never gave it a great deal of thought.'

It was Gregg who made the next enquiry.

'Do you happen to have a photograph of Ellie, Mrs Mollen?'

'Yes, several, but if you want to see them, I shall have to ask you to move your chair a little.'

The old lady eased her wheelchair over to a bedside cabinet and took out a large brown folder secured by three elastic bands. She slid off the bands and began rummaging through the yellowing old papers and photographs inside.

'There you are, that is a photograph of both Ellie and Hans taken just before he went off to war.'

Gregg reached out with the excitement of a youngster who had just been offered a bag of his favourite sweets. He took the sepia coloured photograph from Mrs Mollen and without any hesitation focused his eyes immediately on Weiner's Ellie. She was as beautiful as he had imagined she would be and so much like her daughter that he was taken aback. She had the same oriental mystique about the eyes, the same high cheek-boned face, and the same slender neck that Lorrett had; it was as if one face had been die cast from the mould of the other. He lingered over the photograph as one might over a much treasured possession, totally captivated by the vision of someone he felt he had known all his life.

Weiner sat impatiently, waiting to view the photograph.

'You don't want to see this, do you, Weiner?' Gregg smilingly teased his companion a little before passing it over to him.

'Can you now see the likeness between Ellie and Lorrett, Gregg?'

'Yes, it's uncanny, isn't it, they both . . .' Gregg abruptly stopped mid sentence, for he was suddenly aware of their error and began to wonder whether Mrs Mollen had picked it up. He didn't have to wait long to find out.

'Excuse me, but who is this Lorrett you speak of?'

Gregg, noticing Weiner's hesitancy, realised that he couldn't now avoid answering the question he had refrained from asking earlier.

'Mrs Mollen, were you ever told that Ellie had a child?'

'No, I wasn't.' It was immediately obvious that the news had shaken the old lady, so Gregg paused for some moments before continuing.

'I am sorry if the news has shocked you, Mrs Mollen, but Ellie had the baby in May 1944. It was a little girl and Hans was the father. As for the rest of the facts, they are a little more complex, so do you want to hear them?'

'Yes, I think I should; after all, I suppose, it is in my interest.'

Gregg, ever conscious of the Warden's request, went on to tell how Ellie had in fact committed suicide, how the baby had survived and the reason for their visit that day. It was some time before he had finished his resumé and went on to ask another question.

'How do you feel now, Mrs Mollen, knowing that you have a grandchild?'

'I am not really sure; naturally I am pleased over the news, but I am now also a little worried. For from what you have told me, it would appear that history really does have a way of repeating itself.'

'I don't think I follow you, Mrs Mollen?'

'I am sorry, it's just that since learning about Ellie, I am now forced to tell you something which I had hoped not to mention. You see, Yvette also committed suicide. So knowing that I have a grandchild delights me in one way, but makes me fearful of her future in another; you see, your news now has dual implications.'

'I can see what you mean, Mrs Mollen; you are worried that Lorrett might follow the trend of both her real mother and her grandmother. Well, we can only hope that she won't, Mrs Mollen, and we can only do our best to make sure that things don't turn out that way.'

'I too can only hope along with you, Gregg, but perhaps I should continue to look on the bright side of things, which is what I have always done in the past. After all, it seems as if I have a family to consider now.'

'As you seem quite happy to continue, I would like to ask you about a poem that was written on a piece of paper Ellie had. From what we are able to make out, it appears to have been written some time between the wars, and I am wondering whether you know how she came by it?'

'Now you are asking a lot of my memory, although, thinking back, Ellie did like me to read poetry to her when she was young. Perhaps, if I saw it again, I might be able to recognise it.'

Gregg, not realising that Weiner had the piece of paper with him, was quite surprised to see him take it from his inside pocket and show it to Mrs Mollen.

'How strange, yes, it is a poem that Yvette gave her the last time she came to see us; in fact, it was Ellie's favourite poem. I say strange, partly because I am wondering why she should have given it to you.'

'That is precisely what we have been asking ourselves, Mrs Mollen, but would you happen to know how Yvette came to be in possession of it?'

'I only know that it was given to her by someone she was very fond of, sometime after the great war, that is all.'

'Not to worry, it was just something that has intrigued Gregg and myself. Let me ask, did Ellie like to sing when she was young?'

'Oh, yes, but perhaps more so after hearing her Auntie sing on the radio a couple of times. Then, when Yvette stayed with us for those few days at the time of her last visit, Ellie kept asking her to sing different songs, so that she could join in with her.'

'Did you know that Ellie sang in a night club when she was in Hamburg?'

'Yes, Anton told me, and from what I gathered, she was quite well liked by the clients and many of the troops stationed there at the time.'

'I think well liked is perhaps an understatement, Mrs Mollen, for Ellie was loved by most of those that knew her and I hasten to suggest that even today, she is more than just a memory to many people.'

Gregg, realising that it couldn't be far off Mrs Mollen's bedtime and feeling certain that all the questions that he had wanted to ask had in fact been dealt with, decided it was time to make their departure.

'Weiner, if it is all right with you and you have no more questions, I think we should leave our hostess in peace. Before we do, Mrs Mollen, we should both like to thank you for seeing us and I leave you with the promise that when Lorrett is well again, I will personally ensure that you will be one of the first people she comes to see.'

'That will certainly be something to look forward to, but better still, why not put on a show for Lorrett over here, then I might be prepared to offer my services to you as a top rate dancer!'

The two friends left the old people's home with a wide grin on their faces and, after making some enquiries, found themselves a hotel for the night. In view of their long drive and the sensitive nature of their interview with Mrs Mollen, they were content to forego any further requirement for food and both happily agreed to seek out their beds.

Weiner who had been up some two hours, had enjoyed a full breakfast and was comfortably sitting in the lounge of the hotel reading a newspaper when Gregg came in.

'Ah, there you are, Weiner. I have been knocking on your door; I should have realised you would be down early for your breakfast, that's assuming that you have had it, of course.'

'In the little time I have known you, Gregg, I have never found you to be an assumer, but you are quite right; yes, I have had it, but obviously you haven't had yours?'

'No, unlike you, my friend, I have no antagonism towards my bed and I have also been quite busy on the phone for the last thirty minutes.'

'If I am not being too inquisitive, may I ask who you were phoning?'

'It was in fact two phone calls, one to John Moffit and the other to my boss Robbie. By the way, John has received that report that I completed last Sunday evening before all that drinking at the club began. Again he had nothing specific to say about Lorrett's condition, other than that there has been no change in her situation. As for my boss, well, he has now asked me if I can complete what I have been doing here and nip off to the USA for a couple of months. Apparently he is considering another series along the lines of our last one, but based upon the US air force and the RAF during the war.'

'What a busy man you are, Gregg. Now, I won't ask you if you need an assistant, for I know you will be only too glad to see the back of me.'

'Not true, not true at all, my friend, but whilst I have no intention of letting this problem with Lorrett rest, I do think that I am near the end of my research and it will be nice to give my brain an airing after all this confusion.'

'But will you be leaving convinced of Ellie's gift, I ask myself?'

Gregg sat down in an armchair to one side of his friend. 'Certainly convinced, Weiner, but still quite ignorant about the nature of things.'

'Both you and I Gregg, but at times ignorance can be bliss, so just accept it, otherwise you will always be trying to find the rainbow's end.'

'A satisfactory end to Lorrett's problem would be enough for me at the moment, but I must say I was quite enthralled by our Mrs Mollen last evening. Isn't she a lovely old lady?'

'Yes, so much so, it is hard to believe that Ellie wasn't really her daughter. I am sure, however, the old lady was right, when she suggested that Ellie might have come to realise that Yvette was her real mother.'

'The old lady was very quick in recognising the possible implications arising out of the mother's and grandmother's suicides, wasn't she?'

'Yes, but her thinking is perhaps somewhat traditional, for it was often thought that mental problems were inherited, so she probably sees suicide in the same light.'

'Something else that puzzles me, Weiner. Why didn't Hans write to tell his mother that they had a child and, hand in hand with this, why didn't Ellie write and tell Mrs Mollen of the birth?'

'I am sure that Hans was otherwise preoccupied at the time; after all, he was with an armoured division stationed near the French coast, just as the Allied invasion began. As to Ellie's failure, well, that is anyone's guess, but somehow, I am sure she did either write to Mrs Mollen, or, for her own reasons, chose not to. But returning to your favourite part of the body, Gregg, shall I get you a coffee and something to eat?'

'That would be nice, Weiner; thinking about it now, I was beginning to wonder why I am not myself this morning.'

Weiner called over one of the nearby bar staff and it seemed like only moments before he returned with a large pot of coffee and the necessary china for two.

'Well, here's hoping the coffee and these rather nice biscuits put you back on the road to recovery, Gregg!'

'Going back to the poem, Weiner and being told how Yvette was given it by someone she was quite fond of, I wonder whether that someone was in fact the father of Ellie?'

'It might have been, of course, but on the other hand it could just as easily have been another woman who gave it to her. But as you are in this conjectural frame of mind, what about the other end of this speculative scale? Yvette, according to Mrs Mollen, was a resident singer with a dance band sometime between the late twenties and early thirties, so one might look to find a possible connection between the composer of the song and Yvette's piece of poetry. I also ask myself why Yvette gave Ellie the poem in the first place, especially in view of her suicide later on.'

'I know, Weiner, so many questions still remain unanswered, but that aside for a moment, I have to say that one of the things that has impressed me so much since we first met was this absolute contradiction between what I expected to find and what I have actually found. You see, at times we are all guilty of having deeply entrenched opinions about things that in many cases have merely developed from our own first impression of something or from the heresay evidence of someone else. So I have to admit that over the years I have at times had these wrongly conceived beliefs about the German people. Now I can see how foolish I have been. You see, meeting you, Gunter, Mrs Mollen and all the other wonderful people that I have come into contact with has been such a memorable experience for me, an experience that has taught me a lot about myself and at the same time has given me a great deal of hope for the future.'

'I would suggest, Gregg, that what you have also found is an ideal and that ideal is Ellie, and that what you have really experienced is the spirit of Ellie.'

'Yes, you are right. So what was it that made her what she was, I keep asking myself?'

'Ah, now that is a difficult one. Mind you, you can see how she must have inherited part of her character from her mother Yvette, for she, living on the fringe of survival as she did, had obviously developed this acute sense of awareness from the world of poverty in which she grew up and from the others who shared her existence on the back streets of Paris in those days.

'Then, I am sure that the daughter of this highly perceptive Yvette was nurtured and no doubt treasured by the spirited but level-headed Mrs Mollen who raised and influenced her with the love and patience of a very devoted adoptive mother. Then perhaps, as Ellie grew up, this perceptive quality that she had inherited from her natural mother began to develop into something more than just an actuation of her inheritance. I think it became this gift we have talked about, this ability to anticipate things, this inexplicable cogency to foresee or change things, or, as I have said before, this gift of extra-sensory perception. I think we have also seen how Ellie must have had an instinctive affinity with Yvette from the second time that they met. They both liked poetry, they both loved to sing, so inevitably, there was this immediate compatibility between them. Of course, it is even possible that when they sang together, at the time of Yvette's last visit, the eleven-year-old Ellie subconsciously aligned herself with Yvette and the type of songs that she sang. We then find that Ellie worked with children for some years and I think it was here that she, as a receptive young woman, became imbued with this inner sense of compassion and humility. She then meets and falls in love with Hans who, as we know, must have been quite a sensitive type of individual himself. He and circumstance were to direct her path towards Hamburg and this concern she was to find for the wounded, and now some twenty-five years later we are sitting here wondering how it all came to be.'

'But why this rather angelic figure that I see her as today, Weiner?'

'The war, the war and all its contingencies, Gregg. You see, what I have just tried to summarise for you is what I see as Ellie's apprenticeship in life, but this adorable young woman who was eventually to become our beloved Ellie Mollen simply thrived and grew in eminence out of the turmoil and remnants of other people's lives in war-torn Hamburg.'

'I hasten to suggest, that you have omitted the most important ingredient from that last remark of yours, Weiner. You see, very much like me, Ellie still had a lot to learn about life, but fortunately she had a lovely voice and she loved the song "Lilli Marlene". Well, it was to be this simple combination of both singer and song that was to help her find this missing ingredient I talk of and that was you, Weiner. For it was your meeting with Ellie in those years of war that fashioned this young woman into becoming a legend, the legend that we speak of today, the lovely Ellie Mollen.'

'Gregg, through my embarrassment I must disagree with you for the first time since we met, for in truth, she was a product of her own yesterdays, just as we all are. But this conveniently brings me to the question, what are your plans now?'

'Well, that partly depends on you. You see, I have to write out my final report to John Moffit before I leave for the USA in three days' time. But I have to take the car back to Johanna first, so I shall fly off from Hamburg. Now shall I drive you home, say tomorrow, or have you something else in mind?'

'I think I will return to Hamburg and spend another few days with Gunter, for we have quite a lot to talk over. You see, whilst we were there, he suggested that I should sell up at home and go to live near him, just outside Hamburg. He would also like me to become a part time public relations manager for the hotel and club. So I have a great deal of thinking to do, but whatever the outcome, I am definitely going to make an advance booking for Lorrett to appear at the club sometime later this year.'

'What profound optimism you have, Weiner, but why not, for I am sure there has to be a simple solution to her problems.'

'But there is also the point, Gregg, that by making the booking, I know that you will be back and our friendship will not simply end here.'

Chapter Seven

'Gregg, how nice to see you again. Come along in and sit yourself down. You remember Dr Linley, don't you?'

Gregg renewed his acquaintance with the quiet, unassuming doctor, then, moving across the room, he sought out the armchair he had used at the time of his previous visit to the nursing home.

'How do you like being back in England again after your month or so in Germany and the nine weeks, was it, you spent in the States?'

'It was actually nearer to ten than nine, John, but it is very nice to be back with the team again, albeit I do now have a rather large pile of paperwork that requires my attention.'

'I will not ask if you enjoyed the holiday part of your time in Germany, for if the reports you sent me are anything to go by, I very much doubt if you had that much time in which to relax. I must, however, compliment you on the quality of those reports, for from what I can gather you recorded virtually everything that was said between you and the different people you came into contact with.'

'Yes it was quite a task, I must admit, but it was a memorable experience as well. You see, there was a certain sense of satisfaction in researching Lorrett's past and talking with those who knew of her.'

'I can understand that and it is quite obvious from those reports of yours that you asked all the right questions. But I have to say, I would never have expected your enquiries to have unearthed such a strange turn of events.'

'But in the end, were my findings of any use to you, John, and, perhaps more importantly, have they helped in any way towards finding a solution to Lorrett's problem?'

'Oh yes, there isn't any doubt about that, although perhaps they fulfil their purpose in more of a roundabout way than either of us would have thought possible, but I will come to that later.'

'How is Lorrett, John? It seems like ages since I saw her last.'

'You will be able to find out for yourself soon, Gregg, but I am pleased to say things do seem to be moving in the right direction. One thing is certain, any progress we have made is only as a result of your persuasive ways, for again you were able to break down those mental barriers that we have talked about before.'

'That was as much luck as anything else, although I thought my luck was running out when I first met Weiner. You see, he did look rather formidable standing there in his brown tweed suit, leather leggings and heavy brown boots. But he turned out to be a very gentle and intelligent giant, a really lovely man. In truth, all of the people I met were very nice and even in her absence, Lorrett has already made many friends in Germany. They are now all waiting to meet her and, hopefully, to hear her sing.'

'From what I gather, it was you that made the friends, which is understandable for I am sure people see you as a fellow well met.'

'I don't know about that, but I certainly didn't want to antagonise anyone, for Lorrett's sake. You see, I cling to the hope that perhaps with a fair wind and a good psychiatrist behind her, she might one day still be able to become a really top rate singer.'

'There is no "might" about it, Gregg. I think she still has every chance to be so; in fact, I am almost confident about it, but we still have some way to go. That aside, I do have the feeling that by helping Lorrett, you may have also helped yourself in some way.'

'I am sorry, John, I am not sure I understand your remark, for as far as I can recall I have done nothing to warrant it.'

'I can vouch for that myself, Gregg, but I was merely pointing out that if my thinking is correct, your efforts may be well rewarded in the end, though I am not in any way suggesting that you intentionally set out to reap any reward from those efforts. But let's put that aside and concentrate on the content of these reports you sent me, for who would have thought that so much detail could have emerged from such a simple exercise.'

'Speaking for myself, I found the compounding amount of detail quite confusing and even now I still have difficulty in believing it all.'

'Well, both Dr Linley and myself would have some agreement with you on that, for, to us, it seems as if you have virtually gone out and relived Lorrett's past. But we are at least now able to recognise that we have been dealing with a very unusual and mysterious train of events. So much so and without wishing to add further to your confusion, that we are of the opinion that there is a rather uncanny and impersonal feature about the whole of this case. By this I mean that we have in fact very little to show for our involvement this far. We have many theories as to how her condition might have come about and I believe I can put my finger on a possible reason for it, but I don't think we shall ever really know all there is to know about her problem.'

'So are you saying that you cannot solve it, John?'

'No, but solving it is only a part of our brief: we also need to understand it and, to be perfectly honest with you, I am not sure at the moment whether we ever will. But let me return to these reports of yours and to our friend Weiner, for from what you have said, I get the impression that he is a rather outgoing character, would that be so?'

'He is possibly, at times, but generally speaking I would say that he is quite a serious person, who for much of the time comes over as a sincere and retiring type of individual. Nevertheless, he can be quite funny, although perhaps his humour does have a satirical edge to it.'

'So he is not the over demonstrative type who insists that you believe everything he tells you?'

'No, no, he is a down to earth hard facts man, albeit listening to him as he told me about Ellie was a little like listening to an intellectual trying to explain a fairy story to a child.'

'So was this listening child convinced in the end?'

'At first, no; in fact at one stage I did say to Weiner that there was little point in continuing with my research, but then, when I met Anton and he quite casually mentioned that Hans had been killed in the war, I was so taken back that I had to follow through with my enquiries. As a matter of interest, John, what was your reaction when you read that copy of Ellie's letter I sent you?'

'Initially, I suppose, a little cynical, but after reading it through several times I could see its possible connection with Lorrett's problem. But I think the thing that has struck me the most about your research is the way that the song has continued to link so many people with their past. It is of course a recognised fact that a song or a piece of music can act as a trigger to a person's half forgotten memories, but it has been a great deal more than that in this case. It has been like an adhesive that has somehow invisibly bonded people together without them ever knowing it. Even stranger is the possibility that one of those soldiers in the pub that night might easily have been your father, Gregg.'

'Yes, that is strange, so much so that I have now convinced myself that he must have been one of them.'

'Had you gone beyond that and thought how this research which you have been carrying out could in some strange way be as much about you as it has been about Lorrett?'

'We are not back to this self interest thing you referred to earlier, are we, John?'

'No, not particularly, but if I am to bring Lorrett's problem to a satisfactory conclusion, you are going to have to recognise that you have by association become a part of it. Now I don't wish to pursue this point any further at the moment, but we shall need to come back to it a little later.'

'By all means, John, although I still don't see what you are getting at.'

'You are obviously missing the point at the moment, but let me digress a little and ask, did you manage to find out anything more on that poem of Yvette's?'

'No, but in that last report of mine, I did mention how both Weiner and I speculated over its possible origin.'

'Yes, I am aware of that. I just thought perhaps you may have learned something more about it after having that conversation with Mrs Mollen. Not to worry, but going back to those reports of yours, had you noticed how some of the detail you researched has a way of repeating itself?'

'I am sorry, John, you have lost me!'

'You know how some people think that incidents in their lives often happen in threes: well, strangely enough, this applies to some of the facts mentioned in your reports. For instance, speaking collectively, I was first struck by the fact that all three women, Yvette, Ellie and Lorrett, all loved to sing. They all appear to have been blessed with that same highly developed sensitivity which in Ellie's case seems to have progressed into this phenomenon we call extra-sensory perception; and all three of them have, in one way or another, had sad or disappointing relationships with their menfolk.'

'Well, if you want to add to that, John, what about that point of Mrs Mollen's when she intimated that Lorrett, like both her grandmother and mother, might one day also attempt to commit suicide?'

'Yes, that is quite a valid point and it is something I would like to come back to later, for this is another of those reasons why it is so important for us to understand the whole of Lorrett's problem. You see, until now we have been concentrating our efforts on her recovery, but if we merely solve this part of her dilemma without resolving the stresses which caused it, we could find that we have failed to achieve what we set out to do. However, whilst we are on the subject of family likenesses, let us elucidate on it a little further, for as Weiner said, "Ellie and Lorrett are one and the same". Now perhaps, contrary to your views on Lorrett at the time of our first meeting, I am sure that Weiner is right, for the person you knew prior to the show that night wasn't the real Lorrett, she was only a semblance of her real self. Mind you, I am sure that you had a few snatched glimpses of the real person at times, especially when she was singing on stage that night, but you never really knew her in the true sense of the word. You see, if we can solve this problem of hers completely, I believe that Lorrett will one day be like Ellie, a very happy and delightful person to know. But unlike Ellie, she will not have the need to contemplate her own death, for by then, hopefully, she will have found what she has been looking for.'

'Which seems to suggest that Ellie had no other option than to commit suicide.'

'Yes, I think that is so, for once you accept that Ellie was gifted in the way that Weiner has suggested, it is so easy to understand the reasoning behind most of her actions. For instance, although it may seem impossible to us, she did instinctively know that Hans had died that day and whilst I believe that she had this overpowering desire to follow him, she would not have committed suicide had she not also foreseen the prospect of all their deaths later that same night.'

'So you are now totally convinced of Weiner's belief that Ellie was somehow able to see into the future, John?'

'Yes, although, not knowing Ellie personally, I am unable to evaluate either the scope or the limitations of her gift. However, I once had a patient who had a similar gift, but it wasn't with her all the time and she never knew when or in which way it would manifest itself. But I have to say that, having had two separate telephone conversations with Weiner after you left for the States, I am convinced that her gift, along with the letter Ellie wrote, has been indirectly responsible for Lorrett's problem, for your involvement with it and even perhaps, the final outcome of it. Although that still remains to be seen.'

'I think that all of this is a little beyond me, John.'

'Well, I am no authority on it myself, Gregg, but I have to recognise in my work that there will always be situations which will either totally confuse me, or to put it bluntly, I simply won't understand. However, I hope that by the time that you leave here today, you will at least be able to accept my explanation for many of the strange things that have come out of this case.'

'I can only say, John, that if you yourself are convinced that we are on the right road to finding a cure to Lorrett's problem, then I shall have to agree with whatever you tell me.'

'All right, let me start by suggesting that whilst your efforts have proved to be both relevant and helpful towards the eventual solution of Lorrett's problem, it wasn't so much your findings that led us to conclude as we now do, but rather, those little things you seemed to have missed out. Now, don't go and get hold of the wrong end of the stick for without that information you gave us, we wouldn't ever have found the probable reason for, or the possible cure of, her problem.'

'So a cure is still possible then, John?'

'Yes although perhaps cure is the wrong word. I think "satisfactory result" might be more applicable in this case. You will now have to be patient while I run through the facts with you. Before your arrival here that first time back in June, we, as a team, had decided that Lorrett had in some way suffered a type of catatonic or traumatic shock, so we needed to find out how this had happened. After we had listened to others, you came along to see us and you were eventually able to give us an account of the events covering the show, along with a brief insight into Lorrett's personality. Of the many things that we discussed at that meeting, perhaps the most relevant was that which concerned the atmosphere within the theatre that night and the details you gave to us relating to Lorrett's collapse on stage. Now, whilst you were able to furnish us with such detail, we were unable to do much with it then. However, both the doctor and I found our attention being diverted away from our patient and onto you, for we became fascinated by both the delicacy and the poignancy of the show which you had instigated, and more importantly, we found ourselves interested in you as an individual. So after talking with you for some time that day, we both realised that you were not only responsible for that marvellous show which your team had put on, but that you might also have unknowingly been responsible, in part, for Lorrett's problem.'

'But at the end of that meeting, John, you rejected that idea completely.'

'I know, Gregg, but we had nothing to back up our theory at the time; furthermore, as we were hoping that you would undertake this research for us, we knew that we could pursue the point at some other time. However, by the end of the meeting that day, both the doctor and I were generally to agree on our findings and you had kindly agreed to act as our researcher.

'Now these findings, or conclusions if you will, suggested that Lorrett had quite probably been living in some kind of mental isolation for some time before the show and that if we were eventually to resolve her problem, we would first have to find out quite a bit more about her past. But the thing that bugged us more than anything else at the time was this question of her collapse and precisely what it was that had caused it that night. Now, whilst your research has in fact led us to the reason for her collapse, it didn't actually provide us with it. You see, it was those extra little details that you missed out on that were to eventually give us the answer we had been looking for.'

'Well, I can only apologise, John, but I thought I had covered every bit of information that was available to me.'

'Gregg, I am not in any way criticising what you have done, for both Dr Linley and I, quite foolishly, failed to see something that was staring us in the face. But if you recall, at the end of that first meeting of ours, I suggested that the clue to Lorrett's problem might only be found within those silent or unnoticed moments of her life. Now, whilst you missed out on a couple of things, you succeeded in so many other ways: for instance, you were able to break down the rather strong-willed Mrs Webster. By so doing, she has since become receptive to further questioning and has also been here to see Lorrett on a couple of occasions. This has enabled me to talk with her about both her own life and that of Lorrett's, as a result of which, I was to learn of something that has turned out to be quite relevant to Lorrett's problem. It would appear that when Lorrett was quite small, she often had a rather disturbing dream, but Mrs Webster, knowing that children are often susceptible to bad dreams, quite naturally had never really given it any thought, until I latched on to it.

'Of course, at that early age, the young Lorrett was not able to describe the dream and even if she had been able to do so, it would not have meant anything to Mrs Webster. But as the child grew up, she was to have this dream on several other occasions throughout the years that followed, although it wasn't until she was about eleven that she was able to describe it to Mrs Webster in some detail. Apparently, in the dream, Lorrett first saw the kindly face of a young man, whom she described as being both gentle and friendly, but as the dream progressed the face became increasingly distant, more frightfully distorted and from the child's description, even rather grotesque. The final impact of the dream came when the face gradually broke up into a kind of mosaic of its original self, or, as the eleven-year-old Lorrett explained it, "like a face that had been covered by a spider's web". Now whilst Dr Linley and I felt that the dream might possibly have some relevance to Lorrett's problem, we had no other evidence at that time either to confirm or to contradict our feelings. Then we were to receive that first report of yours from Germany and it was that which gave us the clue to a possible connection between Lorrett's dream and her very confusing collapse on stage that night.'

'I thought that I had questioned Mrs Webster quite well, John, and I can't for the life of me think why she didn't mention the dream at the time I went to see her.'

'She had obviously forgotten all about it. After all, she only mentioned it to me in passing conversation, but, like so many things that we all tend to pass over, this dream sequence was deeply embedded in the back of her mind and perhaps only re-awakened by something I did or by something I said. More importantly, you will see later how this one factor was to play its part in Lorrett's life. But for now, let us look back at some of the other things that were eventually to shake the stability of this comparatively naive young woman.

'I think it would be true to say that Lorrett's life, up to the time she was twenty, was principally that of a happy home-loving young woman, who enjoyed and returned all the love that Mrs Webster and her husband had showered upon her since her adoption after the war. But of course she wasn't to know that she had been adopted until the time came for her to marry her young man, Malcolm Durrant. From your report on Mrs Webster, we can see that Lorrett, as a young woman, was a highly sensitive type of individual, but since your trip to Germany, I am now sure that it goes beyond that and in fact I suspect that she has inherited this sixth sense from her natural mother Ellie. Ironically, Lorrett has never recognised that she had this gift; subsequently it has at times only ever served to confuse and unsettle her. So we find that at the time she was about to get married, she is told of her adoption; furthermore, without actually knowing it, she possibly begins to feel an affinity with the country of her birth, which of course was Germany. A country that by all accounts had at one time openly encouraged the birth of illegitimate children. This, then, is where Lorrett's unhappiness first began.'

'John, I can see how this news of her adoption must have shocked her, but wouldn't she eventually have come to terms with it?'

'Try to put yourself in her situation, Gregg. We have a young woman who had grown up within the security and comfort of a loving and tender upbringing, then she suddenly discovers that she could well have been the bastard child of some dubious war time liaison. It was inevitable that she would react in some way, which, of course we now know, was against the one person who least deserved it, Mrs Webster. Perhaps if Mr Webster had been alive, his presence might have calmed the situation a little, but he wasn't, so it was Mrs Webster who had to bear the brunt of her daughter's sad reactions and the guilt of withholding the truth from her about her adoption.

'You see, Lorrett's world had suddenly been turned upside down and she wasn't really equipped to cope with it. She was undoubtedly quite shaken by the thought of her uncertain origins, she had no way of knowing who her real parents were, and, more importantly, an element of mistrust had begin to seep into her personality. This was to be the beginning of her loss of faith in people and the loss of confidence in herself, so you can perhaps see how this was to affect her proposed plans to marry Malcolm. For it was within this self examining frame of mind that she was to challenge the sincerity of his love by suggesting that they should perhaps postpone their wedding. Now obviously Malcolm, lacking the experience to cope with the immediate impact of such a suggestion, hesitated before attempting to respond. So Lorrett, caught up in this over-sensitive state as she was, saw this as being an indication of his uncertain feelings towards her.'

'Again I don't understand this, for I found him to be a very nice type of individual and, from what I could gather, he appeared to be very fond of Lorrett.'

'I don't for a moment suggest that he was in any way the cause of the breakdown between them, Gregg, I am merely showing you how Lorrett tended to over dramatise things at that time, but let me continue. Within a fortnight of this break up, she decided to leave home and make for London, where, without realising it, she was to undergo a further decline in her mental outlook. She managed first to find a bed-sitter and then a job. To begin with, she possibly felt a degree of exhilaration with this new found freedom, but I am sure that it wasn't long before she began having regrets over leaving the comfort and security of her hitherto happy home. But she had her pride, so she stayed the course and in an endeavour to erase the lonely moments of her life, she joined an operatic society.

'Well, over the years that followed, she was to have one or two other setbacks, but she had at least become moderately successful as a singer with the operatic society, which is how she came to be seen by Martin, who was eventually to become her manager. Martin of course never really saw her as a pop singer, but as pop was the mainstream music of the day, he tried without much success to divert her talents in that direction. But we now know that whilst she failed to make any impact on those in the entertainment business, she was unknowingly to impress at least two characters who had yet to come into her life, one of whom was her now ex-husband, Grant Stevens. To understand why Lorrett married him in the first place confirms how her expectations of life must have been quite low at that time, but marry him she did. Well, some three months or so after the wedding, she did at least find the courage to tell him that she really never loved him. Naturally this wasn't the nicest thing to do, to a rather brand new husband, but without being too unkind to the man, I don't think Stevens was too heart-broken over the situation, for he went along quite comfortably with the divorce that was to follow. But to Lorrett, this was to be yet another stigma, another backward step into this developing abyss of isolation and mental self degradation. The record that Stevens produced for her was played on the radio occasionally, but again, it did nothing to enhance her career, well, not directly that is. But someone who is currently not far away from me must have either heard that record, or have seen her somewhere prior to the planning of that fantastic show, is that so?'

'Yes, in fact, I was to see Lorrett for the first time, strangely enough, on my first day as a researcher with the company. You see, for some unknown reason, she was being shown around our studios at the time and, yes, I did then go out to buy one of her records.'

'So, did you ever find out the reason for her visit there that day?'

'No, John, it is something that I had always meant to ask Lorrett about.'

'But she obviously made an impression on you, for you purchased that record of hers and she was the first person who came to your mind when you were considering singers for that show of yours.'

'Yes, that is so. You see, I liked the sound of her voice, thought that she had a great deal of talent, but realised she was singing the wrong type of songs.'

'That wasn't quite what I meant, Gregg, but let us leave it at that for the moment and continue from where I left off just now. We can see how, over the years since leaving home, Lorrett was to have one setback after another, setbacks that were mainly brought about by her own folly. Nevertheless they all helped to further compound this inability of hers to either rationalise or interpret her own or other people's intentions. Then, from out of the blue, you came along with the offer for her to appear in your show. It is now easy to see how she must have felt at the time, for suddenly spring had replaced winter and once again, she began to find herself wanted, respected and at times perhaps even admired, as she happily and diligently went about rehearsing for that show of yours.'

John Moffit looked at his watch, then glanced across at his silent associate Dr Linley before explaining his sudden change of emphasis. 'Gregg, I am sorry to interrupt my summary of events, but I think it is now the ideal time to take you along to see Lorrett. Before I do, could I ask you to be a little tolerant of my funny ways and do as I ask without questioning my reasoning.'

'It is unusual type of request, John, but yes, whatever you say.'

'Well, it is just that I don't want you to over-react! Oh, don't worry about it, you will soon see what I mean. So, come along, I know you have been itching to see her, since your arrival here this morning.'

The two men left John's office to walk just a few steps along the corridor before arriving at a closed door.

'By the way, Gregg, as you will see, Lorrett is in a private ward for the time being. Shall we go in?'

John opened the door, inviting his guest to lead the way. Gregg walked into the room and as he did he could see Lorrett sitting in a chair over by a distant window. He was about to move forward, when she suddenly stood up and made her way towards him, holding out her hands.

'Gregg, how wonderful to see you again, I am so sorry I have been away for all this time, but I am back now and it is so lovely to see you.'

Gregg was dumbfounded, totally confused and obviously quite shocked, for her once ashened white face was now flushed with colour, her previous silence replaced by the soft gentleness of her voice and her eyes again as clear as crystal. Without inhibition or words, he found himself wrapping his arms around her body and putting his face in close contact to hers.

'Forgive me, Lorrett, but I just don't know what to say, except perhaps, that it is marvellous to see you looking so well again.'

The embrace lingered and John, standing to one side of them, noticed an uncontrolled tear running down Gregg's cheek.

'Gregg.' John had chosen his moment carefully. 'I think you have already met Malcolm here.'

Gregg, not having seen anyone else in the room as he entered, turned in surprise to face the one time boyfriend of the younger Lorrett.

'It is nice to see you again, Mr Jefferson.'

'And you, Malcolm, but please, Gregg is still my name.'

There was a noticeable silence between them, as John again surveyed the scene and in particular, the tell-tale body language of his researcher friend there beside him.

'Lorrett, you won't mind if I take Gregg away from you for a while; you remember, I did say that I wanted this to be just a brief first meeting.'

'Yes, of course, John, I understand.'

'Come on, Gregg, let's go and find a cup of coffee somewhere, for I can see that you are not quite yourself.'

Gregg, who was obviously shaken by the situation and by so many questions left unanswered, felt that he should protest over the brusque way he was being whisked out of the room, but instead, he passively turned to face the couple and said, 'I hope to see you later, Lorrett, and perhaps you also, Malcolm.' Then, in a dazed silence, he followed his mentor back to the office they had left some five minutes before.

The two men settled back into their chairs and John began pouring out the coffee that had been put on the low table between them in their absence. 'There we are, Gregg, drink that and just relax for a few minutes whilst I summon up the right words to apologise for my rather deceptive ways.'

Gregg offered no resistance to the suggestion, and, feeling somewhat weakened by the past moments, he quietly and thoughtfully sipped at his coffee whilst John, viewing him from behind the tilt of his cup, sat silently studying the rather pensive face of his visitor there in front of him.

'Gregg, you will have to forgive me for not telling you of Lorrett's recovery earlier, but I have my reasons. If, however, you feel like giving me a good kick in the pants, can I ask you to wait until I have accounted for my rather unethical ways?'

'Oh, I am sure you will convincingly justify your actions, John, but I do admit that I was both surprised and annoyed by your action, especially when you ushered me out of her room so quickly.'

'Oh, I could see that, Gregg, but disgruntled looks aside, how do you feel now, knowing that Lorrett is with us once again?'

'Naturally surprised, but also very happy for her; in fact, I am happy for both of them, assuming, that is, that they have now come together again after all these years. But how did you resolve the situation, John?'

'Gregg, I do believe you are being a little dishonest with me, but sooner than pursue the point at the moment, let me say that Malcolm came down here today at my request. You see, I wanted to have both of you here at the same time, so that hopefully we could resolve any problems that just might arise out of Lorrett's return to us. But let me correct you on the other point you made, for you will no doubt be quite surprised to learn that neither I or anyone else here had anything to do with Lorrett's recovery. In fact, whilst it could be suggested that it happened quite naturally, I am now sure that, in truth, it came about quite unnaturally. Let me explain. Right from the beginning of this case we, that is Dr Linley and I, recognised that we were dealing with a rather strange set of circumstances. But since Lorrett's recovery, we are now convinced that the cause and the cure of her predicament was both initiated and brought to its conclusion by forces beyond both our control and our understanding. You see, we now know for a fact that some kind of communication has been taking place between Lorrett and her dead mother Ellie, but what we don't know is when it first began. Now, I realise this raises a lot of challenging issues, to which we have but few answers. I also know from your reports, that you have great difficulty believing in such things, So I have no intention of trying to change your beliefs. But I hope by the time the day is over, you will at least accept the fact that there can be no explanation for Lorrett's breakdown and eventual recovery other than that which I am about to suggest.'

'John, after everything I have been through with Weiner, I am prepared to consider anything you say, but I can't guarantee I shall be convinced by it.'

'That's fair enough, so for the moment let me tell you how and when Lorrett's recovery took place. The first signs of a change in her condition started some thirteen days ago with another period of those mumbling sessions that you know about. Still hoping that we might learn something from them, we re-installed our sound recording equipment, but this time we made it a little more mobile, so we were able to monitor her progress continuously. Well, over the next two days, these mumblings slowly began to increase in frequency and just occasionally her body would twitch spasmodically, so we did in fact feel that something was about to happen. I then arranged for our nurses to keep a round the clock watch over her, whilst I continued with my normal day to day routines. Well, on the morning of the third day, I was working in my office when the internal phone rang. It was the duty nurse, who was to tell me of Lorrett's partial recovery. This was ten days ago, Gregg, and whilst her full recovery didn't happen straight away, I have since been able to talk with her at different times. Subsequently, whilst I now know quite a bit more about her previously confused state of mind, I still have to resolve that part of the problem that helped to cause it in the first place.'

'Which from your previous remarks, I assume, has something to do with me, but you still haven't said, John, how I have suddenly become part of that problem.'

'We will be coming to that soon. First, I need to return to that summary of mine, in fact to that point where, after several years of uncertainty, Lorrett and you met and she had accepted your invitation to sing in that show of yours.

'Now obviously, since Lorrett's recovery, we have been able to fill in some of the detail that had been missing from our own pre-analysis of her problem, but naturally, she cannot remember much about her collapse that night and nothing at all about her sustained silence since. So, much of that which I am about to tell you is derived mainly from our pre-analysis of her case prior to her recovery and only part of it from Lorrett's own recent version of events. leading up to the show that night.

'Well, as I have previously said, as Lorrett began to rehearse for that show of yours, she did at first find some of that happiness she had once known, so let us now consider her reaction to the task in front of her. Naturally, she was quite nervous over her forthcoming appearance in such a spectacular event, but she had apparently accepted this as something she could deal with, albeit at that time, no one really knew how emotionally loaded that evening was to become. However, she eventually finds herself on stage for this first time that night and she gives a performance that is to be appreciatively applauded by the audience there. Then she waits in her dressing room until her second call of the evening, when she sings just the one number and, from what I gather, she is again applauded with some considerable gusto. Now the show is nearing its end and Lorrett stands in the wings ready to take up her position on the darkened stage. She is agitated, nervous and certainly very tense as she walks on stage and the mouth organ begins to play. She completes the chorus of the song for the last time and then turns to face this stranger in German uniform, namely our Jimmy Dantry. Let us stop the clock there, so that we can see exactly what it was that caused Lorrett's collapse on stage at that precise moment.'

John left his visitor mulling over what he had just said, as he moved across to a nearby desk and collected some papers together.

'Right, Gregg, let us begin by first picking up on Jimmy Dantry's remarks when you went to see him that time. According to your report, the words he used to describe his impressions of Lorrett, just before she collapsed, were:

' "I remember Miss Lorren's face as she turned to look at me for the first time. It was as if she had seen a ghost, or perhaps the image of someone who had suddenly come back from the dead."

'Now let me remind you of that recurring dream sequence of the young Lorrett, where she described seeing a kind, gentle face pass through its different phases until it became distorted and masked by that spider's web effect. Perhaps you can then see why we began to wonder whether there was some connection between the face in her dream and that of Jimmy Dantry, who of course was the soldier who confronted her on stage that night? Now we had insufficient evidence to connect these two factors at that time, so we looked elsewhere for a possible connection.'

John withdrew something from the file of papers he had in his hand.

'I mentioned earlier, Gregg, that I had phoned Weiner on two occasions after you left Germany for the States. Well, after realising he could speak English quite well, I was able to have a long chat with him, which ended by him agreeing to contact Mrs Mollen on my behalf. As a result of that conversation, I have something here which I want you to look at. It is the photograph of Ellie and Hans which Mrs Mollen showed you at the time of your visit. So, having already seen it once, will you look at it again and describe to me exactly what you see now.'

Gregg took the photograph and studied it, fully aware that for some unknown reason he was being tested by his observing mentor.

'Well, John, I can only return to my thoughts when I first saw this, for I couldn't help thinking then, as I do now, that Ellie, like her daughter Lorrett, was a very attractive woman.'

'That is precisely what I expected and I can now see how you came to miss something so vital to the understanding of Lorrett's problem, something, I have to admit, that both the doctor and I also failed to see to begin with. Let me take your mind back to your first visit here, when you showed us that picture of Jimmy Dantry. You recall, it caused a bit of a jest at the time. Then think about Weiner's remark and how he was able to first recognise Hans in his office that day. Now, take another look at that photograph, but this time, pay a lot more attention to the other person, Hans, standing there beside Ellie, What do you see?'

'Having brought my attention to it, is it that Hans and Jimmy are so very much alike?'

'Well, at last, yes, that is very much the case, but there is something on that photograph of even greater significance, something which actually emphasises this obvious likeness between them.'

'I am sorry, John, I am not with you.'

'OK, let me remind you of Weiner's words, when he saw Hans for the first time, and I quote: "As he walked into the room, the first thing I noticed was that he had a strawberry birthmark on his left cheek." '

'Oh, how stupid of me, John; of course, Jimmy has a similar birthmark on his left cheek. So you are saying that when Lorrett came face to face with Jimmy that night, she thought it was her real father, Hans?'

'Come, come, Gregg, you are not thinking straight. Lorrett never knew her real father, or even his name, so how could it be that?'

'Sorry, John, I didn't stop to think. You are right, of course, she never knew and hadn't ever seen her father.'

'Again, that is where you are wrong, Gregg. She certainly never knew who her real father was, but she had seen his face many times before.'

'Well you will have to explain what you mean by that, John, for Weiner distinctly told me that Hans had never seen the child.'

'And he was right, Gregg, but again we are looking at another of those strange incidents that have somehow engraved their mark on this case. To prevent any further confusion let me return to your reports, in particular to that part of Weiner's story after he found Ellie dead that night. You remember, he had put baby Lorrett down on the floor of the living room just for a moment, while he returned to the bedroom to say his last farewells to Ellie. Now, after reading your reports for the second time, I became more than a little curious over that crying incident of Lorrett's, so I asked myself, what exactly was it that made her cry in the first place? For according to your report it wasn't the gunfire, or even the noise of the object falling on the floor milli-seconds later that caused it. So this was one of the queries I raised with Weiner the first time I phoned him. Needless to say, it took some time before I was able to get an accurate account of exactly what happened that night for, understandably, it was a long time ago and Weiner hadn't paid that much attention to it at the time. But gradually it all came back to him and he went on to say:

' "Amid the noise of the gun going off, I heard something drop to the floor in the living room, so I quickly rushed in to make sure that the baby was all right. As I bent down to pick her up off the floor, I could see what it was that had fallen off the sideboard and had somehow become lodged in an upright position against one of its legs. It was the framed photograph of Hans, which Ellie had always kept on top of the sideboard beside the child's cot. The photograph was still intact in its frame, but the glass covering it had become splintered by the fall and I can now remember how baby Lorrett seemed mesmerised by it. So much so, that as I started to lift her up, she turned her head in an attempt to keep it in view and it was only when she could no longer see it that she began crying."

'Now perhaps you can understand how Lorrett had seen Hans' face before and possibly how that smashed photograph was to give me the answer I had been looking for?'

'I think I can see the point you make about the photograph, but I cannot see any connection between it and Lorrett's collapse that night.'

'Sorry, Gregg, perhaps I am running ahead a little too fast; let me go through it with you. At our first meeting, I suggested that Lorrett might have had some kind of trauma or shock when she was young, but from the information you sent me, the only thing that implied any possibility of this was that extended crying session she had the night Ellie died. You recall, Weiner said, "She had no obvious injury and this sustained crying was inconsistent with her normally happy disposition." So by questioning Weiner as I did, I was able to conclude that I had achieved what I had set out to do: to find the link between Lorrett's past and her collapse that night. You see, up until the night of Ellie's suicide, Lorrett had spent most of her baby days in her cot, next to the sideboard upon which Ellie kept that photograph of Hans. So it was probably always in the child's view throughout the whole of those early months of her life and inevitably the room, the objects and the photograph of Hans all became a familiar part of her every day. In other words, they came to represent all that was passively comforting and reassuring within her contented world. So, understandably, that phototype image of Hans, in particular the face and the German helmet part of it, must have become indelibly imprinted on her young mind. Then, suddenly, this hitherto tranquillity of her life became shattered, first by the violent noise of the gun going off, then by the noise of the object, which fell to the floor beside her, splintering its glass as it did so.

'So, Gregg, within only a matter of seconds, the young Lorrett was subjected to this noisy and visually frightening experience and, understandably, she wasn't able to cry until some moments later, when Weiner was to hurriedly pick her up off the floor and quickly rush her out of the house. It is now easy to see how this experience was to become subliminally impressed on her young mind, for the deafening noise of the gun, the sound of splintering glass, the visually distorted image of the once friendly face and her rapid removal from the security of her mother's presence, had all combined to severely shock the infant Lorrett. Thus the die was cast and those moments of her young life were to remain dormantly concealed within her mind until they eventually re-appeared in the form of a dream. Can you now see, Gregg, how the visual content of that dream was in fact the symbolic re-enactment of her young life up to that night? First the gentle and kindly face of the dream that represented her initial comfort and security, then the sudden distortion of the face caused by the splintered glass covering the picture, which came to represent her fear and the loss of that security and comfort.'

'I think I get the drift of what you are saying, but would a baby of that age be able to remember such things?'

'No, Gregg, or at least not in detail, for at that early age, her infantile mind would have been incapable of rationalising or understanding the cause, the content or the reason for these incidents. But the shock she must have experienced in those moments was to make a lasting impression on her young mind and this was eventually to show itself, in a surrealistic way, through that dream of hers. You see, very much like an animal, a baby is instinctively capable of storing certain bits of information, but too young to be capable of linking them together in a logical or coherent way.'

'So are you saying, John, that the face in her dream was in fact that of Hans and that Lorrett had retained this picture of him in her mind for all those years, without actually knowing it? Then, when she suddenly came face to face with Jimmy Dantry that night, those frightening moments of her early life all came flooding back to her?'

'Well, you are right, in the sense that we are dealing with the phenomenon know as anamnesis, which of course is the recollection of something long forgotten, but there is a little bit more to it than that. To put this into better perspective, let us go back to Lorrett's state of mind in those months leading up to the show that night. We already know how she had suffered one mental setback after another since being told about her adoption and we have seen how, as a result of her inability to cope with these setbacks, she gradually began to withdraw into herself. Well, in those months following your first meeting with her, she did actually begin to feel much happier within herself, but unfortunately this wasn't to last. You see, she was to come up against another problem and it was this which was to prepare her mind for that final shock on stage that night. Now, for a moment, let me return to that observation you made earlier, when you pointed out the possibility that Lorrett might be inclined to follow in her mother's and grandmother's footsteps, by committing suicide, for in fact, that is exactly what she planned to do once the show was over.'

'But why, John? Why would she want to do something like that? She was, after all, on her way to making a break-through in show business, so she had everything going for her.'

'We shall come to the "why" bit of your question in a moment, Gregg. As for your observation concerning her future, well, Lorrett was unable to see herself in the way that you do, especially in view of her state of mind prior to the show that night.

'But let us first look at the circumstances that actually prevented Lorrett from following through with her intended suicide, for if she hadn't collapsed on stage as she did that night, she would no longer be with us. Now, you might just see this as another of those ironies that seem to abound around Lorrett's life, but it is not, for I believe her collapse was destined to happen in precisely the way that it did. Let us see why I believe as I do, by returning to Lorrett's feelings before she went on stage that night, for I think they could best be compared to something like a volcano. She was extremely tense, she saw herself as having no future, she felt utterly alone in the world and, to top it all, she believed that she was just about to face the prospect of possible humiliation at the hands of her audience. She was, as I have suggested, like a living volcano, emotionally pent up, highly volatile and, metaphorically speaking, ready to erupt; in fact, she had all the classical symptoms of someone who was balanced on the edge of a nervous breakdown. Now, the show is nearing its end and at the very peak of this emotional high, Lorrett turns to face Jimmy in his German uniform for the first time. So in those perceptively tense moments, she is suddenly confronted with the face of her dream, and through that dream she recognises an association between it, a face from her distant past and those terrifying moments of her early young life. Now, I suggest that the impact of this upon her was such that her subliminal and conscious mind in unity flashed quickly back over the years to that inexplicable fear she had once experienced as a child. Thus, this latently unexpressed ferment within her came to the surface and, as she was totally unable to suppress or contain it, she simply collapsed under the strain of it. You see, Gregg, Jimmy's face had suddenly become the visual link between both the loving and the terrifying moments of her childhood and her conscious recognition of them as a grown woman.'

'But what was it that kept Lorrett's mind in that suspended state since her collapse that night, John?'

'Well, of course, as we couldn't find a logical reason for her condition in the first place, there was little point in trying to find a logical answer for her recovery later, so the only explanation I can give you has to be based upon conjecture rather than fact. But having said that, I do have certain factual evidence to justify my explanation. However, let us first return to her collapse that night, for normally, it would have only been a matter of minutes before natural recovery would have taken place. So the question has to be asked, what was so abnormal about Lorrett's collapse, that it allowed her body to return to normality but prevented a part of her mind from doing so? Now, I will not attempt to give you a logical reason for this, because as far as we can see there isn't one, but I believe that in those transient moments of collapse, Lorrett's mind became totally void of all normal activity, and subsequently highly susceptible to other more powerful influences. Which brings me back to my earlier remark, when I suggested that some kind of mental contact between Lorrett and her dead mother had taken place. You see, I believe it was this that first isolated and then went on to preoccupy Lorrett's mind, thus preventing it from returning to its normally active state.'

'This all seems so inconceivable, John; I mean all this nonsense about communication between the living and the dead.'

'The occult terminology for it is psychomancy and don't just dismiss it out of hand. Just wait until you have heard all the facts first.'

'All right, John, but if this did actually occur, what purpose did it serve?'

'Be patient, my friend. It had its purpose, believe me, but for a moment let us first discuss how you have become a part of Lorrett's problem. You remember I said earlier how both Dr Linley and I had become interested in you as a person that first time you came here. Well, I think now is the right time for me to explain that interest.

'To begin with, before your first visit here, we had already come to realise that the show itself had been developed around the humanistic ideals of unity and friendship, so naturally, we inquisitively wondered who it was that had dreamt up such a show. Then you came to visit us and we talked about Lorrett and her part in the show and so on, but as the day went by, both the doctor and I found ourselves increasingly interested in you as a person. You see, we both saw you as being a little unusual, unusual inasmuch that your own personality seemed to coincide with the ideals and qualities of the show itself. You were friendly, outgoing, apparently quite unselfish and, as I have already said, a fellow well met, but you also seemed to have an over abundance of humility. Now normally, these particular characteristics in a person are somewhat of a contradiction, so perhaps you can see why it was that we became interested in you. You see, we couldn't understand why someone with so much to offer, by way of a pleasant personality and virtues to match, wasn't married and, on the face of it, didn't seem to be all that interested in the other sex. Now, from what I can make out, Weiner also raised this point with you, but you apparently managed to dodge the issue with him. So, Gregg, whilst normally this would not be my brief, I think as a friend I now have the right to question you on the subject. You see, I suggest that hidden beneath that very pleasant outer coating of yours, you have a slight personality defect and at times you are inclined to hold yourself in low esteem. Now, I know that you are always happy to mix and talk with others about their lives, but why is it that you have this reluctance to talk to them about yourself? You see, from where I stand, you appear to live your life through other people and in so doing, you hide your own vibrant personality away from those who just might like to know you a little better. The irony in all of this is, that you and Lorrett are very much alike, for you both seem to have found sufficient reason to be over cautious, unable to express your inner feelings and, at times, absolutely blind to the obvious. So, Gregg, am I right or wrong in thinking how I do?'

'What can I say, John, other than, yes, you are right. I know that I have become rather introspective in many ways and perhaps I am inclined to express my most profound feelings through my work, but strangely enough, this has only happened since I became a researcher. I also think that this reluctance of mine to talk about myself may be in part due to my own past emotional setbacks, but, more relevantly, to my own inadequacy when I compare myself to the many talented people I come into contact with.'

'This is what I thought; you do, quite unjustifiably, have an inferiority complex, hence my remark about your low esteem. But what you have to remember, Gregg, is that quite a number of those talented people you speak of have at times those same inadequate feelings as you and if they hadn't tried to rise above them, they most probably would never have become the talented people you see them as today. However, your admission does help me with my dilemma over Lorrett and whilst we are on the subject, how do you feel about her as a woman?'

'I suppose, initially, I simply liked her as a person and naturally, I could see her potential as a singer, but I have to admit I have now come to regard her in other ways, especially since learning about Ellie; you see, I think I know quite a bit more about Lorrett now.'

'That I can understand, but what does this knowing do for you? Why, for instance, that tear when you saw Lorrett earlier? Why all this concern over her? This is really what I am asking, Gregg.'

'Well, the concern is something I would feel for any other disadvantaged person, but yes, the tear was out of the joy and pleasure of finding her fit and well again. But if you are going to insist, I also think that I am now in love with her. I would, however, prefer to keep this just between the two of us, for I wouldn't want to complicate her life any further, especially if she and Malcolm are thinking of getting back together again.'

'Yes, that's you, Gregg, magnanimous to the end. It's no wonder people like you so much, for you offer them consideration and kindness and no threat. But, Gregg, there are times in life when you have to reach out for what you want and now is one such time. Let me tell you why. First, you remember how, earlier, I said that Lorrett had come up against another problem in those months running up to the show; well, the problem was you. You see, the reason for some of her erratic conversations with you in those early days was simply because she was falling in love with you and, by your failure to recognise it, she became increasingly unsure both of herself and of her own ability to rationalise her feelings for you. This, then, became the final blow to her already unstable state and as the day of the show came nearer, so her confusion and unhappiness became greater. You see, she had made so many emotional mistakes in the past that she finally felt incapable of either loving or being loved. This, sadly, was the reason behind her thoughts of suicide. Can you now see how you are both so very much alike? You both have this rather high sensitivity, which is so often a characteristic of people with a creative flair, you both share this desire not to offend or hurt others, and you both have this reserve, which makes it hard for you to express or show your true feelings.'

'So, are you saying that Lorrett saw herself as a failure, simply because I didn't respond to her feelings?'

'No, not quite; what I am saying is that her feelings for you became the last proverbial straw on the camel's back. In other words, in her mind, your failure to recognise or react to her feelings left her totally bereft of the little hope that she had left, coming as it did after all the other upsets in her life. It was this that forced her to conclude as she did.'

'I can see now how I have quite innocently become a part of Lorrett's problem, but are you saying that her intended suicide has been the cause of everything that has happened right from square one?'

'Yes. You see, I believe we are now near to the end of a completed cycle of events which began all those years ago with that letter of Ellie's. Our mistake is that we have been trying to solve what we saw as a problem, i.e., Lorrett's condition, when in fact we have simply been witnessing her life as it passed through a pattern of events that were foreseen by Ellie in those days of war.'

'So you are now suggesting, John, that my research, along with your own effort, has all been quite unnecessary?'

'Unnecessary, yes, in the sense that it has not specifically played an effective role in Lorrett's eventual recovery, but very necessary in the sense that had you not carried out your research, then Weiner would not have acted in the way he has now done. Let me explain, by returning to Weiner and that letter he has kept for all those years, for, according to your reports, he said, "I feel that I actually have to do something to solve Lorrett's problem and whatever that is, it is in some way related to the content of that letter." Now the only part of Ellie's letter that suggests Weiner might actually have to act in some way is the part at the end when she wrote, "You will, I know, unite us all again one day." Well, after you left Germany for the States, Gregg, Weiner quite unknowingly fulfilled that prophesy of Ellie's and, in so doing, he has not only been instrumental in bringing about Lorrett's recovery, he has in fact shown how the statements in Ellie's letter have now all eventually come true.'

'John, just as I am beginning to get things clear in my mind, you seem to bring on further clouds of confusion and I become lost again.'

'I can appreciate that, but we are not dealing with a simple down to earth subject. However, you will eventually understand it all, I am sure.

'So, now let me take you back to Weiner's conversation with Gunter, for you no doubt remember that Weiner suggested the idea of having Hans re-buried beside Ellie. Well, when I phoned Weiner that first time, he casually mentioned to me in passing that they had decided to go ahead with the idea and in fact, he went on to tell me the date that the ceremony was due to take place. At the time, my mind was preoccupied with other things, so I didn't really take too much notice of all the details; thus it wasn't until some nine days ago that I suddenly realised the significance of what Weiner had said. Hence my second telephone call to him, for it was only then that I realised how in fact everything had happened as Ellie had predicted it would. You see, Hans was laid to rest in Ellie's grave just ten days ago and what else happened ten days ago? Lorrett's recovery took place. But, even more mysteriously, her recovery happened at exactly the same time as Hans' re-burial in Ellie's grave. Can you see the implications of this? It not only directly connects Weiner's action with Lorrett's recovery, it also completes a hitherto incomplete cycle of events that have finally resulted in the actual reunion of Ellie and Hans.'

'But this must simply be coincidental, John, otherwise you are more or less saying that Ellie's influence has in some way had control over Lorrett's mind since her collapse that night.'

'I am going to go one step further by suggesting that Ellie's influence might even have been indirectly responsible for the whole sequence of events relating to this case, including her collapse that night.'

'But this is all speculation, isn't it, John?'

'Conjecture was the word I used earlier, Gregg, but as I said then, conjecture based upon two pieces of factual evidence. To explain these I shall need to go back to those first few moments of Lorrett's recovery. If you remember, I said that we had been monitoring her progress by tape recorder; well, it was still in operation when her recovery took place. You will see how fortunate this turned out to be, for in those first moments of recovery, Lorrett said something which proves beyond any doubt that communication between her and her dead mother must have taken place and this could only have happened whilst she was locked into that suspended state of hers.'

'What exactly did she say then?'

'I will come to that in a few minutes, but, for the moment, let me tell you about another piece of evidence that backs up that remark. It relates to one of the talks I have had with her since her recovery. You see, I asked Lorrett whether she still felt any antagonism towards Mrs Webster. Well, she went on to say,

' "John, in my heart, Mrs Webster is still my mother, but even from an early age I had always felt that she wasn't my natural mother. So when she did eventually tell me that I had been adopted, I wasn't particularly surprised or even hurt by the news. But the upset between us arose out of her obstinacy, for, try as I would, I could not get her to discuss my early childhood. So my worries came about because at that time, I knew nothing about my real parents, or even why they wanted to have me adopted in the first place. Then, to make matters worse, when I saw the document purporting to be my birth certificate for the first time, I could see that it had been validated with an official Hamburg stamp and signed by someone with a German name."

'Well, there is no need for me to go into any further detail concerning our conversation that day, for as you have just heard, I was being informed for the second time that some kind of communication between Lorrett and her dead mother must have taken place.'

'I am sorry, John, you have lost me.'

'That conversation of Lorrett's: it again proves that there must have been some contact between Lorrett and her dead mother.'

'Well, I am sorry, John, but I must have missed something along the way.'

'Lorrett's conversation with me, Gregg, in it she said, "So my worries came about because at that time I wasn't to know who my real parents were." You see, her words "at that time" imply that whilst she never knew who her real parents were then, she does now. So I carefully questioned her about the remarks and she replied, "Well, John, I don't know now who they were, but at least I know that they were very much in love with each other; they both sadly died in the war and they are now lying at rest together somewhere in Germany." '

'So in what other way, other than through this phenomenon of spiritual communication, could Lorrett have ever known about them?'

'I don't know, John, but there has to be a logical answer to it.'

'So how would she have known that they are now buried together?'

'John, I can understand how you come to think as you do, but I am still unable to believe that the living can communicate with the dead. I can see how some might think they can, I can even see why some would want others to believe that they can, but surely, as a psychiatrist, you can't really go along with this notion, can you?'

'Well, it certainly doesn't fit easily with me, but as I have already said, in our work, we have at least to acknowledge the possibility of occurrences that cannot reasonably be explained. But in this case, it is not just the odd occurrence we have to try to understand, it is a whole sequence of them. Now, whether you believe what I have said or what I still have to say is entirely up to you, but as there is the possibility that you and Lorrett might now have a future together, I think you should delay your judgement for just a little while longer. You see, if we are to prevent further distress on Lorrett's part, she has to be told the full story, for only then will she be able to put the whole of her unhappy past behind her. This is why I think you should also know the rest of the details, especially as you have played such a major part in it.'

'I may be a bit of a cynic, John, but I do want to hear all you have to say.'

'All right; let me take you back to when Weiner told you about his first insight into this paranormal gift of Ellie's. He quoted Ellie's own words, you may remember, which were,

' "When I came to this area for the first time, Weiner, I knew that Hans had been here, for I felt his presence everywhere and, since I don't know where he is now, I shall remain here within the nearness to him, until such time that we can be united again."

'Then a little bit later she suggested that whilst she remained conscious of his persona around her, she knew that Hans was alive and well. So I am sure that the only possible way Ellie could ever have known of Hans' death that day was by the sudden loss of this feeling, or lingering persona, as she described it. Now, knowing that Hans did in fact die that day, we have to accept that Ellie was at that time highly receptive to some form of supernatural understanding. Well, I believe that within those brief but dramatic moments of this apparition, or panoramic insight if you prefer, she had a fleeting glance of the past, the future and the present. The past, where she could see her real mother Yvette, who had committed suicide, the future, where she could see the possibility of her own daughter doing the same thing and the present, where she, Weiner and her baby daughter Lorrett would all die together unless she acted in some way to prevent it. So, for the reasons which we have already talked about, Ellie decided to follow in Yvette's footsteps, knowing that Weiner would react as he did and knowing that she would again be required to interpose in her own daughter's life at sometime in the future.

'So I believe that Ellie has again been waiting, just as she did for Anton and then Weiner at the barrack gates all those years ago, but this time waiting for her daughter to arrive at this point in her life when she would again have to act in some way, to prevent her from ending her life prematurely. That is why I think that Lorrett's collapse on stage that night started off a whole chain of events which were intentionally destined to bring about her eventual peace of mind and, at the same time, to complete something that Ellie had prophesied all those years before.'

'So, John, you see me as being a part of this arranged destiny.'

'Yes, I do, and I will tell why in a moment or two. Let me first summarise some of the detail for you. We have seen how the discovery of Lorrett's adoption, along with the other different problems she was to encounter, all built up inside her prior to the show that night. We can see how confused and saddened she must have felt, thinking that her growing love for you was neither recognised nor wanted, and we can see how this became the final humiliating blow to her already low self-regard. So she decided upon her own self-demise. Thus her collapse, which in general terms is the loss of one's mental and physical activity, was to leave her mind momentarily suspended and therefore highly receptive to the spiritual influences of her dead mother. The reason for this? Well, I am sure it was the only way of protecting Lorrett from herself, until the cause of her anxiety had been removed. You see, because of your meeting with Weiner, you have at last come to both recognise and express your own feelings towards Lorrett and of course, in so doing, you have in fact removed the reason for her intended suicide. So once you tell her how you feel, it will resolve all her problems and at the same time prove that Ellie's prediction, made all those years ago, has indeed finally come true.'

'What do you mean?'

'Ellie's letter, Gregg; more specifically, the part of it that actually predicted Weiner's ultimate action. Don't you remember, she wrote, "Please, Weiner, try not to question or find reasons; just accept that because I die, our daughter will live to find and treasure through you, the happiness and joy that we have known."

'That's exactly what has happened and I am now confident that, just like Weiner and Ellie, you and Lorrett will live to treasure the happiness and joy that they once shared together. The most fascinating thing about all of this is that this was only made possible by Weiner's simple act of actually re-uniting Ellie and Hans after all those years, but as we have seen, this was again predicted by Ellie in her letter.'

'So do you think that the influence of the song in my own early life has directed my progress along a pre-determined path to this point in time, when Lorrett and I were destined to find what in fact we have both been subconsciously seeking?'

'Yes, I believe that to be so, although I think there is just a little bit more to it than that. Weiner's words summed up the song beautifully; now, how did he put it?

' "The song was to become one of those unique random occurrences that was destined to have an unaccountable and unpredictable effect on so many people's lives."

'How true this is, for we have both come to see how Weiner's and Ellie's ideal life together was to materialise out of this common affection for the song. Now, I am sure that you and Lorrett are about to share a love that, like theirs, began with that same song.'

'Is it then, that our lives do in fact follow a route that has in some way been predetermined before we are born?'

'I don't know about that, Gregg, but I am sure that our lives can be re-directed or changed by simple influences as much as they can be by catastrophic events and I think that in fact, we have experienced this in our endeavours to find an answer to Lorrett's problem.'

'But apart from the conjecture, were there any other factors that helped to make her case so unusual?'

'Well, that is difficult to say, because medically speaking, we really haven't had a case at all. You see, we at the home here have done nothing to bring about Lorrett's recovery; in fact, our only real participation in all of this has been either as arbiters or simply as witnesses to an extremely strange set of circumstances.

'But if you are asking me precisely where did this all begin, I would perhaps suggest: with Yvette and the unknown father of Ellie, just after the 1914–18 war. You see, remembering my own childhood and recalling how I loved to hear those words, "once upon a time", I would like to think that Yvette was really the true inspiration behind the words of the song, in other words, the real Lilli Marlene. But in more realistic terms, it had less to do with fairy stories and more to do with genetics. For obviously Ellie inherited some of the genetic characteristics of Yvette and her unknown father, which in turn must have been passed down to Lorrett. This can be seen by the way that they all loved to sing and by the continuity of this transcendental gift, which they all seemed to share. Of equal importance to this historic background of Lorrett's was the coming together of Ellie and Weiner, for it was their life together that was indirectly to create and foster our involvement in Lorrett's life today. But perhaps, most important of all, the catalyst for this complicity of time and place was the war, for war exposes and stimulates both the best and the worst of emotions in people.

'Perhaps one of the more desirable of these emotions is hope, and in Weiner's case, he understandably found this hope in the one person we have all now come to love, Ellie Mollen. For without a doubt, she was to epitomise all that is synonymous with compassion, a love of life and a love for her fellow human beings. She in turn, however, may never have been the person she ended as, if she and Weiner had never seen each other that first time in the Officers' Mess. This is something I still see as being a little unusual, for I would have thought that this aura that was there between them that night was perhaps more sensual than spiritual, yet obviously and quite believably, Weiner has openly said that there was never anything physical between them. But getting back to Ellie's development again, I think it was the suffering of others that really made the girl into a woman and the woman into a legend. You see, tragic and cruel as the war was, it did provide the setting and the circumstance for Ellie's compassion to blossom and, of course, she then sought out those who needed her help and in her own subtle way tried to share the burden of their pain and the despair of their tormented minds. I suppose if I was asked to explain this facet of Ellie's character, I would have to suggest that it came from an inner desire to be sincere, for I am sure that her compassion for people came from the heart, her concern for their problems from deep within her soul and her altruistic ideals from an inner satisfaction that few would understand.

'Standing back from the situation, as you and I have been able to do, one can so easily see why Weiner still remembers her with so much affection, for in a strange way, I now share this feeling of having known her and, if I am honest with myself, I too have gained something from just knowing that her spirit lives on.'

'I know how you feel, for it is as if her presence still surrounds us even today. Perhaps you can now see how, because of my fascination with her life, I failed to find out those odd one or two details that have proved to be so relevant to your understanding of Lorrett's problem.'

'You didn't fail in any way, you merely went off track a couple of times and, believe me, neither I or any of the staff here could have carried out such a task in the way that you have, Gregg.'

'I am still not quite clear on a few things. For instance, is it really conceivable that a baby could have become mesmerised by a photograph in such a way?'

'Oh yes, in fact for the first month or so of a baby's life, its sight is somewhat misty and de-focused, so there is a greater tendency for its eyes to settle on objects of strong contrast; thus a black and white photograph could quite easily have become the centre of attraction to her as a baby.'

'Another thing, John, did you pick up on that remark of Anton's, when he spoke of that phial of cyanide that he once had?'

'Well, if you are thinking that Ellie might have used it to kill herself that night, yes, and there is every probability that that is how she came by it.'

'There is no doubt about it, John, this problem of Lorrett's has given us both a great deal to think over. Tell me, when did you have your first inclination that you had a rather strange case on your hands?'

'I suppose my interest was first alerted by that story of Kerkner. You see, after my initial conversation with your boss Robbie, he kindly sent me copies of those minutes covering some of your meetings and it was then that I first began to wonder. That was, of course, before you came here that first time in June. It was obvious from your account of that incident, that both Kerkner and that Tommy fellow must have gone through some form of profound change in their lives, because of their meeting up there on Monte Cassino that night.

'So I was soon to realise how this and other little incidents you spoke of all seemed to share this common thread of regret and this inner desire for reconciliation. As I have said, Kerkner's and Tommy's story touched upon it; Weiner's, Anton's and Gunter's lives, each in their own way, were to show that they had in fact experienced it; and you, along with Robbie and the team, were to express it as a theme in that show of yours. I suppose in religious terms one might compare it to this experience of "Seeing the light" that some people talk of. But perhaps others, like Ellie, would no doubt think of it as more the first discovery of one's own self. But whatever we call it, it is really all a part of this fantastic *esprit de corps* experience that was to come out of the conflict of war. However, philosophising aside, my first actual insight into these strange events concerning Lorrett's case came by way of that remark of Mrs Webster's, when she spoke of that voice in her ear as she picked up baby Lorrett for the first time. What was it now? "This was intended to be." Now I have come up against other people who have had similar experiences in their lives, so I wasn't so much surprised at that, but what did surprise me was how Ellie at times also used similar phrases in some of her remarks with Weiner. It is as if hers was the voice that had in some way spoken through her daughter into Mrs Webster's ear. Then, of course, as those reports of yours started to come through from Germany, I was to realise that the whole uncanny nature of Lorrett's background was in fact steeped in the mystery of her wartime past.'

'It really has all been quite strange, hasn't it, John?'

'It has, yes, but in another way, the strangeness of what has happened has in its way helped to make the case so coherently clear.'

'Well, that might be your view, John, but I am still not totally convinced about all of this. But let me ask, have you shown Lorrett that photograph of Hans and Ellie, since her recovery?'

'No, not yet, for my conversations with her so far have mainly been about her past problems, but I have planned a meeting so that we can talk to her about your research and her real parents then.'

'So will you tell her of your belief concerning this possible contact between her and her dead mother?'

'We shall have to wait and see how it goes, but, knowing Lorrett, as I think I now do, she won't need too much convincing about it. But as I plan to have you and Weiner at that meeting, we shall tell her the facts first and then play the rest by ear.'

'So does Weiner already know of Lorrett's recovery?'

'Oh yes, naturally I told him of it at the time of my second telephone conversation with him; that was also when he agreed to be at the meeting which, incidently, has now been arranged for the day after tomorrow.'

'So Weiner is coming over in a couple of days' time?'

'No, not exactly, You see, he, Gunter and Anton are at this moment quite probably sitting in a hotel lounge not very far away from here, sitting and waiting, no doubt, for me to phone them. Then, of course, they will be over here like a shot, for I know that they can't wait to see both you and the lovely Lorrett.'

'So you must have anticipated both my feelings and my reactions before I even arrived here this morning?'

'Something like that, Gregg. You see, I don't profess to know a great deal about psychomancy, but people, well, that's another matter. For in the short time we have known each other, I have learned quite a lot about you, so much, in fact, that I even knew at the time of our first meeting that you were more deeply involved in her problem than either you cared to admit or than you realised. So we sent you off on your research, with the hope of you finding out a little more about Lorrett and, hopefully, a great deal more about yourself.'

'But you are not telling me that this was the only reason for the research, are you?'

'No, Gregg, we really did hope you would come up with the reason for Lorrett's problem and, let's face it, you did. But neither of us were to know then what was to come out of that exercise, and I would suggest that it really has been a wonderful experience for both of us. So let me thank you for carrying out that research on our behalf and, of course, letting me into Lorrett's life; you see, on a personal note, the experience has done a great deal towards restoring my faith in human nature.'

'So in spite of all your logical thinking, John, you still believe that Lorrett's problem both began and ended for the reasons you have said and also in the way that you have suggested?'

'Oh yes, but do not forget that I am not the only one to believe as I do, for Weiner, Anton and many of the staff here all agree in principle with my conclusions. The only alternative to our beliefs would be that much of what we have heard has been simply a matter of coincidence. Then, of course, you have to ask yourself, was it just coincidence that everything in Ellie's letter turned out to be true, was it merely a matter of chance that Lorrett's recovery coincided to the minute with the re-burial of Hans? I could go on, Gregg, but it would be pointless, for all that I am saying is that I can offer you no alternative explanation for this very strange sequence of events.'

'So what is the next move, John?'

'Well, just give it a few more minutes and Malcolm will be leaving for home and Lorrett will be anxiously waiting to hear the outcome of our little chat. But before we go in to see her, there are just a few things I want to say and a couple more questions I need to ask. First, I should like to say how much I have enjoyed sharing this experience with you and Weiner, for it is quite refreshing to know that people like Ellie, Lorrett, Anton and Gunter still exist. You see, I often feel that society in general will one day drown in its own selfishness and greed, for, unfortunately, there are very few Ellies left in this world to show us what the real pleasure in life is all about. And perhaps whilst we are on this subject of greed, this might be the appropriate time for me to mention my fees, for as far as I can see, left to your own devices, you might still be wondering about your feelings over the lovely Lorrett.

'So, as a reward for my services, I shall need at least two invitations from you for the first of Lorrett's performances at the club Ellie Mollen in Hamburg. You see, Weiner, Anton and Gunter have already begun to make arrangements for the event and incidently, Robbie, Ned and the rest of your lads have also planned to turn it into another television show. But please, as a favour to me, Gregg, don't let Lorrett sing that "Lilli Marlene" song again, otherwise we could be back to where we started.'

'I won't, but I am afraid Weiner will insist on it, John.'

'Well, I suppose we shall have to put up with it, then. Now I would just like to return to that point about your father and the possibility that he could have been one of the chaps in the pub that night. Would you happen to know how he died, or perhaps even the date of his death?'

'No, we were never told, for just like the mother of Hans, we only had a formal notice saying that he was missing, presumably killed in action. That is all we ever knew, why?'

'Well, I was so intrigued by Weiner's story about the song that I thought I would make a few enquiries on the subject myself and whilst I didn't come up with much, I did find out something which will most probably quite surprise you, Gregg.'

'What was it?'

'I will come to it in a moment, but let me first come back to the matter of your beliefs, for obviously you are still unconvinced about Lorrett's recovery and my explanation for it. You remember how I told you that the tape recorder was still in operation throughout the period of her recovery and how she actually said something as she was coming round; well, I thought that perhaps you might try to give me a simple explanation for it. You see, speaking as if she was talking to herself, Lorrett simply said, "Zero, seven, one, two, four, four, four" and then went to repeat it a second time.'

'But John, that's impossible; that is the number that Weiner came out with in the cemetery that day, the number of Ellie's grave.'

'Oh yes, I know, Gregg, so perhaps you can now understand why I had no other option than to conclude as I have. You see, we know for a fact that Lorrett knew nothing at all about her parents prior to her collapse that night, but apart from this inexplicable fact, the number also has something to do with your own father.

'You see, my friend, it also happens to be a date, the 7th December 1944; and the other digit merely indicates that the grave is situated in the fourth avenue of the cemetery. You may recall, Gregg, it was the day on which both Ellie and Hans died; but sadly, my friend, it was also the very same day on which your own father died.

'So can you now see why I personally stick to my beliefs? The only thing I simply cannot explain is how the writer of this book came to know all about the facts of this case before you and I did.'